# HOUSE *of* SHADOWS

## ROYAL HOUSES SERIES
### *book two*

*USA TODAY* BESTSELLING AUTHOR
# K.A. LINDE

House of Shadows
Copyright © 2021 by K.A. Linde
All rights reserved.

Visit my website at
www.kalinde.com

Formatting and Map Design: Devin McCain,
www.studio5twentyfive.com
Cover Designer: Okay Creations., www.okaycreations.com
Editor: Unforeseen Editing, www.unforeseenediting.com

ISBN-13: 978-1-948427-87-6

# ALSO BY K.A. LINDE

## PRONUNCIATION GUIDE

### *CHARACTERS*

Mistress Alsia: *Al-see-uh*

Alura: *Uh-lure-uh*

Amond: *Uh-mond*

Mistress Anahi: *Anne-uh-ee*

Arbor: *Ar-bur*

Ashby March: *Ash-bee March*

Audria Ather: *Aud-ree-uh Ath-er*

Basem Nix: *Bay-sum Nix*

Master Bastian: *Bast-yun*

Bayton: *Bay-ton*

Benton: *Ben-ton*

Master Boze: *Boz*

Master Callian: *Cal-yen*

Clare Rahllins: *Clair Rah-Lihns*

Cleora: *Klee-or-uh*

Clover: *Clove-er*

Darby: *Dar-bee*

Dozan Rook: *Doe-zen Rook*

Fallon: *Fal-uhn*

Prince Fordham Ollivier: *Ford-um Ah-liv-ee-aye*

Hadrian: *Hay-dree-en*

Mistress Hellina "Helly": *Hell-ee-nuh*

Irena: *Ih-reen-uh*

Isa: *Ee-suh*

Keres: *Kerr-is*

Kerrigan Argon: *Care-ih-gen Arh-gone*

Lord Kivrin Argon: *Kiv-rin Arh-gone*

Master Kress: *Kres*

Master Lockney: *Lock-nee*

Master Lorian: *Lor-ee-uhn*

Lyam: *Lee-um*

Mistress Moran: *Mor-in*

Mistress Movanna: *Moh-Vahn-uh*

Noda: *No-duh*

Parris: *Pear-is*

Prescott: *Press-cot*

Master Raysor: *Ray-sore*

Roake: *Roke*

Mistress Sencha: *Sen-shuh*

Lady Sonali: *Suh-nahl-ee*

Thea: *Thee-uh*

Master Tippan: *Tip-En*

Valia: *Val-ee-uh*

Wynter: *Win-ter*

Mistress Zahina "Zina": *Zuh-heen-uh "Zeen-uh"*

## DRAGONS

Androma: *An-dro-muh*

Avirix: *Uh-veer-ix*

Evien: *Ev-ee-en*

Ferrinix: *Fair-ih-nix*

Gelryn: *Gehl-rin*

Luxor: *Lux-er*

Netta: *Net-uh*

Oria: *Or-ee-uh*

Tavry: *Tahv-ree*

Tieran: *Teer-en*

Vox: *Vaaks*

## TRIBES

The twelve tribes of Alandria were split into four groups based on how they perceived the use of magic: Woodloch to the wooded west, Viland to the hills of the east, Tosin to the mountains of the north, and Moran to the rocky south. Though the twelve tribes are autonomous, the Society rules over all.

### WOODLOCH

Magic should be used for might.

(warriors, weapons, armor)

*Galanthea*

*Herasi*

*Venatrix*

### VILAND

Magic should be used for good.

(healing, medicine, art)

*Bryonica*

*Concha*

*Ibarra*

<u>TOSIN</u>

Magic should be used for efficiency.

(everyday tasks, mining, travel)

*Erewa*

*Sayair*

*Zavala*

<u>MORAN</u>

Magic should be used for nothing.

(magical artifacts)

*Aude*

*Elsiande*

*Genoa*

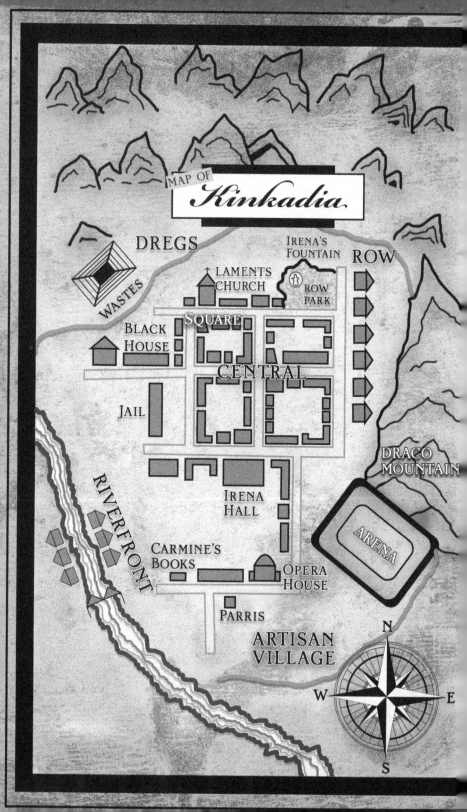

MAP OF *Alandria*

TOSIN

EREWA

ZAVALA

EARLE RIVER

SAYAIR

BAIN BAY

HERASI

HOUSE OF SHADOWS

HOLY MOUNTAIN

GARDIC SEA

WOOD LOCH

ISLE OF SONG

BRYONICA

ROSEMONT

DRACO MOUNTAIN

CONCHA

VERT MOUNTAINS

☆ KINKADIA

EVERIC OCEAN

DAYE RIVER

STRAIT OF URSI

IBARRA

SOUTH RIVER

VILAND

VENATRIX

EDGEWOOD

TANSY CHANNEL

GENOA

AUDE

MORAN

ELSIANDE

ARCHDALE

GALANTHEA

N

CORVIAN SEA

W          E

S

# CHAPTER 1
## *The Celebration*

"Y ou just won the dragon tournament. What are you going to do next?" Kerrigan swatted at Clover. "Stop it. You're ridiculous."

"I'm not ridiculous. I'm beyond excited for my best friend." Clover leaned back against the bar. Her dark bob hanging severely in front of her face, her smile the brightest Kerrigan had ever seen.

When Clover, Hadrian, and Darby had pulled her out of Draco Mountain, Kerrigan had tried to match their enthusiasm. A day earlier, she'd been fighting for her life in a tournament she hadn't entered. She had ended victorious, becoming the first half-Fae full member of the Society and a dragon rider. In two week's time, she was going to start a year of dragon training. It sounded miraculous. If only there wasn't about a million reasons it was anything but.

"Come on, Ker," Hadrian said. His blue hair was coifed elegantly against the golden brown of his skin. The cravat at his neck, half-undone, was the only indication of his inebriation. "Don't look like that. We're celebrating."

"Agreed," Darby said. "I'm out, aren't I? If this isn't a reason to overindulge, I don't know what is."

Darby's midnight skin was coated in a gold shimmer, and her long black tresses gleamed in the dying firelight. She technically wasn't even supposed to be out with them now that she was a member of a royal Bryonican family, but she'd flouted authority and gone out to celebrate.

It wasn't every day that a Dragon Blessed from the House of Dragons became a full-fledged member of the Society—the governmental body of the city of Kinkadia and all of Alandria. Actually, it had never happened. It wasn't even supposed to happen. The House of Dragons was a feeder program for underprivileged Fae to move up in the world. It had worked for Hadrian and Darby, but Kerrigan wasn't like her friends. She was only half-Fae, and no one had wanted her.

"Seriously, you need to let the last forty-eight hours go and have another drink," Clover said, pushing an ale toward her. "Everyone else is buying anyway."

Which was true. The dragon tournament was the most lauded event in Alandrian history. The winners were treated like heroes, and everyone wanted to celebrate, which meant drink after drink after drink. She could feel that she had overindulged.

"My head is already spinning," she said with a laugh.

Hadrian rolled his eyes. "When has that ever stopped you?"

She raised a pint to him. "Fair point."

Kerrigan tipped back the ale and took a long drink. It was the good stuff. Not the swill she and Clover normally drank in the Wastes. No, tonight, they'd had to forgo the underground pit, where Clover worked as a card dealer, for a more reputable tavern. They'd ended up in The Dragon Scales on the Square in Central Kinkadia. It was fancier than anywhere but a royal home but still just a tavern. The same sort of customers and the same sort of drink.

Kerrigan set her half-finished drink on the bar and forced down a yawn. She was about to suggest that they all join the dancing outside when a man sent her drink sprawling.

"Scales," Kerrigan gasped. She jumped away from the spilled ale, but it was too late. The drink coated her dress and down one side of her body.

"Hey, watch what you're doing!" Clover snarled at the man.

The man stood to his considerable height, more than a head taller than Kerrigan. His ears were severely pointed, a clear indicator that he was full-blooded Fae. His skin was creamy white and eyes the darkest brown, and he was currently glaring at Kerrigan, having already discarded Clover's comment.

"Your kind isn't *welcome* in this establishment," he said coldly.

Kerrigan straightened up. "My *kind?*"

"We've been here all night," Hadrian said as if he hadn't heard the insinuation about her being half-Fae. "If you have a problem with that, then you can go somewhere else."

"They should never defile the Society halls with someone like you, *leatha.*"

A sharp intake of breath was heard all around Kerrigan. A buzzing filled her ears at the horrid word. It was ancient Fae language, originally meaning half-Fae, but modern connotation had made it a slur, more commonly meaning half-breed *bitch.* It wasn't slung around in polite society.

Most people in this fancy tavern probably hadn't heard it spoken aloud, except in jest. Not that Kerrigan ever found those jests funny. But Kerrigan had heard the word enough not to flinch from it.

"Creative," she crooned. She was too tipsy for this. "I'm so glad that you don't get a vote."

He took a menacing step forward, but she just laughed. It was the wrong move. She had known it somewhere deep in her brain that laughing at this man would provoke him, but did he think he was frightening? She'd won the *dragon* tournament, and not that he knew this, but she was a prized fighter in the Wastes. He couldn't touch her. His overconfidence was almost endearing, if not suicidal.

"I'll give you something to laugh at," he said and then threw his fist toward her face.

She was drunk, not incapacitated.

She fluidly slid out of his reach. Her reflexes were a half-second slower than normal, but it wasn't like he was Prince Fordham Ollivier. Fordham was the only person besting her four out of five bouts. This was just a Fae male who thought he was better than her.

The male overcorrected for the missed punch and tried to throw another one. She caught his fist in her hand and wrenched it sideways. He cried out.

"That isn't very nice," she slurred slightly. "Someone should teach you some manners."

She jerked the man forward, bringing her knee up to his face with a satisfying crunch. Then, she threw him to the ground at her feet. She could have finished it then with the adrenaline coursing through her, but Darby put a hand on her shoulder.

"Kerrigan, everyone's watching," she whispered.

She came back to herself then, stepping away from the man. Her hands were shaking from the fight. It had happened in a matter of seconds, and she hadn't even needed to use her magic. But this wasn't the kind of place that erupted into brawls. The room had quieted, and all eyes were on her. They hadn't seen this brute attack her, but they'd sure seen her finish it. Were they seeing a Society member enacting justice? Or a half-Fae getting revenge, knowing that no one could stop her now?

She shook her head and backed away from the man on the ground. He'd earned his beating, but she couldn't be the pit fighter anymore. She had to uphold the Society laws. Gods, she'd messed up.

And the fire in the man's eyes said that he hated her all the more. Just like these entitled Fae males always did.

"Let's get out of here," Clover said. Her hand landed on Kerrigan's pale, freckled arm, still sticky with ale.

"Maybe I should ..."

Hadrian shook his head. "Leaving is the right call."

Kerrigan shot an apologetic look to the bartender, a middle-aged woman. She smiled back kindly as Kerrigan slid a dozen marks on the bar. "For the trouble."

She waved Kerrigan off. "I saw what happened. Wouldn't be the first time he needed a good beating."

Kerrigan laughed tightly at the words and then let her friends pull her out of the crowded bar. The noise had returned to the establishment, and the brute had picked himself off of the ground, but Kerrigan still felt uneasy.

"I didn't handle that right," she said with a hand to her temple.

"You handled him just fine," Clover said.

"You should have let it go," Darby whispered. Clover glared at her. All of the usual flirtatious looks between them had evaporated in the last week. Kerrigan didn't know what it meant, but she didn't like it. Darby held up her hands. "What he did and said was terrible, but she's a Society member now. That means something. She can't get involved in bar fights."

Clover opened her mouth to argue, but Kerrigan stopped her. "She's right. I'm going to be held to a higher standard."

"So, you just have to deal with people like him insulting you?" Clover asked.

Kerrigan shrugged. "I don't know. This has never happened before. There's never been a half-Fae Society member. Let alone one who earned her spot below the age requirement, who hadn't officially entered, who didn't have a tribe, and who was part of the House of Dragons."

"It is unprecedented," Hadrian agreed as they set off around the busy Square. A bonfire blazed at the center, and groups danced merrily late into the evening. "But he was wrong for saying something."

"Whatever you say, sweetheart," Clover said, purposely antagonizing Hadrian, as she always did.

"So, what should we do with the rest of our night?" Kerrigan asked before Hadrian could retaliate.

"Wastes!" Clover cried.

Darby yawned and put a hand to her mouth to cover it. "I think I'm done for the evening. Maybe we should all say good night. Don't you have to leave in the morning, Kerrigan?"

Kerrigan frowned at the words. She *did* have to leave in the morning. But she didn't want to think about it. It was half the reason that she'd allowed her friends to cajole her out into celebrating. Tomorrow, she would be leaving for the House of Shadows with Fordham. And he wasn't out here tonight with her because things were complicated, to say the least.

"I'm not ready to go back," Kerrigan said.

"But ..." Darby began.

Hadrian put his hand on her arm to silence her. "Whatever you want to do, Ker."

"Let's go to the Wastes. No one cares that you're a half-Fae there," Clover said.

It was a lie. Someone always cared. But it was the closest thing she had to sanctuary.

"All right," Kerrigan said. "Sure."

"I'm going to escort Darby back," Hadrian said. Such an official way of bowing out of the Wastes. He hated it there.

"Scared, sweetheart?" Clover taunted.

Hadrian leveled her with a gaze. "Some of us have standards."

"Leave it," Kerrigan said, in no mood to fight. "We're still celebrating."

She hugged Darby and Hadrian, telling them to get home safe, and then headed out of the Square with Clover.

"Must you antagonize him?" she asked as they threaded out of Central and to the Dregs—the primarily human slums in the north and western part of the valley that housed the city of Kinkadia.

"I must," Clover said with a laugh.

As soon as they crossed the border into the Dregs, Clover pulled a cigarette out and lit up. Clover's cigarettes were laced with *loch*—the most addictive drug on the market and the only thing that kept back the debilitating pain from which she suffered. Clover's hands immediately stopped shaking. She'd gone too long without, but she couldn't exactly smoke *loch* in the Square.

They were silent as the streets grew narrower and filthier and darker. More and more people were crammed in less space. Taverns were on every corner, blaring with music and laughter. Everyone worked harder and played harder here. Human life spans were so much shorter than the Fae that it was inevitable.

Kerrigan walked into the opening arms of the Wastes. It was a multilevel pit with a floor for drinking, gambling, whores, *loch* dens, and at the very bottom was the Dragon Ring, where she had fought with magic for the last year of her life. It was where she had met Basem Nix, the leader of the Red Masks. He tried to ruin her life after losing to a half-Fae. He slung the same slur in her face as the man in the tavern. The same ignorance made him rise up against her after she won the tournament. They'd fought not two days ago, and now, he was awaiting trial in the Draco Mountain dungeons. And it had all started here.

Kerrigan received the same reception in the Wastes that she had at The Dragon Scales. Except here, the clientele was predominantly human and half-Fae, and she was their *real* champion.

As she passed through the cheering crowd, she found a frowning Dozan Rook, the king of the Wastes.

"Red," he said, slipping his hands into the pockets of his black pants. He was in a full suit with a red cravat at his throat. His burnished hair shone in the light, and his all-knowing golden eyes stared back at her. As menacing and handsome as she had ever seen him.

"Your champion has arrived," she said with her arms wide.

He arched one perfect eyebrow. "I'm surprised you're out on a victory parade."

"Why? Don't I deserve to celebrate?"

His lip quirked at the side as he stepped into her personal space. She fought the urge to step backward. She'd been obsessed with Dozan once. He'd even offered her a place at his side as the queen of the Wastes. She knew he only wanted her for her power, but the connection they'd always shared didn't go away with the logic.

"You deserve everything that's coming to you," he said sensually.

"That sounds ominous."

"You're drunk."

"Still took down a Fae male twice my size."

"I thought you'd have already run back to your mountain." His eyes trailed over her face, as if awaiting an answer she didn't know how to give. "Considering Basem Nix just turned up dead."

# CHAPTER 2
## *The Murder*

"**W**hat?" Kerrigan gasped.

Her mind was spinning. She needed to sober up immediately because she absolutely could not have heard Dozan correctly. Basem Nix was in the Draco Mountain dungeons. The only people with access to him were Society members. The guards were the best of the best and acquiesced to binding spells to prevent any sabotage. It was *impossible* to infiltrate. Except...

"Ah, you've reached the same conclusion that I did," Dozan said as if he could read her mind.

"He can't be dead."

Dozan smirked, a dark, dangerous thing that she'd once adored. "Not if your precious Society is everything that you think it is."

"The only people who can get into those dungeons are ..."

"Society members," he finished for her.

"Gods," she breathed.

She put her hand to it to try to stop the buzzing in her head and the dizzy feeling creeping through her limbs. How much had she had to drink at The

Dragon Scales? More than normal, that was for sure, but it wasn't like she'd had faerie punch. It was a dangerous magical concoction that lowered inhibitions. She'd tried them all for fun, and this headache blossoming behind her eyes reminded her of the green kind she'd had a few summers ago with Lyam. She winced at that recollection of her murdered friend. Another casualty of Basem Nix.

"I have to go," she said at once, turning to Clover.

Clover's eyes were wide. "What's wrong?"

She blinked to right her vision. "I need to get back to the mountain."

"But we just got here, and it's your last night in town," Clover said.

Dozan shifted behind her. "Your last night?"

Kerrigan ignored him. He had to have known that she was leaving with Fordham in the morning. He just wanted to have it out with her about joining the House of Shadows, a place that hated humans and half-Fae alike. No, not just hated them, that tortured and killed them. A thousand years ago, the Society had reviled the House of Shadows so much for their continued enslavement of the humans and half-Fae that they went to war against them—the Great War. The House of Shadows had lost and were trapped forever behind a hidden magical barrier. Until Fordham appeared in the dragon tournament.

Now in a twist of fate, Kerrigan was one of them, and the House of Shadows beckoned. It had been the right decision at the time. Between a lifetime in Bryonica, chained to a life she'd been discarded from by her father at five years old, or a new life with Fordham, she'd chosen Fordham. Even though now, things were problematic.

Kerrigan turned to leave, but Dozan reached out quick as a viper and latched on to her arm. The one still sticky with ale. His face showed distaste. "You can't go run off into the night alone."

"And why not?"

He removed his hand from her, brushing it against a handkerchief from his pocket. "Don't you remember what happened when you went off alone after the last tournament?"

Kerrigan glared right back at him. Didn't she remember? How could she forget? She'd been twelve years old when the first human in history had won the dragon tournament and then left the next day. Kerrigan had gone out to celebrate the victory, was cornered by a group of Red Masks, and brutally assaulted. She'd thought for so long that Dozan had saved her that night, but it turned out that she'd saved herself by the force of her own magic.

That was the night of her first vision. The night of her first using her spirit magic. The start of everything to come.

But things were different now. She was a fighter, a skilled magic user, a member of the Society. Not that she was naive enough to believe that would protect her, but it was not the same as it had been five years ago. She'd made sure of that.

"I'll be fine."

Dozan nodded his head at Clover. "Go with her. Ensure she makes it safe."

"What is Clover going to do that I can't?" Kerrigan demanded. She winced at Clover's irritated face. "Nothing against you, Clove."

Clover was a hundred percent perfectly human. She didn't have a lick of magic in her veins. Few did in Alandria. Even most half-Fae only had enough for parlor tricks. Kerrigan was an anomaly because she was strong enough with all four elements to join the Society. Another target on her back.

"She can watch your back," Dozan said. His finger slipped down her jaw, tilting her head up to look into his bright eyes.

"Dozan," she growled.

He grinned wickedly and released her. "Do try to stay out of trouble and come back to me in one piece, Red."

"I'm not coming back to you." She huffed at the insufferable arrogance and then tipped her head at Clover. "Let's go."

She refused to look back as they left the Wastes the way they'd come in. She wouldn't give him the satisfaction. She also didn't want him to see how much she was flagging. Those drinks had really knocked her on her ass. Maybe it *was* better to have Clover with her.

"And you get on me for antagonizing Hadrian," Clover said with a snort.

"Dozan is … Dozan."

"Yeah, and he wants you bad." She whistled low.

"He wants my power. Nothing more, nothing less."

"That's not what you were saying a year ago when you ended up in his bed."

"Hey!"

Clover cackled. "All right. I'll leave it be, but one day, you two are going to have to figure out this sexual tension. It's uncomfortable to be around."

Kerrigan rolled her eyes. "That's not what's important right now. It's that Basem Nix is dead."

"Gods," she whispered.

Kerrigan couldn't have said it better herself. The gods themselves needed to answer for this crime after all Kerrigan had gone through to get him in prison. There would be no public trial to show the world that what he'd done was wrong. He'd be buried six feet under with no justice.

They passed out of the Dregs and back down the main thoroughfare through Central. Kinkadia was made up of six main quadrants—Dregs, Central, Row, Riverfront, Artisan Village, and Draco Mountain. Row lay to the east, filled with wealthy, aristocratic mansions and sprawling parks. The Riverfront spread across the South River. The newly wealthy who couldn't gain access on the Row were building copycat homes along the waterfront. To the southeast was one of Kerrigan's favorite parts of the city—Artisan Village—with the Opera house, bookstores, and little Painter's Row. Finally, they came upon Draco Mountain—the home of the Society and dragons as well as the tournament arena. It was the largest peak in the semicircle of mountains that surrounded the Kinkadian valley.

And it was home.

"Never gets old," Clover whispered as they stared up at the heights of the mountain.

"It really doesn't."

"I'll leave you here. I'll miss you while you're gone."

Clover bounced back and forth on her feet, as if she were actually anxious. Kerrigan smiled and threw her arms around her friend.

"I'll be back before you know it."

"You'd better be. Dozan said those things to rile you up, but don't let your guard down in the House of Shadows. I want you to come home."

"I won't let my guard down."

"This thing with Fordham …"

Kerrigan shook her head and took a step back. "I don't want to talk about Fordham."

"You're going to be alone with him for two weeks."

"Just don't."

Clover sighed. "Okay. But I'll kick his ass if he doesn't take care of you."

Kerrigan laughed. "I'd like to see that."

"I'm scrappy."

Kerrigan hugged her again and then hurried toward the mountain before she could get sappy. It was two weeks. How bad could it be?

\*\*\*

Kerrigan's steps slowed as she approached the front entrance to the mountain. A few days ago, she'd thought that she would leave the mountain behind, join a tribe, and become a full citizen. Now, the mountain was her forever home. So much had changed in so little time that it was hard to believe any of it was true. One day, she had been discreetly deposited into the care of the House of Dragons by her father. Twelve years later, she was a Society member.

Thinking of her father—Kivrin Argon, First of the House of Cruse—only soured her mood further. He was next in line for one of the four ruling families of Bryonica, and she'd been a princess, the lost Princess Felicity. Everyone had been looking for her after her "disappearance." Unbeknownst to them, her father knew precisely where she was. He'd left her there himself before the softly pointed ears that revealed that she was half-Fae were visible. She'd hidden her heritage from all but her closest friends for twelve years, and now, her secret was out. She was almost happy to be out of Kinkadia to avoid Bryonican royals and the upcoming Season.

Almost.

She nodded at the guards at the entrance and then headed toward the dungeons. If news had already reached Dozan, from his spies inside the mountain, then others likely had already heard as well. Her first indication that something was wrong was the increase in guards. Guards patrolled inside Draco Mountain but not like this. She saw more guards here that she didn't recognize than she did. She didn't know what use it would be if the person who had murdered Basem Nix was a Society member. Guards didn't even usually have much magic. Just enough to keep the populace in check.

"Where do you think you're going?" a guard asked, stopping her at the entrance to the dungeons.

"Official Society business."

The guard looked skeptical. Kerrigan didn't blame her. Not only was she drunk, but she was also an underage half-Fae. Her eyes darted to Kerrigan's softly pointed ears and back.

"I'll look the part when I get my black robes," she half-joked.

"Oh," the guard said, hastily stepping back. "I didn't realize it was you."

Kerrigan shot her a hopefully warm smile before careening down the stairs. The temperature dropped precipitously, the farther she wound her way deeper into the dungeons. Kerrigan hadn't been here in years. Lyam had dared her to run to the bottom of the dungeons one summer. She'd done so just to taunt him. But they'd also thought that the dungeons were empty. She shuddered at the thought of the man she'd found with his guts hanging out.

She gagged on the memory. Lyam had wanted to prove he could do it, too, but she hadn't let him go. That was back before Lyam had confessed his feelings for her, back when he'd been the fourth member of their quartet, back when he'd been alive.

Voices drifted up out of the gloom, bringing her back into the present. Lyam was gone. His compass still tucked away in her pocket. There was nothing she could do to change that, but Basem's death was a different story. A new mystery for her to solve.

"Yes, Corinna. Thank you so much for your assistance," someone said. "We have all that we need here. I'll let you continue with your investigation."

"Thank you, Bastian," Mistress Corinna said. Corinna was the current Chief of the Guard. She'd vouched for Kerrigan before the council when her place in the Society was being debated. "I have my best men here. We'll find who did this."

Kerrigan surreptitiously rounded the corner and found Master Bastian and Mistress Hellina standing before Mistress Corinna. Both Bastian and Helly were on the Society council—the highest rank of any member. Bastian had been a dragon tournament adjudicator this year, as Helly had been five years ago.

She was still listening in on the conversation when her foot slipped on the last step. "Scales," she hissed under her breath.

But it was enough.

Helly whipped around, and when she saw Kerrigan, she sighed heavily. "Kerrigan, what are you doing here?"

Kerrigan straightened and marched forward with what she hoped looked like purpose. "I heard what happened."

"And *how* did you hear that?" Helly asked. "We haven't even announced anything yet."

"Isn't that her specialty?" Bastian asked with a warm smile.

"Sticking her nose in where it doesn't belong?"

Kerrigan shrugged. She wasn't about to say that Dozan Rook had told her. They couldn't hope to purge all his spies. "This concerns me."

"It does not," Helly said. Then, she wrinkled her nose. "Are you drunk?"

"Uh, a bit tipsy," Kerrigan confessed.

Bastian laughed softly. "You can't blame her, Hellina. You couldn't even stand on two feet after you celebrated your tournament win."

She flashed him an irritated look. Black thumbprints from exhaustion were apparent under her eyes. She'd been running herself ragged with the Basem investigation, and now, it was all starting again. "That is beside the point."

Corinna covered a laugh with a cough.

"Is he really dead?" Kerrigan asked.

Helly sighed and put a hand on Kerrigan's shoulder. "Yes. I'm sorry."

"Did we at least get any information from him about the Red Masks before this?"

Corinna shook her head. "No. Nothing."

"This was an inside job," Kerrigan told them.

"Yes, we came to that conclusion," Helly said. "And *no*, you are not part of this investigation. You will let the Society handle it this time."

"I'm part of the Society now."

"You have a year of training first. And if I'm not mistaken, you are leaving in the morning."

"It's not a crime that she's invested," Bastian said. Helly shot him a look full of wrath. But he dismissed her concerns. "I am not suggesting she delay her travels or training, just that you cannot expect her to have no feelings on the matter. She is the one who brought him in."

Helly nodded. "How about this? I will keep you up to date on the investigation."

"I would appreciate that." Kerrigan paused for a moment before leaving. She should let it go, but a part of her couldn't do it yet. "Are you going to question Society members too?"

Helly and Bastian shared a look.

"We're still discussing it," Bastian told her. "But we will do our due diligence."

Society members were supposed to be above reproach. There should have been no reason to think otherwise. But this death was proof that someone in the Society was involved. Because there was only one reason to kill a man in these dungeons—to keep him from spilling your secrets.

# CHAPTER 3

*The Hangover*

*B*ang, bang, bang, bang.

Kerrigan felt every vibration of the fist against her door inside her skull. She groaned dramatically, covering her eyes with her forearm as she rolled over.

"Go away," she muttered.

Her mouth felt like it had been stuffed with cotton balls. Her eyes burned. At any moment, she might expel the entire contents of her stomach. Every single part of her body ached from head to toe. Normally, she'd have Darby create some kind of herbal potion to help with the hangover. Except Darby was no longer her roommate. She lived in a Row mansion, which meant there was no cure for this terrible feeling.

*Bang, bang, bang, bang.*

Kerrigan cursed the gods as she dragged her body out of bed. She ran a hand back through the frizz of her curly red hair. Sure that it looked like a rat's nest. Then, she swung the door open.

"Can you keep it down?"

Her eyes moved up, up, up the layers of black silk to the Fae male towering over her in her doorway. It was a sin for someone to look like Prince Fordham Ollivier this early in the morning. He was six and a half feet of solid muscle with black hair that fell forward into his gray eyes, which were currently set on thunderstorm as they glared down at her. He radiated sinister energy, as if something dark and malevolent were trapped under his skin, so pale that it was near translucent. But Kerrigan had promptly gotten over the anger when he didn't immediately try to kill her. Though he looked like he might try today.

"What are you still doing in bed?" he demanded.

She put her hand up and waved it downward in the general note of keeping it down. "Too loud."

His grip tightened on the door until the wood creaked. "What in the gods' names did you do last night?"

"I might have had a drink." She let her emerald-green eyes meet his, squinting into the hallway light. "Or two."

"Or ten," he growled. "You're a mess."

"I'm going to sleep for a couple of hours."

She started to close the door in his face, but he slammed his hand on it, keeping it open.

"We were supposed to leave twenty minutes ago. If you're not ready in a half hour, I'm leaving without you."

"Fine. That sounds nice."

He blew out an exasperated breath. "Why are you always so much trouble?"

"It's what makes me so endearing, princeling."

He closed his eyes and took a breath. "Half an hour, Kerrigan, and then we're going to the House of Shadows. You need to be *ready*."

Then, he stalked away from her, leaving her floundering with the door. She glared after him. It would have been nice to stay within the confines of the mountain, where she was safe. Except she wasn't safe. If there was someone working with Basem Nix within these walls, no one was safe.

Not that it'd be better in the House of Shadows. She'd be lucky if she ever came out of there again. She could snub Fordham, but despite their problems, she owed him. He'd offered her a spot in the House of Shadows when he could have left her to languish in Bryonican high society. It didn't redeem him of everything else though.

He'd lied to her the entire time they were together. He'd been exiled from his people and decided to join the dragon tournament to earn a place back in the House of Shadows. It was the only reason he'd been able to leave the magical spell that had trapped them. Neither of them knew what would happen next. If they'd welcome him back. If he'd be able to leave again. Where it put them.

Kerrigan cursed again.

She didn't want to think about *them*. And the fact that there was no them.

But she couldn't stay here even if she was mad at him. She was a member of the House of Shadows. She wouldn't let Fordham face it alone.

So, she changed into her traveling gear, plaited her obnoxiously tangled hair down her back, and grabbed the bag she'd packed yesterday. She opted not to eat anything. Not with how her stomach was behaving. Then, she headed up to the dragon aerie. The brighter and brighter it got, the worse her eyes watered, and the more painful her headache, but she hadn't doubted Fordham when he said that he would leave her. He was a man of his word... until he wasn't.

Kerrigan eased past the row of dragons. Some of them said hello as she passed, but most were still sleeping. Then, she found her dragon.

*Her* dragon.

It was still unbelievable to even think that at all. She'd loved flying from the moment she arrived in the House of Dragons. She'd thought that her last flight was a month ago, and now, she had her own dragon that she could fly whenever she wanted.

"Morning, Tieran," she said as she approached the midnight-blue dragon.

He was small for his kind, smaller even than normal, but he was quick and determined.

*Ah, so Fordham got your lazy self out of bed,* he spoke directly into her mind.

And also a jerk.

She sighed. She wasn't ready to deal with Tieran's behavior today. They'd never liked each other, and honestly, she still didn't know why he'd picked her in the dragon tournament. He could have had Fordham or any of the other competitors. Instead, he'd picked her. So, here they were.

"Let's get this over with," she told him.

She could have sworn that he rolled his gold slitted eyes as he turned away from her.

"You made it," Fordham said stiffly.

He'd thrown a thick cloak over his silks. Even in the heart of summer, it was cold in the skies. She'd forgotten hers. Great.

"I'm all ready to go."

Fordham reached into his pack and tossed her a cloak. "Figured you'd forget yours."

She bit her lip. "Thanks."

Their eyes met across the short distance. Tension sparked between them. She wanted to go to him, to bridge that space, like they had in the gazebo of her father's Row mansion. The taste of his lips still lingered. After a month of her visions constantly pulling them together, them learning not to hate each other and then to trust each other, only for her to be rejected …

It still panged in her chest when she looked at him. He'd wanted it too. She knew that he had, but it couldn't happen. Fordham was cursed to hurt anyone he cared about. Even though she would risk it for him, he wouldn't risk it for her. And didn't that make all the difference?

She averted her gaze and settled instead on his dragon. "Good morning, Netta."

The red-jeweled dragon inclined her head. *Kerrigan, it's always a pleasure.*

See, why couldn't she have gotten Netta as her dragon? Netta was as mischievous as Kerrigan had ever been. They would have been a perfect pair.

"Let's get going. We have a few hours in the skies before we reach the House of Shadows," Fordham said.

Kerrigan secured her pack to Tieran's back. Fordham must have already attached a saddle for her comfort. Her throat tightened up, and she tried to ignore how much she wanted to fix this between them. But it couldn't be fixed. That much was clear.

"Did you hear about what happened last night?"

"Beyond your inebriation?" Fordham asked.

"Basem was found dead in the dungeons."

His head snapped to her. "What? When?"

"Last night, when I got back in, I went down to speak with Helly and Bastian about it."

He withdrew into himself. "There is a plant inside the Society."

She nodded. "That's what I think too. Helly told me not to get involved."

He rolled his eyes. "Good luck with that."

"I guess it's good that we're going away for two weeks."

"Perhaps," he said. "Hopefully, they'll have caught the person by the time we return."

*Or we could not go.*

But she didn't offer the alternative. Fordham needed to go home, and she needed to see the tribe that she had sworn herself to.

"Let's hope," she said. "I'd like someone else to step up once in a while."

He just sighed. "Get on your dragon."

She laughed at his exasperation. "So, where exactly is the House of Shadows?"

The archives of the thirteenth tribe had been stricken from record. Their magicked home erased from maps and memory. Only high-ranking Society members had access to that knowledge and unsuspecting humans who wandered across the spell line.

"North," Fordham said before vaulting onto Netta's back.

"North," she muttered. "Right. Super helpful."

"You'll know when you need to know."

"I'm a member of the House of Shadows now," she grumbled. "You could just tell me."

"You're not actually."

Kerrigan froze with her hand on Tieran's leg. "What are you talking about?"

"You're not a member of the House of Shadows."

"But you said to the council ..."

"What they wanted to hear."

"I don't understand."

"You cannot be a member until you swear fealty to my father, King Samael Ollivier." He paused, looking momentarily forlorn. "And he accepts you into his court."

Kerrigan gulped. "You didn't say that your dad had to *accept* me."

"What would have been the point?"

"What if he rejects me?"

Fordham shrugged. "We won't let that happen."

Kerrigan blinked up at him, her headache now the least of her worries. She put her foot into Tieran's leg and hoisted herself into the saddle. She wobbled slightly and felt her stomach clench. She tightened her grip on the pommel.

*If you throw up on me, then you will be walking to the House of Shadows,* Tieran said irritably.

"Noted," she grumbled.

Netta took the lead, gliding toward the exit and then flying out the entrance. Tieran followed behind her. Normally, this was Kerrigan's favorite part—the first free fall into oblivion before they leveled off—but today, it was the last thing she wanted. She should have given up a few extra minutes to run to the infirmary for something to settle her stomach. But it was too late now.

"Take it easy," she pleaded with Tieran, but he either didn't hear her or didn't care.

He vaulted off of the stone opening in the mountain. He tucked his wings in tight to his body as they plummeted hundreds of feet toward the surface of the valley. Kerrigan's stomach rose to her throat. She closed her eyes and held on for dear life, hoping that she wouldn't unleash the drink from last night onto her dragon. She didn't doubt that he wouldn't let her ride the rest of the way.

Then, at the last second, his wings exploded out of him, and they rose as he caught the wind. Going up might be worse, as it jolted her stomach down toward her toes. She leaned hard against the saddle, running her hands along his cool scales to try to settle herself as they pulled up into a glide off of Netta's right wing.

"That was not nice," she groaned.

Tieran's body rumbled, as if he was laughing at her. Ass.

If they were bonded, as they were supposed to be, he would have been able to feel her discomfort. He wouldn't have tried something like that because he would have suffered too. But nothing had gone how it was supposed to.

At the bonding ceremony, they had both drunk the potion that would connect them for life. She went under and saw a vision of her father being beaten by a large man in a white toga. She'd never seen anyone like that before, and when she tried to get the man to stop, he *looked* at her. She had no idea what any of that meant, but as soon as she returned to herself, she knew it had gone wrong. She and Tieran hadn't bonded.

They couldn't tell anyone either. He would have been sent back to the Holy Mountain without getting a dragon rider, and no one had wanted her to have a dragon in the first place. They'd use any excuse to kick her out. So, they had to keep this secret to themselves and hope they survived dragon training together.

Kerrigan had doubts about that, but first, she had to survive the House of Shadows.

# CHAPTER 4

*N*etta says that *we're close,* Tieran informed her.

"Good," she said into the wind. She was as ready as she'd ever be.

Fordham gestured for them to fly lower toward a small depression in the surrounding mountains. It was an uninhabited valley between two mountains, not nearly as large as Kinkadia, but Kinkadia was the oldest city on the continent. It had been here even before Fae began to inhabit it.

"There's nothing down there," she said.

The closer they grew to the ground, the worse she felt about landing. As if she were being repelled from the valley floor by a force of nature. Her stomach, which had finally been settling, began to grumble.

"I don't like this."

*Nor I,* Tieran admitted.

It must have taken a lot to shake a dragon. Whatever was in that valley was not something that she wanted to see. It felt like a physical presence against her mind, telling her to walk away. She swallowed and hoped they weren't making a mistake.

Finally, Tieran landed softly in the moss-filled valley. Kerrigan slid off of his back with her stomach in her throat.

"What the hell is this place?" Kerrigan asked. "And why did we land here? I've heard of this place before, and nothing good can come from being near this valley."

"You've heard of this valley?" Fordham asked as he dropped onto the moss next to her.

"Death's Valley," she whispered as if the air would take up the challenge. "No one flies over it or walks into it and returns alive. It's only on maps to deter wayward travelers from venturing too near. They say the air is toxic and will addle your senses."

Fordham looked amused by the notion. "Interesting propaganda. I feel nothing."

It was the first time she'd noticed that he did seem completely unaffected. Meanwhile, she was practically cowering away from the valley.

"Why?" she managed to get out.

He gestured dramatically. "I give you the House of Shadows."

Kerrigan frowned and followed his gesture, but she didn't see anything. Just that sick feeling washing over her. "*This* is the House of Shadows?"

"You'll see when we cross the dividing line." Fordham shouldered his pack and then patted Netta twice. "You and Tieran should go. My home is no place for dragons any longer."

Netta nuzzled his side, speaking directly to him. He smiled at her in a way that meant that their bond had clearly worked. Kerrigan had to look away from the display. She and Tieran would never have that.

She grabbed her own pack off of Tieran.

*Don't get killed*, he said.

"What is this, sentiment?" she joked.

He puffed a hot breath out of his nostrils. *Hardly. But if you die and I don't, someone is going to know that we weren't bonded.*

She rolled her eyes. "As if that would be your greatest concern."

*Just don't die.*

"I don't plan to," she told him by way of good-bye and followed Fordham across the moss-covered path.

The farther they walked, the more oppressive the sensation got. Whoever had created this spellwork did a magnificent job. It completely repelled her and had ended up so ingrained in their history that Kerrigan hadn't known Death's Valley was hiding the mouth of the House of Shadows.

"How do humans and half-Fae end up on your property if it makes them feel this sick?"

"Usually desperation. The Fae have closed off their hunting grounds or refused them help. So, the only option is to brave *us.*"

Kerrigan sighed. Yes, that sounded very plausible. "Starvation or suicide."

"Basically. Some of them aren't repelled by the land though," he said easily. "We weren't the only people here when we were trapped behind the magical barrier. Humans and half-Fae coexisted with us, and many escaped during the Great War. Their descendants don't feel the oppression and can come and go." Fordham frowned. "It's our one source of trade."

"You *trade* with humans?"

Fordham's face was like stone. "My father doesn't like it, but he permits it. We have a sort of truce with a nearby village."

"Interesting."

So, Fordham wasn't the first to work with the enemy. And they didn't just kill humans and half-Fae, unprompted. Maybe she wouldn't die on sight when she entered. Maybe.

"Here," Fordham said, going suddenly still. "This is the border for the barrier."

Now that Kerrigan was right in front of it, she could almost put the pain aside. She closed her eyes, putting her hand out in front of her. A humming vibrated against her hand as she felt the edges of the spellwork. It was ancient and powerful. Unlike anything she had ever seen before in her life. Completely invisible to the naked eye and yet all-consuming. To be able to have multiple uses—keeping the House of Shadows inside, repelling everyone else, and shielding its location—was a marvel. Even at a lucky thirteen casters, she couldn't imagine any group being strong enough to contain this much power.

A shock hit her palm. She yelped and stepped back, breaking her connection with the invisible wall.

"What was that?" Fordham asked.

"I don't know."

She'd never had a spell react to her like that. And she'd had plenty of strange magical things happen to her.

Five years ago, she'd discovered that she had visions of the future. Gelryn the Destroyer, the formidable dragon of the Great War, called her a harbinger. After her series of visions during the dragon tournament, which brought her and Fordham together and led her to *win* the tournament, Gelryn had discovered that she was a spiritcaster. There hadn't been one in a millennium, and when she returned to Kinkadia, she would have to find a way to control her spirit magic or else be consumed by it.

But this didn't feel like her visions. This felt like the spell was *alive*. Not just alive, but *mad*. Could spells have emotions? She'd never heard of such a thing.

"It's like nothing I've ever seen before."

Fordham nodded. "The lore is that the people who cast the spell all perished after casting it. Its strength is gained by their sacrifice."

"Scales," she murmured. "How terrible."

Fordham made a noncommittal sound. He'd been so stoic the entire morning that she hadn't quite noticed he was in distress until that moment. That he wasn't mad at her because of the hangover. He was taking out his own unease about coming home on her.

"Are you ready?" she asked him gently.

"Yes," he said, straightening his shoulders.

"Fordham, it's me. You don't have to pretend."

But his eyes never wavered to her face. He stared straight ahead, as if he were facing down an enemy.

"Do you think you'll be able to come back through?"

He didn't respond, just lifted one shoulder.

Kerrigan came to his side and stared forward. "Together?"

He tipped his head down. She closed her eyes briefly, working up the courage to take his hand. When her fingers touched his, he didn't yank them away, just twined them together. Then, as one, they crossed the border that led into the House of Shadows.

\*\*\*

Kerrigan opened her eyes in a new world.

She'd grown up in a palace, surrounded by lush Bryonican gardens, and then lived inside Draco Mountain since she was five with the entire city of Kinkadia as her playground. But nothing prepared her for this.

The mossy valley led to a rustic village. It sat on the edge of a lush forest, leading to a trio of peaks reaching for the sky. Purple wildflowers blossomed along the stone walk, which was just big enough for a carriage. Horses grazed in open pastures, birds trilled in the trees, and everything was fertile and blossoming. The air was colder than home, and snow still lingered on the mountains. The view was picturesque. Not at all what she had thought the House of

Shadows would be like.

"Wow," was all she could manage.

Fordham's face was conflicted, as if he'd finally come home and he wanted to be anywhere else, all at the same time. "It's beautiful, isn't it?"

"Yes," she breathed. "As if it were stuck in time."

"It is. We haven't any of the advancements of the outside world. Much is still run as it was a thousand years earlier."

"Kinkadia must have been a huge shock."

Fordham's jaw tightened. She remembered the look on his face when she'd first taken him to the Square and how he'd devoured the meat pies as if he'd never tasted anything like it. He likely never had. Or when they'd gone to Carmine's for a poetry reading. The light in his eyes. She hadn't understood what it really meant to him until this moment.

"We should test the border," he said instead.

Kerrigan faced the valley. Already, Tieran and Netta had vanished into the skies. If they were bound, she'd know in exactly what direction he was. But they weren't, so she didn't.

"Should we walk back through?"

"I'm sure you can. You're half-Fae."

She scowled at him. "Thanks for the reminder. I had no idea."

She pushed forward, back through the oppressive border that held the House of Shadows within. When she looked over her shoulder, the little village had vanished. Just like that.

"Whoa," she breathed as she stepped through. "That's creepy."

Fordham swallowed, not acknowledging her.

"What's the worst that could happen?"

He glanced at her, the words painted on him in a way he rarely let her see. The worst was that he'd be *stuck* here all over again. The barrier would recognize him as a Fae of the House of Shadows, and he wouldn't be allowed back out into the new world he was beginning to love.

"It's going to let you through," she told him.

"It is."

She didn't ask if he wanted her to go with him. He had to face this particular demon alone.

With a deep breath, he put one foot in front of the other and stepped back through the barrier. She thought he would disappear, as the village had done on the other side, but no, there he was. A prince in every aspect. Her heart lurched at the sight of him, the elation on his face. He'd passed the test that had been weighing on him. He could now come and go as he pleased. Whether that was because of his exile or some other new trick of the magic, it didn't matter. He'd be going home with her to start dragon training.

He stepped back through, brushing imaginary lint off of his silk garments. All grace and power returned to his too-beautiful face. "Let's go meet my father."

# CHAPTER 5
## *The House of Shadows*

**K**errigan couldn't stop gawking as they neared the village. The path had been deceptively long. More space than she'd assumed they'd have, but not enough to truly feel free. She fought for neutral as they walked along the cobbled steps and into the town.

"The village is called Cavour," Fordham said. "It's ancient Fae for ..."

"Songbird," she said.

He looked at her in surprise. "Yes. I didn't think you were fluent in ancient Fae."

"I'm not, but ..." She paused on the word and sighed. "My father used to call me his little *cavour de thiery* when I was very young."

"Little red songbird," Fordham translated. He reached up, as if to touch a lock of her tangled red hair, but seemed to think better of it and let it fall. "I've never heard you sing before."

"It was a joke," she said. "I couldn't sing at all. He said I scared all the birds away with my racket."

A real smile hit Fordham's face. As if he'd forgotten for a moment where they were. Then, he quickly let it slip and faced forward. They'd both had complicated childhoods. Neither of their fathers were going to win any awards. It could have been something they bonded over; instead, he'd hidden his exile and his father's wrath.

As they ventured deeper into Cavour, villagers appeared around every corner. Their eyes wide with surprise at seeing their prince walking among them again. A group of women washing in basins curtsied deeply at his approach. A girl no older than Kerrigan looked out at him from a second-story balcony with open want. A group of Fae children, still too young to have grown into their ears, giggled nearby, running across their path.

"Don't bother the prince!" their mother yelled, ordering them inside.

Fordham was impervious to it all. Kerrigan didn't know how he did it. She wanted to scoop up the little bundles of joy and thank them for being welcoming. But this wasn't her court. She no longer *had* a court.

When they made it to the town square with a three-tiered fountain at the center, a woman stepped out of the masses that had now gathered and offered him a single black rose.

"We rejoice in your return, Your Royal Highness."

Fordham nodded his head at her but made no move to take the flower. Kerrigan smiled at the woman and took it for him. The woman put her hand to her chest and backed away quickly.

"Let's go," he barked at her.

His voice held none of the gentleness that she had grown accustomed. Had she made some sort of faux pas by taking the bloom? It'd seemed insulting not to accept it.

But Kerrigan didn't know the customs, and Fordham hadn't prepared her for any of it. She tucked the black rose into her bag and hastened after him. They finally reached the end of the village, she decided it was safe to ask.

"Should I not have taken the flower?"

He shook his head. "It's fine. I couldn't have taken it."

"Why?"

He still looked straight ahead at the forbidden forest that led to the base of peaks. "I will have to maintain a certain appearance through this, Kerrigan," he said, his face like stone. "You may not like it."

She gulped and nodded. The flower was the least of her concerns. "We're going in there?"

"Yes, the court lies within the mountain. You should feel right at home."

"Is it modeled off of Draco Mountain?"

"It predates Draco Mountain," he told her. "When the dragons first landed in Alandria, they didn't go south to the valley where you live. They made their home on Nineveh, now just called the Holy Mountain, and its neighboring peak, Ravinia." He gestured before him. "*This* is Ravinia."

"I've never heard the story told that way."

"Of course not. Draco is now the seat of power for the Society. They wouldn't want anyone to think that power had ever resided elsewhere."

Only a few weeks ago, she wouldn't have believed it. But with everything raging through the Society now, she was sure it was possible. Power corrupted; absolute power corrupted absolutely.

The path cut straight through the forest until it reached an open meadow full of tall, wild grasses, and on the other side of the meadow lay the opening to the mountain. The path across the meadow was empty of people. Not a soul wandered the area before the forbidding entrance.

"I've gone to battle on these fields," Fordham told her almost absent-mindedly. "Killed on these fields."

"It doesn't appear that blood has been spilled in some time."

His gaze cut to her. "Let's hope to keep it that way."

Fear coated her scent, but she could do nothing about it. She'd never been away from her home for this long. Not since she was a child. And she was walking into certain danger. Anticipatory anxiety laced through her.

But Cyrene's words came back to her, as they always did when she was afraid. Cyrene had won the dragon tournament five years prior and was the first person to see Kerrigan for who she truly was. Her mentor and friend. When she'd told Cyrene of her fear, Cyrene had told her that everyone was afraid, but those who mastered their fear, they were the ones who went on to do great things.

Kerrigan lifted her chin and continued forward. Fear wouldn't hold her back. She could do *anything*.

A breeze blew in across the meadow, ruffling her hair. She tilted her head to the sun. She wished that something so evil couldn't come out of something so beautiful. But that was fantasy, and she was in the real world.

The entrance was a wide stone archway, rough on all edges, as if battles had been fought against it and won. Large metal doors were thrown open invitingly with a Fae male standing in the center, awaiting their arrival.

"Prince Fordham," a man said, stepping forward with a stiff bow. He was short in stature and round in the middle. He had flimsy blond hair and eyes like a weasel. "You have returned to tribe Charbonnet."

"Indeed, Langdan. Are you here to prevent me access to the House of Shadows?" Fordham asked, his voice low and lethal.

Tribe Charbonnet? Kerrigan had never heard the House of Shadows called that before. Was this another term lost to time?

"Of course not, Your Highness," Langdan said.

"Then, stand aside."

Langdan sniffed. "First, allow me to direct you to refreshments and a place to freshen up after your long journey."

Fordham narrowed his eyes at him dangerously. He could force his way in. This sniveling little man couldn't stop him. Not with Fordham's skill with a sword and magic. But that wasn't the entrance they wanted to make either.

She cleared her throat slightly, and Langdan's eyes found hers. His nose wrinkled at her appearance.

"Maybe freshening up would be good."

Fordham didn't look at her, but he stiffened at her words. Langdan's smile grew.

"As the lady wishes," Fordham said finally.

Langdan turned on a mark and headed into Ravinia Mountain. Fordham kept his head high, following him into the depths. Kerrigan had no other choice but to do the same.

The doors closed behind them by magic, sealing them inside the Dark Court. The way was brightly lit, and though she should have felt at ease, being in the heart of a mountain, it didn't quite have the ambience of Draco Mountain. This felt like a tomb.

They saw no one as Langdan showed them down a set of stairs and to a bathing chamber. Unlike the hot springs under her mountain, this was a large claw-foot tub already brimming with magically heated water. Fordham was shown to his own bathing chamber. Langdan formally bowed to him as he left but said not a word to Kerrigan.

A pair of twins appeared from behind a curtain and came toward Kerrigan. They were dressed the same in beige dresses with their blonde hair pulled back into severe buns.

"I am Benton, and this is my sister, Bayton. We will be your attendants while in the House of Shadows," Benton said.

Kerrigan frowned. She hadn't had a bathing attendant since she was five years old. "Oh. That's okay. I can do it myself."

Bayton frowned and looked to her sister. "That is unnecessary. We were assigned to you."

"Right. Just doing your jobs," Kerrigan said. "Well, okay."

They hurried over and stripped her down, plunging her into the heated water. Thankfully, she'd lost most of her modesty in the House of Dragons. The bathing quarters were filled with dozens of littlings at any given time. The last year, she'd actually enjoyed that only the senior Dragon Blessed had to share a space.

"So, which is which?" Kerrigan asked.

The twins looked at each other.

"I'm Bayton," the first said. She had a small mark on her upper lip that was her only distinctive feature.

"I'm Benton." Benton might have been just a little softer in the face, but otherwise, they were entirely the same.

"Ben and Bay," Kerrigan said. "Got it."

The sisters giggled, and Kerrigan joined them. Then, they straightened and sobered. Their eyes were wide with alarm.

"Apologies," Bayton whispered.

"We didn't mean ..."

"To laugh?"

"At you, miss."

"With me actually," Kerrigan said. "It's fine. I like to laugh."

But apparently, *laughing* wasn't an approved task because the twins withdrew after that. Saying nothing while they finished with the bath, dried her off, and pulled her hair up and out of her face. A fine silk dress appeared, and they slipped her into it. It was the black and silver of the House of Shadows livery that she had so admired on Fordham. Maybe this wasn't so bad after all.

"Thank you," she told the attendants.

Their eyes rounded, and they curtsied deeply before disappearing from the bathing chamber. She shook her head in confusion. They'd acted like beaten dogs.

When she stepped out of the room, Langdan was waiting for her, but Fordham was nowhere in sight.

"Where has Fordham gone off to?"

Langdan narrowed his eyes. "His Royal Highness has already retired to his chambers."

"Right. His *Royal* Highness," she said, trying not to let the words come out sour.

"If I were you, I would be sure to use the formal denotation while you're here."

"Of course," she said. "I assume that you are to escort me."

"Indeed," he said flatly and then turned on his heel.

She resisted the urge to kick his shin. But she thought about it.

Langdan either took her on the most circuitous path around the mountain or no one lived here. They didn't see anyone. No whispers trailed behind her. Maybe no one even knew they were here besides Benton and Bayton and this insufferable dolt.

"Here we are," Langdan said.

Langdan rapped on the door twice, and Fordham's face appeared a moment later.

"What?" he snarled.

Langdan straightened and gulped at the tone. "I have brought your ... lady."

Fordham arched an eyebrow. "You didn't set up rooms for her?"

Langdan looked scandalized at the suggestion. "Certainly not."

Kerrigan's cheeks flushed at the insinuation that they wouldn't need separate quarters. Why else would a half-Fae walk willingly into these halls?

"Let her pass," Fordham finally bit out. "And tell my father I am ready to see him."

"Of course, Your Royal Highness," Langdan said. He looked over his shoulder once before disappearing down the hallway.

Fordham jerked the door the rest of the way open. "Get in."

Kerrigan didn't object. How would she even begin? She felt wildly out of her depth. She stepped across the threshold into his suite of rooms. They were night and day compared to the corridors. Complete with plush rugs, tapestries and paintings covering the stone walls, and a magnificent set of black-and-silver lounging chairs. An arched doorway led to a bedchamber with a writing desk and fireplace. Only the nicest suites in Draco Mountain had fireplaces that would vent out. And she could tell by the additional set of adjoining rooms that *this* was probably the lushest and over-the-top room she'd ever walked into. And that was saying a lot.

Fordham snapped the door closed behind her. "Well, this is a disaster."

"Nothing has happened yet."

"Precisely. Langdan waited for us at the doors. He's my father's chief buffoon and was there to handle us. I would almost expect the bathing before an official meeting but then depositing me into my old rooms ..." He shook his head. "And you ..."

"Me?"

He huffed. "He didn't give you separate rooms."

"Noticed that. Why is that a problem? I mean, besides the obvious," she said, her eyes drifting to the canopy bed in the other room.

"It's about propriety," Fordham said. He paced back and forth in the sitting room as irritation clogged the very air she breathed. "He must think you're my concubine."

Kerrigan choked on the word. "Is that ... is that a thing here?"

"Yes. Well, no. Usually, it's just a mistress, but I am unwed. So, that makes you a whore."

Kerrigan wanted to be offended that they assumed that, but all she could do was laugh. She doubled over at the thought. That she, Kerrigan Argon—originally Princess Felicity, First of the House of Cruse, and *now* a member of the Society as a dragon rider—could be something as simple as someone else's whore.

"Stop laughing," Fordham said.

"I'm sorry," she said, trying to get it under control. "But it's absurd."

"Where you are from perhaps but not here." He shook his head. "You don't understand. Half-Fae are not treated as equals."

"Obviously."

"The best you could hope for would be to become the concubine of the crowned prince. And I was aware that it was going to be difficult to convince my father that you're a Society member and ally, but now, we're starting below zero in a world where perception is everything."

"Fine. Fine." She wiped her hand down her face and shook off the last of her laughter. "Wouldn't it have been better for us to discuss this before coming here?"

"When would we have, Kerrigan?" he demanded. "While you were out, drinking with your friends, or when you were hungover on the flight?"

"I don't know. Maybe before or after you told me you were exiled," she snapped right back.

He froze at the words. "I wanted to tell you."

"Don't bother, princeling," she said, retreating to his nickname to keep them on solid ground.

"As you wish, halfling."

The word cut just a little bit more than normal.

"What do we do now?" she asked after a moment of silence.

"Wait for my father to see us."

Kerrigan looked at him skeptically. "I don't do well with *sit tight and wait your turn.*"

"We're trying *not* to get either of us killed."

"I can't make any promises."

Fordham chose to ignore her comment and headed into the bedroom, pulling a sheaf of papers out of the writing desk. He sat before it and began to write his sad, broody boy poetry. Meanwhile, she did what she always did when trapped inside with nothing to do—she slowly went crazy.

# CHAPTER 6
## *The Princess*

T wo days went by with nothing.

An interminably long space of time alone with Fordham Ollivier in his bedchamber. Anything could have been happening. They could have been using the big, beautiful bed in his chambers, just to give someone something to actually gossip about. Not that they'd seen anyone, except Benton and Bayton delivering meals three times a day.

But no. No fun bed times.

Fordham retreated to the couch, and she had the giant, fluffy goose down bed all to herself. He left a few times to try to speak to someone who would get them an audience with his father. He only came back angrier every time he left. She'd taken to avoiding him when he returned. They alternated between arguments and cold shoulders, and she didn't have the energy for it. He was out now and had been gone for an hour. She'd wanted out of the room bad enough that she even offered to join him. He'd almost laughed at her. As if her half-Fae presence would make everything worse.

"Miss Kerrigan," a voice called after a knock on the door.

Kerrigan rolled her eyes at the use of *miss* but still hurried to answer. It wasn't yet time for Benton and Bayton to bring lunch for her. Any reason for interaction would be worth it.

She flung the door open. "Yes?"

Benton and Bayton curtsied.

"Will you follow us, miss?" Benton said.

"Where?"

Bayton blanched.

Benton smiled warmly. "We're to prepare you for dinner."

"It's not even lunch."

Bayton nodded. "Yes, but we have our orders."

"Are we finally going to meet the king?"

"That I don't know," Benton said.

"Right. Orders," Kerrigan said. "Does Fordham know? I mean, His Royal Highness."

"We do not know," Bayton said with a shy smile.

They didn't really seem to know anything, or they refused to tell her. But this was her ticket out of this room. She'd go with her worst enemy to escape another day of solitude.

"I'll leave him a note," Kerrigan said. "Just one moment."

The attendants protested, but Kerrigan had already darted back into the bedroom. She found a scrap piece of paper and jotted out a little something to let him know where she was going. He'd probably be angry if he came back and saw she was gone. Even worse, if he had no idea where she'd gone.

"All ready," she said, stepping out of the room and closing the door behind her.

The twins took the lead, navigating the empty corridors with ease. And they truly were still empty. It was so disconcerting. She kept expecting to turn the corner and for the halls to be teeming with people. She found it hard to reconcile it with her home.

"Does no one live here?" she couldn't help asking the twins.

Benton and Bayton shared a glance. Benton answered, "Did His Royal Highness not inform you of how the court functions?" Then, she swallowed at the question, as if she'd already misstepped by asking it.

"Prince Fordham is famously recalcitrant and restrained," Kerrigan said.

Bayton stifled a giggle. "That he is, miss."

"You can call me Kerrigan."

Benton shook her head. "We couldn't."

"I assure you that I would not be offended."

They shared another look that Kerrigan took to mean that she was odd. But they smiled lightly afterward, as if they liked her strangeness.

"We really aren't supposed to discuss the inner workings of the court," Bayton whispered.

"But it wouldn't hurt her to have some knowledge of where she resided," Benton said. Bayton blinked at her sister, but Benton continued right on as they went up a flight of stairs, "The entire court has recently been called back into attendance."

Kerrigan tilted her head. That actually made sense. The court wasn't always in attendance in Bryonica either. People had their own homes and lives. They were called back when the ruler requested it. But there wasn't more land for their estates, just the mountain.

"Where do they normally live?"

"Well, Ravinia is the largest of three peaks, but the tunnels into this mountain expand to the other two—Valeria and Tesera. The three families of the House of Shadows have separated between the mountains. The Ollivier royals in Ravinia. We call the other two the little courts for Houses Laurent and Blanchard."

Fordham had mentioned once about there being three families, but they weren't like what she was used to. These were more factions, always vying for the right to rule. People could move between the factions, depending on their loyalty. They went to war against each other continuously, seeking to depose his father, and then war would start again until he got his throne back. It sounded barbaric. And explained so much about Fordham.

"So, Laurent and Blanchard are traveling back to court for …"

"The prince's return," Bayton whispered. She looked around, as if someone would catch them.

"Is it good or bad that he's back?" Kerrigan asked. She could see it going either way, considering his exile.

"We do not know," Bayton said, glancing uneasily at her sister.

"But court has not been the same since he left," Benton added.

They reached the top of the stairs, and Benton and Bayton went completely still. Then, they dipped into a low curtsy.

"Princess Wynter," they said in unison.

Kerrigan took their lead and dropped low. *Princess?* Who was this girl? The figure before her was hardly how Kerrigan expected a princess to dress, but what did she know about this bloody court?

"What is going on here?" Princess Wynter asked.

Kerrigan rose with the twins and got a good look at the woman. Princess Wynter was dressed in all black—a loose black tunic tucked into tight fighting pants. Her boots were quality leather, laced up to her knees. A bow was slung over her back with a quiver of arrows attached to her hip. Her hair was down to the middle of her back and the same color as her skin—white as snow. She had uncanny light-blue eyes that seemed to suck life out of the world.

"Ma'am, we're escorting Miss Kerrigan to get ready for dinner."

Wynter tilted her head to the side. She was practically ageless. She could have been seventeen, like Kerrigan, or three hundred, but either way, those *eyes* were something altogether different.

"I shall join you," she declared. "I need to prepare as well."

Benton nodded, even as Bayton clenched her hands into fists. "As you wish, my lady."

"Bayton, fetch my attendants as well."

Bayton dipped into another curtsy and then all but fled. Benton, to her credit, held her head up as she directed them down the hallway.

Wynter fell into step next to Kerrigan. Her eyes were forward, but it felt as if she were weighing her. "So, you are Fordham's new interest."

Kerrigan kept her face carefully neutral. *New interest* was such a clever way to say concubine. Though the more interesting part of the sentence was using Fordham's given name. This was his sister. So it made sense. And yet, it made little sense at the same time.

"I suppose that I am."

"Well, you are beautiful. I'll give him that for taste."

Kerrigan tried not to laugh but couldn't help it. "Beautiful? Me? I hardly think that's what did it."

*Beautiful* wasn't usually anyone's choice word for her. Between the uncontrollably curly red hair, freckled face, and mouth that never seemed to know when to shut up, she'd gotten *rambunctious, obstinate,* and *intimidating* before *beautiful.*

And Fordham, of all people, had thought that she was an insult. She'd been sent by the Society to work for him during the tournament because the servants were too scared of him. That didn't exactly go as planned—until she had prophetic dreams about him. The only thing he seemed to like less than a mouthy half-Fae shadowing him was one who actually helped him. Feelings for her enemy had only come later... when she stopped thinking of him as her enemy.

"Well, you're not like the last one. That's for certain," the princess said.

Kerrigan forced herself not to react to that. Surely, Wynter was baiting her. "So, you must know the inner workings of the court then."

Wynter arched a pale eyebrow. "Of course."

Kerrigan hated to show her ignorance, but she needed answers. She couldn't go on, not knowing what she was walking into. "Well, what is this dinner? Am I to meet the king?"

Wynter eyed her skeptically. "No one told you?"

Benton opened the door to reveal a room full of hundreds of stunning gowns. "Here we are, my ladies."

Kerrigan met Benton's gaze, and she shook her head just once. A warning. *Don't confide in Wynter. Don't give her your secrets. You've already said too much.*

But Wynter was waiting for an answer.

"No. No one told me."

Wynter smiled at her. It was supposed to be friendly, but somehow, it only looked a little mad. "We're to have a ball to celebrate my big brother's return."

\*\*\*

*A ball.*

*Big brother.*

These words didn't compute. Fordham had a … sister? Well, that had definitely never come up before. Of course, she should have associated princess with her being Fordham's sister, but she was still so used to Bryonican royalty that these rules didn't exactly make sense to her. In Bryonica, there were four royal lines and all the first of their line were considered princesses. Kerrigan had been a princess. Helly was technically a princess from a different royal house. She hadn't realized that it would mean blood relative. If Fordham had divulged information about his home, then she wouldn't continually be caught off guard. Wynter was apparently relishing in it.

"Well, a ball sounds lovely," Kerrigan finally said. She hated court games and always had. But she was going to have to remember how to play if she was to survive here.

"I bet," Wynter said.

"This way, Miss Kerrigan," Benton said, pulling her into an adjoining room, away from Wynter.

It was a bathing chamber, like the one from the other day, and Benton gestured for her to get in. After a few minutes of Benton scrubbing some kind of salt scrub into her skin, Kerrigan couldn't remain silent any longer.

"She's Fordham's sister?"

Benton nodded. "Half-sister. King Samael has had five wives. The first wife produced one sickly daughter, who died young. She wasn't even a hundred. The next wife was replaced for producing no children. And then Fordham's mother, Queen Kamara, was nearly displaced for lack of an heir when, miraculously, we got Prince Fordham."

"What happened to her?" Kerrigan whispered.

"We do not speak of it," Benton said. "But it was tragic. Wynter's mother was Queen Wisteria, an alliance to appease Laurent family, but she wasn't all there. She was removed from her role as queen as she slowly went mad."

"How terrible."

"Indeed."

"And now, he's remarried a fifth time?"

"Yes," Benton said with a bite in her voice. "Queen Viviana from family Blanchard."

"She's not your favorite?"

"Family Blanchard hates half-Fae more than the other two families."

Kerrigan startled and glanced up at Benton's covered ears. "You're half-Fae?"

"Yes, miss. My mother was a lady from Blanchard. The human male who … seduced her was beheaded."

Kerrigan gulped, reading between the lines. "I see."

"Bayton and I were given to King Samael as a gift with his new bride."

"A gift," I said flatly

"Yes, we don't have rights in the House of Shadows."

Fury burned in her veins, and she had to tamp down the rising magic that wanted to respond to the injustice. "Then, why ever am I being dressed for a royal ball?"

Benton looked at her in surprise. "You belong to Prince Fordham."

"Belong," Kerrigan repeated, unable to fathom these words.

"Of course. To belong to a male such as the prince is a great honor. It's a prized position, even after he weds. You receive much protection from all, except the males."

Kerrigan felt sick. This was worse than she'd thought. Worse than Fordham had even suggested. He'd said she'd be his concubine but nothing more. Had he wanted to save her feelings or suppress her rage?

"And what am I supposed to do at this ball?" she asked, clenching her hands into fists as she came out of the bath and wrapped herself in a towel.

Benton looked startled by Kerrigan's apparent anger. "You truly do not know these things? Prince Fordham has not made you aware that you belong to him?"

"He has not made me aware of that." There was no use in explaining to someone trapped within these walls that this was not how things were done outside.

"Well, you will attend as a sort of ornament. You decorate his appearance. Only the wealthiest Fae have the means to have such a person at their side."

Kerrigan wanted to tear this mountain down from the inside. No wonder they had been trapped away in here for a thousand years. When she had heard that they tortured half-Fae, she had assumed physical abuse. Not... this emotional abuse and, clearly, abuse of the sexual nature. How could property ever say no?

"And did Prince Fordham ever have a half-Fae as an *ornament* before?"

"No, miss," Benton said, fear creeping into her voice. "He was entirely against it, as it was a condition of his exile."

Kerrigan wanted to ask more, but she didn't need to. Fordham had never done this before. It was a misunderstanding. She would go to this ball and be his little decoration if that was how they needed to be seen publicly. Then, together, they would fix this, as they had fixed everything else. They had just over a week to make this backward society see her for who she really was. It wasn't long enough. Not by a long shot.

But she knew exactly how to play it in the meantime.

She wouldn't be going to this ball as she was. Kerrigan of the House of Dragons, the scrappy and rebellious fighter, had to die in these halls. No, tonight, she would don a persona she had long ago discarded, but to survive, it was necessary to become someone else. Tonight, she would be Princess Felicity, First of the House of Cruse, a Bryonican royal.

# CHAPTER 7
## *The Ball*

"**W**ell," Wynter said, her clear gaze sweeping Kerrigan's gown, "this is an improvement."

She spun her finger in a circle, and Kerrigan obliged, swishing in the sumptuous black-and-silver gown and letting her get a full look at the layers of soft satin. Kerrigan had never seen anyone wear a gown like this. The bone-fitted corset crushed her ribs and pushed her breasts up to her throat. A billowy plume of skirt fell to her feet. At least the bodice was more modern than the typical square neckline she had expected with this design. This one pushed the long, diaphanous, velvety sleeves off of her shoulders with a wide-open neck embroidered with Ollivier silver, accenting her pale throat and collarbone.

Her red hair had been straightened in an exercise that tested her patience like nothing else. She'd had no idea that the mass went down to her waist or that someone was talented enough to control the curls and frizz. That she could look like everyone else in an intricate updo. Even Darby had never managed something like this, and as a child, she never would have sat long enough. Benton had then darkened her lashes, colored in her eyebrows, added a line to her lids, applied careful rouge to her cheeks, and painted her lips the deepest, darkest red.

"You'll be the talk of the evening," Wynter said.

"Not next to you."

Wynter's own dress was just as extravagant but dyed the color of Kerrigan's lips. As if the dress were bleeding on her. Her white-blonde hair was up in a braided crown on the top of her head, and a diamond tiara had been placed in it. In fact, she was consummately festooned in glittering jewelry. A blood-red ruby at her throat, diamonds at her wrists, dripping diamonds at her ears, and a silver ear-covering atop one of her finely pointed Fae ears that dangled with rubies and diamonds. Comparatively, Kerrigan looked like a blank canvas.

"You're sweet," Wynter said. "Are you ready for this ball?"

"I'm always ready," she lied.

Wynter grinned, her teeth gleaming. "Ah, I see now."

"See?"

"I wondered why my brother would choose you."

"I don't know what you mean."

"He wasn't a proponent for human and half-Fae rights. He wasn't that stupid," she said, slowly stalking around Kerrigan, as if she were a predator trapping her prey. Of course, Wynter didn't know that Kerrigan wouldn't be easy prey. "But he never took a lover from either kind. In fact, he used it as a shield. As if he wouldn't sully himself. And now, he's shown up with you ..."

Ah, Kerrigan saw where she was going with this. "Do you have a problem with him taking a half-Fae lover?"

Wynter laughed, a throaty thing. "Hardly. I just couldn't figure out why he'd do it now."

"Maybe he came to his senses," she said with a look of carefree ease. She couldn't be caught off guard or seen to have anger about how half-Fae were treated here. It certainly wouldn't win her any points.

"Perhaps," Wynter said with a twinkle in her eye. "Shall we?"

"I believe so."

Benton held the door open for them, keeping her eyes down. Kerrigan touched her hand as she passed, a thanks, and then followed Wynter toward the ball, where she would have to bury her true self so completely that not even Fordham would recognize her.

The walk to the ballroom was shorter than Kerrigan had thought it would be. She had a matter of minutes to steel herself for what she was about to do, and then they were there. She could hear the music on the other side of the door. It was surprisingly comforting to have something so familiar. She'd been to dozens of balls just like this one. She'd be fine.

"There you are," a voice said.

Wynter and Kerrigan turned as one to find Fordham standing before them. Two other people flanked him. Their distaste for Wynter was plain on their faces. One was a well-built Fae male with similar features to Fordham—black hair, high cheekbones, and a cutting look. But the blue eyes were different, and the bounce in his step matched his quick smile. The female was equally raven-haired with a lush, curvy figure and Fordham's stern countenance.

"Brother," Wynter said sweetly. "So, you have come out of hiding? I ran into Kerrigan in the halls, and we have been getting acquainted."

"I have been in meetings," he said stiffly. "You'd know that if you bothered to follow court protocol."

Wynter's hand clenched at her side was the only indication that Fordham's barb had struck true. "And why would I bother with that when your pretty face is back to do it for me?"

"You weren't saying that when he was gone," the male said.

"Oh, dear Prescott," Wynter cooed. "Has Fordham let you off your leash?"

"Enough, Wynter," the female said, cocking her head. "Must we always play these games?"

"What games?"

Fordham's jaw tensed. "It is good to see you."

"As it is to see you, brother." Wynter's eyes flicked to Kerrigan. "And to see that you have come to your senses."

Then, Wynter flounced away, and all of them heard, "Her Royal Highness, Princess Wynter Ollivier."

Prescott breathed a sigh of relief at her absence. "Gods, she's such a bitch."

"Pres!" the female said, smacking his arm. "She's merely misguided."

"Kerrigan, these are my cousins, Prescott and Arbor York," Fordham said.

"Pleased to meet you," Kerrigan said. She dipped a full curtsy for the both of them.

Arbor laughed and put her hand to Kerrigan's arm. "Dear gods, no. Please, we're not even titled."

"You *are* titled," Fordham said.

"Not hereditary titles," Arbor continued. "Which is all that matters here. Technically, because Fordham's mother was our aunt, I am a lady, but you will just call me Arbor."

"All right," Kerrigan said.

"And we're sorry about stealing him away," Prescott said, slinging a casual arm across Kerrigan's shoulders. "See, we were plotting, and he didn't want us to meet you."

"That is not what I said," Fordham interjected.

"Wants to keep you all to himself," Prescott said.

"Pres, you're upsetting him," Arbor said.

"How can you tell?"

"Are you both finished?" Fordham growled.

"Definitely not," Arbor said. "But we'll give you some time since you did abandon her, and now, she has to face your father and Viviana." Arbor shuddered. "Good luck, sweets." Then, she kissed Kerrigan on the cheek and vanished with Prescott.

"They're a pair," Kerrigan said lightly.

"Indeed." Fordham took a deep breath. "So, you met my sister?"

"Yes, the one I didn't know you had."

"My home is complicated. And when I brought you here, I believed that I could control the narrative. If I could speak to my father first and explain our appearance ..." He looked away. "That didn't happen, and now, you are ... I don't know how to explain it to you."

"I've had it explained. Tonight, I belong to you," Kerrigan said with her chin lifted.

His eyes smoldered at the insinuation in the words. And for a second, her breath caught at the thought of what it would really mean to belong to him. Not in the sense of him owning her as a half-Fae, which was barbaric and absurd. But owning her in the way that made him look at her like that. Like she could melt into a puddle at his feet with the calm, sure dominance of just one look.

"Yes. Tonight, you are mine." He stepped forward, bridging the small distance between them. "You don't seem upset by this."

She swallowed, staring up into those swirling gray eyes. This was an act, but belonging to Fordham was something that she could pretend very easily. It was everything else that upset her. So, for a second, she let him see the window into her heart. The place where she kept all of that rage for how her people were treated. He inhaled sharply, as if realizing it.

"I have no place for anger tonight," she said. "Tomorrow and every day after—until we figure out how to stop this hate. But tonight, I can pretend. And then after ..."

"After, we will talk to my father. We'll fix this together."

Fordham held his arm out, and she placed her hand in the crook of his elbow. Together, they walked up to the entrance to the ballroom.

"Introducing His Royal Highness, Crowned Prince Fordham Ollivier."

All eyes turned to face them, taking in their crowned prince and the little half-Fae he had on his arm. The ornament that he had never had before and that would change everything.

Kerrigan ceased to exist in that moment, and Felicity came out of hiding. The Bryonican royal that had been forced to hide her emotions and feelings. *This* was what it meant to be royal to her—hiding. And she was incredibly good at it. But after tonight, she would be through with it and she would never ever again let them control her like this.

She smiled vapidly, imagining the brainless thing she could have been if she had stayed in Bryonica and been forced to marry Ashby March. She imagined hiding the bruises with makeup and forcing a smile, having to weather his moods and fits of anger. She would have been nothing but a conquest for him. And here, now, that was the appearance she had to put on.

The room was elaborately decorated with long, towering black obsidian columns lining the space and white marble floor. The ceiling had been painted with a long-ago battle—dragons flying into a fight and Fae coming home, victorious. As there were no fireplaces, magic must have heated the giant room. All over, it was glorious and perfectly put together.

Members of the court bustled forward to shake Fordham's hand and extend congratulations. Several men circled Kerrigan as if she were for sale. A few women even touched her chin, turning her face side to side.

"Such small ears," one noted. "And completely on display."

Felicity didn't care. She pushed Kerrigan's anger aside and smiled at the woman. All of the women were bejeweled like Wynter, dripping in gemstones. And the pieces that accentuated their pointed Fae ears were clearly the height of fashion. The fact that Kerrigan donned not an ounce of jewelry had to have been deliberate on the twins' part. She stood out more because she was without adornment than all the women in diamonds around the room.

"You look like you could use a drink," Arbor said, appearing at Kerrigan's side as soon as the last insipid courtier moved away. She pushed a goblet into her hand, flush with red punch.

"Faerie punch?" Kerrigan asked hesitantly. Her eyes moved to Fordham, as if to ask whether or not it was safe, but he was currently being accosted by a group of Fae males about some border incident with the other families.

"I wouldn't poison you," Arbor said with a tinkle of a laugh. "It'll just loosen you up."

"I've had enough faerie punch to know what that means. And I'm not sure *loose* is what I should be right now." Because if she lost a grip on Felicity, then Kerrigan would come out, and she was sure that *no one* here would quite like that to happen.

Arbor came in close, running a finger down her ear until she was practically whispering. "People will talk if you're not drinking. Sip it, and I'll replace it throughout the night. Trust me. Fordham does." Then, Arbor giggled. "These ears are just so odd."

She traipsed away, crashing back into her brother and the Fae woman he was courting.

Kerrigan took a breath and drank from the goblet. It was delicious, like fresh strawberries. She had to be careful not to down the entire contents.

"What are you drinking, darling?" Fordham asked then, reappearing at her side. His eyes were storm clouds. The only part of him that made him seem ill at ease.

She leaned into him, looking down at the drink in hand. "Punch."

His finger came to her chin, tilting it up until she looked him full in the face. Her heart pounded at the contact. Gods, she'd barely had any of the drink, and already, she could feel the effects coursing through her.

"And who *gave* you this punch?" he commanded with all the bristling power in his voice that made her knees wobble.

"Arbor."

He plucked the drink from her hand. "Do not do anything without my express permission."

Kerrigan gulped, suddenly feeling like she was on fire. "Yes."

"What was that?" he asked, dangerous and cold.

"Yes, Your Highness."

"Better."

He dragged a finger across her painted lips and turned away from her, leaving her standing there, bereft, with everyone watching them.

She wished she'd had the drink to cool herself down. It should have been humiliating. It would have been if she'd let herself think on it for more than a second. But mostly, she was wondering where in the gods' names he kept that carefully bridled command when he was away from court.

"So," a voice said next to her—another Fae woman dripping in diamonds—"you're the one he chose."

Kerrigan didn't say anything.

"Who knew he could replace Dacia so easily?" the woman mused. Then, she laughed. "Look at your wide-eyed gaze. Gods, the half-Fae are so unbalanced. Dacia was the last girl that he courted, and he's moved on *already*."

Courted? Well, of course he'd courted someone before. She wasn't sure of his age, but based on their discussions, she assumed he wasn't as young as she was. Fae could live incredibly long lives. Some only beginning to fade after one or two *thousand* years. But this woman had made it seem recent.

"You're adorable," the woman said, laughing with her friend. "She thinks that he cares for her truly."

"And after Dacia, of course he went to something easier that he didn't have to care about," the friend said. "The poor prince."

Kerrigan's face flushed at the words. She didn't want to, but she couldn't help it. She'd prepared for half-Fae jabs ... not this. Something that hit a little too close to home. Fordham had been with someone else, someone everyone here even knew about, and yet he couldn't be with her? Was the curse even real? Or was she just someone he'd used to get over the last one?

She took a step back from that thought. This place was vile. It was clouding her judgment, and she couldn't even show anyone the truth. Without a word, she whirled away from the women and went in search of Fordham. Their laughter trailed behind her, and she blocked it out. But Fordham wasn't in sight. Where had he gone?

"Hey," Prescott said, appearing then. "Breathe. What happened?"

"Nothing. Just... I don't know."

"Breathe again. Fast inhale, slow exhale." She took a deep breath as Prescott put his arm around her. He laughed at nothing and gestured to where Fordham was standing with Wynter. "This can't be easy."

"It's fine. These women just brought up... Dacia?"

Prescott stilled, suddenly looking so much like his cousin. "Did they?"

"Yes, but ..."

"Don't say that name to Fordham."

"But ..."

"Listen, Kerrigan," he said, leaning his face into her neck, as if he were nuzzling her. "This is as hard for him as it is for you. We all play our parts here."

As much as she wanted answers, she needed to bury it for now. It wasn't going to help them get through the evening. Maybe she should have had more to drink so that their words couldn't touch her.

"You good?"

She nodded.

"Good, because Fordham is gesturing us over."

Kerrigan's gaze met Fordham's across the room. He looked ever like the imperious prince. She'd learned to read him over the weeks that they trained and worked together, but from here, he was utterly blank. If even she couldn't guess at his thoughts, then no one else would be able to either.

He crooked a finger at her, and as if an invisible line tethered them together, she moved toward him.

The double doors to the ballroom opened then, breaking their eye contact, and Langdan stepped forward, announcing, "His Majesty, King Samael Ollivier, and Her Majesty, Queen Viviana Ollivier."

# CHAPTER 8
## The King

The king and queen of the House of Shadows entered the room. King Samael in the black and silver of his house and Viviana in a midnight-blue dress that matched her sweeping dark hair.

Prescott yanked Kerrigan down, and she stumbled, barely righting herself before she fell into a curtsy.

"Some warning next time," she snarled at him, a little of Kerrigan peeking out.

He shot her an insufferable smirk. "Ah, so you are as feisty as he said you were."

Kerrigan didn't get a chance to respond because the king stepped forward to address his court. He lifted his hand to tell his subjects to rise.

"Welcome," King Samael said. He cut a formidable figure. Not quite as tall as his son, but sturdy with broad shoulders and a booming voice. His hair was long past his shoulders and the same onyx color but with eyes to match. "It is a great triumph of mine to announce that my son, Prince Fordham, has returned victorious to the House of Shadows." The court applauded the announcement as he gestured to Fordham, who straightened, putting his hands behind his back and staring blankly at his audience. "Tonight, we are not just Ollivier, Laurent, and Blanchard. Tonight, we are all tribe Charbonnet, as we once were. Before the Society kicked us out of their halls, killed those of us with dragons who would not submit, and trapped us here forever, branding us the Dark Court. We *claimed* the House of Shadows long ago, and with my son's advancement into the Society and a dragon of his own, we will rise again."

The crowd roared its approval at the pronouncement. The king stepped toward his son, clapping him on the shoulder. They looked at each other not as father and son, but as enemy combatants, waiting for the fight.

"Let the past be the past and old transgressions forgotten," the king said to his only son. "Let's welcome him back properly."

Fordham inclined his head at his father and raised his hand to the adoring crowd.

"That's our cue," Prescott said.

Kerrigan followed Prescott across the room to where Fordham and Wynter stood with their father and his new bride. Upon closer inspection, Queen Viviana couldn't have been much older than Kerrigan. And she was the first to notice Kerrigan.

"What's this?" Viviana asked. "Your pet?"

Fordham brought her close to him. "Kerrigan, this is Queen Viviana."

Kerrigan curtsied deeply.

"And my father, King Samael."

"Your Majesty," she breathed, sinking even lower.

"You trained her up, I see," Viviana said. "Enchanting."

"Well, what do you think of the ball?" Samael asked Fordham.

"Unexpected," he said carefully. "I have been trying to reach you for two days, and you have been busy."

"Save politics for after the party," the king said.

Viviana stepped up to Kerrigan, inspecting her like a prized horse, as the other women had. She leaned in close and pinched her arm, hard. "You'll never have him, *leatha*."

Kerrigan stilled at the comment. Benton had said that the queen was the worst sort of Fae. That she had come from a family of half-Fae haters. That she could handle. But she hadn't mentioned that the queen was apparently smitten with Fordham.

"Viviana, dear, let's dance."

"Yes, darling," she said, winking at Fordham as she passed onto the dance floor.

"Fordham, give that girl a proper twirl."

"Shall we?" Fordham asked, gritting his teeth.

Kerrigan took his proffered hand. As they moved onto the dance floor, she breathed to him, "Viviana?"

He made a small sound of disgust. "I'll tell you about it later."

"Ah," she whispered.

And then the music began, and all thoughts fled her mind. She had taken many dance lessons at the House of Dragons, mostly to satisfy Darby's love of it. But it had never been Kerrigan's love. Not because she was not good at it, but because it reminded her too much of home. Today, she would have to lean into that.

"Follow my lead," Fordham said as they drew close together for the intro.

"I know how to dance, princeling," she teased.

His eyes narrowed. "The way that you knew how to fight?"

"No," she breathed. "The way that *you* do."

He arched an eyebrow at her as the music began, and all the dancers stepped into place.

Kerrigan's love of dance had stemmed from a very young age. She'd begged her father to take her to the balls as a child, learning all of the numbers by heart before she could do much more than toddle around. And the dances never left her. They'd burrowed down so deep as to be a part of her.

As Fordham took her hand and twirled her in place, she realized she knew this number already. She had learned it as a young child. And her very bones settled to have her repeat it.

Kerrigan moved away from Fordham, looking back at him coquettishly. Then, he grasped her hand and drew her in close. She adjusted his grip slightly, and then they were off. Their bodies not quite flush together as he held her waist with ease. Dancing with Fordham was not like dancing with anyone else. He had nimble footwork from all those years of weapons training, and they moved into the perfect rhythm between them. As if they had been born more for this moment than all those times they had fought together.

She twirled away again, and when he pulled her back the next time, he drew her in just a bit closer. And though she was supposed to move her head with the number, she found herself trapped by his gaze and unable to look anywhere else. Her pulse beat a tattoo against her throat. She found that here, there was little acting. Just a girl ensnared by her prince.

"You are full of surprises," he said.

"And do you like being surprised?"

A small break in his facade brought a side of his lip to quirk into a smile. "It reminds me why I chose to help you."

"Because I am irresistible?" she joked.

"Because you are unlike anyone I've ever known."

"And is that a good thing?" She barely breathed the question, feeling them continue to drift together. His mouth now mere inches from hers. The song almost forgotten.

"Yes." The word escaped him, as if he couldn't hold it in any longer.

He released her in the final turn. When she finally stopped and the crowd applauded the show they'd put on, she found whatever ice she'd melted had solidified once more.

He pointed at her. "Dance with Prescott."

She opened her mouth to object. How could he want his cousin anywhere near her after that dance?

But he didn't let her ask it, just turned to the queen and took her into his arms. Kerrigan didn't imagine the smirk on her lips.

"One dance," Prescott promised.

She would have denied it entirely if doing as Fordham demanded wasn't part of her act. They moved around the room effortlessly but with none of the passion she'd had in Fordham's arms.

But when they were finished, Prescott pulled her out of the throng toward Arbor, who was standing against an obsidian pillar with a half-empty glass of punch.

"Here," Arbor said. "You need this more than I do."

"I need to be coherent."

"Your part is done. Everyone saw you and believed that you were infatuated." Arbor eyed her with a little sadness. "Or perhaps it was not all an act."

"Give me that," she said, taking a long gulp of the drink. Strawberries and honey—gods, it was good. "What do I do the rest of the night?"

"Get a little drunk and stay out of the way," Prescott said. "Fordham has already shown you and me together. It is not uncommon to share."

Kerrigan paled. "This place is disgusting."

"It is," Arbor agreed sadly. "But it will get you out of here sooner."

"Thank the gods." She finished the drink and passed it back to Arbor, who laughed. "When will we be able to drop this whole act?"

Arbor and Prescott shared a look. "Fordham is going to address the king tomorrow. I don't know how it will go."

"Poorly," Kerrigan said, looking over her shoulder at the king and his child bride. "And if he doesn't hate it, the queen will assuredly."

"Ugh! Viviana," Prescott groaned.

"She is terrible," Arbor agreed, twirling a strand of her dark hair. "She has been obsessed with Fordham since we were children. I still say that she married the king to get closer to him."

"How do you two survive this place?" Kerrigan asked. "You both seem well-adjusted."

"It's all we have," Prescott said.

Arbor nodded with a shrug. "What else could we want when we can't leave?"

Kerrigan frowned. Right. For a second, she had forgotten that this disgusting court was frozen in time. They had no governing body to stop the atrocities happening here. The Society had cut them off like a diseased appendage. They hadn't considered how it would hurt the ones who longed to break free of the bonds, the ones who weren't as disgusting as the rest of the court they fought against. They'd punished *everyone*.

"I'm sorry," Kerrigan whispered. "I can't imagine how it is here for you. The outside world isn't exactly friendly to half-Fae, but the world isn't like this at least."

Arbor rose to her feet. "We know. We don't blame you." She patted Kerrigan's shoulder. "I'm going to go dance a few rounds, so people don't get suspicious. Have another drink and then leave with Pres. He'll take care of you."

"Thank you," she said. "You two have been a big help."

"We haven't seen Fordham like this in a long time," Prescott said. "Maybe... ever. We'd do anything for him."

Arbor nodded and then disappeared into the crowd.

Prescott grabbed her drink, and together, they endured another hour of the event. Fordham never came to find them, and as soon as they could manage, they snuck out. Prescott deposited her back into Fordham's rooms a little drunker than she'd started.

Kerrigan pulled the stays of her dress loose, and she took a deep inhale for the first time that night. Then, she collapsed back on the bed, the room spinning. She hadn't had as much to drink as the night she'd gone out with her friends, which felt like a full lifetime ago. But the faerie punch here was potent. Maybe even more so than back home.

She didn't know when she drifted off, but she woke again to the sound of a door closing in the darkened room. "Hello?"

And then Fordham's tall figure appeared in the entrance to the bedroom. His cravat had been discarded, the jacket of his suit hanging over his shoulder and the first few buttons undone on his shirt. His eyes were hollow. His body a map of sensuality.

"Fordham," she said, coming up to one elbow. Her mind was still fuzzy. "How long were you at the party?"

"Hours after you," he said, dropping the jacket onto a divan and walking to the bed. His steps were unsteady, as if he, too, were drunk.

"Have you been drinking?"

He kicked off his shoes. "Yes."

She swallowed as he slowly unbuttoned his shirt. The material opening to reveal the smooth planes of his abdomen and the muscular build of his chest. "What are you doing?"

"You responded when I offered you commands," he said with a playful smile on his lips as he let the shirt drop to the ground. "Normally, you just yell at me."

"I couldn't be that person tonight."

He crawled forward on the massive bed. She remained as still as possible. She had never felt quite like she was trapped and wanted to be nowhere else.

"I almost missed that mouth of yours," he said, dragging a finger along her red-painted lips.

"Fordham," she whispered hesitantly. It was one thing to play-act this. It was another to do... this. Because when he was sober, he didn't want this. He'd made that clear. "What are you doing?"

"Kissing you," he said.

His mouth covered hers, hot and tasting of strawberries and honey. She knew that she should stop him. A part of her told her that this couldn't happen. And yet there was no stopping Fordham Ollivier. He was a hurricane wreaking havoc on her heart. His mouth ravaging her.

Everything slowed to that moment, this very second, where his body pressed her into his bed and the taste of him on her lips, arousing her need for him. She *wanted* this. Even if he'd said no before, she never had. It was hard to even process the thought as his tongue delved into her mouth and touched hers.

"Oh gods," she breathed.

And then with the only force of will she had, she used her air magic to physically push him away from her.

She scrambled off of the bed, her chest heaving, stays undone and dress askew. She would have done anything for him that night. Anything. But not like this. Not after today.

Fordham came to himself as the force of her magic hit him. His eyes rounded. "Kerrigan, I ..."

"You should go."

"I shouldn't have—"

"No, you shouldn't," she said. "You told me once that we couldn't be together because you were cursed. That I couldn't have this. Do you feel differently?"

He straightened at the harsh reality. "No. No, I don't."

She nodded, grinding her teeth together. "Is this because of what happened with Dacia?"

"Don't," he snarled, stepping back from her as if she'd slapped him. "Don't mention her."

Kerrigan reared back in alarm. Prescott had said not to mention that name, but she hadn't thought it would elicit this much of a reaction. Was he still in love with her? Was that what this was?

"Fordham, I ..." Now, it was her turn to be at a loss for words.

He bowed dramatically at the waist. "My lady."

Then, he vanished from the room, slamming the door shut between them.

Kerrigan collapsed backward. She had just made a terrible mistake. A mistake in turning him down, a mistake in bringing Dacia up. Why couldn't it have just been fun and easy? This wouldn't have been her first time with a man. It hadn't had to be complicated. But this was Fordham. Nothing was just fun with him. Everything meant more, felt more, needed more. She'd lied to herself for long enough. About everything. She couldn't lie to herself about him.

# CHAPTER 9
## *The Wall*

Fordham was gone the next morning when Kerrigan awoke. The night before was a fuzzy mess in her head. She needed to figure out where they stood and what he was going to do about the king. Now that neither of their brains was addled with drink. But he was nowhere to be found.

Benton and Bayton came to break her fast, and she ate the offering without complaint as they dressed her for the day.

"How was the ball?" Benton asked.

Kerrigan shuddered. "Everything I thought it would be and worse."

Bayton nodded sympathetically as she wrangled Kerrigan's hair into place. "The balls are the hardest."

"Princess Wynter has requested that you go riding with her this morning if you are up for it," Benton said.

"Ah, so that's why you're here."

"It would be unwise to reject an offer from the princess."

"I have nothing better to do," Kerrigan said. And only another week to figure out this situation.

"You know how to ride?" Bayton asked softly.

"Horses? Yes, though I prefer dragons."

Benton shot her sister a look to silence her.

"What?" Kerrigan asked.

"Ignore my sister. It is her dream to meet a dragon," Benton said.

"Oh, you'd hate Tieran," Kerrigan said with a small laugh. "He's the worst. But you'd probably like Netta. That's Fordham's dragon."

"And who rides Tieran?" Bayton asked, eagerness in her voice for the first time.

"Well, I do," Kerrigan said.

Both woman stilled.

"You are a dragon rider too?" Bayton asked. "They let… half-Fae do that?"

"Well, no, not really," Kerrigan said. "They weren't pleased with me for winning the dragon tournament, but yes, Tieran is my dragon."

It still felt amazing to be able to say that out loud.

"Sister," Bayton whispered to Benton.

"I'm sorry," Kerrigan said, turning back to face them. "I wish that you weren't trapped in this place. The outside world isn't much friendlier to half-Fae, if I'm honest, but we're not property."

"That sounds like a dream," Benton said, putting a hand on her sister's shoulder.

"The House of Shadows was stripped of all dragons when we were cut off," Bayton whispered. "All the riders were killed. An entire generation of leadership and all those beautiful dragons. I didn't think I'd ever be able to ride one, but just to see it seems too good to be true, this outside world you speak of."

Kerrigan nodded, swallowing down the lump in her throat. She had been discriminated against by Fae in Kinkadia simply for being who she was, but it was nothing like it was here. She wished there were something that she could do to fix this, to get them out of here. But how?

"Ignore us, miss," Benton said. "Try to enjoy your ride with the princess today. She seems intimidating, but she isn't all bad." Benton pulled her sister away and made her to leave. The conversation had left her gentle soul too upset to continue. "This way."

Kerrigan followed Benton through the corridors and to a disguised exit to the outside. It was mostly obscured by the forest beyond, but she could see a stable visible off to the right.

"I am sorry for what I said to you and Bayton," Kerrigan said.

"Don't think of it at all. We can't do anything to change our stars. It's lucky enough to meet someone such as yourself who has risen above what we could ever dream of," Benton said with a smile and then left her to Wynter.

Kerrigan took a deep breath before pushing her way outside. The chill took her off guard. In Kinkadia, even in the morning, it would already be sticky hot. But here, it was dry and brisk. Wind rustled the trees, and birds chirped nearby. The smell of horses came to her as she closed in on the stables. It had been years since she'd ridden. It wasn't necessary in the city. Most people went on foot. And she'd always been more interested in dragons.

"Ah, you received my request," Wynter said as Kerrigan approached.

"I did. I thought it would be nice to get out of the mountain."

"Well, I know just the thing." Wynter had her hand on a chestnut horse already tacked and ready to ride. "She's for you. This is Sienna."

A man stepped out of the stable with a black stallion. "Your Highness, Caspian is ready for you."

"Thank you, Jeral," Wynter said, smiling warmly at the stable hand. Wynter passed the reins into Kerrigan's hand and then vaulted on top of Caspian without a block or hand up.

Kerrigan gulped and stared at Sienna. She was smaller than Caspian but still much larger than she was used to, and there were no convenient places to put her feet to get up like she did with her dragon.

"Shall I assist you, miss?" Jeral asked.

"Yes, please."

She put her boot into Jeral's awaiting hands. He lifted her as she threw a leg over the beast. Kerrigan settled into the saddle. It wasn't as comfortable as a dragon, but it would do. She wished that she could communicate with the horse the way she could a dragon. It felt safer.

"Good," Wynter said, clicking her tongue at the horse and squeezing her thighs to get it moving.

Kerrigan remembered the moves and got Sienna to fall into step beside Wynter. She was glad that Wynter didn't speak for a while, as Kerrigan needed the time to remember her lessons. She'd ridden with her father but only a pony, and it wasn't quite the same thing.

They came upon a small creek. The horses splashed forward through it, and then Wynter finally spoke, "So, tell me about yourself."

"About myself?" Kerrigan didn't know what she was supposed to say. Were they still pretending like she was property? She'd rather talk about the House of Shadows than about herself. "Nothing to tell."

"Oh, I very much doubt that."

"Well, what do you want to know?"

Wynter's colorless gaze was disconcerting to meet. "Everything."

Kerrigan shrugged. "I grew up in Kinkadia and met your brother at the dragon tournament."

"And you were working there?" she asked carefully.

*In a way.*

"Yes. I worked for him during the tournament."

*Also true.*

"Hmm," she mused.

They passed through an opening in the trees and came to a small clearing. Kerrigan shivered as they stepped out into the open field. Something about it felt different than the rest of the forest they'd ridden through.

"I know that you are not what you say you are," Wynter finally said. She hopped off of her stallion and settled her black leather riding boots into the soft grass.

"What do you mean?"

"This whole act with my brother. It was very convincing, but you are not just some half-Fae he seduced."

Kerrigan dropped to the ground next to her. She didn't know how she would get back up, but what was more important was that she had misjudged the princess. Wynter had seen through the act that the rest of the court believed.

"Why do you say that?"

"Because of this," Wynter said and then set her hand upon the open air behind her.

There was a buzzing, and then her hand stopped. In fact, it was almost *pushed* backward. The buzz turned into a rumble, and Wynter retreated her hand from the invisible wall blocking her exit.

"The barrier," Kerrigan said in surprise. They hadn't traveled that far. They must have been much closer on the outskirts of the mountain rather than surrounding the village. "I didn't realize we'd gone far enough."

"It's not a perfect circle. If it were, we'd have more space. It's more like a corset, tightening the strings."

"I don't know how the wall has anything to do with me and Fordham."

"Oh, nothing to do with Fordham," Wynter said. "And there you go, using his given name." She smiled as if she'd won that round.

"I …"

Wynter held up a hand. "Save it. I don't know your game with him, but I don't care. That's up to my father."

"Then, what am I doing here?" Kerrigan asked.

She drew her magic into her, anticipating the fight that was surely coming.

"Oh, none of that," she said, waving her hand at Kerrigan. "You can let go. It's so blinding."

Kerrigan blinked. "You can see my magic?"

"Clearly. Please, drop it. Gods, how much do you have? You and Fordham together must be formidable."

Kerrigan's magic went out like snuffing a candle. She'd always had a little bit of the ability to sense other people's magic, but that was only when they were actively performing magic. She certainly couldn't see it like, apparently, Wynter could. She'd never even heard of such a thing. Sensing magic was rare enough. Seeing it would be a huge advantage.

"Thank you," Wynter said. "You're already bright enough without drawing on your reserves."

"You knew the moment you saw me," Kerrigan realized.

"Of course. My father keeps me as a silent weapon to judge his enemies. He sent me to judge your magical abilities."

Kerrigan swallowed. "I see."

"I told him what he expected. That you were a worthless half-Fae, bound to my brother."

"Why?" she asked, narrowing her eyes. She couldn't imagine that it was out of the goodness of her black heart.

"I see magic in color. Elementals are the easiest. Their affinity is shown in the color—blue for water, red for fire, yellow for air, and green for earth. The colors blend for multiple infinities. For instance, a fire and air user usually show up orange. For users with all four, they blend together. Arbor, for instance, looks pink at the edges. Fordham, with his inherited black smoke, has black and gray edges. But you ..." She tilted her head at her. "You're altogether different. You're golden and as blinding as the sunlight. I've never seen this sort of magic anywhere else. Except here."

She put her hand back out and touched the wall.

Kerrigan gulped. "The *wall* is golden?"

"Yes. Whatever sort of magic was used to put this barrier up, it was done by someone like you."

Spirit magic. That was the only answer Kerrigan had and one she could never give Wynter. Her spirit magic gave her visions. It'd helped her win the tournament. It let her access the spirit plane as a dragon did—perhaps better than a dragon did. And if she didn't learn to control it, she would go mad.

But that meant that all the lore about thirteen magical users coming together to put the wall up was a lie. No amount of magical users could do this. Which meant that a thousand years ago, another spiritcaster had existed, and *they* had bound all the House of Shadows within.

"Why are you telling me this?" Kerrigan asked.

"Like calls to like," Wynter said.

She took Kerrigan's hand and pushed it against the wall. A charge snapped against her hand. It made her jump in surprise, as if the magic really were speaking to her. And as she had the first time she'd touched the barrier, something was *wrong*. Something was intrinsically broken in the spellwork. She could almost see the edges of it, and then she was through to her elbow. The magic couldn't keep her in, as it did to Wynter. Anger appeared on the princess's face and then disappeared as quickly.

Kerrigan jerked her hand back out of the barrier. "What was that?"

"The walls are weakening. The thousand-year spell is fracturing at the edges." Wynter stared, mesmerized by her jailor, before looking at Kerrigan. "And I want you to bring it down."

# CHAPTER 10

Kerrigan's mind was still reeling when she returned to the rooms. When she found Arbor and Prescott relaxing on the couch, eating out of a bag of chocolate treats, she jumped.

"Gods, don't scare me like that," Kerrigan said.

"Out riding?" Arbor asked.

Prescott grinned. "Wynter?"

"Yes."

"You look like you've seen a ghost," Arbor said.

"What are you two doing here? Has Fordham been back?"

"He's been tied up with princely duties," Prescott said with a shrug. "Sounded boring. We promised to come entertain you."

"I did bring bubbly," Arbor said. She gestured to the bottle on the table.

"I'm in no mood to drink. Why are you always plying me with alcohol?"

Arbor dropped the perpetual smile, and Kerrigan saw the pain etched into her features for the first time. "Look, our cousin and best friend was exiled. There was nowhere to go or anything to do. We thought we'd never see him again. The only way to survive was to become as cruel and terrible as the rest of the court or to drink enough to not have to think about it."

"You don't have to have a drink," Prescott said. "We thought at the party, you'd need to cope. And today, it's more celebratory." He tossed a piece of chocolate into his mouth. "You brought him back to us."

"And happier than ever," Arbor agreed.

Kerrigan relaxed at the words. She was on edge from her conversation with Wynter. At the implications in what she'd said. She didn't need to take that out on Arbor and Prescott.

"Sorry. This place …"

Arbor waved it away. "We get it."

"If anyone does," Pres said.

"Chocolate?"

"Gods, yes."

Kerrigan took a piece from Arbor and popped it into her mouth. She sighed as she sank back into the adjacent chair. It was like getting a special something from the chocolatier in the Square. She could *never* afford it, but sometimes, she along with Hadrian, Lyam, Darby would save up for weeks to buy a special piece of the famous chocolate and share it together. The stuff in the mountain was never quite the same.

"This is amazing," she groaned.

"They have the good stuff at court," Pres agreed.

"Can you tell me about Fordham?" Kerrigan asked, taking another piece.

Pres and Arbor shared a glance.

"What do you want to know?" Arbor asked.

"What was he like before the exile? Was he always so jaded?"

Prescott sighed, and Arbor shrugged. "Yes," they said at the same time.

Then, they both laughed.

"Fordham was always his own person. In a way that his father hated. He wanted him to be a duplicate of himself. But the court, it wears you down. Day in and day out of constant hate, it's debilitating. The only way to survive is to harden yourself. And Fordham had to be the head of it. He had to be cruel, invulnerable, and unyielding," Arbor explained.

"He's done things he's not proud of, and it weighs on him. Despite growing up together, we've never really seen him relax."

Kerrigan laughed softly. "So, he's not much different then?"

"Oh gods, no. The outside world completely changed him," Pres said. "That smile at the party last night—I've never seen him look at anyone like that in public."

"Even in private," Arbor said, flipping her dark hair off of her shoulder. "I don't think it's just the outside world. I think it's you."

Kerrigan shook her head. "I don't think so."

Pres shared a secret look with his sister. "People he gets close to suffer the consequences. If he holds himself back, it's for your safety."

"I've heard the spiel."

"But he's not doing a good job," Arbor said. "Not for someone who knows him."

"Which means Wynter has noticed," Pres filled in.

"And the king."

"Great," Kerrigan said. "Maybe we *should* open up that bubbly."

Arbor laughed. "Now, you're getting it."

Kerrigan only had a glass. Just enough to put out the thoughts of what Wynter wanted her to do from her mind. She couldn't share that with anyone yet. Not without deciding whether or not it was a good idea or if she could even do it. If it was possible, would she be a hypocrite for fearing what would happen if she let loose the House of Shadows? She could get Ben and Bay, and Arbor and Pres out of this hellhole, but she'd unleash the House of Shadows' hate upon her world too. She wished Wynter had never come to her.

Arbor and Prescott kept up an endless litany of trouble they had gotten into with Fordham when they were growing up. She hadn't laughed this much in a while. It was nice to sit and listen to these stories, all while they polished off the rest of the bottle.

"So, there he was, in the treasury, half-hidden behind a statue of the first dragon rider, Irena, and his *father* walked into the room."

"No," she gasped.

The door banged open just then, and all three of them jumped at the sound. Fordham stepped inside with all the force of a tempest. The hinges creaked as he slammed the door shut behind him. He ran a hand back through his perfect black hair. Then, he found Kerrigan seated with his two cousins.

"Rough day?" Pres joked.

"I don't want to talk about it," he growled and then stormed into the bedroom. The door rattled on its hinges again.

Arbor and Prescott cringed. "Gods."

"His father?" Kerrigan guessed.

They nodded.

"We should probably go," Arbor said. "Come hang out with us later. We'll show you that this place isn't *all* terrible."

Arbor brushed a kiss to her cheek, Pres winked at her, and then they disappeared silently through the door.

Kerrigan rose to her feet. She could leave Fordham to brood by himself, but after the conversation with Pres and Arbor, she didn't want to. She wanted to find the Fordham that they'd told her about. The one who hadn't yet been beaten down by his own court and expectations. Even if last night still weighed on her.

She knocked lightly on the door. "Fordham? May I come in?"

There was a heartbeat of silence before a resigned, "Yes."

Kerrigan pushed the door open and found him shirtless with the laces of his pants undone. His muscled back was etched out of marble, and she had to swallow and glance away from where he stood with the wardrobe doors open.

"What happened?"

"My father is a bigot."

Kerrigan almost laughed. "Well, yes."

"He's refusing you an audience."

"I'm not surprised, Fordham. You weren't even sure that he'd see you when you came back. Now, you're the triumphant hero with a foothold in the Society for him. Do you think he wants to see you as someone who is friends with a half-Fae when he can use you for everything else?"

"I'm aware of my father's machinations." He threw a loose white tunic over his head. She'd *never* seen him in anything but black, and it was almost disconcerting. "I thought he'd want two dragon riders in his court. I thought his prejudice would be set aside for his love of power."

"I threaten his power," Kerrigan said. "You have to see that."

Fordham ran another hand back through his hair. "About last night ..."

"You know, let's not. It was a mistake on both of our parts," she said quickly. "I've already forgotten about it."

He pursed his lips, as if he knew she was lying. Because she had hardly forgotten the taste of him or the press of his body against hers. Or the way he'd reacted to his ex's name.

"So, what do we do now?" she asked.

"I have to complete my duties as prince while I'm here. I will keep trying with my father. You should spend time with Pres and Arbor. I trust them."

"I went riding with Wynter," she confessed.

"Be careful with her, Kerrigan. She isn't like other people."

"Don't you think I know that? She can *see* my magic. You should have warned me."

Fordham raised his eyebrows. "She can *what?*"

"Surely, you knew. She's your sister."

"Wynter can *sense* magic, but you haven't used any magic. I also have the gift. I would know."

"No, she can *see* it. And she took me out to the wall and said that I can bring it down."

Fordham actually looked shocked. "She... what?"

"She said my magic is the same as the barrier and that I can take the walls down."

"Can you?"

"I don't know. I didn't try." Kerrigan bit her lip. "Should I try?"

"No," he said at once. "Not under her tutelage at least."

"I want to help the people here," she said. "The people who are trapped."

"But look at what you would be unleashing," Fordham said. "This court is... it's not fit for the outside world."

"I know."

He shook his head. "Do you think this has something to do with your spirit magic?"

"It must, but I didn't tell Wynter that. I'm not stupid."

"Good." Fordham furrowed his brow. "She told you all this for a reason. I'm going to have to dig into it. I've heard whispers since I got here, but I was worried too much about us and not what she was up to."

"Whispers?"

"That she's recruiting from all three families."

"For what?"

He jerked the white shirt off and went back in for black silk. "I'm going to have to find out, aren't I?"

"I'm going with you."

Fordham considered it for a moment. She was sure that he was going to object. He'd done nothing but leave her alone in this terrible room.

"You'd follow me anyway, wouldn't you?"

She smirked. "At least you're getting it."

"Get dressed. I have an idea."

"You sound like me," she teased.

He assessed her. Some of the coolness bleeding out of him. "You're rubbing off on me."

\*\*\*

An hour later, Kerrigan was finally let out of the room for more than getting dressed and a supervised ride. Fordham smiled at courtiers milling about the court hallways. He seemed to know everyone and wanted to be seen by everyone. She thought it was mad to be so visible, but he'd argued it was better cover to have everyone talking about them. Especially since his father hadn't seemed keen on changing his mind about Kerrigan.

After the third promenade of the court's halls, Fordham finally said, "That's enough."

"Thank the gods. How was I ever going to be a princess?"

He glanced down at her and then away quickly. "I thought you did well."

"I know how to behave," she said, nudging him. "I just don't enjoy it."

"Neither do I."

"Then, let's go make trouble."

"You are a devious little thing, aren't you?"

Kerrigan smiled at him, enjoying the camaraderie. This was easier than what they'd been dealing with since that fateful kiss... since coming here.

Fordham turned a final corner, passing through a large stone archway and then down a narrow corridor. "Here," he said, pushing a button. The wall in front of them disappeared.

Kerrigan gasped. "Hidden tunnels?"

"It's a spy network," he said, ushering her inside. "They were used before the Great War to spy on diplomats and foreigners who came into our mountain."

"Also to spy on your own people, I'm sure."

The door slid shut soundlessly behind him, and he snapped his fingers to ignite a flame. "Still used for that. Though far fewer uses than before."

Fordham moved through the spy tunnels with a practiced ease. She'd known he was a soldier and a spy, but it was one thing to know and another thing entirely to live through it.

"Where are we going?" she whispered.

He put a finger to his mouth and then gestured to the right. She trailed him until they came up to a small peephole. He lifted a piece of stone and peered into the room beyond.

"This is Wynter's room," Fordham told her. Her eyes widened. "We used to use these halls when we were younger. But they seem unused."

She had to agree. Cobwebs lined the darkened halls, and she had definitely stepped in something that she didn't even want to know what it was. The air was musty. The few torches they'd passed on the way looked as if they hadn't been lit in years.

"We'll have to be quick. She takes afternoon tea with the queen at this time, but I don't want to chance her return. Look for anything that seems wrong. Anything that would explain why she's recruiting."

Kerrigan nodded. Her stomach was in knots. "I'm ready."

Fordham pressed another button, and the door swung inward. Kerrigan stepped into Wynter's immaculate bedroom. The king canopy bed was all a pristine white. The writing desk had not a thing out of place. Everywhere Kerrigan looked, she saw wealth and meticulous attention to detail. The bedroom door had been left open, and she could see a matching sitting area with pecan furniture and white-as-snow cushions.

"I'll start in her sitting area," Fordham said. "Look through her bedroom. And don't move anything out of place."

Kerrigan nodded. She hurried over to the writing table. She memorized exactly where everything went first and then began to ruffle through the papers. Wynter had hand-lettered stationery with a swooping *W* at the top. The letter was everywhere—embroidered onto handkerchiefs and pillows and the stamp for her wax seal. But she found nothing out of place on the desk. She dislodged the drawers, rifling through them, opening a few letters and reading the mindless missives. They were all placed there, almost as if she had expected someone to go through her things.

She shut the final desk drawer with a huff and went to the wardrobe. It was expansive with dozens of embroidered, bejeweled gowns in varying shades of white, black, and red. She checked the pockets of some of the gowns, but there wasn't even a hair piece or bobble in sight. She returned to the bed, sticking her hand between the mattress, only to find goose feathers. Similarly, there was nothing *under* the bed. Not even a pair of shoes.

She went to the doorway. "Anything?"

Fordham shook his head. "No, it's all wrong."

"Like it's staged and not her actual bedroom."

He frowned. "Yes. Gods, why didn't I think of that before?"

"Think of what?"

But he was already pushing past her and into the wardrobe. "Wynter has had these rooms since she was a child. I thought something felt wrong about them, but I haven't been in here in... I don't even know how long." He knocked on the wardrobe door, and it came back hollow. "Her nursemaid used to have an adjoining room to her. It was a small cupboard of a thing. Hardly big enough for anyone to actually live in."

"Let me guess—a half-Fae?"

Fordham nodded, sticking his hand against the back of the wardrobe until they heard a click. The wood moved inward, revealing a darkened room. He split the dresses in half, stepped over her shoes, and into the room. Kerrigan followed, looking around the space that Fordham had just lit.

It was a madhouse. Papers were *everywhere*. Wynter had even scrawled illegibly on the walls. A pile of masquerade wear was huddled in a corner, and there was a full bookshelf of old, musty books. Kerrigan lifted one off of the shelf with the title in ancient Fae—*Voure hest mas Besremay, Ravinia.*

"What does this mean?" Kerrigan asked.

Fordham frowned, scanning the title. "*History of the Original Mountain, Ravinia.* Where did she get that?" He looked through all of the titles. "Where did she get all of this? A lot of it would have been burned thousands of years ago."

"I don't know." Kerrigan replaced it back on the shelf with the others.

He passed her a stiff card he'd picked up. "Looks like we have our answer."

Kerrigan scanned the page. "She's throwing a masquerade?"

"Wynter's Masq," he said with a frown. "It's coded to look like an exclusive party, but it's something else. It's something to explain all of this." He gestured to the walls. "She's been researching the wall and the mountain and trying to find a way to bring it down."

"The Masq isn't for a week."

He sighed. "Of course it is."

"Well, do you have a mask?" Kerrigan tucked the envelope into her corset. "Because we're going to need one."

# CHAPTER 11
## *The Masquerade*

"**M**aybe I should have taken the potion," Kerrigan said with a shudder.

Fordham shook his head, tugging the hood of her cloak closer around her face. Her red hair was such a dead giveaway that she'd actually taken care to braid it back off her face and tuck it up into a thick bun. The curls still jutted out at odd angles, but there was nothing that could be done for that, short of having Ben and Bay work their magic on her hair. She hadn't been able to find them this evening even to ask, so, that had been off the table. The real problem was her magic. She'd hated the idea of taking a potion to dampen her magic, but it was sounding like a better idea every step they made deeper in the mountain.

"She's not going to be able to distinguish your magic from everyone else's once we're in the crowd as long as you don't use it," Fordham said. "You said that it looked golden and got brighter when you reached for it?" She nodded, adjusting her own black mask that hid her freckles. "Then, don't reach for it under any circumstances."

"Okay," she whispered, following him down the darkened halls. "What if she notices me anyway?"

He shot her a carefully guarded look. "Don't let her."

Right. Great.

Kerrigan picked up her pace to match the prince. The meeting wasn't being held inside Ravinia Mountain, but one of the other smaller peaks, and it was a trek to get there. No wonder they'd had to wait two days for the ball. They didn't look that far apart, but it was a slog through old cave systems, some as big as the dragons that had once inhabited the mountain and some they had to sidle sideways through. They'd had to backpedal once when Fordham discovered a cave-in that he didn't remember.

She was breathless by the time they reached the corridor leading to their masquerade. They filtered into the crowd of people. Fordham's hand reached back for her. Her hand tingled at the first touch as he drew her toward him.

"Don't want to lose you in the crowd," he whispered.

She met his gaze through the white mask that covered more than half of his beautiful face. Her cheeks heated, and she was glad that he couldn't see. "There are so many people."

He nodded grimly. More than they'd expected. There were at least a hundred people milling about. Each handing over an invitation that matched the one Kerrigan had taken from Wynter's secret room.

They waited an agonizing fifteen minutes before Fordham gave up their own invitation, and they stepped inside. Kerrigan's mouth dropped at the sight before her. The space was as large as the ballroom and nearly as full. There had to be more than a thousand people in attendance. No way could Wynter pick her out of all of this.

"Who are they all?"

Fordham also looked around in awe. "I don't know. All social classes though. Look at the clothes."

She saw what he meant. Some people were dressed as elegantly as she and

Fordham, but the majority wore inexpensive spun cloth and practical shoes. She noticed a table along the wall had rows of cheap black masks, and much of the crowd was wearing them. Because Kerrigan had only seen the court and her attendants, she hadn't considered that there was an entire city of people of all social classes living in the mountain. Just as trapped as everyone else.

"I'm surprised she'd go to the masses." It seemed beneath her.

Fordham's jaw was set. "She'd do it if it meant having enough support to go up against our father."

"You think that's what she's doing?"

"Don't you?"

Kerrigan couldn't disagree. With this many people in attendance at one meeting, it was a veritable legion. And Wynter was mad enough to try it.

"Plus, if everything I've been dealing with this week is any indication, these are the people most upset about our continued isolation."

"What does it look like on your end?"

"The poor are taking the brunt of the strain on products. The human village we trade with, Lethbridge, heard about me leaving and are withholding most trade."

"What? Why?"

Fordham glanced at her. "The city of Lethbridge fear it means the House of Shadows is soon going to get out of the mountain. Apparently, a sizable number of their citizens has already picked up and left. They said they wouldn't be subjugated again."

Kerrigan sighed. "Well, I don't blame them."

"No," he agreed begrudgingly. "As a result, prices have increased for all goods. There aren't enough jobs to satisfy everyone. Not enough land to feed everyone. Meanwhile, the court is feasting every night. It doesn't look good. The inequity is going to get my father killed before his enemies ever touch him."

Kerrigan had seen kids starving on the streets of Kinkadia while the Society ate fine and the wealthy on the Row lived like kings. Couple that with a thousand years of forced isolation, their only source of trade evaporating, and she hardly blamed anyone for wanting to do something about it.

"One thing is for sure," Fordham said as he maneuvered them closer to the stage at the front of the room. "With this many people, it cannot be beyond my father's notice."

That pronouncement made the meeting seem all the more precarious. As if at any moment, the king would rush in here with his guards and stop the meeting. Kerrigan tightened her grip on Fordham's hand, and then a flash of light circled the room.

"Wynter's magic," he breathed to her.

But that was clear by the way the room immediately went silent. Everything settled, thick with anticipation. As quickly as it had come, all the candles in the massive cavern dropped at the same time. Gasps of excitement and fear rippled through the crowd.

Before it could crescendo, a figure stepped onto the stage, a flame in her hand illuminating the space. She was taller and broader than Wynter's lithe form with a thin lace mask covering the stretch of her dark eyes. Her clothes were militant and sturdy with a thick blonde braid over one shoulder.

"Welcome one and all to the first annual Wynter Masquerade. I am Aisling of family Laurent, but in these halls, we are one and all the same. For those who are here for the first time, we appreciate your interest in our great princess's vision. For those who have come to meetings before, we welcome you back and into a bigger, brighter future. Rise of Charbonnet!"

The room erupted with an echoing of the phrase. "Charbonnet!"

"Rise of the House of Shadows!"

"House of Shadows!" they chanted back.

Kerrigan's jaw tensed with the effort to keep from doing anything that would give her away. Already, she could tell that Wynter had whipped these people up into zealotry, and she had no way to get them out of the mountain.

"I'm happy to announce your princess, Wynter Ollivier," Aisling said, holding her hand out and offering the stage to Wynter.

Wynter made quite an entrance in a perfectly white dress to match her long, unbound white locks. The stage illuminated around her, showing the barely blue look she cast across the crowd. From here, Kerrigan might even believe she was completely with it. But her sanity seemed tenuous at best.

She held her hands up, and silence settled back into the crowd who had been applauding her entrance. Her nails were painted a deep blood red. The only color on her at all.

"Charbonnet," she said in her low, melodic voice. "Once a term to claim a tribe of Alandria. We were the original Fae who came to this great island. Irena, who they worship, came from our halls. She met the great Ferrinix in the halls of Ravinia Mountain. They were bound in our throne room. The line of dragon riders began with us. And the Society deemed it fit to strip us of that right because they did not approve of our treatment of the lesser races."

Kerrigan winced. Of course, everyone here was Fae. She was probably the only half-Fae in attendance. She doubted any humans were stupid enough to do this.

"They shackled us to this mountain, which had once been the seat of power. And on the eve of our thousand-year imprisonment, what happens? My brother was cast out and able to pass through the barrier."

Fordham tensed at the mention of his exile.

Cheers rose up again, and she waited patiently for them to die down.

"Was this a coincidence?" she asked, casting that terrifying gaze across the room. "I think not. He returns to this mountain and with a dragon."

Gasped whispers scattered throughout the room.

"A dragon now belongs once again to tribe Charbonnet, as it always did before. As it always should have!" She hit her fist into the palm of her hand. A fierceness settled over her delicate features. "And as the anniversary of the barrier approaches, everything is changing. You can feel it, can't you?"

A chorus of responses went up in the crowd.

"I can feel the walls crumbling," she spoke over them. "I alone can see the cracks forming in the foundation of our prison. And I alone am going to get you out of here. The end is near, Charbonnet."

A chant went up in the crowd. *"Wyn-ter. Wyn-ter. Wyn-ter."*

She stood frozen above them, a statue of innocence and power. She was their guiding light out of this madness. Even if it made *no* sense. Even if she had no way of actually getting them out of this place. Even if she hadn't given them *proof* that she could actually see the wall. Everything was blind faith, which had never sat well with Kerrigan. She wanted to save these people, but it certainly wasn't Wynter who was going to be able to do it. She was using their fear and desperation to put herself in a place of power.

Finally, she raised her hand once more, and silence descended on the cavern.

"Many of you are wondering how I am going to achieve this. And I have decided to begin today," Wynter said dramatically.

Kerrigan and Fordham exchanged an uneasy glance. This couldn't be good. Just days ago, she had been asking Kerrigan to take the wall down. She hounded her all week to try to get her to practice. Luckily, Pres and Arbor kept her busy so that Wynter never had the opportunity again. Was there a possibility that she had figured out how the magic worked?

"You must be wondering why I chose this day for our meeting. When the barrier went up, thirteen powerful magical users worked together under a full moon and sacrificed their lives to put it up around us." Wynter held her hand up, tilting her chin with a wicked smile. "Tonight is a full moon. And I have brought the sacrifice."

She stepped backward, and Aisling pushed forward the first sacrificial lamb.

Kerrigan's stomach roiled as she saw the person thrown at Wynter's feet. She jerked forward, and Fordham grasped her arm.

"You cannot let her see you," he warned.

"And I can't let her do *this* either."

His eyes were raw with emotion for the first time. "I'll do it."

"She won't *care*."

Wynter lifted the head of the person, a knife suddenly in her hand. The woman was gagged and bound at her feet. Wynter tilted the person's chin toward the crowd, twisting her sideways enough so everyone could see that it was a half-Fae at her feet.

But that wasn't what captured Kerrigan's attention.

It was the face. She'd recognize the scar above her lip and the roundness of her features and the look of pure terror.

"Bayton," she gasped.

# CHAPTER 12

## The Light

**W**ithout another thought, Kerrigan ripped off her cloak, revealing her bright red hair. She dropped her black mask to the floor and pushed her hair behind her slightly pointed ears. As she stepped through the press of the crowd, she reached for her magic. A blinding light that only Wynter could see.

Wynter staggered backward from Bayton. The knife clattered to the ground, and she covered her eyes.

"Leave her, Wynter," Kerrigan spat.

Someone reached for Kerrigan, but by that point, Fordham was at her side. He disarmed a Fae man with a knife. Then, he dropped his own disguise, and the gasp was loud enough that no one else attempted to stop them.

"You cannot sacrifice these people," Fordham declared with all the force of their crowned prince.

"They are half-Fae and human, brother. Servants and menial workers, nothing more," Wynter said coolly. "Thirteen lives is a small matter when the cost for the rest of us is eternal enslavement."

"You have no *proof* that their lives will bring you what you want. You would kill them all for sport even if it did nothing."

His accusation hit the crowd like a blow. Whispers erupted all around them.

Wynter straightened to her full height, ignoring Kerrigan's magic and staring down her big brother. "You know nothing of my research, brother. You have been gone. You have not seen how our people require more. I was here while you were not, and we look up to you for returning to us as our champion, but you have done *nothing* for them." She threw her hand out at the crowd. "These who suffer."

Fordham looked ready to launch himself across the distance to his sister, but that was what Wynter wanted. No matter that Fordham had been working on fixing the trade issue. That now that he was in the Society, he would have access to more resources. That he could even negotiate new trade agreements, bring people in and out of the mountain. Not that anyone else knew these things were possibilities.

Wynter was the one with the cult standing behind her. And Fordham and Kerrigan were good, but they couldn't withstand an army.

"You will not need a sacrifice," Kerrigan announced before Fordham could react.

A cruel smile slithered across Wynter's face. As if she had been waiting for this very moment, orchestrated it herself, and Kerrigan had stepped into her carefully laid trap. But she couldn't back down. Not with Bay's life on the line. Not with twelve others just like herself set to be killed for an experiment.

"And why is that?" Wynter asked.

"Because I'll take the wall down."

Fordham glared at her. "Kerrigan ..."

"This is the miracle, my fellow Charbonnet," Wynter said, holding her hands out before her. "You have heard me witness about the glow of the barrier around the mountain. That its golden brilliance is bright. I had never seen that color magic until now. Until her." She pointed at Kerrigan. The crowd erupted into excitement. "The answer to our problem has arrived. We bring down the barrier tonight!"

Everyone cheered for her. Everyone, except Kerrigan and Fordham.

"Why do I feel like we walked right into that?" Kerrigan asked.

Fordham continued to glare at his sister. "Because we did."

"Come, Kerrigan," Wynter said, gesturing for her to come to her side.

"Ford," she whispered.

"Together."

They both strode on the stage. Of course, it would look like both Kerrigan, the bearer of barrier magic, and the crowned prince stood with his sister. Even if they had done it under duress.

Kerrigan knelt to help Bayton to her feet. The woman was crying. "I didn't know. She took me. I don't know where Benton is."

"It's okay," she said soothingly. "We'll get you out of here."

Kerrigan walked Bayton to the back of the stage. Twelve more half-Fae and humans were bound and gagged in a back room.

Kerrigan glared at Aisling with all of her fury. "Release their bonds. This is no longer necessary."

Aisling's mouth quirked up on the right side, and she crossed her arms. "Sure thing, honey."

Kerrigan wanted to punch her in her perfect little nose. But she restrained herself, helping Bayton out of her binds.

"Help them," she told Bayton and then took a deep breath and went back onto that stage.

Wynter was speaking, and Kerrigan hadn't been listening. Something about Fordham's return with the half-Fae with the power to save them. She didn't explicitly say that they should be ruling—*she* should be ruling—but the connotation was clear. While the king reveled in his gluttony, everyone else suffered. Wynter seemed to think she could do better.

"That's enough," she muttered. "Let's get this over with."

Wynter shot her a look of pure wrath. So, she was also here for the spectacle. Well, not that surprising.

Kerrigan smiled in the most insufferable way possible. Mischief was in her nature, but she had a way of frustrating anyone with an ounce of authority.

Wynter whipped her head back to her waiting audience. She unclenched her hands and let a smile smooth over her serene features. "Let's begin."

Kerrigan thought they'd have to go back down to the surface, back to the spot that they'd ridden out to. But that was another one of Wynter's performances. Getting Kerrigan out alone before confiding in her about what she knew, trying to make Kerrigan relate to her. She soon found out why this chamber had been chosen above all others.

"Aisling," Wynter said, her voice dipping low at the sound of her assistant's name.

Aisling stepped forward, pulled her hands to her body, squaring her hips, and then pushed out slowly. The chamber wall *shifted*, and suddenly, a wind whipped through the room. The wall was a large stone that filled the opening, leading to a rough balcony and the empty air beyond. It was pitch-black and a crystal-clear night, revealing the completely full moon.

The crowd gasped in amazement. Kerrigan had to admit that it was impressive.

Wynter stepped around Kerrigan and went straight to the opening. She raised her hand into the air, and it encountered resistance at the exit. The barrier had stretched taut over the opening to the outside so that no one could even enjoy the balcony beyond. It seemed a travesty for it to be right there and perpetually out of reach.

"Here," Wynter said, drawing her hand down. "This is where there's a breach." And as she said it, her hand moved just a few more inches forward, as if the barrier could almost *give* under her palm. She smiled triumphantly.

"Come. See for yourself."

Kerrigan jutted her jaw forward and went to Wynter's side. Fordham followed, looking none too pleased, but at the same time, interested. Like he hadn't believed Wynter until that moment. No wonder she'd gained so many followers so quickly.

"What do I do?"

Wynter gestured to where her hand was on the wall. "You cannot see the magic, but its signature matches your own. A bright golden that shines like the sun. The crack is like a fissure in rock. A jagged edge in an otherwise clear film." She took Kerrigan's hand and pushed it against the place that she claimed was a rift in the magical barrier that had endured for nearly a thousand years. "Right here."

Kerrigan closed her eyes, feeling the current of the thing. The wrongness of it. The perfectly rightness of it at the same time. A buzzing and zap against her skin, as if it recognized her. Or was warning her. She wasn't sure which or if it was both. But it certainly gave off a very chilling vibe. She hadn't liked coming through or touching it at all, if she were honest, but she was in too deep now.

But it didn't feel any different. There wasn't this mysterious gap that Wynter had claimed she could find. Even if her hand pushed through the barrier that was there to hold her in.

"Dig deep. Feel the part of yourself that is the same," Wynter whispered beside her. "Like calls to like. Answer the call."

Kerrigan furrowed her brow and pushed deeper in herself. She had no idea what she was doing. And frankly, she felt a little silly, standing with her hand in front of a barrier that she could walk through. But there was a smidgen of resistance right before she would push over, and she concentrated on that.

The resistance was like a jelly right before a fork pierced it—wiggly and amorphous. If she pushed, she'd cut the thing in half. But it was thin air. There wasn't anything else to feel, except the occasional zap.

She gasped and pulled back. "It's not there."

Kerrigan wiped her forehead. She'd been concentrating so intensely that she'd begun to sweat and not even realized the strain.

"There you have it," Fordham said. "Can you stop this charade?"

"You tried once," Wynter said, ignoring her brother. "Try again. Really concentrate. I can see the break. I want you to feel it. To take it in your hand and rip it open from the inside. The spell will shatter around you."

Kerrigan looked at her skeptically. "How do you know that?"

"I've been researching this wall longer than you've been alive," she said calmly. Though her cool veneer was slipping as the crowd behind them whispered at Kerrigan's failed attempt.

"Silence," Aisling called before Wynter had to. "Give the girl another chance."

"Go on," Wynter said encouragingly.

Fordham shook his head. "You don't have to do it."

But there was a mob between them and the door. If she didn't try again, they weren't going to let her leave.

"I'll try one more time," Kerrigan said.

Fordham's features hardened, and Wynter smiled triumphantly.

She ignored them both and held her hand back out, letting her eyes close and going to that place within herself where her magic settled. She reached into the well, and her magic answered bright and vibrant. She'd been careful not to use it here since Wynter's proclamation in the woods. It answered her like a beacon home. Then, she put both of her hands in the empty space once more. She reached for that rip in the world that would set them all free. She breathed in sharply.

"Yes," Wynter gasped.

She could feel it. She could feel exactly what Wynter was talking about. But it wasn't a break from *this* side of the wall. It was crumbling from the outside in and not the other way around.

Kerrigan pulled back. Wynter argued behind her, and Fordham shouted right back, but Kerrigan wasn't listening. She wasn't done. She stepped through the barrier and out onto the stone balcony. A well of shouts followed her casual step across the barrier. Anger and excitement and fear, all a chorus that echoed through her brain. The expectations of so many people, all in one place.

"What are you doing, Kerrigan?" Fordham asked.

But she didn't answer him; she brought her hand back up to that rift. Felt the seams of it wrap around her like a gentle embrace. There it was. *This* was the crack that Wynter had seen. A fracture years in the making. It was as if the spreading of the magic around the balcony had pulled it too tight. Like stretching pie dough to its absolute thinnest and praying to any god who would listen that it wouldn't break.

Except here, she wanted to exploit that weakness and take the whole damn thing down with her.

Kerrigan leaned into it, took a deep breath, and then pulled her hand down. Nothing happened. The moment of anticipation popped like a bubble. She opened her eyes, deflated. It wouldn't work. Not like this. And she didn't know enough about this magic to make it work for her.

She opened her mouth to admit defeat when she felt a tug on her magic. She jumped in surprise but couldn't remove her hand from the barrier. It was as if the spell itself were alive. A bright, blinding light filled the space. The one that Wynter must have seen all along. Kerrigan could suddenly see the entire golden glow of the barrier in all of its glory.

It pulled harder.

Her eyes flew wide. She could hear Wynter's panicked questions. Fordham tried to cross the barrier, and it refused him. He jammed his shoulder against the thing that had once let him out. His eyes were terrified. All of his fears realized once more.

The barrier sank its claws into her. She tipped her head back and screamed, collapsing onto the cold, hard balcony floor. Her vision went black at the edges. The last thing she saw was Fordham's desperate attempt to reach her.

Then, everything went dark.

\*\*\*

*A girl stepped up to Cavour. Her wide, dark eyes looked at the empty village with pity. War had not been kind to the once-beautiful village. Dragon fire had destroyed nearly half the place in one go. Only the mountains had saved the people within, leaving the humans and half-Fae to fend for themselves against a war they didn't want.*

*"I am sorry," she said.*

*"Mei, are you sure?" a voice asked behind her. "These people... they don't deserve this."*

*"They don't." Mei whirled around to find a handsome young man before her. Her heart constricted.*

*Trulian had been the first to believe in her. His resistance meant that maybe even she had crossed the line.*

*"Can you even do it?"*

*She bit her lip and ran her hands back through her nearly black hair. "I don't know, but what other choice is there? You know what they're going to do if we don't stop them. You were in the meeting, Tru."*

*He glanced off to the mountains beyond her head. "This can't be the answer. They're monsters, but ..."*

*"It's the only way. I've seen it."*

*"Seen it?" He frowned. "Again? You didn't tell me."*

*"Oh, Tru," she whispered, all the secrets that lay between them clogging her throat. All the visions she never dared to tell him about as her mind shattered day after day along the campaign.*

*"Please," he pleaded.*

*"Step back. I must work," she said. "To save our very souls."*

*And then, before Trulian could talk her out of it, Mei lifted her brown arms toward the tri peaks of the House of Shadows. A bright, blinding light built between her palms, and she unleashed.*

\*\*\*

"Kerrigan," Fordham said, cradling her head in his lap.

He must have made it across the barrier after it disgorged her. Her eyes fluttered open. Everything hurt. Her magic was barely a flicker within her. She'd never had a vision like that before. Never known that she could glimpse the past and not the future.

"Ford," she croaked.

"I'm here."

"You did it!" Wynter cried. "You made the crack bigger. I can stick my entire hand through."

And for the first time in a thousand years, someone other than Fordham Ollivier stuck their hand through the barrier wall.

"Let's keep trying!"

Fordham ignored Wynter. "We're going to get you to a healer."

"Ford," she repeated uncertainly.

How were they going to get back to the other side of the barrier and through the mountain tunnels? No one would let them pass. Just thinking of it hurt her head.

She heard a sound that was all too familiar. Wings beating on the wind. She turned her head and found Netta flying toward them. Fordham lifted her into his arms and carried her to his dragon, taking off without a backward glance.

# CHAPTER 13
## *The Plot*

ARBOR

Arbor stepped forward out of the gloom of the chamber. Her bright blue eyes cast toward the dragon flying away from their home. Her cousin and their salvation strapped on its back. She dropped her hood, revealing the quintessential raven hair braided back out of her face.

"He stole her from us!" Wynter screamed, seething.

Aisling put a hand on her shoulder, the closest she would come to revealing the true nature of their relationship. But Arbor knew the thing that Wynter could not reveal to her court. How her heart longed for her bodyguard and attendant. Such things were not allowed in this court. Especially not of a royal.

"You were right," Aisling said comfortingly.

"Of course I was right," she snarled. "I can feel the night air. It's coming down."

Already, the carefully placed guards within the crowd were herding everyone out of the room so that no one would see Wynter's meltdown. But not Arbor. Never Arbor.

"They'll be back," she said finally.

Wynter whirled on her, dropping her hand from where it'd crossed the barrier for the very first time. "And how can you be sure?"

Arbor lifted her chin, not bowing to Wynter's moods. It was why she had first begun to keep her around. Everyone else complied with all of her madness. Her unruly tempers and tantrums and outrageous fits. She was a visionary— that much was certain—but with no one to temper that madness, to hone it into something valuable, she would fizzle before it could get anywhere.

Which was where she came in. "Because we're still here."

Wynter waved her off. "You think you and Prescott matter that much?"

She didn't know, truthfully. Fordham was enigmatic on a good day, but their relationship meant something. "Yes."

"Maybe," Wynter acknowledged.

Aisling shot Arbor a narrowed-eye look. Arbor returned the look with an easy smile, sinking into her lush hip.

"I'll write to him," Arbor said. She had already planned to do so, but it seemed prudent to let Wynter think it was her idea.

"Yes," Wynter said at once. "Use one of my birds to get the word out to him."

"I'll have to be careful not to mention you," she said as if it were a second thought.

"Of course. Make it your own mind. We don't want him to know that you work for me."

*With*. With *you*.

Though she didn't correct her. She never did.

"As you wish," Arbor said. Aisling opened her mouth, likely to protest, and Arbor barreled over whatever she was going to say. "I'll get with Pres now and figure out how to craft something in the morning once we've learned of their disappearance."

"Thank you, Arbor," Wynter said, reaching out and taking her hand.

Arbor forced herself not to recoil. Wynter was a means to an end—that was all.

"We all believe in your vision. I'm only your tool." She bowed her head to the princess.

"Where would I be without you?"

Buried in her own mania, for certain. It had been Arbor's suggestion to get all of this moving. To use Wynter's influence to capitalize on the last month of unforgivable grievances against anyone who wasn't titled. Arbor and Prescott had been all but forgotten in the melee of the trade drying up. They needed support for what they planned to do to right this wrong. Wynter had the influence and was influenceable on her own as well.

"We'll never find out," Arbor responded and then backed out of Wynter's presence.

Her smile was feline as she sauntered down the many corridors, away from that cursed chamber. One arm through wasn't enough. But it'd kindled the fire in the thousand who had shown up today for the demonstration. Whispers would follow, and many more would join the movement.

Arbor finally reached the York quarters and stepped inside. She pressed her back to the door and breathed a sigh of relief. Prescott stepped out of his adjoining chambers.

"Well?" he asked, crossing his arms.

"Is Rafael asleep?" she asked of his latest lover.

He had a long string of men and women who came to his bed.

"It's Angelique tonight."

She waved a hand. She didn't remember when he'd given up with Rafi and moved on. "No matter. Are they asleep?"

"Yes. Long since."

"Good," she said and then stepped into his awaiting arms.

Prescott held her close. The way that no one else had ever held her. She pressed her nose into the hollow of his throat and smelled the sex on him. It didn't bother her as it might have bothered others. It was just what her brother smelled like.

"Does she believe you?" he asked.

She nodded, pulling back from him to stare up into his matching blue eyes. "Kerrigan widened the break in the barrier, and then they fled. We're to write to them on the morn when we discover them gone."

"Clever. Your work. Not that incompetent princess, I assume?"

"Obviously."

"You're such a genius, sister."

She beamed at his praise. She brushed a lock of his dark hair from his forehead. He grasped her hand in his and placed a kiss on the top, all gallant and gentlemanly.

"Now, the real work begins."

# CHAPTER 14
## *The Healing*

**K**errigan woke slowly, as if she were stuck in mud and trying to pry herself free. Her eyes were crusty, and she had to blink to clear them. Everything was blurry. And hurt. Gods, every inch of her body felt as if it had been beaten into a pulp. The last time she'd felt this, she had been assaulted. But she didn't remember why she was like this now.

"You're awake," a voice said, the figure jumping from where they were seated and reaching for something.

It ended up being a glass of water, which Kerrigan choked down with a small cough. "Thank you."

She winced as she wiped at her eyes and found Valia hovering over her. Valia was a steward of the Society. Not a full member, but not a citizen either. They worked with Society members for the rest of their days but of their own free will. Kerrigan had almost been one of them. She would have been if she hadn't had a tribe claim her, if she hadn't ended up winning the dragon tournament.

"How are you feeling?" Valia asked.

"Sore," Kerrigan admitted.

"Let me help you sit up." She eased Kerrigan into a sitting position.

She blinked a few times to right her vision. She realized she was in an unfamiliar bedchamber. "Where am I?"

"Training quarters," Valia said. "Your things were moved from the House of Dragons while you were gone, and Helly had you brought here for treatment."

"Treatment?"

"You don't remember?"

Kerrigan shook her head.

"That's okay. She said that might be the case. I'll let Helly explain. Try to drink some more water."

"Okay."

Valia disappeared, and another figure filled the doorway. Fordham looked like he hadn't slept in days. Black bruises pushed against the skin under his bloodshot eyes. He was in days-old clothes, and his black hair was messy, as if he had perpetually run his hands through it.

"You made it."

"Hey," she muttered, taking another drink. "What happened?"

"You don't remember?"

Kerrigan shook her head. He sank into Valia's unoccupied seat. "You tried to take the wall down, started screaming, and blacked out. I had Netta pick us up. We met Tieran and flew straight home."

"Oh," she said, fuzzy memories surfacing. "Did it work?"

He shot her a grim look. "It didn't take the wall down, but it did create a break. Wynter could get her arm through it."

"Gods," she whispered. "I can't believe I did that."

"How *did* you do it?"

Kerrigan shrugged. "I don't know. I don't think that I did."

Fordham frowned. "What does that mean?"

"I don't know." She closed her eyes, wishing that she could explain it. Because now that she was thinking about it, the sensation of what had happened on that balcony all rushed back in. The way the magic had sensed her and then dropped belly deep into her magic, as if it was a life force. Then, the strange vision. She didn't know if she should even mention that. Mei and Trulian and how she had decided to seal the monsters inside the mountain to save the world. It was just as the stories described it. Except it was one spiritcaster and not thirteen of the best magic users of the time. One girl had created *that*.

Could Kerrigan do something like that too?

"What are you doing to my patient?" Helly snapped, jarring them both.

"I was checking on her," Fordham said.

"Out with you. You can see her when I'm finished. It's the middle of the night. You should get rest."

Fordham shot her a hollow look. As if he hadn't slept since they flew away. But it had been the middle of the night when they left, and it was a three- or four-hour flight. It should have been at least dawn.

"What time is it?"

Helly frowned. "You have been asleep for a full day."

"What?" she gasped. "But that means ..."

"Training starts tomorrow," Fordham said.

"Yes," Helly said, shooing him toward the door. Fordham looked like he wanted to argue, but eventually relented. "Your training begins tomorrow, but I can give you a medical exemption."

"No," Kerrigan said automatically.

"Why am I not surprised you don't want one?"

"I wasn't in the tournament until the very end. I can't miss the first day of training as well. No one will take me seriously."

"You're in no shape, but if you drink this draught and sleep the rest of the evening, you might be ready. Or at least, you won't pass out halfway through the day." Helly passed her the drink. "I hope."

Kerrigan took a tentative sniff of the mug and gagged at the smell. "What is this?"

"Just drink it," Helly admonished.

Kerrigan held her breath and then downed the thick, viscous substance in one go. She choked on it but held the stuff down.

"That should speed you up. I did what I could without Fordham telling me what had happened to you. I treated you as if you'd had a vision." Helly arched an eyebrow. "Is that what happened?"

It was easier than the truth. How could she even begin to explain what had happened in that mountain?

"Yes," Kerrigan said, sinking back down into the covers.

"What did you see?"

"I don't know." Kerrigan sighed and closed her eyes. "It was a woman and a man that I didn't recognize. They were together, and the woman did some kind of light magic."

Helly pursed her lips. "I have no idea what that means. You recognized neither of them?"

"No."

Lie. She knew exactly who they were and what they had done. But a part of her couldn't confide in Helly what she had almost done. What would Helly think to know that she had tried to take the wall down? What would she think if she knew it was even possible?

"Well, it always reveals itself eventually," Helly said. She patted Kerrigan's knee. "Get some rest. We will discuss what happened in the House of Shadows after that."

"We will?"

"Of course. You're the first person to enter their grounds with an inside source to their court in a thousand years. We need to know everything that happened, everything you heard."

Kerrigan looked at her, aghast. "I'm not a spy."

Helly shot her a pitying look. "Your allegiance lies with us. Society first, tribe second. This is what that means."

"Did you ask Fordham?"

"Yes. He was quite forward with information, if I'm honest. I don't know why you would want to withhold anything that happened. He made it seem rather mundane. Border disputes, treaty issues, trade issues." She waved her hand. "Anything is helpful."

Kerrigan nodded. Right. Anything but the truth of what they had almost done there.

"Okay. Yeah. We can talk."

Helly nodded, rising to her feet. "Now, sleep. You have a big day tomorrow."

Kerrigan smiled halfheartedly. "Helly, did you ever find Basem's killer?"

"No," she said faintly. "We're still working on it. Don't worry yourself. Your number one priority is training."

"Of course," she said and watched Helly leave. Such a nonanswer and not at all satisfying.

It was only a few minutes before Fordham was at her side again.

"You didn't tell her?" he asked.

She shook her head. "No. How would I even begin?"

He nodded, understanding. The way everyone thought of the House of Shadows was already so set in stone. The monsters that Mei had claimed they were all those years ago.

"You can see my dilemma when I first arrived."

"Clearly."

"What actually happened when you blacked out, Kerrigan?" Fordham asked.

She debated on not telling him, but she could keep nothing from Fordham. Not when he had been there. Not when he'd saved her. Their relationship was complicated, but this bond was as true as it had ever been.

"I saw the wall go up."

Fordham blinked, as if that wasn't the answer he'd expected. "During the Great War?"

"Yes. And it's not what you think. It was someone like me who put it up to protect the Society."

He rocked back in the chair. "So, it is true. We were always the monsters they painted us as."

"I don't know. She believed it. Her name was Mei, M-e-i, and she had a soldier with her, Trulian."

"I've never heard of a Mei."

"Me neither."

"But Trulian is a common enough name," he said.

"It is. At least it gives us a place to start."

"To start?"

She smiled at him with the last bit of strength as the medicine pulled her toward slumber. "I have an idea."

"Gods help us all," he said, but he was smiling.

"If we find out who they were and how she did it, then maybe I can figure out how to take it down without killing myself."

"You still want to do it?" he asked in shock.

"Benton and Bayton are still trapped. Your cousins are still trapped. Whatever her reasons for doing it, they do not deserve to be punished for a thousand-year-old war."

"And how are we going to do this when training starts tomorrow?"

But he wasn't disagreeing with her. He could see the merit. He'd wanted out of there for who knew how long. How could he deny the rest of his people? Even if they could both see the consequences.

"As we do the best things—together."

# CHAPTER 15

## The Training

**K**errigan stumbled into the training facility behind the other four winners of the dragon tournament. The four people, who together, they would dedicate their lives to the Society.

She'd found black Society robes waiting in her room when she woke from her magically induced slumber with a note that read, *Training robes.* They weren't the lush, almost-glossy robes, but a rough spun cotton. She'd slid them over her training clothes with a little thrill of delight anyway. Her entire life, she'd been surrounded by people in black robes with the dragon insignia on them, and now, they belonged to her.

Whatever medicine Helly had given her had worked wonders, but she still felt depleted. Her magic wasn't a hundred percent recovered. Her body still ached. And even though she'd slept for more than a day, she was still tired. But she couldn't be today.

"You made it!" Audria Ather cried, throwing her arms around Kerrigan.

Audria Ather, Third of the House of Drame in the line of Bryonica, had been one of Kerrigan's friends when they were children. They'd played together before Kerrigan's father sent her away to the House of Dragons. It was Audria who had realized that she was Princess Felicity and offered for her family to sponsor Kerrigan. She'd wanted them to be like sisters again. Fordham had given her an alternative—join him in the House of Shadows—and Kerrigan had taken it. Anything to not have to return to the Bryonican life that had been taken from her.

Audria wasn't all bad. They were even friends. Even though she'd revealed Kerrigan's identity to the entire court. Kerrigan still hadn't come to terms with everyone knowing that she was Kerrigan Felicity Argon, once First of the House of Cruse, and her father, the great Kivrin Argon. She'd hidden it for so long that it didn't even seem possible.

"I made it," Kerrigan said, hugging her back.

"Oh my goodness, you look like the House of Shadows chewed you up and spit you out," she said with a giggle.

Not far off.

Kerrigan laughed, releasing her. "How was your break?"

"Excellent! You know that the Season is starting now that the tournament is over. You'll have to come to the parties with me since I can finally tell everyone you're Felicity."

Kerrigan grimaced. "You couldn't *drag* me to a Season event."

"You wouldn't be fit for one anyway," Roake said with distaste.

Roake Brevard was from the south in Elsiande. Traditionally, those from the south believed that magic should be used for nothing, but the younger generation was pushing back on that notion. Roake was the leader of that faction and had won the tournament to prove his point. He was also obsessed with Audria and made his distaste for Kerrigan clear.

"She would too fit," Audria said. "Don't be mean, Roake."

He looked at her with pure devotion. "Of course. I wouldn't think they'd let half-Fae participate."

"We're not prejudiced!" Audria insisted.

But of course, the louder and more often she said it, the more Kerrigan cringed. If they weren't prejudiced, she wouldn't have to announce it. It would be obvious.

"What's the Season?" Fordham asked as he and Noda, the winner from Concha, joined them.

"It's a mating ritual," Noda said dryly, adjusting her teal headscarf.

Audria gasped, covering her mouth. "It is not!"

Roake tried not to laugh. "It's an aristocratic courting system."

"The young ladies are presented to society, and then there are parties in each season to help them get to know the gentlemen," Audria explained. "At the end of the year, weddings are announced for those who courted the whole season."

"And weddings throughout for those who end up pregnant at each season event," Noda added.

Audria's cheeks turned pink.

Roake nodded. "It happens."

"But the best part is that the events take place at different palaces all over the continent," Audria said. "But it all starts in the summer here, on the Row!"

A throat cleared at the front of the room. "Trainees, are you here for the Season events or Society training?"

She was tall and lithe with onyx skin. Her textured hair was braided back off of her face in a protective style that accentuated her high cheekbones and hard eyes. The many braids were pulled into a high, tight bun. Her clothing was fitted black pants and a tunic with overlapping silver metal coins over top. It was the traditional garb of the Venatrix war tribe. It looked *heavy*, and yet she wore it with such grace. The black Society robes hung comfortably loose on her shoulders.

Hastily, the five riders bolted into a straight line and muttered an apology.

"I am Alura Van Horn," she barked. "And you will address me as Mistress

Alura or, preferably, sir. So, let's try this again. Are you here for Society training?"

"Yes, sir," was barked from all five of them at once.

She grinned at them, showing off the bright whiteness of her teeth. "Better."

Alura paced in front of the five winners. She didn't seem impressed by what she found there. Kerrigan was intimidated. Five years ago, three dragons had been up for grabs in the tournament. Alura had won along with Cyrene and Dean, who had both disappeared with their dragons, back to a world in more danger than this one. Which left Alura as the only competitor in her class. And arguably the most talented.

"Society training is not like anything else you have ever experienced before," she said plainly. "You'd be shocked to learn the dropout rate is thirty percent. A full third of all winners can't hack it."

Kerrigan's jaw dropped. Dropout rate? She'd never heard of anyone dropping out of the program. It must have been the most humiliating experience of a person's life to win the tournament and not survive the next year. She wanted to ask what happened to the dragons. Bonding was for a lifetime.

"Look to the person on your right and left." Kerrigan looked to Fordham and then Noda. "One of you *won't* make it."

Kerrigan gulped. That wouldn't be her. It couldn't be. She didn't have anywhere else to go.

"I say this as someone who went through this training *alone* for the first time in Society history: we will not go easy on you." She bared her teeth at them. "We are preparing you for the most important job in all of Alandria. You cannot just be good. You *must* be the best. Because the moment you put those robes on, you are more than yourself. You represent all of us. You *are* the Society."

Kerrigan shivered at the words. Wasn't it exactly what she'd thought that day in the tavern when she was in a fight? She couldn't do that anymore. Even provoked, it would look wrong. She had to be better. Which begged the question, which Society member had turned traitor to kill Basem Nix?

"As I was the last person to go through training, I am set to manage your training."

Roake groaned. Alura's eyes snapped to him.

"Do you have a problem with that, Brevard?"

"No, sir," he chirped.

"I thought not," Alura snarled. "Everything that I endured over my year of training will be carefully honed to make you five representatives of the Society." She curled her lip. Her eyes going flat. "I have my work cut out for me."

Audria's hand shot up in the air.

Alura glared at her. "I didn't open for questions, Ather. Keep your hand to yourself."

Audria slowly pulled her hand back down. Her cheeks were pink. She looked like she'd never been spoken to like that by anyone before. Likely she hadn't.

"I've structured training thus. You'll begin with a thirty-day bootcamp that includes morning workouts with me," she said, pacing back and forth in front of them. "And weapons training with masters who have graciously offered their assistance. You'll have an hour for lunch and then magic training each afternoon. Each day will feature a separate element—air, water, earth, and fire. Friday afternoons will be open for self-guided training."

Which meant working on the things that they were the worst at. Kerrigan had learned that in the House of Dragons, nothing was really *free* time.

"After the first month, if I determine that you are all sufficient enough, we'll move into training with your dragons. As well as a full slot of classes to prepare you to take your place as a government official in Alandria. The three main areas will be: government, philosophy, and history. Everyone takes one elective: maths, literature, or languages."

Roake scoffed.

Alura arched an eyebrow. "Have something to say, Brevard?"

"No, sir."

"Spit it out. You know you want to," she said lethally.

It was not an invitation. Though he took it as one.

"You expect us to take four classes and train with our dragon? When will we have the time, sir?"

"No," she said with a smile that said this would be unpleasant. "I want you to take four classes, train with your dragon, weapons, and magic, *and* keep up your workouts."

"All at once?" he gasped.

"One in three dropout rate," she reminded him, and he snapped his mouth shut.

Alura stared at them, as if waiting for someone else to talk out of turn. But none of them said anything. She could have heard a pin drop, as they'd all stopped breathing under her scrutiny. The next year was going to be plain torture.

"At the end of your year training, if you make it," she taunted, "you will earn the title of Master or Mistress. Only then can you turn in your training robes for full Society robes." She caressed her own robe around her dark shoulders. "Only then can you join our ranks. So, let's begin."

\*\*\*

Kerrigan fell to her knees on the edge of the training room. Sweat poured down her face, and she had the distinct impression that she was going to be sick.

"Get up," Fordham barked at her.

"I need a minute to breathe."

"Alura is going to make you run the lap again if you don't get moving. One foot in front of the other, halfling." He flung the stupid nickname at her to get her moving.

She jerked back to her feet. "I hate you, princeling."

He snapped a smile at her. "I know. Now, let's finish this lap. You can run faster than this."

She could.

She had in the past—when she was running for her life. But there was nothing chasing her here, except disappointment and possible expulsion.

If she hadn't used up all of her energy, trying to take down that stupid wall, she would have been keeping up just fine. Fordham wasn't even breathing hard. It made her look like an amateur. An amateur who didn't belong here.

But there was nothing she could do about it. She'd been incapacitated for more than a day. Her magic flickered in her gut, but it wasn't an inferno by any means. And her strength was practically nonexistent. Not to mention, her coordination. Whatever had happened in that spell had broken something in her. She had to hope that it would all come back.

"Argon," Alura snapped. Kerrigan cringed at the sound of her father's name in Alura's mouth. "Are we taking a rest or completing the circuit?"

"Completing the circuit, sir."

"Get to it."

Kerrigan gritted her teeth and finished. Last but at least she finished.

"A sloppy mess," Alura said. "Gods help us if the lot of you make it through training. Luckily for you, the sword master has already shown up for class today."

And then a tall, dark figure walked into the training arena. Kerrigan's heart dropped. Scales, it was Lorian Van Horn.

Not only was he Alura's father and a revered sword master. He had also been the single loudest voice of dissent for allowing her into the Society. He would stop at nothing to get her to drop out of the program.

She squared her shoulders. Not happening.

# CHAPTER 16

## *The Masters*

Lorian snapped his black robe off of his shoulders, revealing the silver metal attire of Venatrix. He was over six feet tall with black skin like his daughter, a shaved head, and a defined beard. He had a blade strapped to his belt.

Kerrigan had heard stories of that blade. A black blade with a vein of ancient Tendrille steel at its core and a pommel that melded to his hand. It had been in the Van Horn family for hundreds of years and had won him the dragon tournament against Kerrigan's father. Lorian had defeated Kivrin Argon in combat to secure his place and keep her father out of the competition.

She didn't hate him for it. Her dad had no place in the Society. Not that she much respected Lorian's backward view on half-Fae and humans either.

"The sword," he said, dramatically removing his from the sheath, "is an extension of the self. It must become a part of you, an extra length to your arm, for you to truly master the art form. Not all of you will." He shot her a look of disgust. "Some of you haven't even earned the right to be in these halls."

Kerrigan balled her hands into fists as he called her out.

He stepped up to her. The sword held before him. He could have nicked her chin with barely any movement. She held firm. Not moving an inch.

"We'll do what we can with what we have." He split a stray strand of hair, and they all watched the red curl fall to the ground at Kerrigan's feet. The threat blatant between them. "I assume all of you have had proper sword training in the past. I can't imagine you being here without knowing how to use one, but nothing would surprise me at this point."

Kerrigan shifted on her feet, trying to suppress the cramp building in her thigh. Lorian whirled back around to face her. His sword came so close to her nose that she swore that she saw the gods' faces. She jerked backward on instinct.

Lorian shook his head. "Typical."

Kerrigan saw red. She didn't know what he wanted her to do. She wasn't going to get split in half by this Fae standing before her, but she wouldn't be cowed either. If he thought threatening her was going to do the trick, then he would need to talk to Basem Nix about that. Hadn't worked out well for him.

"Stand in a circle and walk through Ravendin's twelve paces," Lorian said.

They moved into place. Kerrigan met Fordham's face for a second. His jaw was set. He was angry with Lorian too. Well, at least she wasn't alone. Not to mention, she and Fordham had run through Ravendin's paces so many times that she sometimes saw them in her dreams.

Everyone else, apparently, had likewise studied Ravendin, the Great War commander.

Lorian moved them into Chutrick's art-of-war formations. Through the basics of Kristoffer's lunge and parry work. And through three more of the greats.

By the end of the hour, not a one of them had picked up even a practice sword. But they were coated in sweat and panting. Each of the paces moving through the next one in synchronization. So, they looked more like a dance troupe than a group of sword fighters.

"Enough," Lorian finally barked. "Tomorrow, be prepared for the ancients and not just the greats. We'll spend a week on footwork before moving into practice play."

Roake looked ready to pass out as he groaned. Noda pushed her headscarf back off of her face. The entire thing was drenched in sweat. Kerrigan had no idea how she'd done the entire morning with it on. Audria—even perfectly prim and posh Audria—looked less than peaky.

"Get out of my sight," Lorian said. "Except you."

He pointed at Kerrigan, and she held back from the rest of the group. Fordham made like he was going to stay for support, but one glare from Lorian, and he relented, following Audria to their awaiting lunch break.

"Yes, sir?" Kerrigan asked.

"You'd do them all better if you cut your losses and bailed on the first day."

"I don't know what you mean, sir."

He arched an eyebrow. "Half-Fae have no place in these halls."

"Sir," she responded amicably.

"You're going to hold them back."

"I won my spot, sir."

"You *stole* your spot," he snarled. "You stole it from someone who deserved it, and you show no remorse for your actions. I don't know what you did or said to the rest of the council to get them to approve you, but I will never approve of you. And I will be here every day of your training, reminding you of exactly what you took from the rest of them."

"Yes, sir," she got out.

If he wanted a reaction from her, he wasn't going to get one.

"Training is all about working as a set, a group. Someone that your team-mates can rely on. It's not all going to be as easy as running and footwork, which you are already abysmal at. You're going to have to trust each other, fly formations together, and anticipate each other's moves. If you hold them back, the entire unit suffers," he spat. "Remember that."

"Is that all, sir?"

The fury on his face at the fact that she wouldn't rise to his bait was quite satisfactory. Though something else must have shown in his posture because Alura finally stepped forward.

"Kerrigan, you eat with your team as you do everything else."

Kerrigan bowed her head to Alura. "Thank you, sir."

She was halfway across the room when she heard Alura and Lorian getting into it. Lorian famously detested his daughter's girlfriend, a human who lived in Venatrix territory on the western sea. He'd trained Alura into the biggest, baddest fighting machine, hardly seeing her as a person, let alone a daughter—until the moment she'd defied him. Kerrigan was taking the brunt of his anger right now, but she couldn't imagine Alura dealing with it all those years.

By the time she made it into the dining hall, everyone else had already dug into their meal. Kerrigan filled her plate with food and took the open seat next to Audria. She drank three full glasses of water before getting any food.

"What did Lorian want?" Fordham asked stiffly.

"Isn't it obvious?" Roake asked. "He wants her gone."

"It's practically barbaric, the way he was treating you," Audria said.

"Seems in line with what I've heard of him," Noda said. "Someone said that last year, he beat a half-Fae girl in Venatrix near to death for supposedly stealing from a vendor in Edgewood Market."

Audria gasped. "He's a Society member!"

"Which means no one would say anything about it," Noda said.

"Isn't the Edgewood Market magicked against stealing?" Roake asked. He pointed a drumstick at Noda. "Why would someone be stupid enough to steal there?"

Noda shrugged. "Just what I heard."

"Anyone would steal if they were desperate enough," Fordham said.

"And how would you know?" Roake asked. "You're royalty."

"I'm not royalty but of the peerage," Audria said. "And I still have compassion for those in need."

"I would know because my people are desperate," Fordham said flatly.

His gaze bore through Roake until Roake finally looked away.

"Yeah, sure," Roake muttered.

"Do you think he actually beat someone?" Audria asked.

"Yes," Kerrigan said at once.

She knew firsthand how people reacted to half-Fae who had supposedly stepped out of line. She doubted that girl had ever even stolen anything. Just the threat was enough. Living as a half-Fae was a crime here.

"What do you think of the schedule?" Fordham asked to change the subject.

"Gods-damn madness, if you ask me," Roake snarled, his southern accent peeking out on the words.

"Agreed," Audria said properly. "I don't know how they expect us to keep up."

"They don't," Noda said. "They expect us to fail a lot, just so we keep trying to get better."

"And how do you know so much?" Roake blustered.

"My mam helped me with Society training. She didn't tell me what I was in for, just that it would test me beyond anything I'd done," Noda explained. Then, she looked at Fordham. "Why are you eating with us?"

Fordham stared right back at her. "Why wouldn't I?"

"You didn't for a month during the tournament. You never spoke more than three words to any of us, except Kerrigan."

"She's right," Audria added.

Roake nodded.

"You were competitors," Fordham said. "And now, we're a team. We have to work together so that we can all make it out of here."

"And why should we believe you?" Roake demanded.

The other two looked like they wanted to know the answer too.

"They don't want the House of Shadows represented in the government," Kerrigan answered for him. "So, they'll gun for the two of us to drop out. You don't have to work with us. I can understand why you wouldn't want to, all things considered, but the only way we'll get through this is as a group."

Fordham nodded once. "Personally, I'd love to prove them wrong about us lot. I'm not dropping out."

"Me neither," Kerrigan said quickly.

"I'm not either," Audria said.

Noda nodded. "All of us or none of us."

They all agreed and then looked to Roake. Waited for him to tell them to all go to hell. It would suit him after all.

But to their surprise, he held his hand out. "All of us or none of us."

Audria covered his hand, then Noda, then Kerrigan, and finally Fordham.

It was a pact that might be entirely meaningless in the end, but at the moment, it felt like it held the weight of the world in it.

\*\*\*

"Oh yes, there you are," an absentminded woman said as she strode into the air-magic room after lunch.

She didn't look like much. Shorter even than Kerrigan with hair graying at the temples and lines around her eyes. Since Fae so rarely aged at all, it was a shock to even see it. They could live for over a thousand of years before ever gaining lines. And many gave in to the abyss before letting that happen. Vanity and all.

"What are you all staring at me for?" she asked in confusion.

"Um, we're here for air-magic training," Audria said quickly. "Sir."

"Sir?" the woman asked, straightening to her tiny height, a sparkle of laughter in her soft brown eyes. "Sir is for military types, I'm afraid." She dropped a giant bag down onto the lone table in the magic training room. "Well, loosen up now. We're not in the military here. The Society is only strict to traitors." She made a slash gesture across her neck, and Kerrigan had to fight back laughter. "Anyway, you can call me Zina or Mistress Zahina if you must. I'm supposed to be teaching you air magic."

She waved her hand, and everything in the room, including the five trainees, rose into the air at once. She clapped her hands, and they dropped back to the ground.

"Good enough demonstration?"

They all nodded with gaping mouths. Kerrigan had never seen anyone with that sort of control before, and she'd spent years sneaking in on air Fae practices.

"Good. Let's get started. I didn't volunteer for this post, but I owed Helly a favor," she grumbled. "So, here I am."

Zina moved them to equally spaced spots around the circular training room. She moved the rocks, water, and oil for the other elements to a spot at the center of the room, as if it were the easiest thing she'd ever done. The entire lot of them had to keep from staring agog at her.

Then, she ran them through wind drills. They had to pass a bit of air between each other as if it were a ball. If a person dropped it, they had to take a step forward until they reached the equipment at the middle of the room.

At first, it was easy, moving the ball of air around in a circle, feeling that tug from one to the next. Still, each of them dropped the ball at least once as they worked through it. Zina made them randomize the pattern. A person could throw it to whomever they wanted, even back to the person who had thrown it. They did all right with that until the blindfolds came out. And within fifteen minutes, all of them were at the center of the room. It was like none of them had ever practiced air magic, which was absurd. Kerrigan herself had done nothing but air in her fights, and Noda was a first-level air-magic user. The exercise made them look like amateurs.

"Where did you go wrong?" Zina asked.

"We don't know who is going to get it, and we're blindfolded," Roake muttered in irritation.

Zina smacked him in the back of his head with a lob of air. "Those are the rules, not your failure."

"We can't anticipate each other's moves," Kerrigan tried.

"But can't you?"

"No," Noda said. "But we should be able to feel the magic moving. It's a basic tenet of Flavia's air teaching."

"Bah! Flavia was a hack! I couldn't teach her anything," Zina said, banging on her head. "And I won't teach you either if you don't embrace what is around you. The air is *already* there. You aren't *catching* a ball thrown. There's no ball. You're embracing the magic that exists in front of you."

They all stared back at her blankly. This wasn't how magic was taught at all. Kerrigan had never heard this sort of rhetoric in all of her time in the House of Dragons.

"Let me show you. You throw the ball with your eyes open. I'll tell you who has it," Zina said. She crossed her legs and sat folded in on herself, floating in the air before them. A blindfold appeared across her eyes. "Begin."

The others shrugged and started up the game again.

Zina couldn't see a thing, and she called out, "Fordham, Audria, Roake, back to Audria, Noda, to Kerrigan, back to Fordham, back to Kerrigan, Roake, to Audria, back to Noda, to Audria, to Noda, to Audria." Zina removed the blindfold. "Stop that."

"But *how?*" Noda whispered.

"I'll teach you if you're willing to learn. Most aren't."

But they were.

# CHAPTER 17
## *The Problem*

The rest of the magic masters weren't half as interesting or helpful as Zina. Water on Tuesday with Master Raysor, who fell asleep halfway through his own lesson and only woke up to talk to Audria about healing lessons outside of class. The rest of them clearly didn't matter. Wednesday earth lessons with Master Tippan, which were not much fun for anyone but Roake, who apparently had an affinity for earth. On Thursday, they met with Mistress Sencha, who Kerrigan had had most of her magic lessons with in the House of Dragons. At the time, Kerrigan had been trying not to draw attention to herself, and so Sencha seemed surprised that Kerrigan had any mastery of the element. But still, the lessons weren't that different, only more rigorous.

Each afternoon when they left magic lessons, they left with their well depleted. Their bodies ached from morning training and their mind and magic were just as bad. Kerrigan, who usually fought with her sleep schedule, crashed face-first into the mattress every evening and didn't wake up until breakfast. No interruptions. No time to do any other research. No time to even think.

When Friday afternoon arrived with another verbally abusive match with Lorian, everyone was ready to call it a day.

"What did you have planned for your extra sessions?" Audria asked, running a hand back through her light hair. She hadn't given up trying to keep it prim and proper despite the rest of them barely finding time for baths.

"I don't know," Kerrigan lied.

"I'm going to meet with Raysor. He said that he'd help me with my healing." She grimaced. "I'm not looking forward to it."

Audria wasn't the best healer. But since that was what Bryonica was known for, it would be an insult to her heritage for her to not at least try. Kerrigan was glad that no one thought it was an insult to *her* heritage, considering water was her worst element.

"It's a good idea."

"I asked Zina if she'd work with me," Noda confessed next to Audria.

"What did she say?" Audria asked.

Noda shook her head. "She said her favor to Helly was to train on Mondays, and I could figure it out myself on Fridays."

Kerrigan snorted. "Sounds like her."

"Yeah, so I guess I'm going to try to get ahead on my ancient Fae. My elective is in languages."

"Boring," Roake said. "I'm going to be working with Lorian. He said I really had something."

Fordham arched an eyebrow in disbelief. "Interesting."

"Why?"

"Nothing."

Roake crossed his arms. "Well, what are you doing?"

"I received dispensation from the council for magic lessons with Gelryn."

Audria gasped. Roake even looked impressed. "Gelryn the Destroyer? He's offering lessons?"

"He's offering me lessons."

"No offense, but didn't he fight a war to kill your people?" Noda asked.

Fordham shrugged. "A thousand years ago."

His eyes met Kerrigan's in the space, and she understood then. He was going to work on his magic lessons with the dragon to try to get information about the war. It was smart. A way to include research in his training time.

"Well, Ker, it's just you," Noda said. "Should we brainstorm what you should do?"

"Nah, I'm good. I have a few ideas. Might try a few different things."

Fordham shot her a questioning look, but she shook her head. She wasn't ready to tell anyone her plans. Not even Fordham. Because not even Fordham knew the secret she was hiding.

They ate together in the dining hall. Audria regaled them with Season gossip. The official opening wouldn't be for three more weeks, but small parties were already cropping up. Kerrigan was thankful she didn't have to participate. That none of them did. She thought Audria felt the same, though she'd never admit it.

As the others branched off to their extra training sessions, she turned to head in the opposite direction.

Fordham jogged to catch up with her. "Hey."

"Hey. Aren't you going to meet with Gelryn?"

"Coincidentally, in the same direction as where you're going. What *are* you planning?" he asked. "I know you well enough to know you have a plan."

She glanced up into those smoky-gray eyes. Her heart lurched. She gulped and hastily looked away.

"I don't know what you mean."

"Come on. It's me."

"Fine," she said with a huff. "I'm meeting with Tieran."

"Flying?" he asked, surprised. "You have to already be the best rider here. You've been riding since you were a kid."

"Tieran and I don't get along," she said, giving him a piece of the truth.

"We never did. Netta and I were always better matched. I still don't know why he picked me, but we have to find a way to work together the next year. We need to figure that out before we're in front of Alura."

"Fair. I didn't realize that you didn't get along. He was worried when you were hurt."

"Selfish reasons, I assure you."

He shrugged. "If you say so."

"And Gelryn? You're going to ask him about the Great War?"

"Am I that transparent?"

She brushed her hand against his pale skin. "Pretty much."

His throat bobbed, his eyes drifting to her lips before his expression returned to his careful neutral. "I figured it wouldn't hurt. I got a letter from Arbor this morning. It arrived by hawk."

"Really?" Kerrigan asked.

"Yeah. She was worried about us after we vanished." He grimaced. "There wasn't exactly a way to let them know."

"No, there wasn't."

"She and Pres heard about what happened with Wynter and said they'd look into it for us there. So, we'll get some intel into what Wynter is doing while we're away."

She relaxed. "That's good news."

"This is my turn," Fordham said, gesturing off to the right.

"Good luck."

He grinned at her, melting her heart. "You too."

She watched him jog away for a minute through the stone hall of the mountain and then buried all of her feelings for him in a place she couldn't reach. The last week of training had been *fine* between them. They were partners, as they'd been during the tournament. There was nothing romantic at all when they were sweaty and exhausted and fighting to survive this place. But one smile, and it all resurfaced.

She turned away with a sigh and headed up into a private aerie. Tieran had agreed to meet her for Friday afternoon training. The dragons also had that time off for private lessons, which was useful for their purposes.

Tieran waited for her as she trekked up the last staircase. Her legs barely allowed her the option. She thought she'd collapse at the top. They'd run stairs all morning with Alura and then been forced to do *more* stairs for footwork training with Lorian. It had been brutal.

"Made it," she huffed, breathing heavy. "How's training going?"

*As to be expected*, Tieran said.

"Great. Yeah. Mine sucks too."

He shot one golden eye her way. *You look like you're going to perish at any moment.*

"That is not inaccurate."

Kerrigan flopped back onto a chair at the back of the room and took a slug from her waterskin. Tieran watched her, a slight look of disdain on his face.

*Why have you called me here?*

"Well, we have three weeks to get this together before we walk into dragon rider training. No one else knows that we're not bonded. We're going to have to be pretty convincing about it. And I thought we should train before we do it in front of everyone else."

Tieran looked skeptical. *You think that we can fake a bond?*

"You're the one who said that we had to try. Do you want to be kicked out of the program? I don't have anywhere else to go. You could always go back to the Holy Mountain …"

*No*, he said automatically, glancing away. *No, I won't go back there.*

He'd made similar comments when they first finished the tournament together. She didn't know what had happened at the Holy Mountain, where he'd been born, but whatever it was, he clearly had no interest in talking about it and definitely no interest in returning. That was good for her because she had nowhere to go. It wasn't like she could set up home in the House of Shadows. Not with what Wynter wanted from her.

"Then great. Let's give this a try."

*Do you even know what the training entails?*

"Not really," she said with a shrug. "Flying?"

He snorted a breath of hot air in her direction. *You are so incredibly naive.*

"Hey! It's not my fault that I don't know what this training entails. Three weeks ago, I didn't think that I'd ever even have a dragon. I wasn't exactly listening in to find out how they trained competitors."

Tieran made a sort of shrug. *You just admitted your own incompetence.*

Kerrigan jumped out of her seat in a huff. "Fine. I don't know why I expected this to work with you. If you want to berate me for not being the person that you wanted, then you shouldn't have agreed to this meeting."

*But it's so much fun.*

"I'm going," she snarled. "I'll do research on the bonds in my spare time instead. Maybe it'll tell us why we weren't bonded." She headed toward the entrance, a deep fury rushing through her. "I've worked too hard to let you ruin this for us."

Tieran's tail swept out of nowhere, blocking her exit. *We can train.*

"Why should I bother?" She crossed her arms over her chest.

*You need me,* he stated simply.

A fact. She did need him. She couldn't dragon train without a dragon.

*Though I believe that researching the bond will be satisfactory as well.*

"Yeah, I should probably do that in all my spare time," she teased. "So, you think we can train?"

*I think we have no other choice.*

"Right. Well, we have a month to try to get this right. Why don't we get started?"

***

Four merciless hours later, she and Tieran were no better off than when they'd started. In fact, she stormed out of the aerie in such a fury after her failure that she overturned a servant carrying a dinner tray. She apologized profusely to the human working within the mountain. Still, she couldn't shake her anger.

It would be one thing if they weren't any good at this. It was another that they both had sharp tongues and knew when to properly wield them. After her bouts with Lorian, she didn't have it in her to deal with Tieran too. It had been a long week. Maybe it would all be better after she slept off the muscle aches.

She pressed the door to her room open, ready to collapse face-first into her bed until she realized someone was standing in the middle of the room. Her danger senses hadn't even been triggered. She was too tired to even recognize who was standing there.

"Go away and come back later," Kerrigan grumbled.

The person laughed. "What in the gods' names happened to you?"

Clover. Right, it was Clover. "Oh, hey."

She laughed. "I haven't seen you all week."

"Training," she said, dropping onto her bed and unlacing her shoes.

"You didn't say hi when you got back?"

"Knocked out."

"Why am I not surprised?" Clover asked. She sank into a seat and lifted her feet to rest on the bed.

Kerrigan kicked her shoes into a corner, stripped out of her training clothes, throwing them into a pile of neglected laundry, and changed into something clean. "What are you doing here?"

"Came to check on you. No word for a week after you were supposed to be back from the House of Shadows. Hadrian and Darby were worried too."

"I'm alive." She sank down on the bed and winced as her legs and back protested. "Barely."

"Send a note next time?"

Kerrigan nodded. She scanned her friend. Her severe black bob had recently been cut even shorter with bangs nearly obscuring her blue eyes. Her cinnamon skin glowed against her white tunic and black pants.

Kerrigan realized why she looked different. "You're not wearing Dozan's colors."

Normally, Dozan Rook had his card dealer in a black button-up with a red vest. It made his employees noticeable. Clover usually wore them, even out of the Wastes.

"Yeah, I'm going to a meeting after this. I came to check on you and... try to drag you along."

Kerrigan closed her eyes and buried her face in her pillow. "Clove..."

"Look, I know that you're tired. Training looks like it's not going well, but hear me out."

She leaned forward, resting her elbows on her knees. The front of her shirt opened, revealing the gold chain she always had dangling from her neck. The piece of metal was nearly the size of Kerrigan's palm and flat as a disc. Kerrigan had rarely seen her without it.

"I'm listening."

"Remember the protest I went to?"

"The one where you got *arrested* and I had to get you out of chains?"

"The one," she said smoothly. "The group that put that together is trying to get more organized. They have real plans. They're having an activist meeting to try to see how much interest there is."

"How much interest there is in what?" Kerrigan asked, afraid she already knew.

"Human and half-Fae rights."

Kerrigan nodded minutely. "I see."

"It's not fair that we have no say in our own government. The Society gets

134

to make all the rules. They get to enforce those rules, and we suffer. We should have people in those meetings, vocalizing our opinions."

"You know I agree with you," Kerrigan said.

"But ..."

"But I have a year of dragon training. I can't protest against the very government that I'm part of."

Clover's eyes shuttered. "Why not? Isn't that the point of being in the government? To enact change?"

"Yes, and you know that I plan to, but right now, I'm not even in the Society. I can still be kicked out in the next year."

"So, you're going to let them censure you?" she asked, getting heated. "Let them keep you quiet for the next year when we have the momentum of your win now?"

"No, that's—"

"Don't be a coward."

Kerrigan dropped an arm over her face. "I don't even have the energy to argue with you. If surviving the next year is cowardice, then fine. I can't change anything if I'm kicked out."

Clover vaulted out of her seat. "I never thought I'd see the day when you backed down over the fear of getting caught. Someone in the Society killed Basem Nix for what he knew about the Red Masks. The very people who beat you in a dark alleyway for being half-Fae. Do you think they're actually going to find the killer if we remain silent?"

Kerrigan moved her arm and looked at her friend. Was she staying here out of fear? Was she letting the Society rules dictate her? Was it worth her principles?

Part of her said yes. It was worth everything to get what she wanted. But at what cost?

"Okay," Kerrigan said with a sigh. "I'll go."

# CHAPTER 18
## *The Meeting*

Kerrigan tugged the hood of her cloak tighter around her face as they moved through the streets of Kinkadia. The city was bustling with the summer energy and late daylight hours. It wouldn't be dark for hours yet, and street festivals would be set up throughout the city. It had long been Kerrigan's favorite time of year. The city truly came alive despite the suffocating humidity, coupled with an oppressive heat and the stink. The city couldn't help but stink in this weather.

They skirted the Square and came up on an inn a few blocks away. Kerrigan was surprised. She'd been expecting something in the Dregs, surrounded by pubs. Something disreputable.

Clover must have seen that on her face because she scoffed. "People in all neighborhoods want this. Not just the people at the bottom. We have to be able to fund it after all."

"Of course," Kerrigan said. "I thought it would be somewhere more private."

"The dining space will be open as normal. There's a garden out back that opens onto a private courtyard. The meeting will be held there. No one else has access, except the innkeeper."

Kerrigan nodded. That made more sense to her.

"This way," Clover said.

She navigated to the back of the property with ease, as if she'd been doing this for a while. They stepped under an archway and into a garden paradise. Vines covered the walls that enclosed the garden and courtyard. Plants of every type filled the area, large enough to hold a couple hundred people. Not that Kerrigan suspected that many people would attend this meeting on a Friday night. This almost reminded her of the greenhouses on the east side of the mountain. Just the sheer expanse of plants. No matter how long Kerrigan had lived in the city, it always managed to surprise her.

Clover walked them through the empty courtyard and to a back entrance to the inn. She knocked three times, and the door pulled inward.

A pale woman with a shaved head and kind eyes answered. "Clover, you made it." Her gaze shifted to Kerrigan. "And you brought a friend. Come in."

"Kerrigan, this is Thea."

Kerrigan stepped inside the darkened interior. "Pleased to meet you."

"No, dear girl, the pleasure is all mine. We could not be happier to have you with us. What you did in that tournament ..." She raised her hands to the ceiling. "A blessing for our cause."

"Oh," Kerrigan said awkwardly. "Well, good?"

"It is good. Praise Lament." Thea touched the Lament symbol at her breast—an X encased in a box.

The Lament was a human religion that had mostly fizzled out in the last decade since the Red Masks persecuted those who believed and burned their churches. A few churches still existed on the fringes of the city, but she hadn't expected them here in this meeting.

"Thea is the leader of the RFA—Rights For All. She's been organizing for years to try to get the Society to listen," Clover explained.

"To no avail," Thea explained. "We got somewhere after Cyrene, but then the mass murders by those horrid Red Masks derailed it all. Everyone was too scared to step forward. That is, until you showed up."

"Oh," Kerrigan whispered again. "I'm glad that I can help."

"Me too," Thea said, putting a hand on her back. "Let me introduce you to the rest of my team."

Kerrigan followed Thea into a private dining room, where a half-dozen people sat around a wooden table. The candlelight was low, and a meal was prepared before them. Not simple food either. A stew that smelled thick with spices, roasted chicken, homemade rolls, summer fruit, and even some kind of decadent chocolate cake. It showed her more and more that this was not some push by a few people with nothing. There were humans and half-Fae with means, and they wanted this as much or more than the rest living in poverty.

Thea introduced her to each of the people present—three women and men. Each of them beamed, getting out of their chair, shaking her hand, offering their thanks. Their effusive behavior made her uncomfortable. She'd never been in a room where this many people thought that she could help them save the world. She was just one girl.

"All right, don't crowd her," Clover said, putting herself between them. "I'm glad that Kerrigan is here, but we don't want to scare her off either."

Kerrigan grinned. Only Clover could get straight to the meat of things. "Thanks."

Thea nodded. "We're pleased that you're here. The streets are full of your name. I must admit that I'm quite excited to meet you in person. We all are."

"I'm just... me."

"My dear girl, you are so much more," Thea insisted. "You defied the odds. You beat them at their own game. You are the only voice for half-Fae in the entire Society. You are more important than you know."

"Okay, but ..." Kerrigan bit her lip. "Look, as much as I want to help, I can't come out publicly for this."

Thea frowned. "What do you mean?" She looked to Clover, who shrugged.

"I have a year of training before I'm officially inducted as a full member. They can still kick me out for any offense in the next year. It might not be public that this is the case, but it's my reality. If you want me to be able to make any change, then I can't be found here."

Thea sighed. "Of course this is their stipulation." She ran a hand down her face and looked to her coconspirators. "Well, this changes nothing about our mission. It would be a lot easier to recruit if we were able to use your name, but we would not like to jeopardize you."

"And why can't you use her name?" a voice said, a figure stepping into the dining room.

Kerrigan whipped around and found herself face-to-face with Dozan Rook. She so rarely saw him out of the Wastes that it was a shock to find him here now in all his glory. His burnished hair was brushed back out of his amber eyes. He wore a crisp three-piece black suit with a black button-up shirt and black tie. Only the red R pin on his lapel suggested that he was a symbol of the Wastes. Not that it wasn't obvious, just looking into his beautiful, hardened face. A sensuous smile played on his lips.

"Hello, Red," he purred.

Kerrigan blinked and stepped backward. She hated this reaction to Dozan. The pull that had always been there. It didn't matter that she'd been obsessed with him at twelve. Her first love at sixteen. Her first everything. She wished that she didn't react to him at all. Because he certainly never saw her as more than a pawn.

"What are *you* doing here?" she asked.

Thea stepped forward, holding her hand out to Dozan. "Mr. Rook, thank you for joining us."

"A pleasure," he said. His gaze swept back to Kerrigan. "We should absolutely use Kerrigan's name. Even if she doesn't directly show her face in support, alluding to her involvement will give us a certain advantage."

"We don't want to harm her chances," Thea said thoughtfully.

"Give her plausible deniability. Use her name to say that she's working with us, but if it comes back to her, she can deny ever being there. We only keep her existence between us."

"It's a good idea," Clover said.

Kerrigan frowned. "What if they don't believe me? What if someone says they saw me here?"

Thea shook her head. "We'll deny it to our grave."

Kerrigan hoped it never came to that. And having Dozan here made it even less likely that it would stay silent. "You never answered me. What are you doing here?"

"How do you think they're funding this little adventure?"

Kerrigan scoffed. "You've never spent a dime you didn't think you could earn back ten times over."

"Then, you understand why I'm doing it," he said with an arched eyebrow.

She didn't. This made no sense. Clover being here made sense. She was an idealist and always fought for those less fortunate. After losing her parents at a young age, she wanted to protect people. To not let others suffer.

Dozan had killed his own family to get ahead. He was the king of the Wastes. He did *nothing* without a direct return on investment. Including his investment in Kerrigan.

"Dozan has generously offered his services," Thea interjected. "He has as much right as anyone else to want to see humans and half-Fae be treated more fairly."

"You *offered*?" she asked skeptically. She stepped forward. "You never of-fer. What's in this for you?"

"In case you haven't noticed, princess, I'm human."

"Don't *call* me that," she snapped at him.

"Why not? Doesn't everyone know you're *actually* a princess now?" he asked with a self-satisfied smirk.

Kerrigan didn't know why, but Dozan always drew this side out of her. All she wanted to do was bury her fist in his too-pretty face. The insufferable bastard.

But Clover saw it coming and tugged her backward. "Why don't we all try to get along? We're here for the same cause, right?"

"Right," Dozan said but didn't drop the look.

Kerrigan breathed in deeply and released it. She was too tired to deal with this. To deal with him. Clover should have prepared her for seeing him. Nothing riled her up more than Dozan Rook.

"I need a smoke," Clover said. "Come on. Let's get some air."

Thea nodded as Clover pulled Kerrigan back out of the room. She brushed past Dozan without a backward look and out into the entrance to the courtyard. Already, the garden was filling with attendees for the RFA meeting, and so they huddled together behind a large gargoyle structure. Clover tried three times to light up a *loch* cigarette, failing with the matches each time and cursing colorfully.

"Let me," Kerrigan said. She hadn't had magic training this afternoon, so she actually had a whiff of magic in her veins. She snapped her fingers and touched the flame to Clover's cigarette.

She inhaled deeply, letting the addictive drug dull the chronic pain that lashed through her body. "Why do you have to let him get to you?"

"Why didn't *you* tell me he'd be here?"

Clover opened her eyes and shot her a look. "You already didn't want to come. Would you have jumped for joy if I'd told you Dozan would be here?"

"No," she grumbled.

"Yeah. So, I thought this would be better. I don't know. Maybe it isn't. You two just need to bang again or something. The tension is… a lot."

Kerrigan snorted. "Not happening."

"Why not?" Clover winked at her. "Waiting for a prince to come to his senses?"

"No," she muttered. "I don't think that he will."

"So, if Fordham has friend-zoned you, why not get some of that pent-up energy out with someone else?"

Kerrigan's cheeks heated at the thought. It'd be as easy as breathing. Hooking up with Dozan wasn't any different than fighting with him. The only time they both relaxed in each other's presence was in the afterglow. Maybe a few rounds would help her get over the prince taking up all the thoughts in her head, but it didn't mean it was a good idea.

After Clover's cigarette, they returned to the room. Dozan still stood, poised and ready. Kerrigan made no further comments about him being there. She sat through the planning session until the sound of voices in the courtyard was loud enough to draw them away.

"If you do not wish to be a part of this, I would recommend keeping your cloak up," Thea said. "Stay out of sight."

Kerrigan nodded and tugged her hood back over her very recognizable hair. Thea retreated to the entrance to the courtyard and greeted the awaiting crowd.

"You'll be okay back here?" Clover asked. "Hadrian said that he'd meet me."

Kerrigan nodded. "Go see him. Tell him I miss him."

"Will do," she said and then darted after a blue-haired Fae who looked out of place in a sea of humans and half-Fae.

Dozan stepped up to her side. It wouldn't do for the king of the Wastes to be seen in that crowd either. His involvement would have to be as secretive as Kerrigan's but for more nefarious reasons. He stopped when he was just off of her shoulder. He towered over her a full head, and she could practically feel him breathing into her ear.

"You did this," he said gently. Not his normal accusatory tone.

"Did what?"

"This." He gestured to the swelling crowd of people from their vantage point. "It wasn't the RFA people that managed to get this many people here. It

142

wasn't the message of equality and unity that Thea has been spouting for over a decade. It wasn't even that they'd *killed* the only witness they had that could get them to the Red Masks. It was you."

"I didn't do anything."

"You proved to them that they could win." He brushed a red curl into her cloak. She shivered at the touch. "You're a symbol."

"I'm just a person."

His gaze caught on hers. "You've never been *just* anything."

Thea raised her hands to the sky. "Today, we speak for those who have long been cast in the shadow, who have no voice, who have no hope. Today, I bring you hope!"

The crowd roared with approval. Their voices raised to the skies, chanting for the end of this oppression. Wanting what the Fae already had—equal rights, a place in the government, a way out from under the boot of the Society.

The same thing that Kerrigan had always wanted when she was pushed aside. When she was called a *leatha* in a dark alley and abused for her half-Fae heritage and abandoned at the foot of the mountain for the state of her ears, the human side of her blood. For all of those times that people had told her no and the one time she'd looked back at them and demanded her place in front of the entire world. People were here because of that moment when she'd told the Society that she belonged and they'd agreed with her.

Hope swelled in her chest. An unfamiliar feeling that flickered to life, tentative and unsure. For the first time, she saw what the world was capable of if they all looked at those who oppressed them and demanded their due— freedom.

# CHAPTER 19
## *The Assassin*

ISA

Isa crossed her arms and leaned against the pillar in the back of the courtyard. The woman with the shaved head had been yammering on equality for an eternity at this point, and she couldn't process any more of this propaganda. Humans and half-Fae were treated poorly. Sure. But they were beneath Fae. So, why was that a surprise to anyone?

If she didn't have to be here, she would have avoided it all together. But no, Daddy's orders.

"And when we finally had a witness, when we finally had the leader of the Red Masks in jail, they allowed someone to murder him."

Boos rose from the crowd. Isa smirked at the depth of her dirty work.

"Basem Nix died inside the mountain, which means our enemy lurks within those hallowed walls. If we don't fight for what is right, they will never listen!"

Isa tuned the leader back out. She wasn't wrong. There were Red Masks in the mountain, but they had no hope of stopping the movement. So quaint.

At least something interesting had come out of being here. She'd noticed Kerrigan's friends amid the crowd. The little blue-haired Fae and the human indentured to Dozan Rook. She had no idea what the former was doing here. He was a full-blooded Fae. He'd been selected into Galanthea tribe by a former tournament competitor. What more could he *want*? Obviously, growing up with Kerrigan and befriending this *loch* addict had addled his brain.

There were a handful of other Fae in attendance but mostly humans and half-Fae. She'd never understand what they were doing here. But then again, she'd grown up with Father.

"Thank you for your time, and I'll see you next week!" the woman at the front said, projecting her voice with some kind of magic. She was only half-Fae but had enough magic to do that. It was almost impressive.

But that was Isa's cue. She'd done her job. Now, it was time to get out of there.

She slipped back through the garden and out onto the alleyway that led toward the Square. Most of the humans were heading west toward the Dregs, but Isa cut east toward the Row. Not everything in the Row was the enormous, aristocratic mansions, the age-old plots of land passed down generation to generation. Deeper in this part of town were rows of townhouses, each a different bright color to match the layout of the streets. Moneyed Fae, who hadn't had families living here since the dawn of time, could still afford the townhomes and were welcome by the Fae Home Association that governed who could and couldn't purchase in the district.

Isa thought it was a fine thing to have rules for all of that, but the association itself was horrid. They had rules from lawn height to exterior paint and everything else in between. It would have been fine if they'd addressed it all the same for everyone, but it was a bunch of petty people on power trips.

She slid into the shadows as the gentry strode by, arm in arm. She ducked down the back alley that led to Father's home here and rapped thrice on the back door. She uttered the magical password that let her bypass his warding.

If she hadn't been keyed to the door, the password wouldn't have worked, and she'd have likely been knocked out.

Luckily, she was. She pushed the door open to the home, slung her cloak on a hook, and then traipsed through the artfully decorated room to her father's study. Most of the servants had already gone home, save for his butler, who always made himself scarce when she appeared.

She took a deep breath at the entrance, reminding herself who she was. That she had no reason to fear him. She had proven herself time and time again. She would continue to do so. So long as he didn't discover the money she'd hidden away. The hope she had to escape this life that he'd richly provided for her. Nothing for free, of course.

"Isa, do stop hovering and come in," Father barked from the study door.

She winced at the tone of his voice. Then, she cleared her face of any expression and pushed her way inside. She was beyond wondering how he had known that she was standing there.

Isa moved swiftly across the room to where he was seated in the lush office behind a mahogany desk that overlooked massive bay windows out to the Row beyond. She bent onto one knee, offering fidelity. "Father."

He placed his hand on the top of her crop of pure white hair. It was the one feature that he disliked on her. Her face could stop carriages. She had been a beautiful child, developing into a distressingly stunning young woman. She could have become a member of the aristocracy, flitting about at the Season, looking for a husband like every other brainless debutante. But Father had seen something else in her and employed her skills to assassin craft. She'd taken to it like breathing.

"You may rise," he said finally. "What is the word?"

"RFA had a huge outpouring at the meeting. Almost exclusively half-Fae and humans. They're planning a protest against the Society. No details yet, just getting people invested and wanting them to tell their friends. It was much more well attended than the last one I went to."

"And the girl?"

Isa shook her head. "No, sir. No sign of Kerrigan. Though her friends were there."

"Which ones?"

"Clover and Hadrian," she said, plucking their names out of memory. "The blue-haired ..."

"I know who they are," he said dismissively. "You're sure *she* wasn't there?"

"I saw no sign of her. They kept alluding to her involvement, but if she was there, then she was well hidden."

Even from her. And Isa knew all of Kerrigan's moves. She'd studied them extensively in the month she tried to kill the girl. Her hands still ached for her knives at the thought. The one who had gotten away.

Father had said she couldn't finish the job, but Isa hoped he would change his mind before this was all over.

"She'll be there," Father said with a nod. His eyes cast past Isa's head to the window. The promenade of families displaying the goods before the Season began. "And when she is, we'll be ready."

# CHAPTER 20

## The Testing

"How'd you do?" Noda asked, panting slightly as she stepped out of the water-magic test.

Kerrigan shot her a thumbs-up because speaking wasn't in the cards yet. Three weeks had passed since the meeting with the RFA. She'd gone back each Friday night after her training with Tieran to listen to Thea's inspirational words. And all the while, she'd gotten better and better at all of her training—physical and magical. They'd all spent hours upon hours working on building their stamina so that they could get to *this* moment—testing.

To move forward at the end of the first four-week boot camp, they *all* had to pass a series of tests. Otherwise, all of them would spend another four weeks training and not working with their dragons. They'd pushed each other even more after they found that out, improving at alarming rates.

"Same," she said. "Water was easier than fire."

"No way," Kerrigan said, finally recovered. "Water was terrible."

"You suck at water though," Noda pointed out.

"Fair."

Then, Roake stepped out of the air final. His face was pale, and he was shaking.

"You okay?" Kerrigan asked.

Roake glanced blankly at them. "That woman ..."

"Air is the hardest," Noda agreed, looking at Roake with pity. "Come on, Roake. Let's grab some food before you do your last magic test."

"Sure. Food."

He stepped past Kerrigan and into the dining hall. Kerrigan was too jittery to eat. She had air to do after passing water and earth this morning and fire a few minutes ago. They had to run Alura's obstacle course this afternoon in the arena and then go straight into Lorian's sword-fighting test, and they didn't know what it would be. Kerrigan had never been in the arena as a competitor. She'd flown in as a winner of the tournament, and that was the extent of it. She was both excited and nervous about the prospect. The others had that advantage over her.

Fordham stepped out of the dining hall. He'd had his break for testing this go round. "She still in there?"

Kerrigan nodded. Audria was in the earth test, which was her weakest element. She'd never fully planted herself in the earth to work with it like the rest of them.

"Wonder how it's going."

"I don't know. Roake looked like he'd seen a ghost, coming out of the air test."

Fordham nodded. "It's brutal, but you'll do fine."

"Thanks. What do you have left?"

"Fire."

Kerrigan nudged his shoulder. "Lucky."

She swept a lock of her plaited hair out of her face and stared up at him. They were both in the black training clothes, black robes thrown over top. His hair falling messily forward over his eyes. Those stormy-gray eyes turning to smoke at the sight of her.

He didn't move toward her. He wasn't going to change what he'd broken, but the want was still there. Blatant, even.

Luckily, Audria stumbled out of the room at that moment. She dropped to her knees, putting her hands to the floor, and looked near to crying.

Kerrigan rushed toward her. "Are you okay?"

"I *hate* that element," she snarled, the lady gone from her voice.

"Did you pass?"

Audria fell onto her back and let her hands hang out from her sides. She stared up at the ceiling. "I passed."

Kerrigan breathed a sigh of relief. "Good. Do you have another?"

"No, that was my last one. Thank the gods."

She looked like she had no intention of moving from the spot. Kerrigan didn't blame her. Each one tested them to their limits, and they had all *four* finals today. And Kerrigan still had the hardest magical test yet—air.

It was fifteen minutes before the doors to the testing rooms opened once more. Kerrigan gulped, nodding at Fordham, and then stepped inside to find Zina absent.

"Zina?" she called.

"Up here, dear," Zina said.

Kerrigan looked up, up, up. And there was Mistress Zahina... sitting on the ceiling.

Zina did any number of odd things during class, including many strange games that she'd apparently made up herself. But usually, she did all of these things on the ground. Occasionally, she'd float around with her legs crossed, like she was meditating, but generally, she hovered a few feet off of the ground. Not sitting *on* the ceiling.

"Hello," she said cautiously.

"Hello, dear. Are you ready for your first test with me?"

Kerrigan looked at her skeptically. "Yes?"

"You don't sound sure."

"You're on the ceiling."

"Am I?" she asked in confusion. She looked around. "Are you sure you're not on the ceiling?"

"Yes, I am definitely on the floor."

"That's a matter of perspective. Don't you think?"

Kerrigan blinked at her and then slowly nodded. "Yes, I could see how that would be a matter of perspective. Considering, to you, the floor must look like the ceiling."

"That *is* the ceiling. You're the one who is disoriented."

Kerrigan frowned. Of course it made sense in its own way. She had never considered it before. Did up always have to be up and down always down? If she was on a dragon upside down, could she also be right side up?

That was at the heart of all of Zina's teachings. Everything they had been told and thought that they knew were building blocks for failure. They needed to close their eyes, forget everything, and relearn their magic.

"Do you plan to join me, or are you going to stand there, agog all day?"

Kerrigan gulped and took a deep breath. Zina had been working with them on floating and hovering in class, but she hadn't had them fly to the *ceiling*. This wasn't something she could have ever prepared for. Yet the other three had passed this exam, which meant she had the building blocks for how to do this.

"I plan to join you," she said finally.

"Excellent. The tea is getting cold."

"Tea?" Kerrigan whispered in confusion.

She closed her eyes and focused on what was important. The elements of Zina's teaching were that energy was all around them. Air was in everything. They were built on air. The world was built on air. They didn't need to *feel* for it because the magic was already there, all around them.

Kerrigan pulled the energy into her, letting herself hover slightly off of the ground. This was where they'd all struggled, trusting the magic to hold them for more than a few inches. But if everyone else could do it, then she could too. Unless they'd all had different exams. It would be the only way to ensure they didn't tell each other what was coming next. They hadn't shared, but the masters didn't know that.

She dropped back down onto the ground. Her eyes flew open. "Did everyone have to complete this final?"

Zina smiled. "Why do you ask?"

"We were only *hovering*," Kerrigan said. "The others were able to sit on the ceiling?"

She shrugged one of her shoulders. "This is the exam that *you* are getting. Whether the others had the same one is none of your concern."

Right. She still had to pass. Even if this one for her was absurd.

The point of this wasn't to fly. They weren't going to suddenly be on Zina's level. There must be another point to the teachings. This wasn't hovering. It was changing her perspective. That was what Zina had said, and she wouldn't have said *anything* unless it was important.

So, Kerrigan let herself go to that place within her magic that was reserved for worst-case scenarios—here spirit magic. She hadn't been there since trying to take the barrier down. And blessedly, she hadn't had another vision either. She didn't have time to even think about finding a spiritcaster teacher. When would she train for that with everything else going on?

She pushed those thoughts aside and focused inside herself. Then, she drew her air magic to her and righted her perspective. She felt as if she were outside of her body when it flipped upside down. The last thing she needed was to think about it. She needed to let her instincts take over.

When she finally opened her eyes, she was on the ceiling, and the floor to the room was far below. Kerrigan gulped and closed her eyes again, feeling dizzy and disoriented.

"Breathe," Zina said, something like a smile in her words. "You're the right way up. The other way was wrong. You know this in your gut. You are sitting on the floor. Everything above you is the ceiling."

Kerrigan heard her soothing words wash over her, and slowly, she peeled her eyes back open. And Zina was right. She was sitting on the floor. The ceiling was suspended above her.

"How am I doing this?" she gasped.

"A change of perspective." Zina gestured at a teapot. "Now, pour us tea. And remember, we are on the floor."

Kerrigan nodded blankly, staring at the teapot in front of them and the two little cups and saucers. If they were the other way around, the tea would be falling out of the pot. But this was the floor. She had to keep reminding herself of that fact. *This* was the floor.

She reached for the teapot and used her magic to leverage everything in place. With a slight hesitation, she poured tea into Zina's glass. It didn't move. Kerrigan gulped, straining to use her magic to keep everything, including herself, in place.

"Relax. Breathe," Zina repeated. She reached for a sugar cube and dropped it into her tea. "This isn't difficult. This is as easy as breathing, as easy as speaking. There is no strain."

Tension released from her shoulders. She'd never thought of magic as easy. She'd always been taught it was a lot of hard work, and the years of training with it had proven that to be true. But the more she *didn't* try, the easier it became to do what she needed to do.

She poured the tea, adding a sugar cube of her own.

"Now, drink," Zina said. She raised her glass with a wink.

Kerrigan took the teacup in her hand and took a sip. "How am I doing this?"

Zina smiled. "Spirit magic."

Kerrigan startled, a drop of her tea leaving her cup and falling onto the floor. She closed her eyes. *This* was the floor. That was the ceiling. Tea fell on the ceiling.

"Relax through it," Zina said. "It'll pass."

"How do you know I have spirit magic?"

"Gelryn and Helly came to me and asked me to be the air master for your training program. I refused until they told me that you were a spiritcaster."

Kerrigan's heart soared with hope. "Are *you* a spiritcaster?"

Zina scoffed. "No. I have some spirit magic of my own in these old veins, and based on what the others have told me, you have much more than that."

Kerrigan stiffened. "They told you?"

"Indeed. You can fear nothing from me, dear. I'm sure it's as much a curse as a gift."

Understatement.

"I have agreed to train you on your spirit magic even though I am not an adequate enough teacher for the job. I cannot access the castings that you can. There has not been one of your kind in a thousand years. But I'm as close to an expert as they could scrounge up. So, I'm what you get."

"Thank you," she murmured. "May I ask why you waited until now to tell me?"

"Couldn't exactly ask you to work spirit magic in front of your classmates, could I?"

"Well, no, but we had Friday training."

"You were always running off with your dragon, for one," Zina said, arching her eyebrow. "And I wanted to see how you'd do under pressure. It's usually when spirit magic is the most effective, I've discovered."

Another understatement. Spirit magic continued to save her life.

"When do we begin?" Kerrigan asked eagerly.

"My dear, we've already begun."

# CHAPTER 21
## *The Course*

$A$lura's obstacle course was a nightmare. She must have been working on it all month. The entire thing was set up inside the arena with various apparatuses along the course. They each had to run it together, working as one timed unit to make it to the end. Slowest time counted for everyone. So, there was no incentive to leave anyone behind. This wasn't a competition, but a building block of the Society. In battle, they'd need to work together. Ingraining it in them now would help when it was necessary later. Waiting at the end of the brutal course was Lorian's final. So, they'd have to walk into the sword fight, exhausted, just as they would in battle. Wonderful.

And worse, they had spectators. Kerrigan could see Lorian standing taut at the end of the line, but there were a dozen other people with him. Kerrigan recognized Bastian and Helly as well as a few other high-profile council members—Kress, Lockney, and Alsia. She gulped.

"Prepare yourselves," Alura said.

The five of them lined up on the white chalk line. Kerrigan looked to Fordham on her right and Audria on her left. They both nodded. They were in this together.

Alura blew a whistle, and they all sprinted forward. Over the last month, they'd all gotten faster. The daily runs had sure helped with that, but now, they were running together as if their lives depended on it.

The flat-out sprint was the first quarter of the race, leading directly to some kind of pond, complete with plant life. Going around would take too long. All five of them dived into the craggy water. It was deeper than Kerrigan had expected, quickly coming up to her waist and then her neck. She swam forward, glad she'd had lessons in the House of Dragons. No one stumbled at this part despite the training program not having a swimming component. But as they all finally cleared the water, they came up to a deep well of mud and no way across but through.

"Gross," Audria grumbled next to Kerrigan.

Kerrigan had to agree. She tramped through the mud, getting the goop up to her waist. When suddenly, she stepped down, and there was no ground. She screamed as she dropped under the mud.

"Kerrigan!"

She fought to reach the surface. Just as her oxygen was depleting, a hand clamped around her wrist. Fordham's face came into view as he and Audria hauled her out of the mud pit. Noda was helping Roake out of similar circumstances. Fordham rushed to help her, towing the lot of them back to the land.

Kerrigan choked and spat up mud, trying to blink it out of her eyes. Fordham gave her a part of his shirt to wipe her eyes. Roake looked worse for wear as well but just as determined.

"That was disgusting," she said as they hurtled forward. She was coated in slick mud from top to bottom. Even the vibrancy of her red hair didn't peek through.

They reached a set of wooden pillars that were roughly fifteen feet high. A fence was placed between each of the poles to keep them from running straight through the pillars.

Fordham got it first. "Scales, we have to climb."

"Ugh," she groaned. There weren't any handholds. They wouldn't just climb; they would have to scale the pole and then *jump* from one to the other. "Gods."

"Let me through," Noda said. "I'm a good climber. I'll go first."

She shimmied up the pole as if it did have handholds. Kerrigan memorized the way she moved and watched as Noda easily jumped from one pole to the next. There were eight poles in total, and she vaulted from one to the other like a dancer twirling on a ballroom floor.

Fordham went next and then Audria, both making it look easy.

Roake nodded at her. A camaraderie had formed between them. They weren't exactly friends, but they were teammates. "You first. I'll boost you."

"Thanks," she said in relief.

He hoisted her up in his arms, and she was halfway up the pole in a matter of seconds. They weren't allowed to use magic on the obstacle course, so she had to rely on sheer strength to claw her way up.

When she reached the top, she lay on her stomach, panting. How had they made that look so easy? Her vision was dizzy as she looked to the other seven poles. With a grunt, she unsteadily rose to her feet, praying to whichever gods would listen that she had the balance for this. As soon as she jumped to the second pole, Roake climbed up the first pole. Kerrigan jumped from one pole to the next. She was to the last pole when she landed wrong and she slipped on the mud still caked on her boot. She cried out as her foot fell out from under her. Her hands pinwheeled. She threw out her hand, her fingernails digging into the wood, ripping and bleeding, but she held on. Barely.

Tears sprang to her eyes as she tried to haul herself up. But she was so slippery; she couldn't make it work.

"I got you," Roake called. "Just hold on!"

He jumped, landing on her pole. She gritted her teeth and dug her fingers in deeper to keep from slipping. Roake grabbed her wrist and hauled her up onto the pole. It wasn't quite big enough for two.

"Thanks," she muttered, holding her bleeding left hand. She didn't dare look at it and wonder if it would be a hindrance.

They jumped to the next pole and out of that obstacle, before racing toward the rest of their team. A set of swinging monkey bars was over another mud pit, leading to a separate platform that had steep metal sheeting to slide down on the other side. Audria had already landed after completing the swings and was waiting for the rest of them.

"Go," Kerrigan yelled.

And they went.

Noda dropped into the mud with a scream when her hand slipped on one of the swings. She half-swam, half-flopped out of the mud as it tried to suck her back into the pit. Audria rushed over and dragged her out of the mess. Meanwhile, Fordham was already rushing across the swings, and Kerrigan was next. She ignored the pain in her left hand and swung across the mud pit. Thankfully she made it across with no difficulty.

The metal slide burned straight through her black uniform as she jumped down onto it. She hissed as she landed into loose rocks at the bottom. Roake landed next to her, and they hustled around the bend to a series of climbing walls. The first two had ropes that they scaled, which Kerrigan managed just fine until she reached the third one. A rope was suspended in front of her but far enough away from the wall that she couldn't brace her feet for support.

"I'll go first and grab you," Fordham said.

He moved up the rope as if he'd been made for it. Kerrigan had been working out, but her upper body strength would never be his. She'd let him have this one. As soon as he was off the rope, she hefted herself up one armful at a time.

"Swing to me," Fordham called.

She breathed out once and then swung the rope toward him. Back and forth. Back and forth. There was a moment of weightlessness, and in that moment, she released her hand. Fordham was there, latching onto her and towing her onto the wall. She stumbled into his body, wrapping her arms around him. Their eyes met for a brief moment. Then, she gulped and stepped back.

"Thanks."

He grinned at her, forgetting where they were for a minute.

Then, they both looked down and froze. Between this wall and the next were a series of pikes, facing up toward them and no rope or swing or pole to jump from one to the other. Just open air.

"What in the gods' names?" she breathed.

Audria landed next to them. Gratefully grabbing Fordham's arm. "What are you ..." She broke off as she saw the pit of death between them and the finish. "How are we supposed to do that?"

Roake and Noda landed safely on the wall beside them. All of them stared down at their failure. There was no way to finish this without impaling themselves.

Kerrigan shook out her arms. There had to be a solution to this problem. Alura couldn't get away with giving them an impossible feat. She didn't want to fail all of them. She just wanted to test them. Which meant there was a way to get across this. She just had to find it.

She ran back through everything that Alura had ingrained in them the last month. She was a vicious and unforgiving teacher, but she got it done. They were better because she'd been a hard-ass. And she always said that there were no impossible problems. Anything could be achieved together. The program had been designed to test them together. Not apart.

Kerrigan turned away from the pit as her friends tried to reason this out. Her eyes slid to the rope they'd used to get here. Then, she jumped back out onto it.

"What are you doing?" Audria asked.

"Trust me," Kerrigan said. Her arms ached, and she was still mostly covered in mud, but she managed to reach the top of the platform that knotted the rope. She swung upward, wrapping her legs around the platform and working the rope knot loose.

"You're a genius!" Audria cried.

They couldn't cross the divide without rope, and they weren't provided rope. But she could make do with what she had. She finally got it loose from the mooring and then swung it over to her friends. Still dangling upside from the rigging, she wriggled across the platform. For a second, her visions shifted. Suddenly, she realized that she was right side up. Her stomach hit the beam holding the platform up, and instead of inching, she crawled toward her teammates. She was so disoriented, wondering why her friends were hanging from the ceiling. She had to close her eyes and right herself again. Zina's teachings had worked a little too well.

Fordham held his arms out, and she dropped into them. He eased her down, sliding her body down his as he did so. "Be careful."

"Careful is my middle name," she said with a wink.

"Well, what do we do with it?" Roake asked.

Noda held her hand out. "I was raised sailing. I can tie knots that you've never even heard of."

"There's a hook," Audria pointed out. "If we can throw it, we can secure it across the distance."

Roake grinned. "I can throw. I played Dragon Eggs back in Elsiande."

"Were you any good?" Noda asked.

"Could have gone professionally in the South," he boasted.

"What's Dragon Eggs?" Fordham asked.

Roake stared at him with a slack jaw. "You've never heard of it?"

Fordham shook his head. "My pop culture is lacking from all those years behind a magical barrier."

Roake winced. "Right, man. Sorry. It's a sport where you have an egg-shaped ball and try to get it into a net. There's a national league and everything."

Kerrigan had no idea that he'd been an athlete. That he'd given up playing a sport to come to the tournament. "You throw."

Noda finished her knot. Roake worked up his arms and then tossed the rope across the divide. It landed on the hook first toss, and he and Fordham yanked it tight, holding it level with the ground.

Audria grinned. "Is this the time to say that I grew up doing acrobatic work? My mother believed in perfect balance."

She tested the end of the rope, putting a foot out, and then without a single ounce of fear, she walked out on the rope. Kerrigan slapped a hand over her mouth. Audria tightrope-walked like a festival performer. She was lithe and graceful. All those lessons had really worked out in her favor.

She hopped off on the other side and properly secured the rope. Fordham tied off the end and sent the rest of them across. It was slow going since none of them had Audria's talents. They went hand over fist across the lot of it. Then, Fordham followed, and they were all across.

They'd completed the impossible.

But as soon as they dropped down at the end of the last wall, they saw what awaited them. Five swords were thrust into the ground at their feet, and an ambush of sword masters raced across the arena toward them.

Kerrigan snatched up the shortest blade and prepared herself for her final test. Lorian hadn't told them what they were up against, but he didn't want her to win. And she had to prove him wrong.

There were five masters in total. One for each of them. Kerrigan only recognized one of the Society members, and of course, he was coming right for her. Master Cannon was a brutal warrior. She'd never had a class with him, but she'd watched him enough to know that he was single-handedly the deadliest swordsman in the Society. How was she supposed to fight him? She was a first year in the middle of her training. And he was the best of the best.

She gritted her teeth and prepared for it anyway. Lorian's work, obviously.

"I'll switch with you," Fordham offered, seeing the beast of a man closing in.

Fordham was the better sword fighter. He might even have a chance against Cannon, but she doubted that would work. She'd put money on it that Lorian had rigged it so that Cannon went solely for her.

"I got it."

"You sure?"

And then there was no time for a response. The trainees crashed together with the masters. She barely had time to raise her sword to meet Cannon's first blow. Her arms shook with the sheer force of the strike. She was already weak from the obstacle course. Her body was slick with mud. Her left hand still bled freely. This was *not* a fair fight.

But the test was that war was never a fair fight. They wouldn't always have the advantage. They wouldn't always be able to regroup and recover. Fordham had instilled that in her while they were training for her fight with Basem. Pain was part of the game. Sometimes, you were exhausted, and you still had to lift your sword, even against a better opponent. You still had to win.

"Little girl," Cannon growled.

"Giant beast," she snapped back, pushing his blade back enough to break his hold on her.

She paced backward, making him come after her. There wasn't much room, but this would have to do. Then, they danced. Strike, parry, feint, strike, dodge. They moved flawlessly through Ravendin's twelve paces and into Chutrick's art-of-war formations. They were evenly matched in footwork at least. Cannon had strength and years more experience than her. But she held her own.

Until he got under her guard. The blades were blunted, but his sword crashing into her shoulder still *hurt*. It would leave a nasty bruise too. Kerrigan gasped. He used the moment to push his luck, slapping the handle down on her wrist and forcing her to drop her blade.

And then she saw, for just a split second, Lorian leering over the fight from the stands. A cruel smile twisted his face as he watched his champion destroy the girl that he didn't believe belonged. That he'd planned to destroy all along. He was using this opportunity to get her kicked out.

She would never give him the satisfaction. That smile turned her gut to lead. Screw him. *Screw* him.

Kerrigan jerked backward out of the reach of Cannon's weapon. Getting far enough out of range that it wouldn't mean a gutting. If Lorian wasn't playing fair by giving her the best sword master in a century, then why should she fight fair? No magic in the arena. Sure. Fine. But that didn't mean that this wasn't like every *other* fight she'd ever had. And she didn't always need magic for those either.

"Fordham," she shouted. "On me."

He didn't even hesitate. He ducked his attacker's advance and then rushed to her aid. He took the brunt of Cannon's attack, holding off both of them for a few seconds as she dive-rolled to retrieve her weapon.

Kerrigan came up again, swinging. Fordham remained at her side, and together, they worked as a team.

Cannon smirked. "Clever trick. More experienced fighters have lost for less."

"Yeah, well, I'm not most."

Then, she showed him the real reason for her dive roll. She threw a fistful of sand into his eyes. He cried out, retreating two whole steps as he blinked the dirt out of his eyes. He was too well trained to fully falter.

But it was enough of an opening. Kerrigan thrust her sword past his defenses, slamming the blunted blade against his ribs. She heard a pop, and he snarled. His eyes were red with tears, and he stepped forward, as if to destroy her for the audacity. But he'd miscalculated. She put the tip of her blade to his throat.

"The fight is over, Cannon," a voice said from the sidelines.

Cannon stilled, his jaw clenching. He whirled around to face who had spoken. It was Master Bastian, and he was smiling. He nodded his head at Kerrigan. Lorian was fuming. The rest of the council members were a mixed bag. Alsia seemed to be considering whether or not what had been done was entirely fair. Kress had his arms crossed, as if he agreed with Lorian's assessment. Lockney didn't say anything. He scribbled in a book and nodded. He was the council secretary, so perhaps it was just his duty.

"She did not fight with honor!" Cannon snapped.

"She did not," Lorian agreed. "It was a disgrace to witness."

"But she still won," Bastian said. "And with both teamwork and ingenuity."

"Cheating is not ingenuity," Lorian said.

"Some would say it is, Lorian," Alsia said. She was a tall woman with brown skin and clear eyes. She had a calm demeanor.

Kress sniffed. "It isn't what we look for in initiates. We'd know that if she had been in the tournament."

"Precisely," Lorian argued.

Kerrigan was breathing too hard to even comment. She braced her hands on her knees and took deep, heaving breaths. Her friends were still continuing their bouts, but hers was done.

"You must admit that she beat our best warrior," Bastian said.

Helly came forward with Alura. "I didn't even think we were using full sword masters for this event."

Lockney's head jerked up. He flipped through his notebook. "It was a recent rule change. I have the official timing for you."

Helly arched an eyebrow. Lorian huffed.

Ah, so he *had* changed the rules to suit him.

"Cannon wasn't on my list," Alura said, fuming.

"Well, she won," Bastian said. "I believe that calls for a pass."

"I pass her," Alura said.

They all looked to Lorian. He ground his teeth together but finally nodded his head once.

She'd passed.

# CHAPTER 22
## *The Season*

"I'll never be clean again," Kerrigan complained, dunking under the water once more in the underground hot spring beneath the mountain. She had been down there with Audria and Noda for two solid hours. The boys had been cleaning up in their own baths.

"Never," Noda agreed. She floated in the water happily.

For a second, Kerrigan's heart panged as she thought about Lyam and how much he would have liked Noda. How much he wanted to be on the sea again. She could have taught him to sail again. But no, he'd been murdered, and there was nothing left.

"What are you thinking of?" Audria asked.

"Nothing." Kerrigan shook off her melancholy. "I'm going to sleep all weekend."

"Seconded," Noda said.

"What? No!" Audria said. "We have plans."

"I don't have plans."

"The Season starts tonight!"

Kerrigan groaned. "I don't want to get dressed up and watch debs flaunt themselves before potential suitors."

"Isn't your friend a deb this year? The one from the House of Dragons?"

Kerrigan sank lower in the water. Darby was a deb this year. It was half the reason she didn't want to go. It was hard to imagine her best friend, who had always loved women, parade herself before a bunch of unworthy men.

"You're going," Audria said. "Both of you. And we're bringing the boys too. We need to get out of here. There's more to life than training."

"Is there?" Noda grumbled.

"Yes!"

Audria didn't let them have an opinion. She forced the boys to put on their suits as well, and they all met an hour later to go to the first Season event. The Society offered up a carriage to take them to the Row. Kerrigan was crammed between Audria and Noda, trying not to look at Fordham and how handsome he was in that black suit with the House of Shadows insignia on a little silver pocket square. His dark hair slicked back and those impossibly gray eyes looking anywhere but at her.

She didn't blame him for the attention considering the scandal of a dress she was wearing. When she'd returned to her rooms, a dress in a pale blue box had been waiting on her bed with the word *Parris* hand-lettered on the top in gold. Parris had once been a member of the House of Dragons. He was moved into a tribe with a female fashion designer who had seen his talent. He'd opened up his own boutique under her tutelage, and he was all the rage. They'd been friends long enough that he always made room for her. Somehow, he'd given her the best dress imaginable.

It was a black lace bodice with just enough material covering her breasts to leave a little up to the imagination. There were no sleeves, and the back dipped nearly to her hips in a generous V. The skirts were full tulle with a slit to her thigh. It was only exposed when she wanted it to be, but in the carriage, it was nearly impossible to conceal it. The Society logo had been threaded into the lace in a shimmery black thread that caught the eye and said *precisely* who she was.

Audria had nearly collapsed at the sight of it. She was jealous of Kerrigan's association with him and insisted she introduce them. Which, if they ever had time away from the mountain, she would be happy to do.

The carriage finally came to a halting stop, and a doorman opened the door for them. He held his hand out to Audria, who gracefully stepped down onto the cobblestone steps. Kerrigan was next, not half as graceful, and then Noda. The boys tumbled out after them.

Kerrigan sighed with displeasure at the state of the mansion. It was so large that it must have at least a hundred bedrooms. Enough space to house an entire section of the homeless population, and no one even cared. She hated this part. The belonging and not belonging.

It was Fordham who held his arm out. "It's a bit much?"

"No different than the House of Shadows," she countered. "It might have been worse."

"Assuredly."

A voice proclaimed Audria's entrance in front of them, and Kerrigan froze, realizing that they were going to announce her.

"I don't want to be announced," she whispered.

Fordham tugged her closer. "We could just *leave*."

She laughed. "And miss all the fun?"

"What fun?"

"Dancing. For some reason, I remember you being quite amenable to dancing and having me... take orders," she teased.

His eyes dipped to her lips. "You were quite good at following orders."

"I was," she breathed. Then she winked at him. "It'll never happen again."

He burst into laughter just as they reached the entrance. The man at the front looked at them both in surprise at the outburst.

"Prince Fordham Ollivier of the House of Shadows," the man called out. "And Lady Felicity Argon, First of the House of Cruse of Bryonica, now of the House of Shadows."

Kerrigan stiffened. Lady Felicity. Everyone in the room turned to look at her in that moment. They all *knew*. They all knew exactly who she was. That she'd been abandoned for being half-Fae. It didn't matter that she'd made her own way. None of it mattered. They were all staring.

"It's Kerrigan," Fordham growled at the man. His shadows flared in the bright room, darkening everything just a touch.

The man took a step backward, his hand flying to his chest in affront. "I must give full titles."

Fordham's seething was next level, and people here didn't know him like she did. To them, he looked utterly terrifying. A frightening sight to behold on any day. That sinister energy that always radiated off of him was choking the room. All for... her.

Kerrigan tugged his arm, looking at all the faces full of fear. "Stop. You're causing a scene."

His magic dropped as his gaze shifted back to her. "My lady."

Kerrigan dragged him into the ballroom and out of the line of sight. "You can't just unleash your magic like that. It was bad enough without you making it worse."

He stilled at the vehemence in her words. His shoulders straightened, and those thunderstorm eyes found hers. He was mad. He was still very mad that someone had presented her like that without her permission. "You wish to allow them to treat you that way?"

"No. But we could have fixed the problem without terrifying everyone."

Fordham lifted an eyebrow. "What would be the fun in that?"

Kerrigan released a breath of tension. "I'm a bad influence on you."

"Certainly."

She fought to keep the smile off of her face but failed. What Fordham had done was for her benefit, and she couldn't be angry with him for it even if it had been extreme. Likely, no one would forget to call her Kerrigan ever again.

"Quite an entrance."

Kerrigan turned to find Hadrian walking toward them with Clover on his arm. His bright blue hair had been tamed into a darker blue, left loose and curling on the ends, as was the fashion.

"You know me too well."

Hadrian laughed and pulled her in for a hug. "Too well to know that you hate that kind of attention."

She shrugged. "Those days are going to have to be behind me. Now, I'm a little faerie princess."

Clover snorted and tugged at a loose strand of hair framing her face. Kerrigan was surprised to see her here, considering she *hated* these kinds of parties and hated even more wearing a dress, which was currently in. A summer green number that highlighted her brown skin and lithe figure. Even her black bob had been tangled up into a perfect little coif at the top of her head. She looked so far from the Wastes card dealer.

"You look... feminine," Kerrigan said with raised eyebrows.

"Oh, shove it," Clover said. She plucked at the swath of silk. "I hate this, but it was the only way we could think to get me inside to see Darby's debut."

"I'm glad you're here."

Clover picked at a loose thread on her shoulder. "Yeah. It should be entertaining at least."

"Darby has waited for this her entire life," Hadrian said.

"I know, sweetheart," Clover drawled, falling into street slang, as she always did with Hadrian. Kerrigan could never quite decide if they were going to rip each other's heads off or fall into bed. "Doesn't mean it's right."

Darby's debut was far from right. Most people didn't care one way or another who a person loved. But the aristocracy was another thing altogether. *Money* complicated things. Love that couldn't produce offspring and keep the money in greedy hands was not sanctioned. It all came down to money since practically every wealthy Row gentry participated in extramarital relations with people of the same sex. It was hard to live as long as the Fae did and not at least try a little bit of everything. Sex and love were a spectrum. Marriage was another matter.

"What am I missing?" Fordham asked.

Kerrigan looked to her friends and then back to Fordham. "Darby favors women."

"So?"

"The Season is for male and female courtships."

Fordham furrowed his brow. "And you call *us* the barbarians."

Hadrian laughed. "House of Shadows doesn't care who you marry?"

"They care," he said stiffly. "They just don't care about someone's gender."

"Must be nice," Clover said wistfully.

"We also have a population control problem." He slid his hands into the pockets of his suit pants. "We don't have the space to expand."

The room buzzed with motion, but the lot of them were silent at that. Kerrigan had never considered how overcrowded the House of Shadows must be if there was only the mountains and every Fae could live past a thousand. She hadn't seen that overcrowding, but it was likely concentrated in the lower classes. No wonder they went to war so often.

"Let's get drinks," Hadrian suggested.

Clover leaned into his frame, and his cheeks tinged pink. "I thought you'd never ask."

Hadrian cleared his throat and nodded toward a waiter. The man stopped and handed them each a glass of dry, bubbling wine. Kerrigan took a sip to steel her nerves. Tonight was going to be a *long* night.

Then, an announcement went up for everyone to head into the ballroom. Fordham offered his arm, and they followed the crush of swishing ballgowns. She leaned into him as they waited.

The ballroom was bedecked in a rush of Fae magic. White sheets were strung on the ceiling with faerie lights dancing and glittering across them. The marble colonnades were festooned in white bows. Dual half-circle staircases framed the opposite wall, and the large wooden double doors had been outlined in hundreds of the softest pink blooms.

An attendant cleared his throat. "I present this year's Season debuts."

The double doors were pulled open, and a promenade of young women in white dresses stepped into the room. They each walked down one side of the stairs as gracefully as they could manage, curtsied gallantly before the assembled royalty—of which there were many from all of the assembled tribes that still had a royal court—and then took their place before them.

Kerrigan was shocked by the sheer number of debuts this year. As if many had waited for the tournament year. She'd heard that wasn't uncommon, as it meant all the eligible bachelors who had entered the tournament and not succeeded usually went for a deb that year. Finally, near the back of the endless line was Darby.

Her black skin was lathered in some sort of slight sheen so that it glowed like a moonlit night. Her dress was the softest swath of fabric Kerrigan had ever seen, and she owned every single step she took down those stairs. Everyone stared at her in that moment. The hint of gold on her lids, the long sweep of her black lashes, the enchanting light pink atop her lush lips. The swish of her lithe hips and the command she acquired in just a head tilt. Her deep curtsy was perfection. She'd always been spectacular at the show of it all, but this was something else altogether. Kerrigan had been practicing sword play and magic work, and Darby had honed her own craft.

Whispers broke out as she took her place at the front of the line. An approving nod from one of the assembled royalty said all that needed to be said—Darby was the star of the Season.

\*\*\*

Clover's lips were pressed so hard together that they practically disappeared. "Well, she did all right."

"Better than all right," Hadrian said.

Clover huffed. She downed the rest of her wine. "I need another drink."

Hadrian shot Kerrigan a pained look. "We'll find you later."

Kerrigan waved him off. "Have fun."

"What's with them?" Fordham asked. "I thought they were together?"

"They're complicated."

*Like us.* That was what she wanted to say.

Luckily, she was saved from having to hide that look from her face by Audria appearing. "Oh my gods, your friend is the talk of the night!"

"She did great," Kerrigan agreed.

She fluttered her eyelashes at Fordham. "You don't mind if I steal Kerrigan for a minute, do you?"

For a split second, he looked like he very much did mind but then came back to himself. "Of course not."

"Great," Audria gushed. She linked arms with Kerrigan and pulled her across the room. "I have so many people I want you to meet."

"Meet?"

"Absolutely. Friends of mine. People you would have known from Bryonica had you stayed in the tribe. Important introductions for you to have."

Kerrigan bit the inside of her cheek to keep from telling Audria exactly how much she wanted to make these people's acquaintances. But it was one night, and Audria was so happy. It couldn't be that bad.

Except it was. It was worse.

Kerrigan desperately want to escape the clutches of these women, but she had no chance of doing so. Audria tugged her around as if she were anxious to impress her friends with her new toy. It was exhausting, and after over an hour of it, Kerrigan had a headache.

It would be one thing if it was just mindless prattle, but it was also the number of these women who continually said uncomfortably offensive things about her being half-Fae. How she'd accomplished so much despite her blood. How she was so *brave* for showing her ears. How they couldn't believe that someone like *her* had snagged a prince like Fordham. And on and on. The endless microaggressions made Kerrigan wish she were back in the Wastes, where at least her heritage wasn't a topic of conversation.

She was so close to fleeing that she startled when Darby appeared at her side. She glowed inside and out. "Kerrigan."

They embraced quickly. It had been weeks since Kerrigan had seen her. The longest the former roommates had ever gone. She hated that they were separated but loved that Darby was coming into her own. Even if it meant this absurd spectacle.

"Well, aren't you the toast of the Season?"

Darby grinned and ducked her chin. "You make quite a sight yourself."

"Ugh, don't remind me," she said with a laugh.

Darby looped her arm with Kerrigan's and tugged her away from Audria.

Audria was chatting with a blue-eyed Fae male she'd had her eye on for the last three dances, giving them the perfect escape route. Kerrigan had no intention of ever returning. She was already planning a way out. She needed to find and tell Fordham before she did so. And she hadn't even danced yet. Pity.

"Thank you," she said to Darby. "You did that effortlessly."

"As if I didn't know that you were ready to escape."

"I've missed you so much."

"I've missed you," Darby said. "It's not the same without you. I honestly thought I'd always want my own room, and now that I have it, I miss having you right across the room to gossip with until the early hours of the morning."

Kerrigan giggled. "We weren't *that* bad."

"Yes, we were, and I miss it."

"Me too. Though you seem to have captured the attention of all the gentlemen this Season." The only indication Darby was displeased was a fluttering of her fingers, something she'd done since she was a child. Kerrigan gripped her hand. "You do know that you don't have to go through with this."

Darby nodded. "I do though."

"You don't."

"I can take lovers, Kerrigan. It doesn't have to be that bad."

"You will have to produce children," she whispered low, worry in her voice for her friend.

Darby squeezed her hand. "You have enough to worry about. You don't have to worry about me too."

"Too late."

"I love you. Now, make your escape before Audria notices. I'll be fine."

Kerrigan didn't believe her, but she couldn't make the choice for Darby. So, she hugged her one more time and then stepped outside for a breath of fresh air. She was only outside for a moment when she realized that she wasn't alone. She jerked her magic to her all at once, instinct taking over. Kerrigan put up a shield of solid air and then shoved it back against her attacker.

The Fae male's shocked face as she crushed him back against the wall might not have hurt his ego, but then she started to laugh in his face.

"What are you doing? Don't you know not to sneak up on a girl?"

He straightened, dusting off the effects of her spell. "My lady."

Then, he hastily retreated.

Kerrigan bit her lip as she watched him disappear. Guess she wouldn't get a dance after all.

"Impressive," another voice said. "That's one way to get rid of unwelcome suitors."

Kerrigan's smile vanished. "What do *you* want?"

Kivrin Argon, First of the House of Cruse, stepped out of the shadows to stand before his daughter.

"Hello, Kerrigan."

Well, the night had just gone from bad to worse.

"At least you can get my name right."

"I see that you've taken on my house again."

"Not by choice," she spat. Nothing could turn her into a mouse caught in a trap faster than her asshole father. "I don't need a surname or a Bryonican house to still be important."

"Certainly not. You used neither when you made it into the Society."

"Oh, so this is what this is about? You only care about me because I have a position?"

"No."

And he was so blatant with the answer that she actually stilled.

"I didn't want to give you up."

She couldn't help herself; she laughed. "I don't believe you."

"I had to do it for your safety."

She put her hand to her chest. "For *my* safety. Right. Right, right, right. I've heard that one before."

"If you'd let me explain for one minute."

"You've had twelve years to explain to me why you abandoned me, Kivrin. You no longer have the right."

She whirled away from him. She didn't want to have this conversation. He could have told her why he'd done it for years. Now that he had to claim her as his daughter again, he was going to make something up to appease the masses. And she couldn't care what he came up with.

She pushed back into the ballroom.

Kivrin followed on her heels. "Kerrigan, wait. There's one more thing I need to warn you about."

"Don't care," she snapped.

The front door to the mansion burst open then, and the attendant called out in a clear voice for all to hear, "Lord Ashby March, First of the House of Medallion of Bryonica."

# CHAPTER 23

*The Lord*

**K**errigan's eyes widened to saucers. She was frozen in place as she stared at the man who had been her betrothed and her worst nightmare.

When they had been children, March's family had been the closest to Kerrigan's home, Waisley. Their parents had tied them together as soon as they legally could do so. A year of courting when they came of age would still be required, of course, but it was known from day one that their bloodlines and *money* would stay together. They would stay together.

But though Ashby March was the handsomest child with round baby cheeks and irresistible charm that got him whatever he wanted, there was something wrong with him. And his parents refused to see what was right there. That he learned early on where to give bruises so no one but her bathing attendants would notice. She stumbled upon him in the woods between their two properties, skinning a squirrel. The poor animal was still alive. She cried all the way home, and no one believed a word from her.

She'd been left at the House of Dragons soon after that. A blessing. A curse.

Even in her final test before she'd matched with Tieran, March had been her biggest fear. The one thing that she could never live through.

And now, he was *here*.

As if he was drawn to her presence like a magnet, March found her face in the crowd. Those endless ocean-blue eyes locked on hers, and a corner of his mouth twisted upward. She couldn't move. Gods, she'd seen that look from him before. She'd seen it that day when he looked at the squirrel. Only now, *she* was the squirrel.

A flurry of debs rushed to his side, eager to gain the attention of the most eligible bachelor at the party. Not to mention, one of the handsomest. He had grown into an exceedingly stunning man. His round baby cheeks hollowing and those eyes almost throwing a glamour across the entire crowd. He was tall, strong, regal. Anyone would be lucky to have him. Anyone but *her*.

March said a few words to the debs and then brushed through them as if they no longer existed. He strode right to Kerrigan's side and bowed deeply at the waist. "My lady."

She stood, stunned. A curtsy was the appropriate response. Instead, she blurted, "What are you doing here?"

His nostrils flared just slightly, and then he smoothed it over. "My darling, how could you expect anything otherwise? I came as soon as I heard."

"Heard?"

"That you had returned to us, of course." He plucked Kerrigan's hand out of the air and pressed a kiss against it.

She nearly wrenched it back. The thought of his lips on her person made her physically recoil. She managed to slowly withdraw it. "I've been here all along."

"Why did you never send word?" His big blue eyes were so sincere. "I was desperate for your return. For years, I went looking for you."

She blinked at him, waiting for the subterfuge. She'd known March like no other person, but it had been so long ago. Twelve years was a long time, and she'd been a child. "I thought that this was what was meant for me."

He grinned brightly. "You were meant for the world."

Kerrigan had nothing to say to that. As far as she was concerned, she *had* the world now.

"This was meant to be our Season," he said calmly, gesturing to the court behind them.

Everyone was watching and waiting to see what would happen. If Kerrigan would so easily snag the most eligible bachelor on her first night here. If things would return to how they had once been.

"Yes," Kerrigan said lightly. "But I don't get a Season. I'm here as a representative of the Society. I train for the rest of the year."

"That's deeply unfortunate. Surely, they can let you all off the hook for a few parties."

Kerrigan shrugged. "This one was in Kinkadia and on the weekend we finished our first month of training. I don't know what things will look like after this."

She waited for his easily kindled anger to rise up at her words. For him to find that soft spot on her elbow that would tinge blue. But he smiled so serenely that she wondered if she knew him at all anymore. Perhaps twelve years was too long to assume to still know a person. Perhaps the behavior from his youth was past him. She didn't know. She didn't want to know.

"It's so lovely to see you again," she said, trying for regret. "But I ..."

"It has been, hasn't it? If I remember correctly, you adore dancing. It would be my pleasure." He held his hand out. "Shall we?"

Kerrigan stumbled on her words. Everyone was watching, waiting, wondering. She hated this part of this world. Before she could even form a word to refuse, March took her hand and tugged her toward the dance floor. The song had just ended, and another one began. It was a quick jaunt that her feet remembered before her mind even caught up. Then, she was in March's arms, being whisked across the dance floor to a perfect tempo.

She had to give March credit. Whatever he'd been when they were children, he had shaped up to be a perfectly respectable gentleman. He'd detested dancing and all courtly things as a child. Now, he moved with a grace that could only be gained from endless hours of practice and a confidence born from birth.

Ashby March was next in line for the House of Medallion. If they had wed, it was entirely possible that when the regents from the House of Drame went into the void, she and March would have succeeded them as king and queen. That showed in every movement. She and March had been built for this moment. They were supposed to be the stars. Even if she was no longer that person.

"You're even more beautiful than I envisioned," he whispered against her ear.

"I didn't know that you thought of me at all."

"Of course I did," he said, pulling back to look into her eyes. His blue ones so sincere that her distrust wavered.

Kerrigan didn't know what to say to that. She hadn't thought of March at all. In fact, she'd been glad to be rid of him. And she was too busy to deal with whatever was lurking there in those blue eyes.

The music ended. Kerrigan stepped back, putting much-needed distance between her and March. Her heart thudded in her chest from the exertion of the dance. There were faint notes of applause all around them, as if they had danced for everyone else's spectacle. She hadn't even noticed.

"Another?" he asked.

And then there was another hand there. "May I have the next dance?"

Kerrigan turned to find Fordham with one hand behind his back, the other before her. His gray eyes were as mercurial as ever, the black of his hair tipping forward toward his eyes. Her heart thudded for a whole other reason.

"I've already claimed this one," March said, reaching out and grasping her arm.

She stumbled a step back toward him.

"Now, March," she said easily, "you cannot commandeer all of my atten-tion." She extracted herself from March's grasp and let it rest in Fordham's hand. The dance she'd really wanted tonight.

She could feel March fuming next to her, but she was unprepared for the next words out of his mouth.

"I must object. Unhand my fiancée," March declared.

The ball went silent at the pronouncement, and then, whispers tittered around the room. People were too polite to point, but their eyes did the talking for them.

Kerrigan's face was beet red. Her stomach flopped around on the floor like a fish. Her jaw unhinged as she turned to see the man she had been betrothed to twelve years earlier. Fordham's hand still held her own. And though the whispers only grew, Kerrigan heard none of it. Only focused on the singular word that had left March's mouth—*fiancée*.

"Excuse me?" Kerrigan forced out, quickly removing her hand from Fordham's.

March shot her a beguiling smile. "We're still betrothed, my lady."

"No," she whispered. "That's not possible. I was gone for twelve years. I'm not even Bryonican anymore."

"I assure you that the proper betrothal documents are still in place, signed by our parents all those years ago."

"But surely, they're not still *valid*. Everyone thought I was dead."

"I didn't," he insisted. "I never gave up hope that I would find you again one day. And the documents are only invalid if either you were found officially deceased or I chose to marry someone else."

Kerrigan looked into those blue eyes in shock. And he hadn't married. He'd *waited* these long twelve years for her. Of course, it mattered little when a Fae male married, if he ever did; her father certainly never had. But to have left the betrothal in place was absurd. What would be the point?

"I think... I need some air," Kerrigan said, plucking at her very hot throat. "If you'll both excuse me."

She curtsied and rushed out of the room. Audria grabbed her arm as she hurried past.

"Kerrigan," she cried.

"Leave me alone, Audria."

"I had no idea you were still betrothed."

"Nor did I."

"I wouldn't have contacted March otherwise."

Kerrigan froze and whirled on her. "You contacted him?"

"I was sure that you wanted to see our old friend again."

Kerrigan took a step toward her friend and Society teammate. "Audria, we must work together for the next year, and I will honor that. But what you did—telling everyone that I was Princess Felicity and contacting March—without consulting me beforehand was a breach of trust."

"I'm sorry," she said slowly, putting her hands out in front of her. "I thought you would be happy."

"I am not happy. Do not do me any more favors in the future."

Audria nodded. "I understand."

Kerrigan hurried out the front doors and onto the busy Row street beyond. She had no carriage and was in these ridiculous heeled shoes. She pulled each one off of her feet and then stood barefoot in front of the first event of the Season. What a mess.

"May I assist you?"

Kerrigan huffed a sigh when her father motioned for his carriage to be brought around. "Did you know?"

"I tried to warn you, but you wouldn't listen to me."

"And why would that be?"

Kivrin sighed heavily. The carriage appeared, and they were helped inside before he spoke again. He ran a hand back through his dark brown hair and looked out at the city beyond as it drove toward the mountain. "I did wrong by you, Kerrigan. I acknowledge that I'm not a good father by anyone's standards. But I did what I thought was best for you."

He shot her a pained look, and for the first time in her entire life, she wondered if maybe he was telling her the truth. Not that it made up for the abandonment. Nothing could. But he wasn't playing the playboy prince here. He was being honest.

"Why didn't you break the betrothal?" she asked.

"I couldn't. I tried. I would have had to admit to your death."

"There was a funeral," she snapped.

"Not on my account," he snapped right back. "People wanted closure. I refused, and it was done anyway. But since I never sanctioned it, the betrothal documents were still valid until March married. In what world did I imagine that you would be back here as *yourself* for a Season—your *own* Season at that?"

Kerrigan shrugged. No one would have thought that. She certainly hadn't ever planned to let anyone know who she was. Nor join in the Season. That wasn't the world she'd wanted since she left. She still didn't.

"How do I make it go away?"

Kivrin shook his head. "You can't."

"I do not have to marry someone that I do not wish."

"Bryonican law ..."

"I'm *not* Bryonican," she ground out.

"I'll figure it out," he said as they came up to the foot of Draco Mountain. "Just focus on your studies. I've heard horror stories about Society training, and Lorian is gunning for you."

"As you once said."

Kivrin frowned. "I do not enjoy being right about this."

The door opened to the carriage, and she let the footman assist her out.

"Kerrigan," he said, leaning out the door. She turned back to him in surprise. "I'm proud of you."

A lump formed in her throat. She'd never thought that she would want to hear those words, but she did. She smiled and sent him a small nod of acknowledgment.

# CHAPTER 24
## *The Star*

**CLOVER**

Clover had been drinking too much wine.

"You need to slow down," Hadrian said, trying to pry the gold goblet out of her hand. He managed to take it out of her grasp, but it was already mostly empty anyway.

"I'm fine," Clover muttered.

"No, you're not. You're going to make a fool of yourself."

"This is a ridiculous spectacle." She thrust her hand out toward Darby. Hadrian grabbed it and pulled it to their sides. Their fingers laced together in the space, and she looked up into his face. The handsome boy she had always teased and mocked and joked with to get him to shed his perfect skin.

Hadrian was a street rat through and through. He'd grown up on the streets, and though he was Fae, he was as much a part of this city as Clover was. He might dress in silk and cravats and top hats now, but she could *feel* the city on him. Drawing it out of him was the real work of her life. It was how she'd convinced him to come to the protest. It was why she was standing with him right now. Because despite how she felt about Darby, Clover and Hadrian were *the same.*

Darby was from a middle-of-nowhere farm town. She'd had family who loved her enough to give her up to the House of Dragons for a better life. Clover and Hadrian had nothing and no one. Then, he'd been picked for the House of Dragons, and she'd found the Wastes.

"I know it's a spectacle," he finally said, dissolving his anger and releasing her hand. "But it's what Darby wants."

"She doesn't know what she wants."

"Don't do that," Hadrian said. "Don't diminish her choice just because it wasn't you."

Clover winced. She hated that he'd gotten to the heart of it.

Darby was too good for a lousy human. She had always been too good for Clover. Still, they'd shared one perfect kiss at a party just like this. Clover had thought this would be easier. It wasn't.

"Fine. We've seen what we came for. Can we go?" Clover asked.

Hadrian nodded. "Clove …"

"It's fine, sweetheart," she teased. "You don't need to coddle me. I'm not breakable. Unless you want to try." She winked at him.

He flushed from his neck to the tips of his sharply pointed ears. "That isn't …"

She laughed. "I know, Hadrian."

He cleared his throat again. "I don't want to hurt Darby."

Clover startled at the words. Was he saying that he was interested?

"What are you saying? Speak plainly."

"Don't you know?"

"Say it," she commanded.

His gaze traveled to her lips and back up. "I shouldn't want this, but I do. She wanted you first. Her feelings matter."

"So, she gets to do *that*"—she gestured to Darby standing with a tall gentleman, her hand on his sleeve as she laughed—"but we can't do *this*?"

He gulped. "She still likes you."

"She *chose*. And you said so."

He nodded and then took a step back. "She chose, but it's still wrong."

Clover wanted to tell him to live dangerously, but she could feel this thing between them was strange and precarious. If she pushed, he'd shut down. Darby was one of his closest friends. Clover still ached for Darby. But she'd wanted Hadrian in other ways for too long to ignore it when he admitted to wanting her back. She'd have them both as lovers if she could. If they'd let her.

But not yet.

Then, they heard the room go silent. Clover stared at Kerrigan stuck between Fordham and some unknown male. She heard the word *betrothal*, felt Kerrigan's shock from here, and then she was leaving.

"Oh gods," Clover gasped.

Fordham rushed out after her. The other man, whoever he was, looked at Kerrigan with a smug smile on his face. Clover didn't know anything about him, but that smile told her all she needed to know. He had done all of that on purpose. And it hadn't been for a good reason.

She didn't think. She just dashed across the room with Hadrian on her heels. Kerrigan was speaking to Audria and then was out into the night. Fordham was going to catch her, and Clover couldn't tell him how big a problem that was. Kerrigan's feelings for Fordham were so blatant that he could only make things worse.

She grabbed his shoulder. "Wait," she gasped.

He whipped around. His eyes set and hard. "Clover... what? I need to catch Kerrigan."

"Let her go."

They stood at the entrance to the party. A crowd milled around, waiting to see what would happen next. But then Kerrigan's father appeared at her side.

"He's handling it."

"She hates her father," Fordham spat.

"I know, but you will only make things worse."

"Me and not him?"

"Oh, he probably will, too, but she expects that from him."

He turned back to look at Clover. Hadrian had finally reached them as well.

"Explain," he commanded.

"Have you changed your mind about Kerrigan?" Clover demanded.

His jaw clenched. "No."

"I don't understand," Hadrian said. "Why are you two not together?"

Fordham shook his head. "It's a curse."

Clover rolled her eyes. "Melodramatic."

"A *literal* curse," he explained. "I am doomed to hurt the ones closest to me. It was given to me at birth."

"Have you considered that simply by denying yourself the person you want, you are already hurting her?" Clover snapped.

Fordham's face cleared for a moment. "No. I don't want to hurt her, but ..."

"But?"

He shook his head and turned to find Kerrigan piling into a carriage and leaving the party. Hope died in his face. "I don't want to get her killed either."

Hadrian put his hand on Fordham's shoulder. "We all think we're doing the best by her, but as someone who has known her most of my life, let me tell you that she does not like choices to be made for her. She would rather suffer the consequences than live with regret."

Fordham's face was pained at the words. "I'll consider that."

Clover watched him deal with the consequences of his actions. She wasn't ready to return to the party to deal with the consequences of hers. So, she slipped into the night without Hadrian or Darby. Away from the life she could only ever halfway occupy as a human and back to the Wastes that accepted her wholly as she was. She lit a *loch* cigarette, wondering who that was anymore.

# CHAPTER 25

## *The Dragons*

"**W**e can do this," Kerrigan said to Tieran as she stood at his side in the arena.

*You are incredibly optimistic. It would be endearing if it wasn't so ill-advised,* Tieran grumbled.

"Thanks." She rolled her eyes at her dragon.

Seriously, how had they ended up together? Not that she wasn't a sarcastic jerk sometimes—a lot of times even—but Tieran took it to the next level.

Now, if Alura could just show up and tell them what they were all doing.

The trainees hadn't been given any directions the rest of the weekend. Kerrigan had spent it sleeping and trying to forget the Season party that had ruined her life. She only left to eat, making sure to do it at odd hours to escape the others. Which worked. She didn't even see Fordham, who must have been avoiding her to accomplish that. He always seemed to have a sixth sense to her movements.

Then, this morning, she'd woken up to a note slipped under her door that said to meet in the arena. So, here she was. The dragons were already waiting for them when the others trickled in as well.

Audria was paired with Evien, a majestic purple-scaled dragon, who Kerrigan used to sneak out with at night to fly. Roake had the sapphire-blue dragon, Luxor, who had never understood Kerrigan's sarcasm or really any figures of speech. Which might have been a problem for Kerrigan, but seemed to suit Roake just fine. Noda's dragon, Avirix, had seafoam-green scales that nearly matched the various patterned teal headscarves she always wore. Avirix was the largest of the lot. Not as large as Gelryn, who was the size of a large house, but hardly as small as Tieran.

Kerrigan tried not to look to where Fordham stood with Netta in all of her ruby-scaled glory. She didn't want to know what he thought about March. Or maybe... didn't think about March.

Roake tapped his foot. "Is she ever going to appear?"

*She must*, Luxor said evenly. *She is duty-bound.*

"She's taking her sweet time," he grumbled.

"She's allowed to do what she wants," Audria said.

*Indeed*, Evien said. *But maybe we could fly around the arena while we wait.*

Tieran nudged her. *Maybe we cut a break.*

Kerrigan rolled her eyes. "We're not that lucky."

Tieran couldn't even argue.

Noda was the first to see her. She gasped and pointed to the skies where Alura soared in on her dragon, Gemina. She was a stunning metallic blend of silver, gold, and bronze. Her scales almost matched the silver metal armor that Alura had fastened down her front. She looked like an avenging goddess from legend.

Gemina zoomed in low, and Alura executed a perfect dive roll onto the sand floor. She whipped up, removing the sword strapped to her back, and ran at a full sprint. Gemina dipped down, grabbed her in one claw, and tossed her upward. Kerrigan's eyes widened as Alura did a flip and landed in a standing crouch on the back of her dragon, an effortless shield forming around them. She thrust the sword back into its sheath and then side-rolled down the leg of her dragon, dangled from the ankle, and released, using air to cushion her descent and landing on one knee.

She slowly rose to her feet and surveyed her charges.

"Congratulations. You have completed your thirty days of basic training and are moving on to dragon training."

Gemina soared around overhead once and then landed primly next to Alura, whipping her tail in tight around her.

*Hello, littlings,* Gemina mind-spoke to them. *Today is the first day of real training. You will leave here a different person, a different dragon, a different bonded team.*

Kerrigan glanced at Tieran worriedly. A bonded team was anything but what they were.

"The training will progress over the next eleven months with a final test with your dragon next summer. Passing that test means getting official robes and membership into the Society. But first, you have to be able to do everything that I just did and more. Any questions?"

Audria, of course, shot her hand into the air.

Alura glared at her until she pulled it back down. "Good. Then, we'll begin."

\*\*\*

Begin wasn't quite the word. Thrown in headfirst without warning was more like it. Alura had a very unique method of teaching. Which basically meant *figure it out until you get it.*

"Shield up," Alura shouted from the distance.

Kerrigan lay in the sandy arena, staring up at the clear blue sky, drinking the humid air, and trying desperately to breathe.

*Again*, Tieran grouched.

"Yeah, yeah," she grumbled.

She hoisted herself back to her feet, prepared, and ran at top speed. She completely understood the last thirty days of training because to execute this move, she needed to be in top shape and to land with the shield up, and not floundering would use all of her magic skills. And she was still struggling.

Tieran flew in low, snatching her up in both of his claws. She winced as his nail dug into her shoulder. Then, she was soaring through the air. She flipped backward with her eyes closed, a shriek escaping her mouth. She landed on Tieran's back.

"Scales," she yelled as she scrambled for purchase on her dragon.

"Shield up!" Alura barked again.

"Crap." She reached for her shield, but she was off-balance. She certainly hadn't landed on her two feet. Her body slid sideways, and then once again, she was falling through the air. She dropped a few feet and landed hard on her back.

The air rushed out of her lungs. Her shoddy shield dropped.

"Oh gods."

She coughed and coughed, worried that she was going to vomit up breakfast. Her eyes were blurry at the edges. Tieran sank back down onto the ground and huffed in her direction.

"Shove it," she ground out.

But they were actually the best of the lot. Kerrigan had had a lot of time with dragons in her life. She'd been flying since she'd been left at the House of Dragons. She had a distinct advantage with it as the others had never really been around dragons. Not for an extended period of time at least.

Audria was better at the flipping with her acrobatic training. Noda had perfect balance from sailing. Roake was sturdy and strong in his movements.

Fordham executed everything with military precision, and his shields were top-notch. But they all still fell over and over again. Most of them hadn't even managed to get onto their dragon.

*Again,* Tieran said.

"I can barely breathe."

*We have to work twice as hard.*

Kerrigan waved a hand at him and rolled over to her knees. Her vision dipped. She closed her eyes until it passed and then got back up to her feet.

"Ready," she told Tieran.

She let loose again, running at top speed. She felt like she was flying before Tieran ever swooped in and picked her up. She forced her eyes open this time as she rotated backward over Tieran's body. Her eyes focused in on where she wanted to land, and she dropped into place on her knees on Tieran's back.

She gasped. She'd done it! She certainly hadn't done it with a sword in her hand or anything, but she'd *done* it.

"Shield!" Alura cried again.

"Oh, right," she said sheepishly, pulling a shield around them. Not perfect, but she'd done it.

She whooped loudly and fell backward on Tieran's back as he soared above the arena. He trailed back down to the arena edge.

Alura nodded her head as Kerrigan slid down Tieran's leg and dropped into a crouch. "Good. Now, do it again."

Kerrigan beamed at her. "Yes, sir."

She couldn't help it; she threw her arms around her dragon in celebration.

He snorted. *You're embarrassing us.*

Kerrigan laughed. "We did it."

*So far.*

"See, it wasn't too bad."

Tieran shot her an exasperated look. *We'll see.*

\*\*\*

"That's enough for today," Alura called as Roake landed in the sand heavily. "We're going to be working on these mounting and dismounting maneuvers until you have them down seamlessly and then as a group. So, if you don't have them today, it'll take some time to get used to, and that's normal."

Kerrigan beamed. She'd spent the rest of the hour trying to get to her feet. She'd managed it once before face-planting into Tieran's back. But she was so happy to be flying in any way, shape, or form that she could hardly even care. Only Fordham had also been able to land on their dragon by the end of the session.

"Now, I want the trainees on one side of the arena opposite their dragon on the other side."

Kerrigan winked at Tieran. "Partner."

He blinked at her. *You're in high spirits.*

"We're doing it," she whispered.

*It's the first day. You're incredibly optimistic.*

"And you're a pessimist. Now, get over there."

Tieran blew hot breath into her face. She rolled her eyes at him and jogged to the other side of the arena, lining up between Fordham and Roake.

"Nice job out there," Fordham said.

She grinned. "Getting over your fear of heights?"

"It's a fear of falling," he corrected her. "And, yeah. Falling this much in one day is making it go away."

"Didn't I tell you that facing your fears makes you master them?"

He bowed slightly in her direction. "Forgive me for ever doubting you."

It was the most they'd said to each other in days. Color heated her cheeks at the way the words flowed over her. They'd been avoiding each other with good reason. Fordham had made it clear this wouldn't happen, and now, she was betrothed… always had been apparently. Not that she'd let that stand if she had anything to say about it. But she didn't want it to change their friendship. If it was all she could have, it was what she would take.

Alura came to a stop before them. "Dragon bonding is the core to the entire Society. It is the foundation of our government and the establishment of Fae and dragon relations. However, the bond is a fragile thing. When you're first bonded, the tether between you and your dragon is a little light within yourself. Something that flickers on, and if you're not careful, it can go out."

Kerrigan chilled at those words. She'd never heard of that before. Bonds could be severed and not kill the dragon and human rider? No wonder this was only spoken of to initiates.

"What we're going to spend the next eleven months on is working that bond like a muscle until it's big and strong. It generally takes about a year to get a bond strong enough to be fully functional. You should be able to feel where the other is even if you were on a different continent. On a different world entirely," Alura said with an arched eyebrow. "It would be your beacon home."

Kerrigan shivered. Her eyes found Tieran's across the arena. The bond that they never had… and had to fake for the next eleven months. Scales.

"Today, we're going to work on very basic bond strengthening. I want you to look at your dragon and then reach deep within your chest." Alura tapped the center of her torso. "Try to find the flickering light and then touch it. Don't pull on it yet. I simply want you to acknowledge its presence. Once you've found it, don't say anything, just raise your hand."

Kerrigan looked deep in her magic, dived around down there uselessly. Of course, she wasn't going to find a bond. But she had to pretend to be concentrating on it at least.

Fordham's hand shot up first. Within seconds. Even Alura's eyebrows rose. Apparently, it was much faster than she had expected.

Noda rose her hand next. Then Roake.

Kerrigan wondered how long she could fake this. She didn't want to raise her hand too early, but all she found down in there was her magic. Just the well of space where she could dive and pull up whatever she needed... just not a bond.

Audria's hand finally went up, reluctantly. No one looked at Kerrigan, but she could sense that they were all still waiting. Twenty minutes had gone by, and really, there was nothing to do but put her hand up.

"Good," Alura said. She pointed to Fordham. "You found your bond quickly. Explain."

"I found it before this. I called my dragon to me before we started training."

Alura managed to smother her approval.

Kerrigan, however, remembered that very moment. Her eyes flicked to Fordham's, and he nodded once. When they'd been in the House of Shadows and she'd been dying from trying to take the walls down, Netta had flown to them, as if called. She had been called. From who knew how long of a distance.

"Were you in danger?" Alura asked intuitively.

"Yes," he said flatly.

She nodded. "Bonds strengthen faster when they have to. In war, bonded dragons and riders snap together like magnets. Without that immediacy, we have to build it up ourselves. Ollivier, call your dragon."

Fordham looked to Netta, and something seemed to ripple between them. Then, Netta flew across the arena distance and landed before them.

"That's what we want, people," Alura said. "We want to find the bond within ourselves and tug on it. Light at first. It can be disorienting to be bonded. Now, give it a try."

One after another, the dragons flew across the arena toward their rider. It wasn't instantaneous, but it left Kerrigan standing there without Tieran.

She gritted her teeth and nodded her head at him. Come on, she wanted to scream at him.

Eventually, he got the picture and flew across the arena. But there was no bond, no tug, nothing. And as they looked into each other's eyes, they both knew they were in way over their heads.

*Not too bad, huh?* Tieran spat sarcastically into her mind.

# CHAPTER 26
## The Protest

**K**errigan spent the week excelling at the various mounts and dismounts that Alura had shown them and failing miserably at every single bond exercise. They skidded by when they could look at each other or Tieran could speak into her mind what he was planning to do. They suffered through blindfolded bond training. And while everyone seemed to get better, she stayed exactly the same.

Alura looked at her strangely through much of it. She didn't know that Kerrigan was faking it, but how long could they keep this up?

She was more exhausted from faking a dragon bond than from the rest of her classes combined. She did fine in her new subjects—government, history, and philosophy. She excelled in her magic classes. She was even pulling away in her air and fire lessons. Water was always her worst subject, but even that was nothing compared to the bonding.

She kept waiting for Zina to start their spirit training classes, but anytime Kerrigan asked, Zina shooed her out the door and claimed that she'd contact her. Which was fine by her since she was swamped with papers in the evenings now. Her nose buried in a book as she scratched on parchment until late into the night. Only to wake up for dragon training all over again.

The only joy in all of this was that weapons training had been moved to twice a week, and they were fighting with staffs, knives, and spears, too. Lorian only came to taunt her, frustrating but manageable.

The one thing she did know was that she couldn't stay inside this mountain another moment. She missed the Wastes. She missed how easy her life had been in the House of Dragons. While there, she'd complained that it was hard, but boy, had she been wrong.

"What took you so long?" Clover asked once Kerrigan slipped through a secret exit out of the mountain.

"Sorry. It's been a very long week."

"Tell me about it on the way."

But Kerrigan didn't want to tell anyone about it. She knew that Clover wouldn't judge her for not bonding with Tieran. She'd even encourage her to fake it until she made it. She just couldn't do it. Something about saying it out loud would make it real.

"Well?" Clover asked, pulling out a cigarette as they wove through the streets.

"You're going to smoke that here?" Kerrigan asked dubiously.

"I need one before we're in the protest for hours on end," Clover said. Her voice hardened at the words. She clearly hated admitting to it as much as Kerrigan did.

"All right. Be quick."

Kerrigan tugged on her hood and glanced around nervously to see if anyone was watching. Loch was still illegal even if Clover smoked it for medicinal reasons.

She stamped out the smoke before they made it to the Square. People milled about the interior of the Square, making signs and chatting. For a Friday night, the Square was relatively empty. The traffic had been reduced by barricades that kept the horses and carriages out of the center.

"There are fewer people here than I thought," Kerrigan said.

"Yeah. Thea can get people out for the secret meetings, but to actually stand up to the Society, that's an entirely different thing."

"Makes sense. No one wants to get in trouble."

"We're allowed to protest," Clover said defensively. "It's protected speech."

"I know, but …"

Clover shrugged. "I get it. It's stupid."

Kerrigan agreed. But fear laced the protest. No one was approaching anyone else. None of the signs were being held high. The protesters were huddled together and looking around anxiously. Only a few people were doing much of anything, and Kerrigan instantly recognized Thea as one of them.

"Come on. Let's say hi."

Kerrigan followed her to where the leader of Rights For All was standing, speaking to a Fae male. Well, the man was arguing with Thea while she kept a perfectly level head.

"I understand, sir, and appreciate the information, but we actually are allowed to be out here today."

"I'm going to call the Society Guard."

"You may do so, but I have a permit from the Society for this demonstration," she said cheerfully.

"No one wants your kind here," the man said. "You're going to lose us all our business."

"I apologize for the loss of business. We do not want to harm you in any way. We would like to request the same from the Society and the city guard. We deserve to be heard."

The man grumbled something and then turned and trekked back to the glass-blowing business he apparently owned.

"Need me to take care of that?" Clover asked defensively.

"Clover!" Thea said with a wide smile. She took Kerrigan's hands in her own. "You made it."

"Are many people talking to you like that?"

"Oh no," she said with a twinkle in her eye. "Nothing I can't handle. Let's get you set up somewhere in the Square."

"Everyone seems afraid," Kerrigan noticed.

Thea sighed. "I know. We gave them a pep talk, but it didn't help. They believe in the cause, but they fear the consequences of being here. Despite the fact that this is sanctioned by the Society."

"They don't want to give us rights, but they'll let us march for them," Clover ground out.

Kerrigan tapped her finger to her lip as she thought about what to do. This wasn't going to do anything. She could feel it in her bones. These people weren't prepared for what was happening. They needed inspiration to make them stand up for what they believed in.

What had Dozan called her at the last meeting? A symbol.

Scales.

"Where are you going?" Clover cried as Kerrigan marched across the Square to the protestors.

But Kerrigan couldn't answer because if she did, she'd second-guess herself. And she needed every ounce of reckless confidence in her system.

She drew her hood back enough for her red curls to frame her face. She looked into the eyes of the couple dozen people standing around, clouded in fear.

"Do you know who I am?" she asked.

The people at the front of the group gasped. Eyes widened into saucers. Whispers broke out. That answered that question.

Kerrigan held her hand up. And when they all fell silent, she put her finger to her lips. "I'm not here right now. Do you understand?"

A girl in the front nodded. "The Society can't know?"

"That's right. They can't know."

"Why not?"

"Because," Kerrigan took a deep breath, "they're afraid of me."

More whispers.

The girl at the front shushed them. "Listen to her."

"We're not here today because of me. We're here because of *you*," Kerrigan insisted. "But I did what the Society thought was impossible. I got into their sacred halls. I'm going to challenge them and help you. But first, *you* have to prove that my cause is valid. Let them hear your battle cry. Tell them no longer will you live in the shadow of the Fae. Only through you can I succeed. Will you fight with me today?"

This time, there were no whispers, only cheers as the crowd swelled with excitement. She'd given them what they needed—a reason, not just a cause.

She put her finger to her lips again and ducked back fully under the hood of her cloak. Excitement glittered in their eyes. They were in on the secret. They were part of something bigger. Fear was still there, but now, it mingled with purpose. And through purpose, they could all succeed.

Kerrigan went from group to group, reciting the variations of the same speech. A hundred people saw her face that day, knew who she was, and came to her battle cry. She wasn't ready to reveal herself publicly, but this was as close as she could get. It was likely that it could reach the Society after this, but she still had plausible deniability.

When she returned to Thea and Clover, they stared at her in awe.

"Thank you," Thea said, tears coming to her eyes. "You have no idea what this means to us."

"I think I do," Kerrigan told her. "I know what it would have meant to me to have someone fight for me when I felt like I had nothing."

Thea squeezed her hand. "You're a blessing from the Lament. I will pray for you."

Kerrigan's eyes widened as Thea whispered something unintelligible over her hands. "Uh, thanks?"

Clover tried not to laugh. "We're ready when you are, Thea."

"Yes, let's begin the march."

Thea led the charge. Kerrigan could see that Clover wanted to be up there, leading with her. She pushed Clover forward.

"I'll hang back with you."

"No, go on. You deserve it," Kerrigan said.

Clover waffled for a moment and then fell into step with Thea. Kerrigan waited until she was near the back of the group with the stragglers and then entered the protest. Fae came out of their storefronts to hear Thea's protest cry—*rights for all*—on repeat. Some people sneered and called them names, but many more of them nodded along and even called out chants in agreement. Kerrigan would never have guessed so many Fae would agree with them.

"Amazing, isn't it?" Dozan said, slipping to her side at the back of the protest.

His own brown-red hair was covered by a cloak. He'd swapped out his Wastes red for another all-black suit. His amber eyes flitted with danger and lust.

"Even you can't ruin this for me," she told him.

"Why would I ruin it, princess?" He reached for her hair, but she grabbed his wrist on reflex.

"Haven't you heard, I'm betrothed?"

Dozan smirked seductively. "Shall I tell your fiancé what a bad girl you've been?"

Kerrigan threw his hand back at him. "I wouldn't mind actually."

"Ah, would you prefer a prince to a lord?" he sneered. "Because I remember you falling into bed with a king."

Kerrigan rolled her eyes. "Your title is made up, Dozan."

He winked. "So are theirs."

"Is there a reason you're here tormenting me?"

"And here I thought this was foreplay."

"You're insufferable."

"That's what makes us such a team. But yes, I'm here for a reason."

"Spit it out."

"I thought you would like to know that the Society has ceased investigating Basem's killer."

Kerrigan froze in place. The person behind them nearly ran into her before she realized she'd stopped in the middle of the march. She continued forward. "They stopped? You're sure? And they didn't find out who did it?"

"You doubt my contacts?"

*No.* Though she didn't have to say it.

"A little birdie told me that not only did they cease, but they also never even questioned anyone in the Society."

"What?" she gasped.

"Only the Guard."

"But it *had* to be an inside job."

"You and I know that. I'm sure even they know that. But they protect their own. And you aren't quite one of their own yet."

Kerrigan fumed. "I cannot believe this."

"But can't you?"

Yes, she could. She'd been so wrapped up in training that she hadn't even had time to think about the investigation. But if they hadn't even spoken to anyone in the Society, no wonder it had gone nowhere.

"I'll figure it out," she said. "Let me know if you hear anything else."

"Ah, you want me to spy for you now?"

She glared at him. "Ah. So, you didn't give me this information freely? I won't fight for you."

"I wouldn't expect you to. Let's call this one on me."

"You don't offer anything for free."

"I want you to find out who killed him," he said, lethally calm. "And I want you to make them pay."

Kerrigan gulped at those words from Dozan. She knew exactly what he meant. What he'd done to get his throne. The throne settled on the blood of his enemies.

She nodded anyway. "I'll do what I can. Tell Clove I went back to the mountain?"

"My dealer will be taken care of," he said with a small bow, and then he disappeared into the crowd.

She watched his back, feeling conflicted by his help. She doubted this was all really free. He wanted something out of it. The killer being punished wouldn't be enough for Dozan. But she couldn't see the threads in front of her.

Instead, she took the next turn and hurried back to the mountain. She didn't bother sneaking back in through her side entrance; she went straight through the front doors. The guards looked at her in confusion until she flashed the Society insignia on her trainee robes. They wouldn't stop a Society member from entering even if they hadn't seen her exit.

She stopped by her room first when she nearly ran right into Valia.

"Kerrigan," she gasped. "There you are."

"What are you doing in my room again?"

"Helly sent me," Valia said quickly, looking down.

The power dynamic between them had shifted. She hated feeling the gap between them.

"Good. I was on my way." Kerrigan flung her cloak onto her bed and then followed Valia out.

"You were already going there?"

"Yes. Why did she send you?"

"She didn't say. Something about training."

Kerrigan frowned. Well, that could be anything, considering how poorly

Kerrigan had been doing with bonded training. Not that she had any interest
in talking about that.

"How does it feel?" Valia asked as they approached Helly's rooms.

"How does what feel?"

"To be one of them?"

Kerrigan sighed. "Tenuous."

Valia didn't speak after that. The topic was closed. Nothing could change
that Kerrigan had been given what Valia had been denied.

Valia knocked once, and Helly called, "Come in."

Kerrigan stepped inside, closing the door behind her. "Helly."

"Oh, Kerrigan, good. She found you."

"I was already on my way."

"Oh? What for?"

Kerrigan crossed her arms. "You closed the investigation."

Helly sighed. "You heard about that?"

"Yes! What were you thinking?"

"It wasn't my call. The head investigator found no evidence to trace back
to the perpetrator. No one had any information."

"And you didn't get any because you refused to question the Society
members!"

Helly frowned and slowly sank into her seat. "I was overruled in that
as well. You must see how it looks. As someone now in the Society, we go
through vigorous training. Our life is dedicated to this place. To question our
own would mean to question the very methods that put them there."

"Maybe that's a good thing."

"Maybe it is," Helly said. "But you're young, and you change much more
willingly. The others ..."

"So, you're going to let them get away? Someone within the Society did
this, and you aren't even going to find out who it was?"

"That is the way of things. We have suspicions, and we're waiting to see if they slip up."

"You're waiting for another murder?" Kerrigan gasped.

"Gods, no, Kerrigan. Don't you know me better than that? I have people being watched. I am doing what I can through the means I have. I cannot publicly accuse people, but I can search out evidence my own way."

Kerrigan finally sank into a seat next to Helly, her anger turning into resignation. "Why must it be this way?"

Helly took one of Kerrigan's hands. "The Society has been around for thousands of years. We're changing incrementally all the time. We'll do what we can, I promise."

It wasn't enough, but it would have to do for now.

"And I called you here because Zina sent me this."

Helly passed Kerrigan a slip of paper with Zina's scrawl on it.

*I can start training the girl on the Night of the Dead. Let her know, will you, Hell?*

Kerrigan shivered. The Night of the Dead was still six weeks away, and just thinking about it made her nervous. "Why do we have to wait so long?"

"With Zina, who knows? If she says the Night of the Dead, then she knows what she's doing."

"All right. The Night of the Dead it is," Kerrigan said, rising to her feet.

Irritation about the investigation hit her. She hated that this place was still so set in the past. And she was starting to worry that one girl wasn't going to be able to fix it.

# CHAPTER 27
## The Library

"**Y**ou're doing just fine," Audria said, clapping Kerrigan on her back as they headed to lunch later the next week.

"I suck," she grumbled.

Bond training was a nightmare. By the time she finished every morning, she felt like she'd been run over by a carriage. At least yesterday, she'd gotten to take it out on Lorian. She'd fought ferociously until even Lorian seemed almost impressed. Not that he'd ever say it out loud.

"The bond is hard for me too," she confessed. "I've never had anything like this. Fordham makes it look easy."

Kerrigan glanced over to him and found him already watching her. He met her gaze evenly with an arched eyebrow until she hastily looked away. "He does, doesn't he?"

"What's going on with you two anyway?"

"Nothing," Kerrigan said slowly.

Audria rolled her eyes. "Look, I made the mistake of inviting March to the Season, but you can tell me. Are you two involved?"

"No," she repeated. "We're really not. He's not interested."

Audria pulled her to a stop. "Kerrigan, you'd have to be blind not to see that he's interested. It's palpable."

Kerrigan shrugged. "It's not my story to tell. Just know that it isn't happening."

"His loss," she said with a giggle. "If it's not Ashby March, the most eligible bachelor of the Season, that you want, then we will find you someone!"

Kerrigan wanted to tell her that she didn't need the help, but it was easier to let Audria ramble than to argue.

They finished up lunch as a team and headed into their history lesson. Luckily, it was the easiest of the three classes. Far easier than her language elective, which she'd taken to brush up on her ancient Fae. She'd had a lot of these lessons at the House of Dragons. By a lot of the same teachers too.

Kerrigan took a seat in the row of chairs before their instructor, a bubbly Fae with long, braided blonde hair, light-blue eyes, and a peach-colored pin on her black Society robes to mark her as a member of tribe Zavala, far in the northern mountains.

"Welcome back," Mistress Movanna said cheerfully. She bounced slightly with each step and pressed thin spectacles up the bridge of her nose.

Kerrigan had rarely seen a Fae have to wear the enhancing glasses. Though Movanna joked it was because she was always deciphering tiny lines of ancient Fae.

"Today, we're going to discuss the Irena Bargain."

Roake groaned softly.

Movanna laughed. "I know. I know. We've all heard it before. Of course we know all the details. No need to even discuss it, right?"

Kerrigan wanted to nod but had a feeling that Movanna was joking.

"I'll tell you the story, and you tell me what you think," Movanna suggested. "Thousands of years ago, Fae discovered an uninhabited world. To their shock, dragons existed here already. The Fae wanted the land for themselves and began a battle between Fae and dragon, which the Fae were losing. One Fae maiden walked alone into the belly of the beast and struck a truce with the dragon leader, Ferrinix. Together, it was the first dragon bond and the beginning of the Society. The Fae agreed to live under Society rule, and twelve tribes split the land for themselves based on their belief of magic. Three tribes to the west in Viland, who believed magic should be used for war. Three to the east in Moran, who thought magic should be used for good. To the north in Tosin, who used magic for efficiency. And three more to the south, who believed magic should be used for nothing or menial things, depending on the translation. Is that what you learned?"

Kerrigan nodded. Everyone else was nodding along as well, except Fordham. He had his arms crossed and looked dubious.

"Fordham?" Movanna asked.

"They tell it differently in the House of Shadows."

"I believe they would," Movanna said eagerly. "In fact, I would love to learn the tale from you one day. Tell us one thing that stands out starkly to you."

"There weren't twelve tribes," Fordham said.

"Correct. Correct. There weren't even thirteen," Movanna added eagerly. "Thirteen is what we landed on after many of the tribes combined through marriage, enslavement, or war. We started with *hundreds* of tribes. Not to mention, all Fae didn't show up at once. We showed up over hundreds of years, different tribes claiming land and warring with the dragons as their territory diminished."

Audria's hand shot up. "Why is it taught the other way then?"

"Myth, legend, nationalism, a good story? You take your pick." Movanna bounced around the room excitedly.

The door opened at the back of the room, and Master Bastian appeared.

"Can I help you, Councilman?"

"Just here to observe. Pretend I'm not here," he said, shutting the door behind him.

Movanna shrugged. "As you wish. Now, Irena. What do we know about her?"

Noda held her hand up. "She's a maiden."

"And Fae," Roake added.

"Indeed. That's about all despite depictions of her all over the city. But in the history books, there's a different picture. She could have been the chieftain of her tribe, sent to kill the dragon, Ferrinix, and instead made a different choice."

The room was hushed at the pronouncement.

"It's all fascinating, isn't it?" Movanna said. "Now, let's back up and discuss the tribe arrival and what they found."

Kerrigan listened, rapt, as everything she'd thought that she knew about history was carefully dismantled by a small, bubbly historian. By the end of the lesson, her mind was whirring a thousand miles a minute, and she had three parchments on the Irena Bargain to write before next week.

They all groaned as they got out of their seats to head to magic training.

Bastian clapped his hands once. "I came to inform you that Mistress Zahina is gone for the week, so there will be no air lesson this evening. You are on your own. Use your time well."

Roake whooped. "Might actually get to bed before midnight."

Audria laughed as she looped arms with him. "This calls for cake."

"Everything calls for cake."

"You have never said anything more right," Noda said with a laugh.

"Kerrigan, if I can have a word," Bastian said as she passed him behind Fordham.

"Of course," she said, waving Fordham on with the others.

"I'll be in the library. Come find me later," he said.

She nodded and then turned her attention to Bastian.

"Walk with me, Kerrigan," he said and waited for her to fall into step beside him. "That was quite a lesson. Mistress Movanna is energetic."

"She is. It was fascinating."

"She's constantly dredging up new information about the founding of the Society. You'll get to more modern times, and she'll stop caring," he said with a laugh. "She considers the Great War modern."

"That sounds like her."

"I must confess that I showed up to your lesson for a reason," Bastian said with a smile. It stretched the side of his face that had been burned from an accident as a child. He grew up in a village in the south, where the closest healer was miles away. It was what had sent him to participate in the Society and try to help those who most needed it. She respected that about him. "I heard a rumor that you were at a recent protest in the city."

Kerrigan gulped. So much for no one telling anyone that she had been there. "Sir?"

"Don't worry. I'm not here to stop you. I understand your reasoning for doing it. I was the one who signed the form that sanctioned the protest in the first place."

"Oh. Well, that was nice of you."

"It was legal. But there are others who, shall I say, would prefer to quash the protests entirely. I believe they would not look favorably on you attending them."

"I understand."

"I want you to be careful. We need people like you in our ranks."

"I'm being careful." But was she? She'd shown her face on purpose. It could have gotten back to anyone.

Bastian stopped her with his hand on her arm. "Don't let Lorian find out, Kerrigan." Kerrigan shivered at the words. "He is your strongest detractor and will do anything to get you removed from your position. Helly and I can only do so much if he sways the rest of the council."

Kerrigan gulped and nodded. "Thank you for the warning, sir."

He patted her shoulder. "Good girl. Now, run off with your friends. I remember my own training and having very little time to relax. Zahina's absence should free you up for the evening."

She thanked him and then hurried away. She thought about finding the others for cake, which sounded delicious right now, but her head was buzzing about the protest and Bastian finding out. How much she didn't want Lorian to find out. And instead, she found herself in front of the library.

The massive oak double doors were open to reveal the stacks beyond. Rows and rows and rows filled with parchment and thick, musty books. The librarian was a stodgy, old Fae male who was a steward like Valia but treated everyone as if they were beneath him. She didn't mind him that much. She could deal with his ill humor when she was surrounded by the books. The smell of parchment and the feel of endless memory all in one place. It was enough to make her want to skip through the halls.

She bypassed the librarian and searched for Fordham. A part of her felt more connected to him than her dragon. She couldn't feel a bond with Tieran at this distance, but something about Fordham pulled her to his hiding spot before she ever knew he was there. He scratched out a verse on a piece of parchment. Several had already been discarded next to him, likely burned to ash later if he hated them that much. Her sad, broody prince writing his sad, broody poetry. The only thing he kept entirely to himself. She'd read a sliver of it once and immediately felt as if she was invading his privacy. She'd do anything to know what was on that paper. What he wrote about when he thought no one else was watching.

"There you are," she said finally.

Fordham startled. He shoved the paper under a book half the size of the large oak table. The poetry vanishing that quickly. "Kerrigan, you found me."

"Indeed."

"What did Bastian want?"

Kerrigan sighed heavily and plopped down in the seat next to him. She hadn't even planned to come see him. They had barely seen each other outside of classes. They were careful and professional and not at all what she actually wanted from him. But in this moment, she wanted her friend.

"I know that look. What did you do now?" he asked.

She glanced up into those smoky-gray eyes. Her stomach fluttered with that one look. How had she once thought him so sinister? She knew objectively that he was terrifying, but when he looked at her, it wasn't there anymore.

"I might have gotten involved with a group called RFA—Rights For All."

Fordham waited. He didn't interrupt. Just sat there and let her tell her story.

"It's an organization that is trying to petition the Society for equal protection and rights under the law. A representative on the council, a say in the government, better treatment by the Guard, that sort of thing."

"I'm sure that's popular," he said sarcastically.

"Yeah. Well, more people than I thought, honestly. I went to a meeting with Clover and found out that I'm"—she huffed in annoyance at the next words—"some sort of celebrity."

He arched an eyebrow.

"I know. It's ridiculous, but I'm here right now, and believers are taking that as a symbol that the Society is ready for change."

"Okay." He still sounded dubious.

"So, I went to a protest and spoke to some people there. We marched through the streets, and it was amazing. I felt so supported. I've wanted this for so long." She shook her head. "But Bastian found out I was there."

"Is he going to kick you out?" His voice was laced with concern.

"No, he wants me to be careful. If Lorian gets wind of it ..."

Fordham grimaced. "Don't let him find out."

"I know. But how do I get people to participate and the Society to listen if I stay hidden?"

Fordham was silent for a moment, as if he didn't have an answer. But then he finally met her gaze again. "I haven't been the best advocate for human and half-Fae rights. I was raised to see them... you, as lesser. Though I am trying to be better."

She nodded, knowing what the admission had cost him.

"Could I join you the next time you go to something for the RFA?"

Kerrigan blinked. That wasn't what she'd thought he'd say. "You want to come to a protest?"

"You shouldn't stay hidden. You can't be contained, and no one should try to force you. Wild and untamed are the only ways in which you should exist," he said, his hand sliding across the distance between them and settling on hers. Her pulse jumped in the hollow of her throat at the bare touch. "I want to be there to see you change the world. Because I already know that you will."

Kerrigan's throat bobbed. She didn't have words.

She wanted to kiss him. To pull their bodies together in the stacks and get lost in him entirely. Their bodies hovered in that space, a beat between them. She moved a few inches forward, and he mirrored her. She could have reached out, but she couldn't keep asking for something that he wouldn't reciprocate. And here they were, in this moment, and all they had to do was finish, push their lips together and forget the world.

Just as she was about to say screw it and dive in anyway, Fordham closed his eyes for a second and then pulled back. He took his hand with him, and suddenly, she felt bereft.

Kerrigan crossed her arms over her chest and turned away from him. Her eyes struggled to focus, accept what had almost happened. She was so stupid. Why did she keep putting herself in this position with him? He'd made himself clear.

"Kerrigan..."

"What's this?" she asked, focusing on the book finally. Anything to keep him from saying whatever was next going to come out of his mouth.

"What?" He saw what she was looking at and then said, "Oh. It's records from the Great War."

"You've been researching the Great War?"

"Well, I was working with Gelryn to see if I could get information about your vision, but he had no interest in talking about the war."

"Unsurprising," she said, paging through the book. "Considering what he went through there."

"Yeah. So, I thought to see if there were records for all of the Society members at that time, but there were just long lists of names. They were almost indecipherable." He shook his head. "I decided to try to search through the Great War rosters and see if I could find anyone by the name of Trulian or Mei."

"Any luck?" she asked.

He shook his head. "About what I expected. Trulian is a pretty common name. I found five of them so far. Four Fae commoners and a Society general. The general seems pretty important."

Kerrigan wracked her brain. Trulian had looked like someone important in her vision, but with five options already, she didn't know if that was right.

"And Mei?"

"No. Plenty of Mae spelled M-A-E but none M-E-I."

"Huh," she said. "Thank you for doing this. I never would have thought there would be records."

"We keep them in the House of Shadows, and sometimes, as a child, I had to copy them word for word as punishment."

Kerrigan frowned. "That sounds torturous."

"It was," he admitted. "Who knew it would be useful?"

Kerrigan pulled the book closer to her and paged absently through it. She didn't know what she was looking for. If there were that many Trulians, she wouldn't find them, but a Mei might be the key. She had been the one to put up the wall around the House of Shadows after all.

But there was nothing here. She spent an hour thumbing through the records and found nothing.

"What we need," Fordham said, "is someone who was alive during the Great War, who would remember and talk to us about it. I don't know anyone old enough though."

Kerrigan shook her head with a sigh. "I don't either, but I'm going to find someone."

# CHAPTER 28
## *The Bond*

"Congratulations, trainees. You have completed the introductory bond training. Your mount and dismounts have greatly improved. Though we will continue to focus on them as we go into the next section, they will not be the primary concern of the second set of training."

Kerrigan grinned, knowing what this meant. They were finally going to be able to *fly*. Flying was her true passion. The first time she'd ever ridden on a dragon, she'd known that she had been made for it. Nothing in all of her life had ever prepared her for finding joy on the back of a dragon high above the city. She'd wanted nothing but her own set of wings from that day forward. That way she could go up into the skies anytime she wanted. But as she'd gotten older, she'd realized two things: she'd never get her own wings and no one was going to give a half-Fae a dragon. She'd been right on both counts even if she'd made her own destiny with the second. It had been luck or fate that gave her Tieran. She couldn't wait to do more than hover around the arena with him.

"Before we move on," Alura said, "I have a series of bond tests to determine the strength of your bond."

Kerrigan's stomach dropped. That wasn't going to be good.

"Afternoon classes have been canceled for us to perform these tests. There will be two tests—one for you and one for your dragon. Each test will be scored based on how well you perform together."

Kerrigan looked to Tieran with a frown.

His face revealed nothing of his own anxiety, but she swore that she could feel it radiating off of him. They'd fumbled through most of bond training so far with him speaking into her mind or her gentle nodding. She'd actually come up with a few signs and magic signatures for him to follow. There was no bonding, but they were beginning to understand each other in ways that they'd never managed in their earlier training sessions. It hadn't been dire enough. Now, it was do or die.

"Dragons and riders, to opposite ends of the arena," Alura declared.

Kerrigan patted Tieran's neck. "Good luck."

*We need more than luck. We need a bond*, he grumbled.

He wasn't wrong.

She'd spent the last couple weeks researching the bond. She found the spell to brew the bonding potion. It was incredibly simple. She filched the supplies from the greenhouses on the eastern side of the mountain and put all of the materials together herself. Tieran was skeptical but willing to try anything. Maybe the bond hadn't worked because she had thought that she shouldn't be picked. Maybe it was a mental thing.

She read over and over about mental fortitude for the spell. That the pair had to want to be linked. Which, in the beginning, had been far from the case. But this time, there was no other choice. They had to bond, and they both wanted it despite their differences.

They took the potion. Kerrigan passed out again. She saw her father in a strange world, being beaten by a giant of a man. The man turned at the last moment and *saw* her. She could still hear the screams from inside the villa. She had just been getting over that particular nightmare, but here it was all over again.

She had no idea what Tieran had seen, but he awoke, shaking with real fear in his eyes. But the bond continued to evade them. It hadn't worked, and Tieran refused to try again. She didn't blame him. If what he had seen was as bad as what she had seen, then she hardly wanted to go through it a third time.

Now, they were on opposite sides of the arena prepared to trick everyone into believing they had a bond. Scales.

Gemina went up to each of the dragons as Alura strode over to the trainees. "Gemina is giving each dragon a location outside of the city, and you will have to trek to reach them by following the bond. It is the farthest bond that we've tried, and I suspect it will take a lot of stretching for you. But we can't get better if we don't stretch." She was firm and unsmiling but somehow made it sound encouraging.

Kerrigan sweat with fear. She had no bond to follow. It didn't matter how far away Tieran was; she wasn't going to find him.

"We want you all back by lunch, and then we'll start the second part of the test. Once Gemina returns, you'll begin. Any questions?"

By now, even Audria kept her hand at her side. Alura didn't actually want questions. She wanted them to be soldiers.

"Good." She grinned viciously.

The five of them waited with nerves biting at them. Audria still looked as prim and proper as ever. Though she'd been letting her hair down more. Fordham hadn't loosened up an inch, but he also had the easiest time with his dragon. Roake was constantly frazzled. He hated the schoolwork. In Elsiande, where he was from in the south, he hadn't been big on book work, especially when he'd been playing Dragon Eggs. The endless rolls of parchment set him to ranting. But it was Noda that Kerrigan worried the most about. She was homesick—though she wouldn't admit it—and the constant pace was running her ragged. Her cuticles were stripped raw and her nails bitten to the quick.

Kerrigan wasn't sure where she fit with the rest of them. The bond was fake, and she was terrified to be kicked out. She hadn't even had time to go to the few other protests the RFA had put together these last couple weeks. She wasn't sleeping, but that wasn't unusual. Nor were the nightmares. She was hyperfocused on not getting kicked out.

Gemina soared back into the arena then, and all five of them took off at a run. Kerrigan had no *clue* which direction Tieran was in. She had to get close enough that he could speak into her mind. Surely, he was shouting to let her know wherever he was.

Fordham was going to finish first. That was obvious. Once he was out of the arena, he set off at a run toward the South River. Netta must have been across the water. But the rest of the pack slowed once on the other side of the arena walls. They didn't exactly travel together, but Kerrigan figured that each dragon had been sent in a different direction, and maybe process of elimination could get her to Tieran.

"This is insane," Roake grumbled. "I can't feel anything."

"Just keep trying," Noda said.

"We'll get there," Audria agreed. Her face was pale. Despite being top of the class in studies, she was worst after Kerrigan on dragon bonding. She couldn't work extra hard to make it happen.

"I think I'm west," Noda said with an uncertain look. "I'm going to head in that direction."

She jogged off, leaving the other three to contemplate the rest of the directions.

"Do you think they put the dragons all in different places? Or is Alura tricking us?" Roake asked.

"It's a test. Not a trick. She wants us to succeed," Audria said.

Roake looked at Kerrigan behind Audria's back in disbelief. She didn't know what she thought about Alura, but she at least seemed fair. Strict but fair.

"I'm going to try north, I guess," Roake said. "See if I can feel anything from Luxor."

Audria waved him off as he started jogging north. "She knows we're bottom of the class in bonding." She winced. "Sorry."

"No. It's true," Kerrigan agreed.

"Maybe she put our dragons closest and Fordham's farthest."

"Maybe. Worth a try."

Audria and Kerrigan headed east around Draco Mountain and down the Row. They jogged for about an hour before Audria gasped.

"I feel it!"

"Which direction?"

She pointed northeast. "I can't believe I can feel it. I thought that for sure, I would never be able to pass this test." She looked so relieved. "Good luck with yours, Kerrigan."

Kerrigan watched her go with deep regret. What was she going to do now? East was the most likely direction, but she didn't know if Roake's dragon was actually north, which could mean that she spent all this time heading in the wrong direction, only to find Tieran had gone north.

Indecision bit at her, but logically, she decided east was the simplest answer. There was no bond to tug on, and she had to follow her gut. It had served her well in the past.

She jogged east for an hour until she felt like her lungs were going to explode. She was stranded in the middle of nowhere in the mountains outside of the city with only her magic. She'd passed a few traveling tourists, here to see the city as it bloomed in the fall. The trees all changed almost at once from vibrant green to a myriad of orange, yellow, and red. The leaves fell in a heap right before winter, leaving it all bare. But right now, it was stunning as the first wisps of cold came down off of the mountains.

Kerrigan was a summer child at heart, but she always enjoyed the cooler temperatures for a few days until the snow hit. Then, she'd rather huddle inside and never leave until spring revealed itself once more.

Right now, she couldn't even be thankful for the cooler weather. She needed to find her dragon.

Three more hours passed in the blink of an eye. She'd missed the lunch deadline. She was lost. She had no dragon. She didn't care who heard; she screamed at the top of her lungs. All of this, only to fail their first bonding test. How in the gods' names was she supposed to survive this?

Just when she was ready to give up and turn back around, she heard a small voice in her head. *Kerrigan?*

"Oh, thank the gods!" she cried. "Tieran!"

A dragon flew into view, landing in a meadow near her. She dashed through the trees and straight to him.

*I've been circling the area for hours, looking for you,* Tieran said.

"Same," she said. She actually hugged him as hard as she could. "I am so glad I found you. Where were you?"

*A half hour on foot south of here.*

"I never would have found you," she groaned.

*No. I think this proves that. And the next test, they'll drop you off, and I am supposed to find you.* He sounded dubious. *How will we not fail as miserably next time?*

Kerrigan didn't have an answer to that as she climbed onto his back and he shot into the air, heading back toward the mountain.

"Maybe we should plan a place to meet. One in the north and one in the south, just in case. As soon as I'm dropped off, I'll run to the meetup spot."

*What if you're hours away?*

She huffed, too tired to argue. "Do you have a better idea?"

He was silent a full minute before conceding, *I do not.*

So, they made their plan. They picked the locations that both of them knew and agreed to meet up. She didn't know if it would even work, but at least they had a game plan.

They landed back in the arena, and Alura awaited with her arms crossed.

"What happened?" she demanded.

Kerrigan shook her head. "It's the distance. I can't find the bond that far away."

"That shouldn't be possible. You've been working on it for months."

"Maybe I'm blocked," she said.

"Blocked? No, that's in your head," Alura assured her. "You simply aren't trying hard enough." Her eyes shifted to the horizon. "It's too late to set you up for the next test."

"What?" Kerrigan gasped.

"If it took you this long for the first one, you could be out into the evening for the next one. Light is fading sooner now."

"What does that mean then?"

She frowned. "That I cannot pass you to the next level of training."

Kerrigan gasped. "Are you kicking me out?"

Alura considered it and then shook her head. "No. We'll have to have a makeup for the second part."

"A makeup," Kerrigan breathed. "When?"

"Monday. It's a holiday weekend," Alura reminded her. "I won't keep you from the Night of the Dead celebrations in the city. Plus, I am to return to Venatrix this weekend for the Season event and the market opening. You and Tieran will have to make up the second test then. But if you don't pass, then you're out."

Kerrigan gulped and nodded. "I understand."

Tieran looked at her bleakly. *We're screwed.*

And he wasn't wrong.

# CHAPTER 29
## The Night of the Dead

**K**errigan didn't participate in any of the Night of the Dead festivities. She and Tieran spent all weekend flying around and scoping out locations to figure out how to beat this test on Monday. There was no other option. They ended up with a half-dozen places to meet all around the city perimeter. If she didn't send them near those, then Kerrigan didn't know what to do. It was the only shot they had.

Her friends tried to pull her out for the street festival the day before her exam. They wanted her to get her mind off of the test, but even if she wanted to go out, she couldn't. She had plans with Mistress Zahina.

Helly had sent word to meet Zina in the aerie at nightfall, wearing all black. Kerrigan arrived right on time to find Zina in her black robes, her graying hair tied back and her face distant. A dragon nearly the size of Gelryn waited nearby with milky eyes and scratches down its neck and back.

Kerrigan swallowed as she approached the pair. "Mistress Zahina."

"Zina, dear, is fine. Don't let Vox scare you. He's really a very sweet creature. He did his duty and now spends his days as he wishes, as I did until Helly called me back."

"Hello, Vox," Kerrigan said, bowing deeply to the ancient dragon.

*Kerrigan, it is a great pleasure to make your acquaintance. The stars speak your name.*

Kerrigan rose and stared in confusion. "The stars?"

"Don't listen to him either. He fancies himself an astrologer."

Vox nosed her. *I study the stars, and they speak plainly about so little. Do not diminish the ones that they highlight. It is why you heeded your apprentice's summons.*

"Apprentice?" Kerrigan asked in surprise.

"Yes, yes, I taught Helly. She's a handful and a half, isn't she?"

Kerrigan didn't know what to say to that. Helly was having her own master teach Kerrigan. It must have taken a great deal to get Zina back here. No matter what Vox had said about the stars.

"Anyway, we should go, dear," Zina said.

She climbed onto Vox's back with ease, and Kerrigan followed her without question. To ride such a dragon was a great privilege. Many people didn't even like to carry guests on their dragon's back. They weren't pack mules after all. They were sentient beings.

Kerrigan didn't ask where they were going. It didn't really matter after all. She needed to learn to control her spirit magic or else the spiritcasting would consume her. She hadn't had a prophetic vision since the tournament, but they used to wait years between visions. The only thing she'd seen at all lately was Mei putting up the barrier, and she didn't know how much of that was her connection to the wall. Either way, she wanted to stay sane.

Vox didn't fly far before landing in an open lane inside the city. No one even seemed to care that a dragon had landed on the road. A giant at that. But that was the way of Kinkadia. Dragons were as common as horses.

Kerrigan slid off of Vox's back and then balked when she saw where the dragon had brought them. "Black House?" she gasped, whirling on Zina.

"Yes, yes, I know the stories people tell of the place. It's abandoned, haunted, a home for orphans who were drowned." She waved her hand, hauling a large bag onto her shoulder. "All that. It is still the best place to practice on this night."

Kerrigan shuddered, remembering the last time she'd stepped into Black House. She'd been with Fordham, investigating the weapons that Basem Nix was selling with illegal magical artifacts. Her spirit magic was erratic, and the spirits of the dead swarmed her. Fordham didn't feel a thing, and Kerrigan was overwhelmed with their presence. And that had been in the middle of the summer. Not on the actual Night of the Dead.

"Come, girl. Nothing is going to reach you with me beside you," Zina said.

A healthy lot of Fae children prowled around the house, stepping close to it and then screaming at some bump in the night. It was tradition to try to touch the door to prove your mettle to your friends.

Everyone gaped as Zina strode right past the entire lot, up the stairs, and yanked the door open without even a backward glance. The kids all screamed and ran away. Kerrigan bit her lip, her stomach twisting, but she didn't want Zina to look back for her. It was just a house. A haunted house on the Night of the Dead. But just a house. How many times could she say it to convince herself?

She pushed her shoulders back and strode inside after Zina. The house was musty with signs of disuse everywhere. The old staircase was rickety with missing boards. Cobwebs littered the corners. Dust covered the creaky hardwood floor. The Red Masks had been using the abandoned house to store weapons, so it hadn't been entirely abandoned, but it looked worse than the last time she'd been in here.

"Help me with this," Zina said.

She dropped her bag onto the ground, and Kerrigan helped her extract a few dozen candles from inside. Zina directed her to put them in a circle large enough for them both to sit in. Even before she was finished, Kerrigan could feel the house come alive.

She closed her eyes as she felt the brush of little fingers on her hair. She shuddered.

"Leave her be," Zina commanded. "She's here with me."

"You know the spirits?"

"Know them? No. No one can really know the spirits that still inhabit this land, but I can feel them, and they've come to respect my presence. They're not used to you. They're inquisitive. The circle will keep them at bay."

Kerrigan gulped and hurriedly put the rest of the candles in the circle. Zina settled into a seated cross-legged position and gestured for Kerrigan to sit, facing her, which she did.

"Now, light the candles," Zina said.

Kerrigan didn't even have to snap her fingers anymore, and flames burst from all of the candles at once. Her fire training had really taken off. She'd never had this level of control.

"Dimmer," Zina said. Kerrigan put her hand down, and all the candles burned low so only their faces were illuminated in the space. "Better."

Zina put her hands on her knees, palms up, and closed her eyes. Kerrigan mirrored the position and waited for something to happen. When nothing did, she opened her eyes and looked around the haunted house.

"Not a fan of meditating?" Zina asked.

"I don't dislike it. It's hard to forget where I'm at though."

"That seems reasonable." Her eyes opened to stare at Kerrigan. "Today, we're going to work on guiding you into the spirit plane. Helly said that you've done it before with Gelryn, but it came with risks. I want you to very easily be able to flow between the two."

"Okay."

"But it's not easy, even for me, and I've been doing it for nearly a thousand years," Zina informed her. "The spirit is the realm of the dragons. The bond should link you deeper into the spiritual world, but because we each have spirit magic of our own, we can cross without them. Though that bond is a useful tether. We can reach for it and pull ourselves back out."

Kerrigan flushed in the dying light. Even here, that stupid bond was ruining everything. "I understand."

"You don't understand anything," Zina chided. "You just wait. The reason that I wanted to do this on the Night of the Dead is because crossing the spiritual plane is easiest at those times when we're closest to that liminal space. The summer and winter solstice, the Night of the Dead, midnight of the full moon, for instance. Witching hour is a good place to begin practicing on your own.

"First, take my hands."

Kerrigan scooted closer and reached for Zina's hands. They were cold to the touch, and Kerrigan realized that she could see her breath fog up in the house. It wasn't even that cold outside. Perhaps Zina had been doing something other than meditating.

"Now, close your eyes and reach down past your other magic to the center of yourself. Grasp on to the seam of your spirit magic, and I'm going to guide you into the spiritual plane once you have ahold of it."

Kerrigan did as instructed. She found her spirit magic much quicker than when she'd had to find it for her air-magic test. It came to her almost giddy with excitement. That must have been the liminal space. It never hit this easily.

"I have it," she told her.

Then, Zina had connected them, and the world disappeared all around them. They shot out of their bodies and up into the spiritual plane. They were still within Black House. In fact, she felt almost trapped within the bounds.

"You won't be able to leave. That is another reason for choosing this space. It already contains so many spirits that its purpose has shifted to containment, and I didn't want us to get too far away," Zina told her.

Kerrigan looked down at her body, just a wisp of what she had been down below. "I can't believe I did it."

"I did it," Zina corrected her. "But we will get you there. The important point is that you should feel safe in these confines. The last time you did this with Gelryn, you were out of control, and I want a safe learning environment. Now, we're going to push back down into our bodies and let you try."

Kerrigan nodded, and before she finished doing so, she was rushed back to the surface. She blinked awake in shock. "Whoa."

"Your turn."

She gulped and then reached back for her spirit magic. It jumped to her as if it had a life force of its own. She didn't know what she was doing, but she fumbled for Zina as well. Nothing happened the first few times as she slipped around her teacher. Then, with a jump of force, she jerked them both upward.

"Slow down," Zina commanded.

Kerrigan stopped and found them a floor up. She'd pulled them straight through the floorboards and nearly out of the house. Something Zina had said was impossible.

"That wasn't too bad. How did it feel?"

"Good," Kerrigan admitted. It had felt powerful. Like she had been meant for this.

"Excellent. Now, put us back."

That was harder. Her magic didn't want to release. It was so happy to be flexed that the return took a full half hour before it relaxed enough to let them soar back through the floor and into their bodies.

Kerrigan didn't even feel tired. Normally, spirit magic of any kind drained her reserves. Visions made her pass out. The Night of the Dead must have had such a profound impact that it wasn't even hurting her. No wonder Zina had waited.

They did it a dozen more times. Each one with more accuracy and control. It was still hard to pull herself back into her body, but by the final time, she was doing it in a matter of minutes.

Zina nodded at her once. "Good. That will be all for tonight. We'll meet back at the winter solstice."

"Wait," Kerrigan gasped, grasping her hands harder. "Please. I'm not ready. This is so necessary."

"I don't want to drain you, dear."

"I'm not. I feel like it's refilling my magic rather than draining it. I've never felt anything like it."

Zina considered. "I am being drained."

Kerrigan startled. She hadn't even realized. Zina did look wan, as if the life were being sucked out of her.

"Using too much all at once drags on you. It's why I only use my spirit magic in bursts throughout the classroom. Plus, I have trained it for hundreds of years to obey me." Zina tilted her head. "But you do not look drained, as you said."

A flush came to her cheeks. She honestly felt like she was glowing. Everything was heady and exciting. So close to the surface. Like she could reach out and grasp what had been claiming her for so long.

"We'll try one more thing. Though I will not participate. I will guide you through it."

Kerrigan breathed a sigh of relief. "Thank you."

"Close your eyes."

Kerrigan did as she had been told.

"Grasp your spirit magic and feel for the plane. Pull yourself into it but do not go far."

She exited her body onto the plane with wide-eyed excitement. It was the first time that she'd ever been here by herself. First with Gelryn for her test to get into the tournament. Second with Fordham as they'd crossed Alandria by the help of a raven. And then finally, with Zina tonight. But this was the first time she was in complete control to do as she pleased.

Zina was still speaking, and Kerrigan could hear her as if she were underwater. "I want you to feel the spirits all around you. Each one has a unique signature. You also have that unique signature. I have one as well. You should be able to feel the shape of each person and locate them by that signature. You have surely felt mine since we have been on the plane together."

Kerrigan realized that she had without even knowing it. Zina felt like the first freeze in the mountains and the smell of purple wildflowers that grew on the northern side of the mountain. If she concentrated, she could feel the other spirits in Black House. They all left her alone. She was in control on this plane, and even though they were residents, they had no body to return to. But each had their own smell and feel and sense. It was like a stamp of who they had once been.

"I want you to stretch as far away from me as the house permits. Then, I want you to find my signature and pull me into the spirit plane from a distance."

Kerrigan frowned at that thought. She could tug Zina in when she was touching her, but could she do it from across the house? How was that even possible?

"I can still sense you. Go," Zina told her.

So, Kerrigan left her teacher behind and found the farthest corner of the house. She closed her eyes and concentrated on Zina's signature. The frost that hit so hard and beautiful. And those purple flowers that bloomed right after the first snow, as if they only came out of adversity.

She gasped as she felt her, even two stories away. She tugged on the signature and pulled.

Zina came into the spirit plane with ease. But something else reached for her. Kerrigan gasped. Her eyes flying open. She'd never felt another presence in the spirit plane like this. They were supposed to be safe in the circle, contained in this house.

"Kerrigan?" Zina called, concern in her voice.

Then, something touched her hand, and she disappeared from Black House.

# CHAPTER 30
## *The Camp*

Mei tramped through a dirty war camp. She was in mud up to her ankles and wanted nothing more than to rid herself of this place. Nothing had gone as planned. No one would listen. Ten long years, they'd been at war with no end in sight until tonight. Tonight, the war could end.

She brushed a hand back through her hair. She wouldn't even be here if it wasn't for her daughter. She had joined up like the rest of the youth who thought they could make a difference and had no idea of what war was actually like. So self-righteous and certain that they were going to change the world.

Fae should have been slow to go to war and quick to retreat. The long lives afforded them space to see reason. But no one would see reason.

The tent flap shoved open before Mei could do so. Her daughter stepped out. They were nearly the same height with the same black hair and dark brown eyes. She had none of her father in her. Only twenty turns of the sun and dragon bound. How had she failed her so completely?

"What do you want, Mother?" her daughter sneered.

"You know why I'm here."

*"I won't go with you. You're a coward."*

*Mei winced. The words hit hard despite the youth in them.*

*"You have no idea what you speak of."*

*"I'm here to help us win this war against those barbarians. What are you doing, Mother?"*

*Mei clenched her hands into fists. "Please, come with me."*

*"Where? Where are you running off to? How dare you run away from your obligation to the Society."*

*"I have no obligation to the Society," she snarled. "The Society only cares for itself."*

*Her daughter took a step backward. "You include me in that assessment."*

*"Yes," she bit out.*

*"Then we're done. Trulian will never leave either. How does he not see you for what you are?"*

*"Your father has nothing to do with this."*

*Her daughter narrowed her eyes. "He is not my father."*

*"We don't have to go through this again."*

*"I have no parents."*

*"Please," Mei whispered, broken.*

*She knew what she had to do. She had to go to Cavour. She had to put up the wall that would end this war. She didn't know what would happen when she did it, if it was even possible. But she knew what would happen if she didn't try.*

*She had seen it.*

*Everyone would die.*

*"Please," she repeated.*

*"Good-bye, Mother." The girl turned away from her and flipped the tent flap back open.*

*"Zahina, please ..."*

*But she was already gone.*

*And Mei had to save the world.*

***

Kerrigan jolted back into her body full force. She rocketed forward, pushing Zina over and breaking their protective circle. The spirits zoomed in all around them. The wind picked up, and the spirits grabbed at both of them. The energy was so erratic that Kerrigan couldn't help the scream that ripped from her throat.

Zina jumped to her feet and threw her hands out. "Cease."

The spirits popped out of the space, leaving everything suddenly empty. She smothered the skittering flames and spilled candle wax before turning back to Kerrigan, who was huddled on the floor in a ball, shaking.

"What happened?" Zina asked, calm but firm.

"I don't know." She squeezed her eyes shut.

"One minute, you pulled me into the spirit world, and the next minute, you disappeared."

"I was... I was pulled into a vision."

Zina sat back on her heels. "A vision? Have you had one before?"

Kerrigan nodded.

"Helly didn't tell me."

"She's been protecting me," Kerrigan said, slowly coming up to a sitting position. She wiped the stray tears from her cheeks. "I've had a few visions of the future in the last couple years."

"Harbinger," Zina whispered.

"That's what Gelryn said. And recently, I had visions of the past."

"What have you seen?"

Kerrigan closed her eyes and took a deep breath. "I saw your mother."

Because it was clear that was what she had witnessed. The night that Mei had put up the magical barrier around the House of Shadows, she had gone to her daughter. A daughter named Zahina with black hair and dark brown eyes. The woman sitting right before her.

"My mother?" Zahina whispered, coming back to a seated position.

"Mei."

Zina exhaled. "I haven't heard that name in a thousand years."

"I saw you arguing in a war camp during the Great War. She asked you to leave."

Zina held up her hand. A tear welled in her eye. "I have relived that night more times than I care to recount. She disappeared that night. The Society… they said she was killed in the war. But I know my mother… and she was already leaving."

"She put up the magical barrier around the House of Shadows."

Zina's head snapped up. "What?"

"She left that night with Trulian and put up the barrier. It was the first vision I saw. When I went to the House of Shadows before I began training, I connected with the wall, and it showed me Mei doing it, but I had no idea who she was. I've been researching it."

Zina came to her feet again. "My mother had spirit magic but not… she couldn't have done that alone."

"I believe she was like me," Kerrigan said. "You didn't know that she was a spiritcaster?"

Zina's eyes shot to her. "What did you say?"

"She was a spiritcaster."

"No. I haven't heard that word in a long time either. She would have told me. She wouldn't have kept it from me." Zina looked frazzled.

"Someone went to great lengths to keep what she did from you and the public."

Zina paced the room. "That bastard!" she snarled. "I need to go."

"Wait, go?" Kerrigan asked, jumping up after her.

"There are things I need answers to."

"But I thought you were training me."

"This is as far as we go," Zina said dismissively as she headed for the door. "If what you said is true, then I can't help you any more than I have. You will need a spiritcaster trainer."

"But your mom was the last spiritcaster in Alandria!"

"Then look beyond Alandria," Zina said at the door.

Kerrigan balked. She'd never considered that as an option, but she didn't even know how to find someone like that. She couldn't exactly leave training. Zina had been her one hope to figure this out.

"Where are you going?"

"To get answers," Zina said.

Zina bundled up their supplies and rushed out of the house. Kerrigan followed her in a huff. Vox appeared in the street, and they were airborne in an instant. Kerrigan would give anything to call Tieran right now and have him sweep her away from this moment. She was shaking from exhaustion. The vision had snapped it all out of her, and the last thing she wanted was to wander through the streets of Kinkadia at night alone.

A thought hit her as she huddled against the side of Black House. Zina had taught her that every person had their own signature and she could draw them into the spirit world. Dragons had dominion over the spiritual, which meant Tieran could be pulled in. Her idea bloomed bright, forming in her mind, giving her a way to fix what was broken.

Kerrigan was drained from the vision, but she had enough energy to drop back into the spirit plane one more time. She sat on the mossy ground with her back to Black House, closed her eyes, and pulled herself out. She had no idea of Tieran's signature. But she *knew* Tieran now. She knew the heat of his breath on her neck. The sarcastic tone he used when she said basically anything to him. The relief in his body when she'd found him that day in the mountains. The smile he sometimes shot her when they succeeded in duping Alura. The feel of his warm body beneath hers as they soared around the arena. The gentle pressure of him speaking in her mind. Tieran belonged to her in a way that had nothing to do with the bond.

And so she reached out with her spirit magic for the essence of him. She had no idea where he was. Did the dragons stay in for the Night of the Dead? Or did they go out? She couldn't remember.

It didn't matter. All that mattered was that she needed him. And there was no bond to connect with.

She didn't know how long she sat there, reaching out for him in the spirit plane. It could have been hours or minutes, but time ran differently on the plane. Finally, she smelled baking cinnamon and hearth fire. The scent and warmth curled around her. Familiar. It knew her.

With just a brush, she eased against that signature and drew Tieran into the spiritual plane.

The dragon looked at her in astonishment. *Kerrigan?*

She breathed a sigh of relief. "Tieran, I need you."

*How have you accomplished this?*

"Surprise. I have spirit magic."

His golden eyes blinked at her slowly. *And you were able to find me in the spirit plane?*

"I was working with Zina tonight, and she mentioned that every person has their own signature. I thought about what I know of you and searched for that signature. I'm at Black House, and I don't feel safe walking home. Can you get me?"

*You know what this means, don't you?* He grinned devilishly.

She smiled at him in that liminal space, relief flickering between them. "We're going to pass our bonding test tomorrow."

# CHAPTER 31
## *The Celebration*

Alura was baffled.

And it was glorious.

"You pass," Alura said. She shook her head. The little metal beads she'd braided into her hair clacking against each other. "I don't know what you did over the weekend, but you pass."

Kerrigan grinned from ear to ear.

Alura had dropped Kerrigan off at a spot an hour outside of the city and said to call her dragon to her. She moved into the spirit plane and spent the next hour stretching herself to locate the smell of cinnamon and that feel of hearth fire. She told Tieran her location and he'd flown right to her. They'd beaten everyone's time except Fordham. They might have done it, too, if she hadn't still been learning how to find him on the spirit plane. This would work.

"Thank you, sir."

Tieran bowed his head low. *Mistress Alura.*

"Go. Both of you. Kerrigan, the air lesson has been moved to the top northern aerie. Mistress Zahina left for urgent business, and you'll be working with Master Carr instead."

"Of course."

Urgent business. Which basically meant she was missing and no one knew where she was. Kerrigan knew why, but she wasn't about to reveal that information. She had no idea what had made Zina fly off into the distance and not look back. Her mother had been dead for a thousand years. How could she learn more about it now, except through Kerrigan's visions?

Kerrigan left the arena and found Helly waiting for her on the sidelines. She applauded. "Well done."

Kerrigan beamed. "Thanks. What are you doing out here?"

"I heard that you were having trouble, and I wanted to watch for myself instead of waiting for word."

"Oh," Kerrigan said faintly. "Well, I passed."

"Good. I'm so proud of you." Helly gestured for her to walk as they headed back up the hill toward the mountain. "I did want to ask you about Zina. I have reports that she left Kinkadia altogether. Weren't you training with her last night?"

"Yes. I had a vision while we were together," Kerrigan confessed.

"Really?" Helly asked. "I hadn't told her that you had visions. Just spirit magic. It must have been a shock."

"Yes. I, uh, saw her mother."

Helly stopped, her eyes wide. "A vision of the past? Because Zina's mother is long dead."

"Yes, it was in the Great War when Zahina had just joined the Society. They argued, and then Mei left. It was the last time she saw her. She said, 'That bastard,' and then just left. Left me there."

"Gods," Helly whispered. "What a mess. Well, at least that explains why she vanished. Thank you for the insight. And if you have any more of these visions, let me know."

Kerrigan nodded. She felt guilty that she hadn't told Helly about the one about Mei putting up the wall. But her gut told her that she wasn't ready to let anyone know that she might have the ability to take it down.

Kerrigan waved good-bye and then hurried to her afternoon lesson. Her friends actually cheered when she walked back into the room.

"You did it!" Audria cried, throwing her arms around Kerrigan.

"I did. We figured it out. I really must have been blocked."

"I'm glad you passed," Fordham said.

"Wouldn't be the same without you," Roake said with an eye roll.

She laughed and settled into her seat for history. While Movanna rattled on about the foundation of the Society, Kerrigan scribbled out a note to Fordham and dropped it onto his desk.

*RFA event tonight, princeling. Join me?*

He secretly glanced over at her and then opened the note. He scratched something out, scribbled a note, and then passed it back to her.

He'd scratched through *princeling*. She almost snorted.

*Someone has to keep you in line.*

She grinned down at the paper. Her toes curled as she imagined him keeping her in line. She was so relieved to not be kicked out of the program that she might even do something crazy and kiss Fordham Ollivier tonight. Might be stupid. Might be worth it. Only tonight would tell.

\*\*\*

"Do I look ready for subterfuge?" Fordham asked when Kerrigan opened her bedroom door.

Her breath caught at the sight of him in all black silk. His black hair loose and tumbling into those ever-changing eyes. A half-smile on his sensuous mouth. His body so big and tall that he took up her entire doorway. He towered over her, and she loved it.

"You look ready for a ball," she teased.

His smile dropped. "Our last one was quite eventful, wasn't it?"

Despite sharing the library space frequently over the last months, they'd never brought up her betrothal to March again. She didn't want it to be real. She hoped her father had figured out a way to break it. Because she had no intention of marrying that man even if he had changed into the upstanding gentleman that he appeared to be. The only gentleman she wanted was the sinister and domineering one in front of her.

"It was," she said. "Let's not repeat that night, okay?"

He nodded. "I'd like that."

"Then let's get going."

She veered left instead of right, and he fell into step beside her.

"This feels like old times. Sneaking out of the mountain to get in trouble."

"No trouble tonight," she said with a wink. "Just trying to make people like me as important as people like you."

"You already are."

She hid her blush by ducking into the secret passage that led out of the mountain. Valia had shown it to her during the tournament. It was shocking that someone knew this mountain better than Kerrigan did.

They exited out of an old wooden door and slid it back into hiding before heading out onto the streets of Kinkadia. Fordham still had a bit of wonder to his expression when he gazed around the city. After having gone into the depths of the Dark Court, she understood his awe. He'd spent countless years trapped inside a mountain with hardly any space to wander. Just enough for a small village stuck in time and a war field soaked with blood. Nothing like the vibrant, industrious city that Kerrigan called home.

They headed to the Square, where the protest was to begin, and found Hadrian's blue hair as a beacon near an erected stage. Already, hundreds of humans, half-Fae, and Fae congregated in front of it.

"Hey," Kerrigan said, grabbing Hadrian's arm to get his attention.

Kerrigan had her hood up, so he jolted when he found her standing there.

"Gods, Kerrigan, you scared me."

"Sorry. You with Clover?"

His gaze swept to the stage. "She went around to speak with Thea. Can you believe the number of people here?"

"It's much bigger than the last one," she agreed.

Hadrian nodded at Fordham. Fordham nodded back. Boys.

"Are you going to speak?" Hadrian asked.

She shook her head. "I can't be seen. I'm on thin ice as it is in the program."

"But they need you."

"Look at this place. The Square is full. They don't need me."

"If you say so."

She'd done her part. She'd helped to energize the RFA when they were getting the protests off the ground. She didn't need to be up there on that stage now. It was enough.

"How's Darby's Season? I haven't heard from her much."

"Good, I think," Hadrian said. "She was in the east for the Venatrix Night of the Dead event. So, she's been out of the city all week." He shrugged. "It was a whole thing that Lady Sonali insisted on."

"Is she... courting someone?"

"Not that I know of. Not yet. Lots of interested parties," he grumbled. "Not that Darby seems excited about any of them."

"Yeah. How could she be?"

"Why is she putting up with this?" Fordham asked. "Forgive me, I don't understand this courting ritual."

"She feels obligated," Hadrian said. "As a lady of the Bryonican court, it's part of her duty. She loves the parties and dancing."

"She wants to do it," Kerrigan said. "Even if we all think it's ridiculous, we will respect her wishes until she says otherwise."

Fordham made a noncommittal noise.

That was about what Kerrigan thought of it too. But Darby had made herself clear. So, that was what they'd do.

Clover appeared then, and they all dropped the topic immediately. No reason to bring it up with Clover around. She'd been depressed enough.

"Oh, Kerrigan, you're here!" Clover grinned widely. "I'm so excited. Look at the crowd!"

"It's amazing," Kerrigan said. "I can't believe there are so many people."

"All thanks to you!"

Kerrigan laughed. "No way. This is the movement. I was just a small part of it."

"Give yourself some credit," Hadrian said with a smile.

"Surprised you brought him along," Clover said. She glanced at Fordham. "Prince."

"Clove."

"Fordham is here to support us."

Clover shrugged. "I'm into it, but a lot of other people will be hesitant."

"I am not a representative of my people," Fordham said formally.

"Yeah, I know you're into my girl," Clover said with a mischievous grin. Kerrigan smacked her arm. "Anyway, Thea was wondering if you'd speak."

Kerrigan frowned. "I can't."

"I told her as much but thought I'd ask. Will you come back and say hi at least?"

"Can Fordham come too?"

Clover worried at her lip. "Someone is going to be upset with me, but why not?"

Hadrian waved them off, promising to stay there until they returned.

Then, the three of them ducked behind the stage. Thea stood proud and tall with the rest of the leaders of RFA behind her. Her bald head was on display today. No hat or headscarf in sight. She looked ready to take on the world.

Her eyes lit with excitement and then flitted behind Kerrigan and found Fordham. They rounded wide, like it was the last person she'd expected to see.

"Thea," Kerrigan said brightly, "I'd like to introduce you to Prince Fordham Ollivier."

"It's a pleasure, ma'am," Fordham said, bowing low for her.

Thea's eyebrows shot up in surprise. A prince of a Fae kingdom known for detesting humans and half-Fae was *bowing* to a half-Fae woman. It was a sight to behold.

"Well, I can't say I'm not surprised to see you here."

"Fordham asked to join us," Kerrigan said.

"I can speak for myself," he said, holding his hand out to stall Kerrigan. "My people are known for their prejudice. I can say that I was one of those people, but I have come to find out how wrong I was. I would like to apologize for my previous actions and do what I can to help."

Thea's smile warmed, the longer he spoke. "Well, we can always use an extra set of hands."

"I suppose we're just letting anyone in now," Dozan said, striding out of the fog of people to square off with Fordham.

Fordham immediately went on high alert. She could practically breathe in the scent of his magic, and she wasn't even in the spirit plane. He just radiated that same threatening energy. Dozan brought it out in him. Dozan brought it out in everyone.

"It appears so," Fordham said coolly.

Thea laughed. "I see you've already met Mr. Rook."

"We're acquainted."

The hatred was mutual. No matter that they'd had to work together during the tournament to save her life, it didn't change how they felt about each other.

"Let's not do this today," Kerrigan said.

"This isn't exactly the place for Fae nobility," Dozan said.

"*I'm* Fae nobility," Kerrigan snapped. "As you continually remind me."

"It's different."

"It is," Fordham agreed. "I was raised to it, and she managed to escape the worst of it. She's much better than I'll ever be."

Dozan blinked slowly, as if almost in surprise. "You're not wrong."

"Oh, look, you can get along," Clover quipped. "Now, can we get this thing started?"

"You're sure that you won't speak?" Thea asked Kerrigan.

She shook her head. "I don't want to risk it."

Thea sighed and nodded. "All right. I'll get up there. Wish me luck."

"You don't need it," Clover told her.

Thea strode onto the stage, calling for silence from the ever-growing crowd. Kerrigan stood between Fordham and Dozan, her skin prickling as they both weighed on her in that moment. The boy she'd always wanted but given up and the boy she never should have wanted, who had given her up. Too complicated to be this close to them.

And Dozan, as always, pushed his luck. He drew even closer, ignoring the glare from Fordham. His lips nearly pressed to her ear. "Any luck inside the mountain finding the killer?"

She gulped as his breath tingled down her neck. She shook her head. "Suspects in the Society are being followed, but I don't know who they are."

"What if I said I did?" His hand trailed down her arm, and she stiffened. "What would you give me for that information?"

"Dozan, stop it," she growled.

He laughed, and Fordham's hand shot out, grasping Dozan's arm at the wrist. "The lady said stop."

Dozan looked ready to throw a punch. That wouldn't end well.

She pulled them apart. "Both of you stop." Kerrigan faced Dozan. "Who is being followed?"

"As far as I can tell, only one Society member is any longer."

She waited, crossing her arms over her chest. "Tell me."

"You're no fun," he teased.

"Dozan," she snapped.

"The only person still being followed in relation to the murder is Lorian Van Horn."

# CHAPTER 32

## The Suspect

"Lorian? A Red Mask?" she whispered.

Fordham shot her a look of alarm. "Are you sure?"

Dozan ignored him. "That's what the little birdies in the mountain tell me."

"But… he's on the council," Fordham said.

Kerrigan's head buzzed with that information. Lorian Van Horn was being watched as a suspect for the murder of Basem Nix. The only one still being watched by Helly's spies. Did that make him a Red Mask? Did that make him the leader?

She remembered every interaction she'd had with him. Every single one had been unpleasant. He was the one who refused her a spot in the Society. He tried to get her kicked out of the program. He sent his best fighter after her on her testing. He told her countless times that she was worthless and her kind didn't belong. Why hadn't she seen it for what it was before? She had just assumed him a bigot, an annoyance.

But all the warnings were there. Bastian had told her not to let Lorian find out that she was here. Helly had stood up for her time and time again against him. She had just been too tired to put the pieces together.

"It's Lorian," she said. "It all makes sense."

"We cannot accuse him without evidence," Fordham said hastily.

"Then we get evidence."

Dozan nodded. "I'm working on it."

"Good."

She would do the same. If Lorian wasn't the killer, then she would find out who had done it. But it was the only suspect they had, and it would be sweet justice to see him put away by her.

Before they could say anything more, Thea had whipped the crowd up into a frenzy, and the march was beginning.

Dozan grasped her hand once more before she could be pulled away by the crowd. "Be careful."

"Not really in my repertoire."

"They tried to kill you once."

"Aww, Dozan, is this sentiment?"

His amber eyes gleamed. "You know how I feel about protecting my investments."

She rolled her eyes. "I can take care of myself."

She snatched her hand away and hurried after Clover and Fordham. He was no more than two steps ahead of her, waiting.

"What did he want?"

"Nothing. He's just Dozan."

"Why do you put up with him?" he asked.

"I don't really believe you're in a position to judge my actions or associates."

"That's not what I mean."

Kerrigan whirled on him. She'd wanted today to be celebratory. For her and Fordham to reconcile. To even sneak that kiss in, but now, it was clear that wasn't happening. No matter how jealous and defensive he acted around

Dozan, it didn't change anything.

"Then what do you mean? Because last I checked, you made your stance perfectly clear."

He froze at her words. "You're right. I did."

"Good. Then, if I want to *associate* with Dozan," she said, letting the insinuation in the words linger, "you have no right to say anything."

His thunderstorm eyes swirled at the words. As if the thought sent him reeling. Like he'd expected her to wait and pine for him. Which she was—not that she'd admit it. But let him get a taste of how she was feeling all this time.

"He's not good enough for you," Fordham couldn't keep from saying.

Kerrigan took a step forward and poked him in the chest. "Then man the fuck up."

She didn't wait for his response, just jogged up to Clover and Hadrian.

"Everything all right?" Hadrian asked.

He'd known Kerrigan for so long that he could judge her moods by a glance. She missed him so much sometimes.

"Fine," she lied. "Let's go."

They fell into step with the rest of the march. A swell of protestors chanting and yelling out for others to join them. Fordham was a step behind them. Near enough that he wouldn't lose them but far enough back that he was giving her space. She hated it. Hated the position they were in. Hated getting her hopes up that he'd change his mind, only to be reminded that he wouldn't.

She threw herself into the march. They were with so many people that no one even pointed her out in the crowd. She wasn't the only redhead in the bunch, and with the sheer numbers taking over the streets, she felt safe enough to go as herself and not hide.

"Rights for all!" Kerrigan cheered along with the crowd.

It felt good. Right.

Five years ago, the streets had filled with Red Masks. They'd killed people and destroyed property to protest their hate of a human winning the tournament. Now, those humans and half-Fae were banding together to fight for what they believed in. The Red Masks were the past. This was the future.

As the sun set on the horizon, the crowds only grew. Society Guards were posted at many of the alleys they passed. Their hands on the elemental weapons on their belts. Their eyes uninterested in what was happening, only judging each person as they passed, as if they were waiting for someone to slip up. They should have been cheering the crowds on. Not looking at them like they were the enemy.

Kerrigan had never gotten a bad vibe from the Guard. Most of them knew who she was since she'd grown up in the mountain. But here, it was as if they were altogether different Fae.

"Keep moving," one barked at her.

She narrowed her eyes at him. "We have the right to be here."

"Are you talking back to us?" the guard asked, stepping forward threateningly.

Clover put her hand on Kerrigan's shoulder. "Don't provoke them. They don't need a reason."

Kerrigan frowned and backed down. What the hell was with the power trip? It was so unnecessary. She let Clover drag her away. She wished that she'd gotten his name. It would have been good to report him to his superior, Mistress Corinna. There was no reason for that response.

"What are they doing?" Clover asked, standing on her tiptoes to look ahead. "That isn't the approved path. We're supposed to turn right here and head toward the Artisan Village."

Fordham came closer. "It looks like the Guard are herding them in the opposite direction. Using some kind of magic to force them left. What's left?"

"Row Park," Kerrigan said. "We'd never get permission to walk through the Row."

"Then why are they directing us there?" Clover asked.

None of them had an answer, and as they turned the corner, guards blocked off their retreat. Kerrigan looked back in confusion as barriers were put in place behind them. Suddenly, the march stalled, leaving the huge crowd stopped in the middle of the road, almost to Row Park.

"What are they doing?" Clover asked.

Fordham shook his head. "It's too far ahead. I can't tell."

A chill ran down Kerrigan's back. "Something's wrong."

"What?" Hadrian asked. He was straining his neck. "There's some kind of light ahead."

Fordham followed where he was looking. "Fire."

And then the screams began as the last rays of light died on the horizon, plunging them into near total darkness. People jostled all around them, but they were stuck.

Kerrigan grabbed on to Clover's hand. "Stay close."

Fordham put his chest to her back protectively. "We need to get out of here."

"Lead the way." She slid her hand into his.

He nodded and pulled the four of them through the crowd. It was slow going. Everyone was trying to escape at once, but there were no exits. They were trapped in a part of Central district with high buildings on either side. The alleys were clogged. Fordham tried to move them back the way they'd come but stalled when he saw what awaited them.

Red Masks.

Kerrigan's stomach dropped. The Guard had vanished from their posts, and in their place were men standing in all black with red masks over their faces. Or... the guards *were* Red Masks. That thought was chilling.

A loud bang exploded behind them. Screams grew to a deafening volume. And to Kerrigan's horror, she watched one of the buildings shift. Rubble rained down on the crowd. The building listed sideways and collapsed, trapping countless people.

Kerrigan gasped. "We need to help."

Another building exploded nearby. Kerrigan ducked to the ground, ash and rock falling down on her. Her eyes darted left and right as the world that she knew and the city she loved dissolved into chaos. Fear crept up her throat. She was paralyzed with inaction. All she could think and feel was that night so long ago when she'd been trapped by Red Masks. When she'd seen her life flash before her eyes and known it would be her last.

"Kerrigan!" Fordham yelled. "We have to get out of here. Help me get through the Red Masks."

She stared up at him with tears in her eyes. "How?"

"Call Tieran. I'm going to get Netta here. We can bust through them ourselves while we wait and get people out of here," he said, calm in the face of danger.

A plan. Yes, she could execute a plan. She wasn't helpless here anymore. That was in the past.

Kerrigan braced herself to slip into the spirit plane and call Tieran, but then the Red Masks lobbed black orbs into the crowd. One fell right in front of Clover and Hadrian, who had been huddled together, waiting for direction. Black smoke exploded out of the shattered orb, wrapping around Clover and Hadrian and the people nearest them.

Fordham jerked her cloak up over her face. "Don't breathe it in."

Kerrigan couldn't see anything, but she could hear the shouts as Fordham wrenched her backward, away from the smoke.

"Clover," she screamed, pulling the cloak down.

But Clover and Hadrian were gone.

Kerrigan turned in a circle, panic seizing her. "Where did they go?"

"I don't know," Fordham said. "Gods."

More buildings were coming down. Kerrigan couldn't see anything in front of her. The smoke was everywhere. More of the orbs being lobbed into the crowd and taking out the demonstrators.

"I can't reach Netta. She must be too far away. Tieran?" Fordham asked as he continued to pull her away from the smoke and toward the opening.

"No," she said. Her throat was scratchy and painful. She must have inhaled some of the smoke because, suddenly, she was coughing and couldn't seem to stop. Her eyes itched, and tears welled in them. "We need to get out of here. We need to get the others out."

"Charge the line with me," he said.

She pulled her magic to her, weak with terror, and followed behind Fordham as they approached the Red Masks at the entrance. But they must have seen them coming because one threw an orange orb into the nearest building. People screamed as it tilted sideways.

"Fordham!"

His eyes widened in fear. Then, in a second, he had his arms around her. Black smoke enveloped him. This was an altogether different feeling, like being trapped in darkness. Secure and content. One minute, the building had been falling on top of them, and the next, she was in shadow.

She dared not breathe as Fordham's magic swept them away.

# CHAPTER 33
## *The Smoke*

**CLOVER**

Clover couldn't breathe.

Smoke filled her lungs and burned her eyes and choked her throat. Everything was hazy with the substance. Fire burned in the distance, a fiery blur. Screams and screams and more screams. All around her. Coming from her.

"Clover!" Hadrian yelled next to her over the cacophony.

She coughed, trying to form words but she couldn't manage it. Her hands were starting to shake. It made no sense. She'd had a *loch* cigarette before she arrived. A nice long one that should have left her buzzing for hours. But it was as if the black smoke was filling her up and pushing all of that healing out of her. Everything that kept her from the chronic, debilitating pain.

And now, it was creeping in. First along her spine, where it always started. Then up to her neck. Just twisting in place sent a spasm through her. She wanted to vomit from it wrecking through her body.

Hadrian must have seen it on her because he grasped her arm and slung it over his shoulder. She cried out as the shoulder joined the neck and spine. Then, he carefully slid his arm around her waist and supported most of her weight.

That helped some. It took the pressure off of her back.

He was speaking, but she couldn't gather what he was saying. He started to walk, and she picked it up. He wanted her to go with him.

It had been a long time since she'd hurt this bad. In her early years, before she'd found *loch*, before her parents had dare dreamed of giving it to her, knowing she'd be addicted her entire life, pain had been a constant companion. This level of hurt would have been manageable. But now, it felt like sharp stabs of death at every step.

At least they were moving, avoiding the worst of the crowds and the rubble. There were dead bodies splattered all over the ground. Heaps of bodies. She tried not to look at faces, to remember seeing her world upside down like this once before. The dead all around her in the catacombs.

She blinked away the memory. She couldn't think of it. She couldn't think of anything but this moment. Because they'd lost Kerrigan and Fordham. No use in looking. They needed to get to safety.

Red Masks flooded through one of the open alleyways. Hadrian pressed her against the remains of an overturned building as they passed. They held their breath, not daring to move a muscle until they were gone. Clover's back seized, and she gritted her teeth to keep from groaning.

Then, they were past the worst of it, and Hadrian hurried down the alley. Their feet thundered against the rubble. Neither daring to speak. They needed to escape this horrid place. She couldn't believe the protest had dissolved into this. How had it even happened? The Society Guard were never their friend, but they were supposed to protect and serve the people. Did that only mean Fae? Had they sold them out to the Red Masks?

Her breathing was ragged as she pushed those intrusive thoughts away. They'd just bring more fear. And they had to survive first.

Hadrian helped her out of the mouth of the alley. This side of the street was much better than the other, but the people who had escaped were now being targeted by awaiting Red Masks. Blasting them with the black smoke bombs or using magic to hurt them. It was a war zone, and Clover had no magic. Hadrian barely had enough to get by. Certainly nothing like Kerrigan or Fordham.

"Scales," she coughed out.

"There." Hadrian pointed to a grate back in the alleyway.

They pushed back out of the way of the Red Masks. Hadrian rested her against the building wall and then pried the grate up to reveal the sewer system beneath the city.

"This isn't going to be fun," he yelled over the explosions. "I'll go first, then you lower yourself, and I'll catch you."

She nodded because speaking hurt too much. She didn't know if she had enough strength in her arms right now to lower herself down. But if she didn't, she'd die. Hadrian dropped into the sewer tunnel as if he'd been doing it all of his life. She went to a place in herself where pain no longer existed. She shut a gate over the pain and then crawled down to the grate. Her body shook with exertion as she put her legs into it and then slid the cover back over part of the opening, hoping it was enough to conceal where they'd gone.

"I've got you," Hadrian yelled up.

And then without letting herself consider what else might be down there, she fell into the sewer.

Hadrian's arms came around her tight, and this time, she couldn't stop herself from screaming.

"I'm sorry. I'm sorry," he whispered into her hair.

He set her on her feet and then hustled down the sewer with no light to guide them. The street above them rattled, sending dust and the gods only knew what else raining down on them. She coughed again as fear that the tunnel would collapse seized her.

"Here," Hadrian said.

He was shaking. She realized that he'd been keeping it together for her. But fear and pain lanced through his face.

What he'd found was a small break in the wall big enough for the two of them to huddle together, unseen in the tunnel. She didn't care how he'd found it or if he had known it was here all along. The only thing that mattered was safety.

Hadrian sat down first, holding his arms out so that he could cradle her in his lap. He put his arms around her, hugging her tight against his firm body. Both of them could barely breathe. Her body was catching up with her. Everything was shutting down.

"How'd you know this was here?" she whispered, her voice hoarse.

"Benefits of being a street rat," he murmured. After a minute of her body shaking uncontrollably, he asked, "Do you have a smoke?"

She nodded. "But I can't light the match."

"Give it to me."

She dug through her pockets, her hands shaking too bad that she couldn't even reach them. Tears fell down her cheeks. Hadrian put his hands on hers to still her and then carefully looked for the smoke and matches she carried with her everywhere. He pulled one out, lit the cigarette, and put it to her lips.

She inhaled sweet *loch*. Her very life force. The shaking didn't completely subside—some of it had to be shock—but it wasn't as debilitating.

She took the cigarette out of her hands and pressed it to his lips. It was a testament to how terrified he was that he actually inhaled. Straitlaced Hadrian smoking *loch*.

After she finished the cigarette, she stubbed it out next to them and settled back into Hadrian's arms. She turned her head to face him. "You saved my life."

"We did it together," he said, his voice raw.

Clover put her fingers to his lips to silence him. She could barely see the outline of his face, just a bit of blue hair and a sharp jawline and those big brown eyes. "Thank you."

He pulled her hand away and crushed his mouth onto hers. The last hour vanished as he devoured her. She didn't care if it was the terror still coursing through them. She needed him in that moment like her life depended on it. And there was no world where she would stop him.

# CHAPTER 34
## *The Martyr*

ISA

Everything had gone to plan.

Isa smiled through her red mask as the world turned to utter chaos. Humans and half-Fae ran for their lives. Bodies littered the ground. Buildings were toppled. The Red Masks were on top of the world. They had *won*.

They'd waited it out until the protests got big enough that even the Society took notice. Attacking the small ones would have given them more notice than was necessary. But if they were going to actually become a threat, that was a different story.

And now, they were nothing.

This was Father's great undoing. He had been misguided to ever let Basem Nix do as he pleased. It had set back their cause. But then Kerrigan had been named to the Society, the protests had started along with petitions to the government for humans to be treated as Fae were. It had turned the tide.

The Red Masks were innumerable. They would wash this city in blood before allowing the humans and half-Fae to take a place beside them. And it was all Father's doing.

She'd seen Basem as a way out of the Red Masks. Away from her fanatical father, who had raised her but did not see her as anything but the assassin he had created. She'd wanted more. And now, standing on the battleground in the wake of their victory, she understood his vision. Why he had always treated her so. A part of her still wanted to escape, but how could she be anything but this? The only thing she knew how to do was be an assassin.

And tonight, she wanted to finish it.

She'd seen Kerrigan's red hair in the crowd. Watched her now struggle with the prince who should have hated her. He should have been on their side. Not siding with some half-Fae.

She could complete her mission.

She could kill the girl.

Father had told her to abandon the task. It had been given to her by Basem, not Father. He didn't approve of it.

The last thing he wanted was for Kerrigan to go from being a symbol to a martyr. There would be no turning back the wave of support then. Her death could mean the end of the Red Masks.

But still, she hated her. Hated the life she had and the prince and the role in the government. How could a half-Fae have it when she didn't?

Isa defied orders and strode across the barricade line. She would end this here, today. Then, something happened. The prince grabbed her. His black magic swept around them, and they popped out of existence.

"No!" she screamed into the crowd.

Isa whipped around, looking for them. His magic wasn't that strong. She'd gathered from her spying that he couldn't travel much distance at once. Which meant they might still be within reach. She could still end this if she found them. And even better, he would be depleted of his reserves.

She turned back the way she'd come and watched the smoke reappear.

They'd made it across the line and into safety. Or so they thought.

She pushed past the remaining Red Masks on the line and ignored them as they tried to focus her elsewhere.

"Father's orders," she snapped.

Kerrigan looked around herself in terror, as she must have realized that she wasn't completely out of danger. The prince had fallen to his knees next to her. He didn't look like much as he was now. Not like the last time she'd gone up against him. She'd been practicing too. Maybe she'd forfeit both of their lives. Two less half-Fae sympathizers was all the better.

Kerrigan scrambled to her feet. She saw Isa coming toward her and put her hand on Fordham's shoulder. He shook his head. He couldn't get up to help her.

*Good.*

"Miss me?" Isa called to Kerrigan.

Kerrigan stiffened. She didn't have to see Isa's face. It was clear she recognized the voice. "Isa," she snarled.

"I do love that I made such an impression."

"Why are you doing this?"

"It's fun, darling," she trilled.

"Who are you working for?"

"Father, of course."

Kerrigan's eyes narrowed. She brought her fists up, as if that would save her. "What do you want?"

"You dead," Isa told her flatly.

And then she stopped walking as she heard the flapping of wings.

Kerrigan looked up at the same moment as a giant black beast landed in the space behind them. Dragons were in the skies. Dozens of them heading in their direction, answering the call of their city.

Isa wiggled her fingers at Kerrigan in a mock wave. Maybe next time, she'd kill her but not when Father could see her misbehaving.

# CHAPTER 35
## The Arrest

"Isa!" Kerrigan screamed into the night as the girl got away. As she always did. "Gods!"

Fordham groaned next to her, but his head was tipped up in fear. "Kerrigan, look."

She'd only half-recognized the dragon who landed behind them. But now, she turned fully away from the assassin and to the man striding toward her in black Society robes—Lorian.

"No," she whispered.

"Look what we have here," Lorian said with a smile that practically glowed. Here was his excuse to have her kicked out. Here was his excuse to get rid of the half-Fae while his Red Masks terrorized the city.

"Fordham, you have to go for help," she told him.

"I can't. I'm drained."

"You're not," she insisted. She didn't know if it was true, but it had to be. "Go get Helly. Or Bastian. Just go to the mountain. You can do it. I know you can."

"I won't leave you."

She looked down at him with determination in her eyes. "You can't carry us both that far. Now, go!"

He squeezed her hand. The only confirmation she needed. Then, his black magic enveloped him one more time, and he vanished into thin air. She released a breath of relief. Lorian might have seen Fordham, but he couldn't prove it. So, even if he couldn't get help, he wouldn't be in the thick of it. It would only be Kerrigan facing down the head of the Red Masks.

"I always knew that you were more trouble than you were worth," Lorian taunted.

"Funny, I could say the same thing about you."

Lorian bristled. "You dare talk to your superior like this!" His hand went to the pommel of his sword.

"Yes, I dare!" Kerrigan threw her hand to the carnage behind her. "Look at what is happening on the streets of Kinkadia. And you're here, talking about how much trouble I am. People are lying dead, and you care more about *me* than *that*."

"That is being taken care of," he snarled.

That was when she saw the Society Guard rushing into the bottlenecked streets. A strange vapor emanated from their water magic. People were coughing and falling over.

"What are they doing to them?" Kerrigan gasped. "They're innocent."

"No one is innocent in a riot."

"The Red Masks started this! Not the protestors."

"A convenient answer. I don't see any Red Masks, do you?"

Kerrigan rubbed her still-burning eyes and looked around at the destruction before her, but he was right. She didn't see any Red Masks. He'd let them get away. By the time the Guard had returned, all of the masks had been safely hidden. No one the wiser. She wanted to scream.

Just then dragons rained water down on the burning buildings. Society members were in the skies, taking care of what the Guard hadn't cleaned up in the streets. Kerrigan could already see shackles coming out. Arrests were being made all over the place. It was wrong. So wrong. This wasn't even their fault.

"You can't do this!"

Lorian scoffed. "What? My job? You'll find that I can."

Then, with her senses still addled from the smoke and his superior footwork, he whirled her in place, kicking her knees out from behind. Kerrigan gasped as she fell forward—hard. Gravel and bits of building dug into her knees. Tears streamed down her cheeks as she watched the devastation.

Lorian wrenched her arms behind her back. "By authority of the Society, I am placing you under arrest."

Shackles circled her wrists, closing so tight that they nearly cut off circulation. She gasped, doubling over as she realized they were magic-dampening manacles. It felt like a punch to the gut when she reached for her power and found only a yawning emptiness. And not just that, but they were also *iron*. Her half-Fae heritage kept them from making her completely recoil. Iron wasn't exactly poisonous to Fae, but it was a deterrent, and many refused to go near it. The fact that Lorian had on protective gloves proved that he'd *known* what he was walking into.

Without another word, Lorian dragged her back to his dragon. Getting onto the beast with her hands behind her back was a feat, but Lorian shoved her into position, and without a backward glance, they were in the air. She leaned forward and gripped the dragon tight with her thighs.

She didn't want to do this. She couldn't believe that Lorian had the audacity. Why hadn't she had a vision of *this*? What was her magic even good for if it didn't warn her about impending doom any longer? She reached for it then, searching for that connection to the spirit plane. Demanding its release. Her head buzzed and buzzed and buzzed. Only getting louder and more persistent as she attempted to force it to do her business. Her vision swam and then went black at the edges. Still, she pushed.

The last thing she remembered was her magic leaching from her core and everything falling into darkness.

\*\*\*

She woke again inside the mountain. Two Society Guards hauled her by either elbow. She got her feet under her and blinked. There hadn't been a vision. Not a single thing. She'd just expended her magic and passed out. Thanks, universe!

"Oh, good. You're awake," Lorian said at the bottom of the flight of stairs. "Here will do."

The guards deposited her in an iron-lined cell. The Fae guards hastened back out as quickly as possible. The walls felt as if they were leaning. So much iron that it was nearly oppressive to Kerrigan, whose Fae blood was so diluted. They hadn't even put Basem Nix in a cell with this much iron. How telling that they'd shove a half-Fae in one who had done nothing, but not a murderer.

Lorian stood before her, seemingly unperturbed by the iron. He looked smug as he watched her take in her surroundings—a smelly straw pallet, a metal bucket, and cold, hard stone.

"This is where you've always belonged."

"You're not going to get away with this," she told him.

"Arresting a rioter that I caught in the act?" He shook his head at her as if she were so naive. He was the sole witness. She wished more than anything that she had an ounce of her magic to wipe that look off of his face.

Lorian turned then, as if that was all he was going to say on the matter. Just leave her down here to rot. A commotion on the steps stilled him. And in that moment, Helly burst through the doorway.

"What is the meaning of this, Lorian?" Helly demanded.

"Hellina," he said mildly. "What a pleasant surprise."

"You have overstepped." Her eyes were wild. She looked half-ready to throttle him. "You have no authority to arrest a Society trainee when she has done nothing wrong. This is outrageous. I will request an inquest from the council."

"I must agree with her, Master Lorian," another voice said, following in Helly's wake.

Kerrigan craned her neck to see Mistress Anahi step into the prison. She was nearly as short as Kerrigan with long, perfectly glossy box braids and deep black skin. Anahi barely suppressed a shudder at the iron all around them. Kerrigan was surprised to see Anahi here with Helly, as they didn't always see eye to eye. They must have been meeting at the time or else Helly wouldn't have brought her along.

"I do not approve of the protests outside, but they are legal. Arresting a Society trainee is outside of the bounds of your jurisdiction," she said with a flat northern accent, indicating her Sayair tribe high in the Vert Mountains.

Lorian glared at both of them. "It was not a protest. It was a riot. I have every right to arrest someone inciting violence in Kinkadia. That is our express purpose—to govern and protect the people. And I must protect our people from her."

"He's lying!" Kerrigan cried. "I was at a protest, but we weren't rioting. We were marching through the streets. We were herded away, and the exits were closed off. Red Masks destroyed buildings, threw smoke bombs, and were killing people."

"I saw nothing of the sort," Lorian said.

"You came too late. You let the Red Masks escape."

Lorian actually had the audacity to roll his eyes. "There were no Red Masks. Their leader was murdered months ago, and they have dissolved, if they were ever what you claimed in the first place."

"Lorian," Anahi admonished. "We know of the Red Masks' existence."

"And their threat," Helly added.

"Five years ago maybe," he said lightly.

More footsteps announced another person's entrance. Bastian appeared then with a huff. "I don't move quite as fast as I used to," he said with a small smile. "Now, what is this I'm hearing about what is going on? You are discrediting the existence of the Red Masks? Even after Basem's blatant use of them after the tournament?"

"I believe in their existence, but I saw no threat, except what you see before you. She is turning the city against us, initiating riots in the streets and infiltrating our sacred halls. Can none of you see what she is doing to us? How she is trying to turn us against one another?"

"I wouldn't have to do any of that if you weren't leading the very people you allowed to escape," Kerrigan snarled.

She shouldn't have said it. She had no proof. Not yet at least. Just Dozan's word, how Lorian had treated her these months, and what he'd done today. But she knew he was the leader. He was the one who had been trying to kill her. Why else would Isa have run away like that at the sight of his dragon? She'd known.

But the looks of disbelief, coupled with Lorian's stark laughter, hurt.

"Kerrigan," Helly said softly, "we cannot accuse people of such things."

"Aye," Anahi said with displeasure in her expression. She had gone from helpful to neutral to disapproving. "Master Lorian still deserves your respect. Whether or not you should be behind those bars."

"Of course, Mistress Anahi," she said in haste. "I only meant—"

But Lorian cut in with another laugh. "You believe I am the leader of these Red Masks?" He turned back to his colleagues. "Do you not see now? She is trying to place the blame on me. It's absurd. You can take this to the council if you wish, Hellina, but I am going to move to have her expelled."

"Expelled?" Kerrigan gasped.

Helly looked dismayed for one second before straightening and giving him an imperious look down her nose. "If you do this, it will end your career. The council election is next year, Lorian."

His nostrils flared. "Are you proposing that you will oppose me?"

"It is not the time to make enemies," she said pointedly.

He balked at the blatant threat. A part of Kerrigan cheered for her. That she'd go up against Lorian for her.

"This is not about you two," Anahi said. "It is about the girl."

"Agreed," Bastian said, coming between them. "None of that. What we need is a compromise. Lorian wishes to see the girl expelled. Helly believes that she should be let go. Surely, there is a middle ground."

Anahi nodded. "I concur with the honorable Master Bastian."

Lorian and Helly huffed at the same time and looked away from one another.

"Kerrigan was in the wrong place at the wrong time. She likely shouldn't have been at the protest in the first place." Bastian looked to Kerrigan, as if to say *I told you so.* "But unless you can prove that she started all of this, Lorian, I believe that her infraction is more a problem with political action during her training and less to do with inciting violence. For that, I would offer a third choice—probation. Kerrigan would be monitored for the duration of her training and grounded from flying for a month."

"What?" Kerrigan gasped. "But we start flying tomorrow!"

"It seems fair to me," Anahi agreed. "A compromise."

Lorian's lips tipped up at her objection to the punishment. It wasn't getting her kicked out, but it was something she clearly cared about.

Helly sighed and shot Kerrigan a pained expression. "I agree with Bastian if you do, Lorian."

"Helly," Kerrigan breathed. "But…"

"No, Kerrigan, you were warned about the protests already. This is a fair alternative."

She shut her mouth. Because if Helly was saying it was fair, that likely meant she thought that Lorian had a chance with convincing the council to kick her out of the program.

"Fine," Lorian ground out. "Probation it is. But I'll be the one watching."

Then, he whipped his black robes around him as he vanished. Anahi shot them a pained look before following in his wake. Helly produced a key and opened the iron gate. She bristled as the iron touched her skin as she removed the manacles. The rush of magic returning to Kerrigan sent tears to her eyes.

"Thank you." Kerrigan threw her arms around Helly. "Fordham found you?"

"He did," Helly said. "And he's fully depleted. Nearly killed himself doing it. We were lucky that Bastian was already with me at the time. I gave Fordham a tonic, and he should be out for the rest of the day."

"Gods," Kerrigan whispered.

Helly patted her back comfortingly until the tears dammed up. Kerrigan brushed the back of her hand under her eyes and looked to Bastian. "Thank you for your help. I can see that Lorian could have come out ahead."

Bastian bowed his head to Kerrigan. "Indeed."

"I still think he's behind the Red Masks," she told them both.

"Even if it's true," Helly said, "you cannot go around saying so. We'd need definitive proof before we could bring it to the council, and you're already on thin ice."

"Do you really believe that he's behind the Red Masks?" Bastian asked carefully.

"Yes," she said and then frowned. "I don't know. I want to say yes. He just let them all go. And the way he treats humans and half-Fae." Kerrigan sighed. "We need more proof."

"What you need to do is keep your head down," Helly said.

"I agree," Bastian said, "with Kerrigan."

Helly looked at him in alarm. "What?"

"We've been investigating for months. If Lorian is working with the Red

272

Masks, then we need proof."

"Yes, of course, but Kerrigan needs to finish training first and foremost."

Bastian nodded. "Let us work on it in the meantime." He patted her arm. "We will get to the bottom of this."

# CHAPTER 36
## *The Probation*

Fordham opened the door to Kerrigan's room bright and early the next morning. "You're all right."

She half-opened her eyes to see him standing in the doorway. She'd slept terrible. It had taken ages for her to fall asleep, and then she'd been racked with nightmares about the riot.

"I'm not in chains anymore," she murmured.

"Gods," Fordham growled. He sank into the bed next to her.

"Helly knocked me out when I found her. She wouldn't let me come see you. This morning, she said you're on probation?"

She groaned. "Yeah."

Fordham shook his head. "That's disgusting. You didn't do anything wrong. And if you're in trouble, then shouldn't I be?"

Kerrigan grasped his hand to keep him from barging off and doing something stupid. "Don't. I don't want you to get in trouble too. You wouldn't have even been at the protest if not for me."

"That's ridiculous. The way everyone is talking about it, it's like the Red

Masks weren't even there and we destroyed those buildings ourselves."

"Welcome to being a minority in Kinkadia."

She was just so tired. So, *so* tired. No matter what happened, the blame befell them. And they could try and try to dig themselves out, but they were still always seen as the problem.

"I hope I'm not interrupting anything."

Fordham rose to his feet. "Not at all."

Audria shot Kerrigan a knowing look. "Time for our first day of flying."

Kerrigan groaned and pulled her pillow over her face.

"What's wrong with her?"

"She's grounded. No flying for a month."

"What?" Audria gasped. "That's absurd. We just started flying. She's going to be behind. How do they expect us to be a unit without her?"

Kerrigan shot Fordham a look, and he ushered Audria out of the room and explained in a whisper. She was glad that she didn't have to be the one to do it.

The first thing she'd done when she got out of the cell was send a letter to Dozan, asking about Clover, and one to Fallon's residence in Central to ask over Hadrian. She hadn't received any word back yet, but she couldn't exactly leave to go find out if they were okay. Even sending the letters had felt risky with her probation hanging over her head. But she had to know.

It hung over her head as she got ready and headed out to training early. Alura eyed her without a trace of pity. She hadn't expected any from the trainer, but it was still frustrating. None of this was her fault.

Tieran was waiting when she arrived. *What did you do?*

"I'm sorry," she said at once. "You'll still be able to practice the maneuvers."

*Little good it does me without you.*

She winced. "Look, Lorian is gunning for me. This wasn't my fault. I get you being angry, but keep your condescension to yourself."

Fine, he snapped and then flew off.

She glared at his retreating back. She couldn't even call him back to have this out. If he wanted to be petulant about it, then fine. She couldn't change the outcome, and she didn't regret going.

The worst part was sitting in the arena and *observing* the flying lessons. All she wanted to do was get on Tieran's back and put the work in. Flying was her favorite thing in all the world. Bastian had probably known she'd feel cut out for missing these lessons, but he couldn't have known that it would feel like she'd lost a limb. Flying was the one thing about all of this that had always made perfect sense. And now that she *finally* could do it whenever she wanted, she was barred.

The other four trainees came off of the arena, covered in sweat but laughing and jovial. Kerrigan kept her face carefully blank. She couldn't let them see her in distress. Kerrigan was quieter than normal, but no one commented on it. How could any of them blame her?

She still had to go to all of her regular lessons. The new air instructor was nothing like Zina with her eccentricities. Frankly, he was boring. The rest of the lessons were even more grueling. She'd received no word from Zina after her disappearance, and it took two whole days before she heard back from Dozan. A short missive that said Clover and Hadrian had made it out of the massacre. Clover hadn't come herself to deliver the message. She'd gotten it from one of Dozan's little spies. It was at least a relief that they were alive, but she couldn't imagine what was keeping Clover away.

She felt very lonely without any word from any of her friends and isolated from the four that she had been making these months of training. Probation loomed overhead like a dark cloud threatening rain.

"Pst," Audria said, peeking her head into Kerrigan's bedroom one night a couple of weeks into her grounding.

Kerrigan looked up from the parchment she'd been working on for her philosophy assignment. "Hey."

Audria pressed a finger to her lips and nodded down the hall. "Come with me."

She arched an eyebrow. "Are we going to get in trouble?"

"No, of course not."

But Audria had mischief in her eyes. Kerrigan recognized it because it was like looking in a mirror.

"I can't. If I get in trouble, then I'm kicked out."

"You won't get in trouble," Audria insisted. "We'd never let that happen. It's a spot of fun."

Kerrigan frowned and shook her head. No fun for her.

Audria huffed. "You can't shut us all out like this."

Shut them out? She wasn't doing anything of the sort. "I'm not."

"Maybe you don't see it, but you are. You're even shutting out Fordham." Audria gave her a pointed look. "Just come have a fun night with us. You need it most of all."

Kerrigan should argue. The last thing she needed was to do something that would get her in trouble. She couldn't be kicked out of the Society. She had little else in her life, and it would mean being without Tieran forever.

But she didn't argue. She wanted to get away from her studies and be with her friends. Audria usually had a good idea about whether or not she'd get in trouble. Not that she knew what it was like to be half-Fae. Kerrigan would take the fall even if the others were caught as well. That was how it always was.

Still, she pulled on her cloak and left her room. They met up with Fordham, Noda, and Roake a floor up, waiting together in a landing.

"See, I told you that I'd get her to come with us," Audria said.

Fordham's eyes were only for Kerrigan as he shot her a look that she couldn't read. Noda cheered, and Roake just winked. She couldn't help but grin. Kerrigan followed the lot of them through the mountain. She gathered where they were going first. Long before Audria pulled the door open and gestured behind her.

"Ta-da!" Audria said.

The others gaped at the lush greenhouse beyond. Thousands of marks' worth of glass lined the walls and ceiling of the incredible structure. It had been the work of magnificent ancient earth Fae masters. They'd designed the building to not only produce crops year-round for the mountain, but also for medicinal use. Kerrigan had spent one or two nights here with Lyam, trying out the forbidden herbs and laughing at the ceiling all night. They'd gotten in so much trouble. She clutched at her skirt, where his compass lay in her pocket, as it always did now. A constant reminder.

But that night was gone, and what lay ahead were new friendships.

"I've never been in here," Noda whispered reverently, lighting a few faerie lights to illuminate the path.

"It's massive," Roake added.

Audria pulled a bottle from the bag at her hip. "I thought we could loosen up a bit."

Fordham shook his head. "Who would have guessed you were the troublemaker?"

"I am more than just a title," Audria said indignantly, tilting her nose up.

"What kind of faerie punch is that?" Kerrigan asked, stepping inside and letting the door close behind her.

"I've no idea," she said with a laugh, linking arms with Kerrigan and winding through the plant life until they came upon the small circle at its center that was used for lessons. "I filched it out of the storeroom and didn't even bother looking."

"And you said this wouldn't be trouble."

"It's the middle of the night. No one saw me take it, and no one is going to find us."

The words cast a spell about the greenhouse. As if by saying them aloud, they were true.

They dragged cushions into a small circle and drew their faerie lights in close, so just the five of them were brightened. Audria passed around the faerie punch. She'd apparently taken a few bottles. Not conspicuous at all.

"We're all frazzled, and we need the break," Audria insisted.

Roake didn't complain as he took the first swig, passing it to Noda. She held it aloft and then shrugged, taking a drink. When it reached Kerrigan, she looked at the label, but it gave nothing away. A red bottle of faerie punch had once knocked her on her ass for two days straight. Helly refused to heal her, and nothing Darby did made it better. She'd had to suffer the consequences. Gods, she hoped this wasn't the same stuff.

She took a drink, and the punch went down smooth. Not usually a good sign. The more potent it was, the sweeter the punch, as if it were lulling you into a false sense of security.

"Let's play a game!" Audria insisted after she took her drink. She pulled out a second bottle with a green liquid swishing inside and handed it off.

"What kind of game?" Roake asked, burping. They all groaned, and he just laughed.

"Truth or Dare."

"What's that?" Fordham asked.

Kerrigan looked at him skeptically. "Surely, you played Truth or Dare in the House of Shadows."

Audria laughed. "It must be so dull there if you haven't. Either you choose to answer a question truthfully or you perform some action. If you refuse one, you must do the other."

"Ah. We called it Challenge or Consequence," Fordham explained. "Everyone was challenged with a question, and if they refused to answer, they were given a consequence."

"Ooh," Audria gushed. "Let's play *that* way!"

Kerrigan nudged him. "Look what you've done."

"My apologies," he said with a smirk that said he was nothing of the sort.

"I'll start," Audria chirped. "I challenge Noda."

Noda sighed heavily. "Fine."

"What is your deepest, darkest secret?"

Noda frowned and thought for a long minute. "That I'm not good enough for the Society and I can't hack it."

"That's not a secret," Roake said. "You already are good enough."

Noda withdrew at the accusation. "Well, that's what it feels like to me."

The circle was quiet for a moment. That would be a heavy burden to hold.

"Your turn, Noda," Audria said.

Noda swallowed. "I challenge Fordham."

He sat up straight, anticipating the blow. Kerrigan guessed that the ones in the House of Shadows were brutal. If her short stint there was any indication.

"Who is your one true love?"

He balked. Whatever he'd been anticipating, that hadn't been it.

Kerrigan held her breath. She waited to see if he would name Dacia. He'd bitten her head off at the mere mention of her name. She never brought it up again.

"Consequence," he ground out.

Everyone blinked. They'd all thought it would be an easy question. He could have named anyone. Could have said he'd never been in love even. Instead he thought it so private that he wouldn't even answer.

"Oh," Noda said. "Uh... your consequence is to strip naked and run a lap around the greenhouse."

Roake burst into laughter. "Oh man, this should be good. No way you're going to do that."

But Fordham rose to his feet, and then as they all watched, he unbuttoned his silk shirt. Kerrigan gulped at the first inch of exposed skin and then all the way down to his abdominals. He wrenched the shirt off, exposing his chest and arms. The group was in a hush as he went for his pants, releasing the ties and dropping them to the floor.

Audria gasped and turned away at the sight of his muscular thighs. Noda, too, blushed and covered her face. Kerrigan was peeking. How could she not?

Only Roake laughed through the whole thing. Perhaps he'd expected him to stop.

Kerrigan's mouth was dry. She could no more look away than make a joke of it. For his eyes found hers in the dim lighting. She wanted to blush, but all she felt was... need.

But Fordham didn't stop. He arched an eyebrow at her. A challenge, waiting for her to be embarrassed. But she wasn't embarrassed. Just interested.

He hooked his thumbs into the waist of his undergarments and dragged them off too. Every muscled inch of him on full display. Her mind went fuzzy at the sight of him in all of his naked glory. A pulse shot through her body, straight to her center. And still she didn't look away.

Fordham threw his pants into the circle, whirling away from the lot so they all got a flash of a perfectly muscled butt. Then, he was running.

Kerrigan's eyes rounded as he dashed away.

Roake whistled. "Well... I might be more into males than I thought."

All the girls broke down into giggles.

"A body like that would make anyone interested," Noda said.

Audria shook her head. "I have a horribly embarrassing question." They all looked at her in question. "Does it always look like that?"

"Does what?" Noda asked.

"*It*," she said, gesturing between her legs.

Now, they all fell backward in laughter at the question. No one answered, and Audria just snatched the green bottle back and downed it to hide her blush.

Fordham returned moments later, pulling his clothes back on as efficiently as he had taken them off. "My turn. I challenge Roake."

"I'm ready. Lay it on me."

"How old were you with the first woman you ever lay with?"

Roake sputtered. He puffed his chest up, and they'd all been around him enough to know when he was about to bluster.

"The truth, or you take a worse consequence," Fordham demanded.

Roake deflated. "I mean, how old was I? I was… well, I haven't… precisely."

"You haven't?" Audria gasped.

"You just asked if it always looked like that! As if you'd never seen one!" Roake shot back.

Audria giggled. "Yes, but I'm not the one always bragging about my conquests."

"It's fine that you haven't," Kerrigan said.

"Agreed," Noda said, her voice solemn. "It's better than regretting it."

And no one had a response to that.

"Well, I suppose that I challenge Audria," Roake said.

"Big surprise," Audria said, flipping her hair.

"If you could have your first time with one person in this circle, who would it be?"

Audria gaped. "That's… that's not fair."

Roake shrugged. "That's the question."

"I…" Audria looked around. Her gaze jerking between each person and then shrugging. "I can't choose. Consequence, I suppose."

"Then, you have to kiss Noda."

Audria huffed. "That's a terrible consequence."

Noda looked offended by her response for one moment, but then Audria was on her hands and knees, crawling across the small circle. Her movements were unsteady. The alcohol was getting to them all. Kerrigan's head felt fuzzy. But she was unprepared for Audria to gently take Noda's face in her hands as if she were precious and kiss her so soft and slowly.

Roake gaped at them. Kerrigan's eyebrows rose. They were kind of hot. She was definitely into guys, but still… it was hot.

Audria pulled back and winked at Noda. "I'm an excellent kisser."

Noda nodded, dazed. "That you are."

Audria giggled and returned to her spot. "I challenge Kerrigan."

"Of course," Kerrigan said, taking a fortifying sip of faerie punch. "What do you have?"

"What did you see in your bonding ceremony?"

Kerrigan froze. Her head spun. Did Audria know that she and Tieran weren't bonded? Had she guessed and then gotten her drunk so that she'd reveal it?

"We all know what the others saw, but you've *never* shared it," Audria continued. "I've been dying to know."

No, she didn't know. She was just being Audria and nosy. But of course, Kerrigan couldn't say. Because they *weren't* bonded. And Fordham would know if she was lying.

"Come on. It's an easy one," Audria encouraged.

But it *wasn't* an easy one for Kerrigan.

"Consequence," she murmured.

"Well," Audria frowned, tapping her lip. "Your consequence is to go off into the greenhouse and kiss Fordham for three minutes."

"What?" she chirped.

"It was an easy challenge. So, I'm giving you a bigger consequence," she informed her haughtily. A twinkle was in her eye. As if she'd planned this all along. The little matchmaker.

"Fine," she said, coming unsteadily to her feet.

Fordham rose beside her, and she stomped into the greenhouse. She walked until they were far enough away from their friends before she spoke, "I know that you don't want to do this. So, we can just wait…"

But she never finished her statement because there was Fordham. His fingers pushed up into her unruly red hair, and his lips descended on her own until there was nothing else in the entire world except the feel of him. Those perfect lips against hers and the taste of faerie punch potent between them.

She tripped, the alcohol making her legs wobble. He caught her easily with a breath of laughter on his lips. Her head was fuzzy, but she still couldn't believe he was kissing her. After all the effort not to show how much she wanted to kiss him, here he was, with his mouth sealed against hers.

Fordham laid her down amid the out-of-season flowers and cradled her body against his. His hands moving from her back, across her stomach, and up her sides. She arched into him, wanting so much more. Her hands ripped his shirt out from his pants and ran over the hard contours of his abdomen. She dragged her nails over the pale skin, wanting nothing more than to let the faerie punch take over. To forget the three-minute rule from Audria and pull him to her. She could take what she wanted right here in the greenhouse.

"Fordham," she murmured as he broke away to look at her.

But whatever he saw in her glazed gaze made him dive back down and claim her mouth once again. His tongue delved into her mouth, stroking against her own until there was nothing but heat and need. Gods, she wanted him. She tried to remind herself that this was just part of the game. But the way he moved against hers and the heat from his body made her forget everything entirely.

"Ford," she groaned as he moved from her mouth to her ear and neck and down to her collarbone. She dropped her head backward, arching into his touch. "Oh Gods."

He stopped before diving lower. His chest rising and falling like they'd just run a marathon. His pelvis was pressed firmly against her hip, and she could feel precisely what their kissing was doing to him. No matter that they were drunk on punch and under the spell of a game, they both *wanted* this.

Then, his hands trailed lower and lower and lower. They slid under the waistband of her pants, and everything stilled for a brief moment. His swirling gray irises met hers, a question, a comma, a pause. She nodded once. *Yes.* Yes, she wanted this. All of him.

He moved down deeper until his finger pressed against her most sensitive area. Her back arched against him. A soft moan escaped her lips, and he drowned it out with a swift kiss. Then, he was at her opening. He pressed one finger experimentally into her, a slow upward thrust that made her shiver from head to toe. He added a second finger as his lips became more insistent against hers.

She was consumed by him. There was nothing else in the entire world except his body flush against hers. The length of him hard against her hip. And those fingers... oh Gods, those fingers. He brushed this thumb against the small bead at the apex of her core and everything collapsed inward all at once.

He muffled her small whimpering cries with his mouth as she contracted around him. Her vision went in and out. Then, she slowly returned to earth and stared up at the incredible male before her.

A lazy self-satisfied smirk played on his too pretty lips, and the effects of the alcohol swirled through those big gray eyes. She reached up and ran a hand down the stubble of jawline. "What are you thinking?"

"I could devour you," he said immediately, nipping at her bottom lip.

"Devour me," she urged.

For a second, his grip tightened on her waist. She could feel the more insistent press of him as he shifted to try to release the tension. Yes, it had been a game, but it was a game no longer.

"Please," she murmured against his lips.

His head fell to her shoulder, and he pressed a kiss there. "What is in this punch? It makes me want to throw caution to the wind."

She laughed hoarsely, the spell broken. "Magic." She already felt him withdrawing. "Is this all we'll ever have?"

He didn't answer. She saw the sorrow cross his face. They could have this. They could have the world. If only he'd let them. But he wouldn't.

She pressed one more kiss to his swollen lips, adjusted the laces of her pants, and stood up out of the flowers. She returned to their friends, and he returned a few minutes later, after he was fully in control of himself once more. The game was forgotten as the others had discovered more recreational herbs.

It was for the better. She'd gotten the hardest consequence already.

# CHAPTER 37
## *The Holiday*

"**Y**ou are all excused from the remainder of lessons this week," Alura announced. "You have been personally invited by the king and queen of Bryonica to come to Rosemont and partake in the winter holiday Season events for Geivhrea."

Geivhrea was the ancient Fae winter holiday, celebrating the end of the night and the coming of spring. It was the biggest event of the year.

"You've been given accommodations within Belcourt Palace. It is a great honor, and I expect all of you to treat it as such. As always, you represent the Society while you are there. Anything that would look bad for us there will directly affect you here. Any questions?"

No one raised their hand. And then at the last second, Kerrigan put hers up.

Alura glared at her, but Kerrigan didn't put it down. She might be a good little soldier, but there was one important question.

Alura blew out an exasperated huff. "What is it, Argon?"

Kerrigan sighed in relief. "How exactly will I be getting there?"

"Since classes are canceled, today is your final day of being grounded.

You'll leave tomorrow, and you are free to fly Tieran there."

Kerrigan breathed a sigh of relief. She couldn't have been happier. No more grounding. It had been a grueling month without him in the skies. They didn't get along, but a part of her missed him like a giant ache in her chest. Maybe she was actually coming to like this sardonic dragon.

"You'll resume training after the first of the year," Alura continued, her gaze never leaving Kerrigan. "I expect you all to look exactly the same. No matter if you've had a break from training or not."

Kerrigan gulped. Well, great. That was ten days. Ten days to make up for a month of training that the others had been given. And she had to attend Season events. How was she supposed to accomplish that?

But Alura just asked, "Any *other* questions?"

She kept her hand down. That wasn't an invitation.

"Go pack and be ready to be in the skies by high noon," Alura said. "Dismissed!"

Kerrigan jumped at her shout and hastened behind the others. They had a matter of hours to get ready. Audria gossiped the entire way about who was going to be there and what the Belcourt Palace would look like this year for Geivhrea. She forced herself not to think about it.

Kerrigan hadn't been to Bryonica in twelve years, but she remembered her last night as if it were yesterday.

She'd gone out riding with her father, cutting through Corsica Forest, which made up the bulk of their lands. Kivrin was unusually quiet. He'd never been a taciturn kind of father like everyone else. He was fair, kind, buoyant. He was as interested in teaching her the intricacies of court to have her grow into a fair lady as he was to teach her the art of deception and warfare. The son he'd never had.

They stopped at the stream on the far side of their family estate, Waisley. Her horse should have been a meager pony, but her father never would have allowed her such a small beast. He'd wanted her on stallions by the time she could toddle around.

He'd looked far away and said the words that never left her all these years, "You will survive this, Felicity."

He'd known even then what he was going to do. She'd thought he meant that she'd survive the beast and March coming to the estate and all the many petty problems a young girl could have. But when she woke the next day, she was not in her bed with the white drapes cresting the posts, the cushions so soft that she always felt like it must be the same as sleeping on a cloud. She was in the mountain. And everything had changed.

Now, she was to return.

\*\*\*

It took a matter of minutes to pack her bag but an hour to traipse through the Artisan Village and find Parris' dress shop.

"I can't help you," he said, crossing his arms. He was a slight thing, not more than a spattering of inches taller than Kerrigan and all skin and bones. Not even getting out of the House of Dragons had changed that. His Fae ears were delicate and on display. His long blond hair tucked behind them in a ponytail at the nape of his neck.

"Parris, come on," she said. "Imagine me at the Geivhrea party in *your* gown. I'll be before the king and queen."

"I have a dozen other gowns to finish before then," he grumbled.

"Will all of *those* people need to make an impression on the king?"

He tried to shoo her out of the place, but she'd spent months training and always been stronger than him anyway.

"You've ruined too many of my gowns," he complained.

"It's not *my* fault."

"You don't even pay me!"

She laughed. "I'm free advertisement."

"That doesn't pay the bills, Society mistress," he joked, poking her in the ribs.

"Parris..."

He huffed. "I'll need all new measurements." He gestured to her arms, chest, and back. "Everything has gotten *bigger*. Must you keep training with that useless sword?"

"Afraid so."

He tweaked a dress to her measurements on the spot. He'd already been working on a new design for the Season with her in mind. And he'd been right; it would do the trick.

With the dress safely tucked into her traveling bag, she went to the aerie at high noon to find Tieran waiting for her. He hadn't been talking to her this last month. It had been agonizing.

Now, he turned his head to glare at her. *Are you through trying to ruin all of our plans?*

"Completely."

*I don't believe you.*

"Don't blame you," she said with a laugh as she attached the bag to his saddle. "But the king and queen called us to court. So, to court we go. Plus, we're going to need to train the entire time we're there if we're to catch up to the others."

"I'll teach you," Fordham said, striding away from Netta.

She flushed. Her mind returning to that greenhouse. They hadn't discussed it. What was there to discuss really? They couldn't deny their attraction to one another. They kept ending up tangled in each other's arms, like idiots. And if she wasn't comfortable with that being all it was, then she was going to have to cut him off entirely. Because she couldn't keep doing this if her heart wouldn't shut up.

"I appreciate it, but … I'm going to see if Audria will work with me," she said carefully.

*Fordham is better*, Tieran grumbled in her head.

She glared at the traitorous dragon.

"Audria is going to be knee deep in Bryonican gentlemen," Fordham said.

"Maybe I will as well," she challenged.

He frowned. "Just one, I'd wager."

Kerrigan winced. She'd walked right into that one. March was another issue entirely.

"Just let me help," he commanded in that general's voice she hadn't heard in so long.

Her spine straightened at the words. "I don't think we should be spending time together. And even if we should, don't use that voice with me."

"Rightfully, I am your crowned prince," he said, pulling a trump card.

She stepped up to him, meeting his challenge. "Respectfully, I'm not a member of your court. Your father made damn sure of that."

His eyes darted around the room. "Don't let anyone hear you saying that. Lorian just needs an excuse."

She deflated. "I know."

"Just let me help, gods. Why is it always an argument?"

*Yeah, Kerrigan, why is it always an argument?* Tieran asked.

"Enough out of both of you," she muttered and then climbed onto Tieran's back. Fordham arched an eyebrow, and she reluctantly nodded. "Fine. You can train me."

He smiled, slow and dangerous. *Gods, help me.* She remembered exactly what his military training had been like. She was up for some sleepless nights and exhaustion. But what was the difference at this point?

\*\*\*

Late in the afternoon, they landed in the Bryonican capital city, Rosemont, wind-whipped and half-freezing. The sea came into view long before they reached the sprawling city and the gray stone of Belcourt Palace. With no mountains in sight, the dragons had been given accommodations in Society housing with plenty of fresh meat while the trainees were escorted across the palace grounds.

Kerrigan kept her eyes straight forward as they crossed the frost-covered yard from the stables. Belcourt Palace was a jewel at the mouth of the Seven-Finger Bay leading out to the Gardic Sea. It was well guarded and damn near unbreakable. One of the first cities to ever be built by the Fae in Alandria. They'd settled in this natural defensive position and dedicated the space to the gods, which was why everything was gilded and bejeweled. Or so they said.

Their bags were carried to their rooms ahead of them while attendants directed them to bathing quarters and brought out fresh clothes in their tribe colors.

Kerrigan stepped out of the bath and was toweled off before a navy dress with embroidered silver roses was put before her. She blinked at it. "This is Bryonican colors."

"Yes, my lady," the attendant said, curtsying deeply.

"I'm of the House of Shadows."

They frowned and glanced at each other. "Many here still see you as Bryonican, my lady."

She wanted to argue. Wearing this color would give them the wrong impression. She wasn't returning to Bryonica. No matter what anyone thought. But causing a fuss would surely be noted as well.

She frowned and let them drape her in the colors she'd long ago given up. When she stepped out of the chamber, she saw Audria in a similar attire with the House of Drame insignia emblazed on her chest. Kerrigan was glad that at least her father's House of Cruse wasn't on her own dress.

"You look wonderful!" Audria gushed. "Oh, I love seeing you back in our colors."

That made one of them. Though she didn't say it.

Fordham however frowned when he saw her. "Blue?"

She sighed. Of course, he was dressed in all black for the House of Shadows.

"I tried to tell them this wasn't my color."

He touched the fringe of lace at her collar. It was definitely more ornamental than what she normally wore. "This doesn't suit you."

"Really, Fordham?" Audria gasped. "You're such an ass!"

He stepped forward, ignoring Audria, until he was in Kerrigan's space. She took a deep breath and met his gaze. He bowed slightly, taking her hand in his and pressing a kiss to it. "Charbonnet black is better," he said low.

She startled at the tribe name for the House of Shadows. She'd never heard him use it before. But before she could ask about it, Roake and Noda returned from their baths. Noda in Concha teal blue and Roake in all black with an Elsiande pink cravat at his throat. Then, the attendants were ushering them through the palace and straight to the throne room.

Audria squeezed Kerrigan's hand. "Here we go."

Roake shook slightly. "I'm going to be sick."

"They're not *your* king and queen," Noda said with a laugh.

"They're still royalty."

Fordham sniffed. As if he wasn't royalty in their very midst. As if she and Audria weren't from a royal line as well. Not that Kerrigan wanted anyone to think of her like that.

The doors to the throne room creaked open.

"His Royal Highness, Crowned Prince Fordham Ollivier of the House of Shadows," the attendant called. "Lady Kerrigan Felicity Argon, First of the House of Cruse of Bryonica, now of the House of Shadows."

Kerrigan winced at her title. The use of her given name. Then, she took a breath and stepped up next to Fordham.

"Lady Audria Ather, Third of the House of Drame of Bryonica."

Audria joined her with her head high.

"Master Roake Brevard of Elsiande and Mistress Noda Hoake of Concha. The latest representatives of the Society."

As a unit, they strode forward down the aisle that led to King Mydran, First of the House of Stoirm of Bryonica, and Queen Littany, First of the House of Stoirm, formerly First of the House of Medallion. Courtiers milled about the room, assessing their entrance. And to Kerrigan's dismay, Ashby March stood at the front of the room. She nearly froze at the sight of him beside the queen until she remembered that the queen was his great-aunt.

Was *this* why they had been called to court so abruptly? Scales.

"Welcome, representatives from the Society," King Mydran said grandly. He wore Bryonican navy in a series of sweeping robes with gold glittering about his person. His hair was graying at the temples. He'd fought in the Great War, and he was much beloved by his people. "We hope that your accommodations are to your liking and that your days within Rosemont bring much joy. It is always a pleasure to have members of my court back within the halls." He paused as his eyes dropped to Kerrigan. "Some whose return was a long time coming."

She curtsied lower at the acknowledgment.

He issued more pleasantries before releasing them to the court. All Kerrigan wanted to do was turn and run the other direction. She'd had a long day. It was the first she'd flown in a month, and she was exhausted. But one look at March, and she knew that she would have to speak to him before fleeing.

"Lady Argon," March said formally as he approached her. He took her hand and bowed deeply.

Kerrigan could feel Fordham stiffen next to her. "March," she said with a curtsy. "Do I have you to thank for this trip?"

His eyes gleamed. "I might have suggested it to my dear great-aunt. I missed you at the fall Season in Venatrix. It wasn't the same without you. I hope we'll get to spend more time together at this one."

"Perhaps," she said coyly, searching for an excuse to get away.

"I'd like to call on you while you're in Rosemont for the week."

Kerrigan gulped. How could she say no to that? "I would like that," she lied. He grinned, as if triumphant, and she continued, "However, I have training."

"Training? You have the week off."

"Not me," she said.

"Well, I could come watch your training," he offered. "Or meet you afterward."

Gods, he was persistent.

"I'm leaving tomorrow morning."

He blinked. "Whatever for?"

She hated the words that were about to come out of her mouth. This wasn't what she wanted out of this trip, but if she stayed in Rosemont, she'd be stuck with March the entire time. There'd be no escape.

"I'm going home."

His eyes rounded. That was the last thing he'd expected. "To Corsica?"

"Yes. To Waisley," she whispered. She hadn't uttered that word in twelve years. Couldn't even think about Waisley without a fresh pang of despair. And now, she was committed.

"I didn't think that you still considered the House of Cruse home."

"It's the first time I've been back. I'd like to see the estate and train on my own lands," she told him, her heart aching at the very thought.

"I could... accompany you."

They both knew it wasn't proper for him to even suggest it. Courting had rules. Seeing her here was one thing, but returning home with her when they were betrothed without an invitation from her father was something else entirely.

"You could write to Kivrin," she said easily. "If he's there…"

He nodded. "I'll do just that." He bent at the waist once more, bringing her hand to his lips. "I look forward to seeing you again in your home. I have many fond memories of Waisley myself."

She shivered as he departed. Yeah, she remembered him skinning live squirrels and tormenting her. He didn't seem like that boy any longer, but she couldn't shake the feeling. She needed a way out of this engagement and fast. Perhaps her father would be home at Waisley, and they could correct this egregious error.

# CHAPTER 38
## The Estate

"**W**e can't train here," Kerrigan told Fordham the next morning as she threw all of her clothes back into her traveling bag.

He blinked at her in confusion. "Why ever not?"

"Ashby March."

"Ah. And what does your fiancé have to do with this?"

"He wants to court me. I had to think of a way to get rid of him."

Fordham was quiet for a moment before asking, "And what did you decide?"

"I'm going home."

"All the way back to Kinkadia?" he asked in confusion.

She sighed and looked back at him finally. "No. I suppose you will get to see my home, as I saw yours. We're to go to Corsica, where the heart of the House of Cruse is. My father's estate, Waisley."

Now, his eyebrows rose, and he crossed his arms. "All this to escape Lord March? Couldn't you just break off the engagement?"

"I don't know. Kivrin said he'd look into it, and I intend to find a way to do it. I am *not* marrying him." She sighed and threw her last cloak into the bag. "I have enough to figure out, Fordham. Basem's killer is still loose, and we have no proof that it's Lorian. Zina disappeared into the wind with our only hope of getting information about Mei. Not to mention, my probation."

"I understand," he said, stepping up and holding her shoulders. "You've dealt with a lot. I should be on probation right there with you."

"But you never will be."

"Only because you sent me for help."

"We're not having this discussion again," she said, slinging her bag over her shoulder. "If I hadn't sent you ahead, then I'd have been kicked out."

"I still think—"

"Well, it didn't happen. Now, get your bag. I have a month of training to make up for in ten days, and we have to be back for the party."

He glared at her interruption, but he went for his bag and came back with his pack. Kerrigan left a note for Audria, explaining as much of the situation as she dared. She'd gone into the spirit world this morning to explain to Tieran where they were going. He agreed to meet her in the stables. Though he objected to the name since he was not some ridiculous horse. Kerrigan laughing at the comparison hadn't helped his ego.

Still, Tieran waited for her when she came out of the glory of Belcourt Palace. Netta was beside him. She and Fordham saddled their dragons in companionable silence.

"I thought I might find you here."

Kerrigan winced at the sound of March's voice. She schooled her features and whirled around with a wide smile on her face. He held a small present in his hand.

"Why, March, the holiday isn't for another week."

He strode forward, narrowing his eyes at Fordham. "I thought you were going alone."

"Fordham is training me."

"Won't he also need an invitation from your father?"

Kerrigan swallowed and spoke the truest words. The ones that hurt the worst. "We're not courting," she said with a breezy laugh, as if unaffected. "It's like bringing a riding coach with me."

Fordham's shadows closed in tight around her at the words. The easy delivery. She could practically feel him wanting to snatch her away from March. But it also wasn't wrong. No amount of time in the greenhouse could change that.

"I see," he said, rather skeptically. "Well, happy holiday."

She took the proffered box and opened it. A small gasp escaped her throat before she could stop it. A yellow diamond sat amid a halo of diamonds on a gold band.

"March," she whispered in what she hoped was awe rather than horror. "What... what did you do?"

He plucked the ring out of the box, stripped her riding glove off of her left hand, and slowly slid the giant diamond onto her ring finger. "There. You always deserved a ring, and now, we are properly engaged."

She gaped at the giant thing on her hand. It was gorgeous and gaudy and way over the top. She loved it and wanted it off of her hand this very second.

Instead, she put a hand to her chest. "I... I don't know what to say."

He squeezed her hand, drawing her a step closer. "Come home to me soon, my love."

She nodded mutely.

March flashed a smug look to Fordham. "Take care of my fiancée, will you?"

"Oh, I will," Fordham snarled.

Her stomach dropped out as March just laughed and walked away.

"Don't say a word," she snapped at Fordham. She dragged the ring off of her finger and threw it into her saddlebag. She couldn't get the blasted thing off of her fast enough. She shoved her hand back into the glove and jumped on Tieran's back.

*Can I say something?* Tieran asked with mirth in his voice.

"Not a word," Kerrigan snapped.

And then they were in the skies, and Kerrigan lay against Tieran's back. What the hell was she going to do? Kivrin had better have a damn solution to this problem. She was going all the way to Waisley to get it.

\*\*\*

The flight to the Bryonican countryside took hardly any time at all. The seat of the House of Cruse was on thousands of acres of Corsica Forest. They bypassed the town of Lillington with its beautiful thatched-roof houses. Then, Waisley rose high on the next hill.

Kerrigan's breath hitched at the sight of it. She hadn't thought about the house that she'd loved so dearly as a child. The various gray stones that created the exterior. The gardens were bare in the chill. Frost covered everything in a soft winter wonderland, making it almost glow ethereally.

When she'd been young with only a strapping father for company, she'd wanted to bring her mother to Waisley. She envisioned showing her the grounds and making her fall in love with the estate the way that Kerrigan was. But she'd never had a mother. Not really. Her name was Keres. She was a human woman, and she'd died in childbirth, giving Kerrigan nothing but her name. Human women rarely survived birthing a half-Fae child. The magic depleted and killed them. Which was still horrifying, considering most half-Fae were born of human mothers. So many unnecessary deaths.

So, she'd never met her mother or taken her around the grounds. But still, when she looked at Waisley, she saw her there. All the hopes for a future that never came to be.

Kerrigan signaled for Fordham to begin his descent, and they landed in an open field near the western gardens.

*This place smells of dragons,* Tieran told her.

"I descend from a long line of Society members. My grandmother, Enara, and great-grandfather, Coen, were both dragon riders," she informed him.

But not Kivrin. He'd lost the tournament to Lorian, and the feud had existed ever since. A feud she was currently embroiled in.

*One of the greats was here,* Tieran explained. *This will be fertile training grounds.*

A lump formed in her throat, and she could just nod. As much as she hated what had been done to her, she'd never thought she'd see Waisley again. She still loved it so.

She slid off of Tieran's back and retrieved her belongings, patting his back. "We'll call when we start training."

*Good. I'm more than ready.*

"Me too."

Fordham dropped off of Netta and stood passively by as she collected herself. She'd seen his home in the House of Shadows and his love-hate relationship with it. Now, it was his turn to witness it on her end.

"Might as well go," she said.

He nodded and fell into step beside her as they walked to the north side of the house and up the gravel trail. A butler awaited their entrance, bowing deeply.

"Mistress Argon," he said formally. "Master Ollivier, welcome to Waisley."

"Hello, Warby," Kerrigan greeted him. "Is my father in?"

"Indeed, young mistress. He arrived last week and has been informed of your presence."

"Swell," she muttered.

"Allow me to escort you into the residence. Bedrooms are being prepared for you at present. I have refreshments in the sitting room."

Kerrigan nodded. Warby was exactly as she remembered him. A tall, rounded Fae male with thin blond hair and an angular nose. He wore House of Cruse livery and had been with the family for generations. His father before him and his father before him had worked for the Argons. Now, his children resided in Waisley and would take over for him.

Warby opened the enormous double wood doors, and Kerrigan stepped back in time. Everything was precisely the same. As if no time at all had passed since she had last been here. Tightly woven rugs lined the hardwood floor. Gilded framed paintings of Argons past littered the walls. An enormous life-sized portrait of Mistress Enara Argon, the last Society member and revered mistress of Waisley, sat in a place of prominence at the top of the winding staircase.

Her throat tightened, and before she could say a word, Kivrin strode into the room, plucking gloves off of his hands. "Kerrigan," he said in surprise. Though she had no idea if it was genuine. "I thought you'd be in Rosemont."

"That was the plan," she said. "But Fordham and I have some training to do. I thought I'd show him around in the meantime."

Fordham bowed to her father. "Sir."

Kivrin shot the prince a look that said his presence was less than welcome. "Don't you have the holiday off?"

"We do, but circumstances dictated this being necessary."

She was purposely opaque about her answer. But he nodded as if he knew all about her probation. He liked to stick his nose in her business. So, he probably did know.

"Though March seemed upset that we were leaving Belcourt," she said.

"Ah, did he?"

"Indeed." She felt the yellow diamond that she'd transferred into her pocket like a brand. "He said that he would be writing to you about coming to visit for courting."

Kivrin arched an eyebrow. "We'd be honored, wouldn't we?"

"Honored," she said dryly.

"Well," Kivrin said, clapping his hands together, "I'm sure you've had a hard day of travel and would prefer to change into something more suitable for the luncheon."

"We have training. We won't be stopping until evening."

"Dinner then," he said.

"Unfortunately, no. The hospitality is appreciated but unnecessary," she said. "We'll make do as we train."

Kivrin showed no outward sign of displeasure at the words and just nodded. "Very well. Kerrigan, may I have a word in private?"

Warby teetered back and forth. "I can show Master Fordham to his room."

Kerrigan winced and glanced at Fordham. "Do you mind?"

"Not at all."

She nodded at him and then followed her father through Waisley. Her feet carried her through the grand house by memory. He opened a side door, leading to his study. A giant desk and three walls of books took up the majority of the room. The fourth wall was a row of windows that opened to the gardens beyond. It smelled of ink and parchment and the particular softness she'd only ever associated with Waisley.

"I didn't think I'd ever see you here again," Kivrin said when the door closed behind her.

"I didn't think I'd ever come back."

"It suits you."

She shrugged. The house had seemed to warm at her first step through the door. As if it remembered and welcomed her.

"What made you change your mind?"

"March," she said simply. "It was the only way I could think to avoid him." He nodded. "Ah."

"Did you discover what to do about that? You said you'd look into it. What did you find?"

He leaned back against his mahogany desk, crossing his arms over the navy-blue doublet, and stared back at his daughter. The playboy prince and the lost princess. They were quite a pair. "Not much."

She huffed. "I'm telling him at the Season party that it's over. Is there no recourse?"

"You can call it off, but you would be in breach of contract. If he wanted to, he could sue you... us." He sighed. "He could come after the estate for it."

"After Waisley?"

He nodded once curtly. "I signed the betrothal agreement. How serious do you think he is?"

Kerrigan produced the yellow diamond ring and showed it to him. "I think he's serious."

"Gods," Kivrin said, plucking the ring from her hand. "What a rock."

"So ostentatious."

"Is this about the dark prince?"

She rolled her eyes. "As if I would ever marry a man that I didn't love."

"Love is not usually in the cards, I'm afraid."

"I'm not Bryonican."

"No, but can you afford to lose the support of the tribe?"

"What do you mean?"

He shrugged one shoulder. "Nothing," he said, obviously not meaning it. "I'm prepared to deliver payment if that's what he wants. I never relinquished your dowry. It's a considerable amount."

"Oh," she whispered. "That's quite generous."

"I got you into this. I suppose I should help get you out."

"Indeed."

She looked at her father again. The man she had despised for so many years. She'd sworn she'd never forgive him for what he'd done, but he seemed so much... less , alone in this big estate, than he when he was surrounded by so many others at his Row parties. As if the last twelve years hadn't been as kind to him as he wanted her to believe.

"Thank you," she said finally.

He nodded at her. "How long will I expect you to stay?"

"We'll fly back the day of the party."

"I'll have the cook prepare food for you while you're here."

"And if March writes…"

"I'll give you plenty of time alone with your prince."

She rolled her eyes. "That's not what this is about."

"I was once young and in love, Kerrigan," he said easily. "I can recognize the signs."

"We're here to train."

Kivrin smiled knowingly. "If you say so."

Damn, if she couldn't even fool her father, then who was she fooling?

# CHAPTER 39

## The Flight

**K**errigan was born for the skies. Watching the others fly while she was grounded had been pure torture. And now that she and Fordham were at the clearing to begin training, she just wanted to lie back on Tieran's back and let him take over.

Not that it was possible. They had a lot of work to do if they were going to keep up with the others. Ten days to catch up with what the others had been doing for an entire month. And they had to do it without a bond. It was impossible as far as she was concerned, but she refused to give up.

"We will make this work," she said, letting the words whip away into the wind.

*I'm willing to try,* Tieran said into her mind. *If you're willing to try.*

It was the most he'd said to her other than to make fun of her. He was still pissed that she'd been arrested. Which was all well and good because she was pissed too. What Lorian had done was outrageous. She wasn't going to let him win this one by giving up.

"I'm definitely willing to try," she told him.

They descended into Enara Meadow, named after her grandmother. She'd been on the Society Council for nearly a hundred years and leader of it for several decades. Kivrin never spoke of her. So, all Kerrigan had were legends.

"This is sufficient," Fordham said as he jumped from Netta's back.

"I would hope so, considering this was where my grandmother trained before the Great War."

Fordham glanced around at the beautiful meadow—as if seeing it for more than the barren, snow-crusted land it was—to the stunning visage of wildflowers, grasses, and blossoming trees. It was easy to imagine this as the perfect place to train during the springtime when everything was alive in Corsica Forest.

Kerrigan jumped down next to him, landing hard in the snow. "Ready when you are, princeling."

Fordham's eyes snapped to hers. "I thought we were beyond that nickname."

"Ah, but it's so fitting."

He shook his head and then moved into a military stance. She didn't know if he even did it knowingly. "We're going to begin with steering. Like with a horse, we can direct our dragons with the use of the bond."

*I take offense to the metaphor,* Tieran grumbled.

*As if we could ever be as dumb as a horse,* Netta said, nettled.

Tieran shot Kerrigan a look, as if to say, *See.*

"Regardless," Fordham said, smiling at Netta, "it's the same principle. And as with horses, we want to use a light touch. Jerking a horse around is going to do nothing but make them mad at you, possibly buck you off. Bond-strengthening exercises help keep the bond taut but not painful for either involved."

"Okay," Kerrigan said uneasily.

"So, first, we'll work on strengthening the bonds each day through meditation. And then we'll begin steering."

Kerrigan gulped and met Tieran's stare. Well, this was going to be fun.

She and Fordham burned away the snow in a small circle and then sat cross-legged on the dead grass. She put her hands on her knees, closing her eyes, as instructed. Then, Fordham took them through breathing exercises. She spent an hour on the frigid ground, breathing in through her nose and out through her mouth, pulling on the bond to grow it between them. Except, of course, there was no bond. By the time they rose and stretched their muscles, Kerrigan felt nothing but tense.

"We'll begin with basic maneuvers," Fordham said in his commander voice. She wanted to laugh, but this was who he was. When he instructed, he reverted to who he'd had to be to survive the House of Shadows.

"Excellent."

"We'll start with showing you how to use the bond to steer. You should be able to do it when you're not on the dragon, but I find it much easier the first time while astride."

Kerrigan nodded and then followed his lead, getting on Tieran's back. Fordham sat on Netta across from them in the meadow.

"Now, there are two ways to move the bond. The first is with your hand, as if it were reins." Fordham held his hand out in front of him and gently moved Netta's head from side to side and then moved her body backward and then forward. "This is the easiest way, but in combat situations, you'll need both hands for magic casting. Go ahead and try."

Kerrigan gulped. "It's been a while. I might be rusty."

Fordham crossed his arms and waited without a word.

She muttered under her breath, "Here we go."

She held her hand out gently in front of her, grasping for a bond that didn't exist between them. She moved her hand right and then left, but nothing happened. She blushed at the look on Fordham's face as he watched them together. Then, she went back to concentrating. Not that any amount of concentration would fix this.

She squeezed Tieran's sides with her thighs and coughed out, "Come on."

Tieran huffed and then spoke into her mind, *Right. Now, left. And backward.*

She followed his directions, moving her hand to follow his head. But the look on Fordham's face said that he could tell something was off. Maybe it was the split-second difference between Tieran's head movement and her hand. Maybe she was just imagining it. Could he know that Tieran was the one issuing the commands? And if he didn't see it here, would he see it later? Because this might work in practice, but it wasn't going to be practical in a battle.

"Good," Fordham said with a nod. "The second way is mental. You don't move your hand at all. Just use the strength of the bond to guide Tieran, which we'll do later in the week. Once you have a handle on hand-steering." He turned Netta to stand next to them. "Normally, as you know, we'd have obstacles set up around the arena for us to veer around. We're going to have to use the forest for that. Netta and I will guide you through the first pass to get the hang of steering with the bond."

Kerrigan nodded. "Sure."

Tieran backed up a pace and then settled. *This is ridiculous, Kerrigan. You cannot steer. There is nothing there for us to connect with. It will just be me flying with you on my back. That isn't what the program is for.*

"Shh," she hissed.

Fordham glanced at her in confusion. "Set?"

She nodded. "Yeah, we're ready."

Following Netta through the trees was as exhilarating as any other flying she'd ever done, but Kerrigan wasn't in control. She had no reins or tether to her dragon. Each time she reached for something—*anything*—to get them through it, she found open air. She gritted her teeth and pushed herself to do more than just sit there.

But Tieran was right. It was ridiculous. She wasn't doing anything. And she didn't know how they were going to hide this from everyone else.

Fordham directed them to try a pass of their own. The first one was easy. But as they progressed past the beginner's course, Kerrigan realized why the bond was so necessary. She couldn't feel Tieran beneath her. Not really. She only had an abstract sense of what he was going to do at any given point. And when he decided to take Fordham's instructions literally, as he would do in battle, she had no concept of what was coming next, and that resulted in her slipping and crashing down into the trees.

Her shield collapsed with the fall. She yanked on her air magic to cushion her fall, but still, she landed hard on her back, torn up from the trees on the way down. Air rushed out of her lungs, and her eyes burned.

"Gods," she groaned.

Tieran circled around and came back for her. *You don't look so good.*

"Let's do it again, jerk," she said, groaning as she came to her feet and climbed back on her dragon.

But a dozen more runs, and she was still falling off of his back. Her shield stayed in place almost every time, but that hardly made a difference. It was muscle memory, not talent. Even when Tieran started to warn her, she'd still lose momentum and cling to him for her life. It was obvious they were out of sync.

Four days later, when they hadn't progressed to mind-to-mind bond control and she was still landing on her ass in the snowy forest, Fordham called it quits for the day.

"No," Kerrigan ground out. "We have to keep practicing."

"We have been out here all day, every day for four straight days, Kerrigan. You're not improving, and there's no healer for all the myriad of bruises atop your body."

"You once said that pain was part of the program. You had to learn to live with it."

"Yes," he ground out. "When we were running five miles a day. Not when your spot in the Society is at stake."

She balked. "You think that I'm not good enough to stay in?"

He ran a hand back through his hair and looked across the meadow toward the sun lowering on the horizon. "I don't know what's wrong with you two. It's like you are always one second behind. I'm not qualified to say what the real problem is, but there is a problem. Maybe the month grounded hurt the bond."

Kerrigan gasped. He'd hit so close to home that she actually stepped back in horror.

"That came out worse than I meant," he said with a harsh breath, facing her.

She wanted to tell him. A part of her ached to let him know the truth. Maybe they could figure this out together. But she recoiled at the thought. Not because she thought that he'd turn her in to the Society, but because of the way he'd looked when he said the bond could be damaged. That it was the worst thing he could imagine. How would he react if he found out it'd never been there?

"You go," she told him, crossing her arms over her chest. "Tieran and I will stay and try to figure it out."

"Kerrigan..."

"We'll start again fresh tomorrow."

Fordham blew out an exasperated breath. "You don't have to stay out here."

"I want to," she said. "Just... go eat some real food." She climbed back onto Tieran. "We'll keep at this until we get it right."

Fordham looked skeptical. She hardly blamed him. If they were going to get it right, they needed a lot longer than a few hours. But it must have been a testament to how poorly she was doing that he didn't object to them staying out and working alone.

"Don't do anything stupid."

"What would be the fun in that?" she asked with a smirk.

He shook his head and then steered Netta away from the clearing. She watched them go with a sigh.

*What exactly are we going to do out here in the cold? I could use some dinner and a warm bed.*

Kerrigan rolled her eyes. "You're such a baby. We have to figure this out. No warm bed until we have it."

*We're not going to figure it out!* Tieran all but yelled, shaking his body until she slid off of his back. *This is the end of the line. Someone is going to know that we aren't bonded.*

"We figured everything else out! We can figure this out too."

*How? Because all you've done is fall off of me all week.*

"It's not my fault that they grounded me."

*Isn't it?* he snarled, stepping away from her.

"Fine! Just walk away. Just let us fail. I'll be kicked out, and you'll go back to the Holy Mountain."

Tieran stopped. His body heaving with anger. *Don't ever say that again.*

"What happened in that mountain, Tieran? Because whatever terrible thing it was, it's going to happen again if we don't work together."

He cracked one pained eye open and glared at her. *You want to know what happened? I grew up there. I had a mate. We found each other as hatchlings, and were together for thirty years. Her name was Risa. She was blood red with the widest wingspan and bright green eyes. I loved her.* He choked off on the word.

Kerrigan froze. "What happened?"

*The Society took her for the tournament.*

Kerrigan racked her brain for a Risa. She didn't know any dragons with that name. That had to be before her time.

*They took her, and she did her best. She had a dragon rider. She was supposed to come home after her year of training, and she never did. When I asked what happened to her, no one would tell me. I only found out years later that her rider had perished in an accident after the tournament. Their bond cleaved her in two. She died on the spot.*

Kerrigan froze. Her heart went out to him.

*She died for no reason but that stupid bond. I hate the bonds.*

"Oh Tieran, I'm so sorry," I said, tears coming to my eyes. "I had no idea. Why did you enter the tournament if you hated it all so much?"

*You think I had a choice? I spent fifty years purposely botching the entrance exam. So that no one would force me into a bonding. But the Holy Mountain decided that I had grieved long enough and sent me to the tournament anyway. They said if I returned without a bond, then my life would be forfeit for my failure.*

Kerrigan balked. "What? They'd kill you?"

*Dragons are still animals,* he ground out. *They cull the weak.*

"And after all of that, we still didn't bond."

Tieran nodded, turning his head away from her. *I sometimes wonder if it didn't work because I never wanted it to.*

"But you can't go back."

*No, I can't.*

"I can't go back to my life either," she told him. "It's this or nothing."

*Then, we really are in this together.*

"Until the end."

He nodded and then dropped down next to her. She leaned her head against his side. Something had shifted between them. That old animosity burned off. It had never been personal for Tieran. It had been about the loss of the love of his life. And she couldn't blame him for wanting to avoid the very place that had shattered his heart.

They stayed like that until the sun finally fell on the horizon, and then they got to work. Neither of them could be left behind. So, one way or another, there had to be a solution.

# CHAPTER 40
## *The Confession*

**W**hen the moon rose to its zenith, Kerrigan and Tieran finally called it a night. She was bone-weary and could probably sleep through a full day if she were able to. But they didn't have the luxury.

They'd tried everything short of bonding again. They didn't have the materials, and the last thing she wanted was a third look at her father being beaten by some unknown man. She'd really thought that they'd had it when they tried going into the spirit plane. But it didn't work here.

For one, she had to be out of her body for the spirit plane to function. She'd fallen clear off of his back the first time they tried. She hadn't been holding on tight enough, and she just plummeted. Tieran dropped back into his body long enough to catch her, but it had been problematic. The second problem was that while Tieran could fly straight while out of his body, he couldn't make any other movements until he returned. So, even after figuring out how to keep her attached to him, it took precious time to drop onto the plane, explain what they were doing, and come back to make the maneuvers. It wasn't like she could direct from the plane. Which would have surely been too convenient.

*We'll try again tomorrow,* Tieran said, nudging Kerrigan lightly after he dropped her off in front of the estate.

She shot him a forced smile. "Sure. Tomorrow."

She watched him fly away before creeping through the empty estate. She stepped into her room, stripping out of her warm gear, and collapsed into the bed. Theoretically, she should have been so exhausted that she passed out. That was what normal people would do. But her brain was going a thousand miles a second, and she couldn't shut it off. This thing with Tieran was a huge problem. There had to be a way to fix it, but she couldn't figure it out. And she needed sleep to be able to get there. Only she couldn't sleep.

She tossed and turned for what felt like ages, but she huffed and pushed herself out of bed. Tossing on a pale nightgown, she eased back out of her room. Her feet moved before she knew exactly where she was going. It wasn't until she stood before the door to her old room that it dawned on her.

Kerrigan gulped and then pressed the door open. She blinked in the moonlight. The room was perfect. It was set up exactly how she'd left it twelve years ago. As if it had been preserved in history. She drew a finger over the dresser, and no dust had collected there. It was well kept.

The four-poster with thick, gauzy white curtains, the palest of pink coverlet, and light-honey-colored furniture all brought her right back to that moment when she'd been taken away from this life. But what drew her eye was the open balcony door and the breeze flowing through the window. That should have never been allowed.

Kerrigan drew her magic to her and headed toward the balcony doors. If there was an intruder, she would stop them from hurting her home. Even if the word home made her chest hurt. But when she got to the balcony, she only found her father leaning against the railing. She released her magic at once.

"I wondered when you'd come up here," he said without turning around.

She didn't know how he'd recognized her. She'd been as silent as a mouse.

"Your shadow," he told her, as if reading her mind.

Kerrigan glanced down and saw where her shadow overlapped with his. Smart. "What are you doing up here?"

"Enjoying the view."

Her room always had one of the best views from Waisley. She could see for miles from her vantage point. She leaned forward against the railing. The moon cast enough light to see the edge of the forest and the tops of the homes in Lillington. Many of the House of Cruse subjects lived and worked in Lillington. Though there were other farming villages all across their feudal land.

After a moment, Kivrin said, "The village sent a missive this morning."

"About what?"

"It's apparently common knowledge that you're here, and they would like to throw a Geivhrea celebration in your honor."

"What?" she gasped. "But... why?"

His gaze swept to hers. He looked sardonic. "You're their lost princess too."

She glared at him and looked away. "When would they like this?"

"The day before you leave."

She was silent a moment, staring off toward Lillington. Her father had dropped her off on the steps of the House of Dragons, in the shadow of the mountain. She'd become a story—the lost princess of Bryonica. But she hadn't been lost; he'd known exactly where to find her. And now that she was back, everyone wanted to go back to how things had been. The king acknowledged her. March still wanted to marry her. Waisley was as if she had never left. And now, this...

It was a lot.

But it wasn't anyone's fault but the man standing in front of her. She wouldn't take this from them, just because everything had been taken from her.

"I'll do it."

He nodded. "They'll like that."

"Why did you do it?" she asked, trying for calm and failing. "Why did you leave me in the mountain? I had a life here. It wasn't perfect, but it belonged to me. And while I wouldn't trade what I have now for anything, I still wish to understand."

Kivrin breathed out slowly. He withdrew a cigar from inside his sharp black suit. He used a flicker of fire magic to light the end and took a deep inhale. He let the smoke out in rings before answering, "Many years ago, I was to have my own Season. As with your Season, it was the same year as what I assumed would be my dragon training. I was an eligible bachelor, and my mother wanted two things from me: to join the Society and marry to a station befitting my heritage." He wrinkled his nose. "Mistress Enara ran a tough household."

Kerrigan had never met her grandmother, but besides her genius, not much was said about her. She imagined the cold, hard green eyes from the painting downstairs and believed wholeheartedly that she had been a tough mistress.

"Unfortunately for her, I fell in love with a commoner."

"Scandalous," Kerrigan said.

"It wouldn't have been if I'd had taken her as my mistress. No one cared about status when it was just sex."

Kerrigan held up her hand. "I don't want to know who you're sleeping with."

He laughed softly and nodded. "Fair. But it was more than that. I was in love with her, and I wanted to marry her. I thought I could get away with it if I won the tournament and forsook my Season."

"But you didn't win," Kerrigan whispered.

"No," he said, taking another puff on his cigar. "I didn't. Nor did I marry."

"Well, what happened to the girl?"

"I brought her to the tournament. I got her accommodations in the Square so that she could be near the mountain. We ignored the warnings of her family and the distaste from mine. We were young and stupid." He shrugged. "You have that propensity too, I hear."

Kerrigan shrugged. He wasn't wrong.

Kivrin breathed in the smoke again. "Behind my back, she began to see another man."

"No," she gasped.

Kivrin nodded. "By the end of the tournament, she broke my heart, married another, and left me with nothing. I lost the Society and the girl I'd believed to be the love of my life in one fell swoop."

"That's terrible," Kerrigan murmured.

He laughed mockingly. "That man was Lorian Van Horn."

Kerrigan blinked. "Wait, Alura's mother is a Bryonican commoner?"

"Yes. Anya Van Horn used to be Anya de Leland. She's from Lillington in fact."

"Gods, no wonder you hate Lorian."

Kivrin tipped his head at her. "He's earned every ounce of my hatred."

"Mine too."

"Ah, yes, we would have that in common."

"But… how does this explain why you abandoned me?"

"I'm getting there," Kivrin said. "I was a wreck, as you can imagine, after what happened with Anya. It was how I gained my reputation as the playboy prince. When your grandmother passed, the House of Cruse went out of favor with the throne. Your great-grandfather had been king in his own right, and with my desolation and lack of marriage or heir, I had nothing to offer. For a time, it was all I could do to hold my head above water and keep others from invading our borders." Kivrin shrugged and took another drag from the cigar. "Things eventually settled, and there was talk of me marrying again to secure the line. I had no interest. To escape, I told the court that I was going on a five-year journey of the continent." He glanced to her and then away. "That's how I met your mother."

"Oh," she whispered. "She was living in another tribe?"

"Of sorts." He paused to consider and then continued, "She was married."

Kerrigan sighed. "Father!"

"I know. At the time, it didn't seem to matter."

"Of course you'd say that."

He shrugged. "I was in a low place. She was unlike anyone else I'd ever met in my life. Her husband found out about our relationship and nearly beat me to death."

Kerrigan froze. She'd seen this. The man larger than life who had beaten her father while a woman screamed in the background of her nightmares. The vision she'd had at her bonding that made no sense at the time. Was it possible that she'd seen reality?

"This man," Kerrigan said quietly, "was he massively tall with blond hair and wearing a white almost drape across him?"

Kivrin froze. His calm demeanor disappearing as true horror crossed his face. He dropped the cigar and grasped her by both shoulders in alarm. "You have seen him?"

"No," Kerrigan said quickly. "I... I had a vision of him. I saw it at my bonding ceremony."

"Gods," he said, releasing her and running a hand back through his hair. "If you see this man, you must run at all costs. Tell me you will run, Kerrigan. Promise me."

"Kivrin, what are you talking about?"

"Promise me!" he demanded, shaking her slightly.

"All right," she whispered. "I promise."

"I tried to protect you," he said hollowly, releasing her. "Your mother made me leave after I was beaten. She showed up here nine months later with a baby girl in her arms. She told me to keep you safe and that if her husband found out, he would try to kill you."

"And did he find out?"

Kivrin nodded slowly. "You had just turned five years old, and word reached me of a giant man in Lillington village. You were out riding, and I met you. I tried to remain calm and show you that everything would be okay. But then I bundled you up and ran. I told Helly that you were in danger, and we left you with the House of Dragons. You were far safer there than with me."

Kerrigan held her breath. "Did he ever find you?"

Kivrin swallowed. "Yes. He came to Waisley shortly after I returned. It was why I'd spread the rumor that you'd disappeared. So, by the time he came calling, everyone already believed you were gone. I had to bury you or else he would keep looking."

"But... but why? Why would he want to kill me?"

"Vulsan cares about one thing and one thing alone: power. The fact that you existed at all was anathema to him. I did what I could to protect you." He put his hand out and covered Kerrigan's. "I am so sorry that I made you believe you were not wanted all those years. I've always wanted you, but I wanted you to live more than my selfish desire for you to be my daughter."

Kerrigan looked up into his eyes and saw the sincerity there for the first time. The act of playboy prince that he continued to wear to this day to keep her safe. To keep a crazed man from slaughtering her because of her very existence.

Tears welled in her eyes, and for the first time in twelve years, she stepped into her father's embrace. He wrapped his arms around her shoulders and held her tight. They couldn't make up for the twelve years they'd lost, but they could at least start today on a new foundation.

# CHAPTER 41
## The Village

"I don't believe this is the best use of our time," Fordham said.

"Well, I already promised that I'd go."

Fordham crossed his arms over the black silk of his shirt. "What is this really about?"

Maybe she had. They'd stopped early the last two days and sat down for dinner with her father. She wasn't improving, and the extra practices didn't seem to matter, so she might as well spend the time with her father.

"I haven't been to the village in twelve years, and they want me to join them, Fordham," she said quietly. "I didn't hate everything about Bryonica. I loved this house and my lands and my people. I don't want to disappoint them. Surely, you can understand that."

He nodded and sighed. "I can."

"Good. Then, grab your coat, and let's go."

He muttered something under his breath but followed her out anyway. Warby had horses saddled for them, and she hoisted herself up into the saddle. The beast felt strangely small after riding Tieran all week. He was the smallest of the lot of dragons but still significantly bigger than a horse. She took up the reins and directed her horse out onto the road.

"If it were only this easy," she grumbled.

"What's that?" Fordham asked, trotting up next to her.

"Nothing."

They continued the short ride to Lillington in silence. The village was a mere mile from Waisley. Likely the only reason her father had been able to carry on a relationship with a local girl without anyone knowing the extent of it. She was surprised to find that guards circled the village before they crossed into the village limits. She didn't realize that her father had a patrol this close to town.

The village was comprised of a few hundred cottages with thatched roofs and wooden doors, congregated around a central town square. A circular fountain took up the center of the square, lying dormant in the chill. It had been festooned with faerie lights and shimmering ribbons. The entire square had been transformed into a faerie dream world. Courtesy of her father, of course.

He'd clearly sent ahead enough decorations and food for the entire village. It was an incredible expense that she'd had no idea he was going to incur for her. Sure, he usually helped throw a party for his subjects, but she doubted it was anything this extravagant.

"My lady," a man said as they pulled their horses to a stop. He bowed deeply. "May I assist you today?"

"Yes, please," she said.

He helped her down and then took both horses away to be stabled.

An elderly woman approached then with a dozen littlings, each holding a string of frost drops—a white winter flower that only bloomed after a snowfall. They'd laced them together and made a small crown.

"It is with great pleasure that we welcome you back to the House of Cruse, my lady," the woman said with a deep and powerful voice. She curtsied, and the littlings fell over themselves to follow. "We present you with the winter crown."

"Oh, thank you," Kerrigan said.

She bent down to allow one of the littlings to place the crown of flowers on her head. When she straightened, she felt a shift in the world. In faerie, symbols had meaning. The queen of Geivhrea with a crown of frost drops meant something to these people. And the world responded in kind, illuminating all of the faerie lights, intensifying the glitter on the ribbons, and brightening the smiles on all the village faces. If she had to guess, the food would taste better and the wine more potent. Nine months from now, there'd be a whole new cropping of littlings to look after. A blessing on the people since it was so hard to have Fae children in the first place.

"You bless us," the woman said. "Come. Let us celebrate."

Kerrigan walked into the center of Lillington just as the music started up and dancing transformed the square. They were local country dances, and she remembered every one of them as if she'd learned them yesterday. She'd always cursed Fae memory for how much she remembered about her time in Bryonica, but now, she was glad that she could keep up.

A smile crossed her face, and she grasped Fordham's hand. "Well, princeling?"

He laughed. A real, joyful laugh. It made her toes curl. "As you wish, my lady."

She flushed at the words before he caught her up and swung her into the dance. She didn't need faerie punch to survive this, as she had in the House of Shadows. She didn't need anything to enjoy Fordham's company. Cut off from the constraints of his people and the Society, they could live in the moment. She was a princess for her people, and he, her prince consort for the evening. Everyone accepted that as fact, and for tonight, it was.

They stopped only long enough to dance and accept the toast before returning to the dance floor. Her father appeared at one point, and Kerrigan only realized it because the rest of the village paused at his approach. As if the power of him swelled and magnified what was around them.

323

But he came no farther, accepted no food or drink, nor did he offer a smile of his own. He just cast sad eyes upon the crowd and watched their merriment. Was he thinking of Anya? Had he spent a Geivhrea here with her? Had they been prince and princess of their holiday?

When she thought to ask him, she found he had already left. It was appropriate for him to appear before his subjects, but he didn't owe anyone anything more. Especially with Kerrigan here in his stead.

She fell back into Fordham's arms. The music slowed to a syrupy cascade that she melted into.

"What is that face?" Fordham asked. She scrunched her nose in response. "You seem sad."

"I'm worried about my father." She shook her head. "I can't believe those words just left my mouth. I hated him for so long. It's weird to have any other emotion related to him."

"I'm glad that you've reconciled. You deserve to take back what was stolen from you."

"I don't know."

He tipped her chin up, forcing her to look at him. "You do."

"It's just hard. I always thought he was ashamed of me."

Kerrigan had confided in him about her problems with her father. He'd wanted to know why the sudden change of heart when she asked to start eating dinner with Kivrin.

"That's what he wanted you to think. It was safer for you."

She nodded. "I know that now. But I'm so confused." Her eyes roamed Lillington's square, all the people out here for her. This was the life she could have led. It was what she could have again. She voiced the treacherous thought. "Did I make a mistake by not returning to Bryonica?"

Fordham tugged her in closer. She rested her cheek against his chest. "It was the only choice you had at the time. Your father spent twelve years convincing you not to come back here. And he did it successfully. You would have picked anything over coming back."

"Not anything. You."

He held her closer in silence. Things neither of them could say hung heavy in the space between them.

As the party came to a close, the littlings were put to bed, lovers held each other tighter, and the magic of the evening faded. The faerie lights dimmed. The food was gone. The ribbons no longer glowed. Even her frost-drop crown withered on her head. Once picked, they only ever lasted the course of an evening.

She plucked the white flowers from her hair with a sigh. "It was lovely while it lasted."

"Let's get you back," Fordham said, taking her hand and guiding her to the horses.

She let him help her back on the horse, and they leisurely took the road back home. They passed a contingent of guards again. They nodded their heads as Kerrigan passed with Fordham, and she smiled brightly at them. She was glad that her father's men were protecting the village. It made her rest better at night.

Halfway back to Waisley, she decided that she wasn't ready for the night to be over.

"Come with me," she said, turning the horse off onto a well-worn path.

"Kerrigan," he called. He huffed behind her from the path. "Where are we going?"

But she didn't respond. Just kept leading the horse deeper into Corsica Forest. Then, she heard Fordham trot in after her.

"You'll be the death of me," he grumbled.

A smile quirked on her lips. She'd heard that before.

After fifteen minutes, she pulled off onto another trail, and the forest opened to reveal a series of pools. Despite the snow coating the ground and the chill in the air, none of them were frozen over.

"What is this place?" Fordham asked.

"The Corsican Hot Springs."

Kerrigan dropped down and tied her horse to a nearby tree. Fordham did the same but with a furrowed brow. "I can see that. What are we doing here?"

Kerrigan answered by plucking at the laces on her dress. His eyes went wide as she dropped the dress onto the forest floor, leaving her in nothing but her shift.

# CHAPTER 42

## The Hot Springs

"**K**errigan?" he said softly.

"I thought you were the one who didn't care about nudity," she challenged.

"Yes, but…"

She turned her back on him and let the shift drop. He sucked in a sharp breath as her bare backside was exposed. She hastily stepped into the water, letting the heat lick at her cold extremities. Once she was in up to her chin, she met Fordham's eyes.

"Come on, princeling. I wasn't ready for the party to be over."

His jaw was set and his eyes hard. As if she'd tricked him into something he didn't want. She opened her mouth to tell him that, of course, he didn't have to come in, but then, he was jerking free the laces of his pants and stripping. When he'd done so in their game, she'd watched with intent interest. But that had been a game, and this wasn't. Her cheeks bloomed red, and she hastily faced away from him until she heard him gently splash into the water.

She slowly turned back to face him, her eyes snagging on the steam hugging tight to his abdominal muscles, the broad sweep of his shoulders, and then finally that stormy gaze, as inimitable as ever.

"What are you thinking?" she whispered, sliding backward into the water.

"Are we back to Challenge or Consequence?" He sank deeper into the pool as he approached her.

"Truth or Dare," she teased. Her cheeks flared hot again as she thought about how far they had gotten in their consequence.

"A truth for a truth," he countered.

She nodded, intrigued. "Okay. What are you thinking?"

"That a siren has ensnared me in these waters."

Her breath caught. "Oh."

He stepped forward again until there was only steam between them. His face was still a mask. If he hadn't just said that he found her to be a siren, she'd never have guessed his true feelings.

"What are you thinking?" he asked.

"I don't know how you hide your true self so easily."

He startled at her words. "I don't."

She choked out a laugh. "You do. You hide from everyone, even me."

"I was raised to do it," he admitted. "I'm not sure I could break the habit. It's a defense mechanism."

"Against me?"

He paused. "Especially you."

She opened her mouth to ask what he meant, but he arched an eyebrow.

"I believe it's my turn."

She huffed. "Fine, princeling. Ask away."

"What did you see in your bonding ceremony?"

The air left her lungs in a rush, as if she'd been punched. Of course he would ask the one question she hadn't wanted to answer. The one that she'd taken a consequence for in their twisted little game. But it was just the two of them here. If she couldn't trust Fordham, who could she trust?

"I saw an estate much like Waisley though also like nothing else I'd ever seen. I was on a bridge in a garden. I crossed the beautiful visage toward the mansion home and found a giant of a man. He was in some kind of white dress draped across his huge figure. He stood proud over my father and beat him near to death. Someone was screaming from inside the house, begging him to stop. I could do nothing to stop it myself, but at the last second, the man turned, and he saw me. I screamed and was launched out of the dream."

Fordham, who was normally so stoic, looked truly shocked by her words. "But that makes no sense."

"I'm aware."

"You never saw Tieran? You never faced the three challenges with him?"

"No."

"You never chose each other above all else?"

"No," she repeated.

"Then... how are you bound?"

She frowned and looked down. He inhaled sharply, as if suddenly everything made sense. All the pieces of the last week fit together for him.

"You're not," he whispered.

"No."

"That's why you've been failing all these months. Why you seem off during training."

She met his gaze head-on. She had told him. He knew the truth now. She wouldn't back down from it.

"Yes. We've been faking the bond all this time."

"How?" he gasped out.

"The spirit plane," she said.

"Like the raven psychopomp in the forest during our final trial in the tournament?"

"Sort of. Zina showed me how to access the spirit plane and find the signature of another's magic. I can locate Tieran and speak to him anytime I want. We faked the second test that way."

"So, what's stopping you now?"

"We have to exit our bodies to enter the spirit plane. We can't be present and on the spirit plane at the same time. When we try, I end up slipping off of him or not making the turn fast enough. He can fly just fine, but I can't lead him."

Fordham nodded. "That explains so much."

"I guess so."

"Why didn't you tell me?"

She crossed her arms over her chest and sank lower. She didn't want to answer that one. "I think it's my turn, princeling. You've asked a few questions."

He straightened, as if forgetting they were still playing a game. "Of course. I simply meant that I could have helped you through this. You didn't have to do it alone."

Kerrigan nodded, her throat tight at those words. "Thank you."

"We can still figure this out."

"Fordham," she whispered. His eyes were bright on hers. "Who is Dacia?"

He went perfectly still. She'd asked him that question once before in a mountain room when she could have had him, if not for her mouth and her honor. He'd snarled at her then. He didn't owe her an answer now. He'd made it clear that he owed her nothing. Still, if she was spilling secrets, she would see how far she could push him.

"I hoped you had forgotten."

She laughed acerbically. "As if I could."

He clenched his jaw. "Dacia was my... lover," he said, choosing the word carefully. "We had been together many years. She wanted me to properly court her. She was a noble and of marriageable age, and everyone expected it of us. But the curse..."

Of course, the curse. The curse that made him second-guess everyone he cared about. For he was destined to hurt them.

"She tried to tell me the curse was fake—I'd only lost my mother to it; what did I know?"

She winced at those words. She'd said something similar.

"Finally, I agreed. I told my father that I was going to begin courting her publicly." He ground his teeth. "The next day, she was captured on the outskirts of Ravinia Mountain, helping a group of humans and half-Fae escape their prisons."

Kerrigan's jaw dropped. "What?"

"She was a revolutionary, who believed in the rights of humans and half-Fae. She wanted to see the end of their enslavement and torture. I had no idea. She never once mentioned it to me in all of our years together. But when she was caught, she was brought before my father. I stood there while they accused her of treason and beheaded her on the marble floor of the throne room."

Kerrigan gasped. "Holy gods, Fordham."

His eyes were empty while he looked back to that moment as it all unraveled for him. "She denied my involvement to her last breath, but it was too much for my father. He didn't believe her testimony. It was the moment that he turned on me, sending me into exile."

Kerrigan covered her mouth, horror on her face. She'd known that he'd been exiled from his people. That he hadn't known if he would be welcome back. But not all of... this.

"No wonder you hated me on sight," she whispered.

He laughed without humor. "I hated everyone on sight after that. I'd lost the woman I was to be with, my kingdom, my entire life in one fell swoop. I'd done nothing but care for her, and look at how the curse repaid me."

"Is that why you wouldn't answer your challenge question?"

His eyes found hers across the moonlit spring. "You believe that I loved her?"

"You wouldn't talk about her. You just said you were to marry her."

"I thought that I loved her," he confessed. "I believed it at the time. But how could I love someone that I didn't know?"

"Then, why?"

"Can't you see why?"

She tilted her head in confusion. She'd been certain that she knew why he hadn't answered. Now, as his mask finally fell away, she wondered if she had been perfectly, horribly wrong.

"I..."

"It was you, Kerrigan," he said, closing the distance between them. "It was always you."

"Me?" she could barely get out.

"I know you. All of you." He stroked one of her red curls out of her face and tucked a wet strand behind her ear. Her heart thrummed wild in her chest. "I have tried to resist wanting you and failed time and time again. I did not answer the question because I was not prepared to tell you that I loved you for the first time in front of an audience."

Her gasp was nearly silent. She reached out with trembling hands and cupped his cheek. "You... love me?"

"With all of my heart."

He drew in a step closer until their bodies were nearly touching. His lips hovered over hers. She could barely breathe as his hand slipped from her slightly pointed ear down to the hollow of her throat and across her collarbone. He continued his descent along her arm, to her waist, and landed on her hip. Then, he dragged her that last step forward, skin to skin. She hitched a breath, in shock at the feel of all of him pressed hard against her stomach. Her eyes widened as her hands came to brace against his chest.

It had been one thing the game they had played in the greenhouse. It had gotten too far. They had been drunk on faerie punch. It had been amazing, but not enough. Never enough. This was so so much more than that.

"I want this," he told her. "And I'm terrified I'll lose you."

"You won't lose me."

"You don't know that. You're engaged to someone else. We're both in mortal danger quite frequently."

"I'm breaking off the engagement tomorrow," she assured him. "And if we're already going to be in danger, then we should enjoy what we have while we have it."

He pressed a finger to her lips. "Don't say that. I never want to rush with you. To take what we can in scraps of moments."

She took his finger from her lips, pressing a soft kiss to the tip. "If we don't take our moments, someone else will take them from us. You love me, Fordham. I love you. You want this. I want this." She drew his head down to hers, just a breath between their lips. "Please."

A growl erupted from deep within him at that one word, the ounce of begging in her voice. She knew that they should wait until everything was settled. Until there was no March between them. Until they were finished with Society training. Until the world no longer burned. But if they waited, they'd never have time. She was done waiting.

His mouth collided with hers with a ferocity born from primal longing. As if he'd spent all of his energy staying away from her, and now, he could no longer contain himself.

They crashed backward in the hot spring. Her exposed back hammered against the rock wall, cutting into her skin. He bit down on her lip at the same time. Blood welled in her mouth, but the pain was nothing compared to his hands on her skin and his mouth on hers and the feel of him pressing hard against her body. She had waited for this too. Waited in agony for him to see what was right in front of him.

"Gods, I love you," he said, kissing down her neck.

She dragged her nails along his back, just wanting more, more, more.

"Please," she repeated.

His teeth dragged along her neck, and she shuddered all over. This was what she had been waiting for. The stolen kisses and moments would never be enough. Not from him. His hands slicked under the water across her bare skin. They caressed her hips, angled over her backside, and then slipped under her thighs. He lifted her effortlessly and she wrapped her legs around his waist. Her eyes rounded at the first feel of him pressed so achingly hard against her.

"Ford," she ground out.

But he was already moving, carrying her across the spring. She could have come apart at any moment. He was her undoing. He always had been. She had given herself up before, but it had been childish obsession. Not what they had. Not what was happening today. Fordham was her one and only. She had learned that the hard way. She refused to surrender this moment.

Fordham laid her backward on the steps of the hot spring. She lay naked against the wet stone for his eyes to rove over her. And he took her in appreciatively, as if she were the most glorious thing he had ever witnessed. She took in her full at the same time, her eyes widening at the sight of him as he came out of the water naked in all of his glory with water streaming down his beautiful body.

He smiled something fierce and primal. "Mine," he growled, as he pressed a kiss to her swollen lips.

"Yes," she breathed, beckoning him to her.

His body moved over her, discovering her in a whole new way. Her back arched, and she shifted, wanting more of him. He must have recognized that and his lips came back down on her. He shifted into position against her, and everything narrowed so closely. She groaned softly, a wave releasing through her body. Then he moved and finally, finally, they were joined.

The feeling was unfamiliar, almost painful. But then he was seated entirely and that pain passed. She released a harsh breath and opened her eyes to look up at him. A coupling during the winter festival was more than a blessing. Fordham was unequivocally more than her heart could ever encompass, and to have him here, now, was almost too much to bear. Here, they were united as one. As they always should have been.

Water lapped at them as Fordham began to move, and soon they were meeting the fluidity of the water all around them. A stroke as perfectly timed as the tide and just as inevitable. Magic lit in response to them, as if the faerie lights from the party had never truly dimmed. It had just followed them to this moment. The moonlight touched the surface of the hot springs, brightening the water and forest beyond. Right before her eyes, frost drops bloomed to life. And then, miraculously, snow began to fall as if the very elements approved.

Fordham pushed a hand up into her hair and drew their lips together. Heat sparked through her as she hit the crest of a long wave. And everything crashed down all around her. She quivered in his embrace as he grunted and came unleashed in her arms.

After a moment, they lay, sprawled on the steps of the hot springs. They breathed heavily, releasing hot puffs of air into the sky. Snow touched their lashes.

Fordham pulled her body closer. "I fear to ask…"

"Ask," she said, kissing his chest.

"Once your engagement has ended, may I court you properly?"

She laughed, leaning on an elbow. "And how do you explain this?"

His eyes were so sincere though. He wanted to do this right.

She pressed one more kiss to his beautifully swollen lips. "Yes. Once I break everything off, you can court me."

He grinned devilishly. "Then, I believe we should do this a few more times before we get to that point."

She laughed in relief and fell into his arms all over again.

# CHAPTER 43

## *The Geivhrea*

Geivhrea dawned the next morning to a bright winter wonderland. Snow blanketed the ground in thick drifts, cloaking the forest and beyond. The temperature had dropped precipitously in the middle of the night, and Kerrigan might have noticed if she'd ever made it to her bed.

"No, don't get up," Fordham groaned as she tried to slip out of the covers.

She laughed and snuggled in close again. "We have to return to Rosemont today for the party."

"Maybe we could stay here instead."

"I wish. We were invited by the king and queen."

He sighed and ran a hand back through his hair. "Politics," he said dismissively.

"Come on, you," she said. "We have to get moving."

He dragged her in for another lingering kiss. "We didn't sleep. Maybe we should stay in bed a little longer."

"And I thought I was the bad influence."

He grinned devilishly and pinched her rear as she slid out of bed. She swatted at him and pulled her shift back over her head. She found a thick robe in a wardrobe and drew it close around her shoulders.

"I should probably change before someone notices."

A sharp knock at the door had her heart racing. She waved at Fordham as she hastened to hide behind the curtains.

"Yes?" Fordham called.

A servant, Mereda, peeked her head in. "Sir, Lord Argon sent me up here. Lord March has arrived from Rosemont for Geivhrea breakfast with the House of Cruse."

Kerrigan bit her lip so hard that she reopened the bite from last night.

"We will break fast as soon as you have arrived. I must locate Lady Argon," she said, purposely looking around the room, as if Kerrigan would jump out at any moment, "and prepare her. None of us would want Lord March to suspect she was not in her bed last night."

"Thank you very much," Fordham said with a nod. "I will be down promptly."

The door shut behind Mereda, and Kerrigan breathed out a sigh of relief. "Gods, March is *here*? What is he doing here?"

"I don't know," Fordham said, shucking off his sheets and pulling on breeches. "But I intend to find out while you're getting dressed."

She dashed to him and pressed one more firm kiss upon his lips. "I'll only be a moment."

Kerrigan peeked her head into the hallway, and when she found no one, she darted into her rooms, where Mereda was waiting. She cocked an eyebrow. "My lady?"

"Yes, yes," Kerrigan said, waving her hand. "Let's skip the lecture."

She grinned. "He is quite handsome."

Kerrigan laughed. "Quite."

\*\*\*

A half hour later, she descended the grand staircase in a dress fit for a queen attending an audience. Mereda had insisted that she'd change her again for traveling but that she had to make an appearance if her betrothed was in attendance. She'd been right. The minute March saw her, something hungry shone in his eyes. He was pleased with her appearance, especially the giant ring she'd retrieved and put back on her finger.

"What a surprise," she said, hoping for enthusiasm.

"My lady," March said. He bowed extravagantly and kissed her hand as soon as she finished her descent. "Happy Geivhrea."

"To you as well. How did you manage the roads in these conditions?"

"Me," a voice called, and Audria Ather stepped out of the foyer, looking radiant and also perfectly apologetic. "He insisted that he had to see you for Geivhrea, and the roads were impassable."

"Audria," Kerrigan said. She pulled her into a hug, squeezing her a little too tight. "You shouldn't have."

"I know," she whispered, barely a breath. "I'm sorry."

Fordham strode out of the foyer as well with Kivrin at his side. His eyes landed on the ring on her finger with disdain. He looked ready to skewer Ashby March. Her father smiled at the irony of it all.

"Shall we break our fast and then open presents?" he suggested.

They entered the dining room. She was seated beside Audria and across from March. Fordham was across from Audria while Kivrin sat at the head of the table. He blessed the gods before eating, and then they dived into the food. Kerrigan ate as daintily as she could while also shoving food in her mouth at every opportunity to keep from speaking to March.

Kivrin and Audria filled the holes of the conversation with ease. But by the time they were finished and ushered into the sitting room, Kerrigan was well aware of March's foul mood. His animosity toward Fordham was becoming clearer and clearer. And Fordham's shadows hovering tightly around him helped nothing. Her betrothed and the man she loved in the same room was a disaster waiting to happen. If Dozan were here, it would have been the icing on the cake of the most awkward Geivhrea ever.

Kivrin distributed presents like Father Geivhrea delivering the goods of spring. He must have been quick with new gifts because he had a ruby bracelet for Audria and an embroidered coat for March. She hadn't thought she would receive anything from her father. It was her first gift from him in twelve years, and when she peeled back the brightly colored paper, a diamond brooch landed in her palm. Her eyes rounded as she saw the livery of the House of Cruse in the design—a raven and a rose twined in flight.

"It belonged to my mother. Mistress Enara wore it on the battlefield and the ballroom. I thought you might wear it tonight," Kivrin said softly. "You no longer claim the House of Cruse, but I believe it still claims you."

Her eyes were wet as she looked up at her father. "Thank you ... Father."

He smiled, letting her know that using that word was present enough.

Audria broke the moment by standing and clapping her hands. "While this has been wonderful, Lord Argon..."

"Call me Kivrin, Audria."

She nodded her head in acknowledgment. "We do have to get back to Rosemont for the party tonight, and Kerrigan and I have much to do to get ready."

"It was a pleasure having you all here. Regrettably, I won't be able to make the party, but happy Geivhrea, and send the king and queen my regards."

Kerrigan tucked the brooch into her pocket and then pulled her father into a final good-bye. "Will I see you in the city again?"

"Yes, I'll return with the snow melt. You can't keep me away."

She smiled. "Good. Perhaps we can do more of this."

"I'd like that."

He released her, and she hastened up to her room to change into her riding outfit. Mereda had already directed for her bag to be packed and taken to Tieran. When she arrived, Tieran, Netta, and Evien were clustered together, as if gossiping. Fordham stood stoic next to Netta while Audria chatted endlessly with March. As soon as he saw Kerrigan though, he broke off with Audria and came to her side.

"I rode here with Audria, but I would prefer to return with my betrothed," he said with a wide smile. He truly was incredibly handsome. More so than she ever remembered. As if Bryonica suited him more than anywhere else in the world.

"How do you find dragon riding?"

He wrinkled his nose. "It wouldn't be my first method of travel. I'll always prefer a horse, but I can't deny how fast it is."

"Certainly," she said.

Her eyes found Fordham's in the distance. He waited for her to break off the engagement, but she couldn't do it here. Then, she'd have to ride all the way back with him in their party. She'd do it after.

"Of course you can ride with me."

\*\*\*

Having March at her back for the entirety of the flight felt like a violation. It wasn't that he'd ever done anything precisely *wrong* to her in the present. It was her memories of him that stabbed at her mind. It was unfair to assume he was the same person when he'd shown no such inclinations, but she loved Fordham, and having March's hands at her waist made her feel slimy.

They landed in Belcourt Palace before lunch. March looked a little green in the face when he clumsily dismounted from Tieran's back. Tieran huffed in irritation and then flew away with Netta and Evien.

"That was bracing," March said. "I don't know how you do that all the time."

"It's my favorite thing in the entire world."

"Well, probably because you grew up with those people."

She blinked. "What people?"

"Oh, you know, in the House of Dragons rather than nobility."

She visibly bristled at his choice of words. "Why would that matter?"

"I mean that you had more time for dragon riding and less time for things that really matter."

She opened her mouth to demand to know what the hell he was talking about. But he must have realized he'd put his foot in his mouth because he bowed deeply and then drew her in close. "My lady, I have missed you deeply and hope that I might escort you to the ball tonight."

"I have to make my appearance with the rest of the Society members."

"Surely not."

She smiled innocently. "It's tradition. I'll save you a dance."

"All of the dances, my dear," he said, circling the ring that she'd put back on her finger for his appearance. He kissed her hand and then disappeared into the palace.

Audria rushed to her side as soon as he was gone. "I am so sorry. I never wanted to bring him. He'd asked me when you would be back and said that he'd written your father and never heard back. But then something happened last night. I don't know what, but in the middle of the night, he banged on my door and demanded that I fly him to Corsica."

Kerrigan's face paled. "In the middle of the night?"

She nodded. "I have no idea what happened last night that made him change his mind about it all."

Kerrigan gulped. She knew precisely what had happened last night. But the real question was, did March know she'd been with Fordham? And if so, how?

# CHAPTER 44
## *The Winter Party*

A knock sounded at her door. She was behind schedule. She should have already been at the party, but she couldn't shake the horrible feeling about March. If he knew about her and Fordham, that would be horrible. Maybe one of the worst things she had ever considered. And if he did, was it the curse working against them? She hated considering it, but she couldn't stop thinking about it.

If what had happened with Dacia was any indication, then whatever was coming for them would be coming quickly. She needed to get ahead of Ashby March, but she had no idea how.

"Come in," she said, expecting Audria.

Instead, Darby stepped through the door, looking resplendent in a full white gown, threaded through with diamonds that glittered like starlight. It made her onyx skin stand out rich and luminous. Her black hair was up in an intricate design with a hint of shimmer along her lids and lips.

"Oh my gods," Kerrigan gushed, throwing her arms around her friend. "Darbs, you look like a dream."

"Me? Look at you!" Darby said.

Kerrigan laughed. "What are you doing here? Shouldn't you already be at the ball?"

"Probably. Sonali isn't going to be pleased, but a grand entrance never hurt anyone. I haven't seen you in months. It's been far too long."

Kerrigan pulled Darby over to the divan. "Much too long. Tell me everything. Is someone courting you?"

She glanced down, picking at her nails. "Not officially, no. I thought this would be easier."

"Did you? Why would you think that?"

"I trained for this," she explained. "I thought I was meant to do this. But I really don't like men."

Kerrigan snorted. "I could have told you that."

"Why are they all so boorish? None of them are..."

"Clover," Kerrigan offered.

Darby sighed. "They're really not. But no one else is like Clover."

"That's a fact."

"How is she? I never see her anymore."

"Do you blame her?"

"Of course not. I was the one who ended it," she whispered sadly. "I just haven't seen her or Hadrian much for that matter. I heard what happened at the protest but not even from their mouths that they were there. I had to hear it from you."

"I'm sorry. I wish it could all be how it had been when we were still in the House of Dragons."

Darby sighed. "Me too. It was much easier then."

"Shockingly, yes."

"And what about you? March?"

Kerrigan wrinkled her nose. "I'm breaking it off tonight."

"Really? Because of Fordham?"

A small smile came to her face at that question. She didn't even know how to hide her affection for him any longer. And after tonight, she would no longer have to. "He asked to court me properly after I end things tonight."

"Oh my gods, Kerrigan!" Darby squealed. "Wait... can you do anything proper?"

She nudged Darby. "Hey!"

Darby giggled. "Gods, I have missed you so much."

Kerrigan couldn't even describe how much she had missed Darby. They'd been roommates in the mountain since they were little. That bond didn't just evaporate overnight. She could sit in this room with her all day and giggle like schoolgirls and have more fun than at the party. But that wasn't their life anymore. Darby was a Bryonican noble. Kerrigan was very nearly a member of the Society. Their absence would be noted.

"Come on. We can't stay here forever," Darby said, coming to the same conclusion.

Kerrigan rose to her feet and followed her friend to the door. "Oh wait, one more thing!" Kerrigan dashed back to the table and retrieved the brooch her father had given her this morning. "Would you help me attach this?"

Darby's eyes rounded into saucers. "Wherever did you get this?"

She took the ornament in her hand and gently affixed it to Kerrigan's Parris original gown. The diamonds glittered like star beams, somehow bringing the whole look together.

"My father gave it to me. It's the House of Cruse livery."

Darby clasped her hand. "Oh, Kerrigan. I know how much this means to you."

Kerrigan swallowed and nodded. They didn't have to say anything else. Years together meant that everything had already been said.

"Together?" Kerrigan asked.

Darby smiled. "Together."

They stepped out of Kerrigan's room and headed toward the ballroom as a unit. Music and laughter and chatter filled the hallways as they approached. Audria, Fordham, Roake, and Noda were waiting for Kerrigan near the entrance.

"Took you long enough," Audria said with a laugh. "I mean, I would want to make an entrance if I had that dress too."

Kerrigan turned in a circle. "Right?"

Darby squeezed her hand. "I'll go first. See you in there."

"Good luck."

Darby was announced behind them as Fordham stepped forward. He held his hand out to her. "My lady."

She swallowed, meeting his gaze. They were the foggiest of gray today. His face all sharp edges, but those eyes... those eyes were only for her. Something had shifted between them, and she never wanted to get it back. She put her hand in his and turned to face the ballroom.

A gasp came from the room as they were announced. Kerrigan could understand why. They matched in every sense of the word. Parris had designed her dress in the House of Shadows black and silver. The plunging neckline reached nearly to her navel with a shimmer mesh over the décolletage. A matching exposure was visible in the back as well. The same mesh covered her arms and tied off tight at the wrist and waist. The skirts were lush and full with hints of the silver shimmer throughout, as if he'd imbued the very material with his artist's magic so that they glimmered all on their own. And with Fordham in a black-and-silver suit, complete with a black cravat, they were a vision together. As if they had always been meant to be.

Their titles were called before the court, and all eyes turned their way. In the crowd, nearest the throne, Kerrigan could see Ashby March narrow his eyes.

Her heart skipped as the enormity of what she was about to do came over her. She had to break off this engagement. And she had to do it with a man who had demanded a dragon rider take him into the mountains without explanation… and actually accomplished it. Somehow, he'd known that she and Fordham were together. Which meant he must have had spies at Waisley. That thought turned her stomach. How much did he know? And how much more difficult would it make this if he did?

March left the queen's side, bidding his great-aunt adieu, and then walked right to her. "Lady Kerrigan, may I have this dance?"

She had steeled herself for this moment and nodded. She forced herself not to look at Fordham as March whisked her away. One dance, and then she'd end things. She didn't need to be here any longer than was necessary.

"You look lovely," March said as they fell into step with the waltz.

"Thank you. You're as handsome as ever," Kerrigan said.

It wasn't a lie as much as she wished it were. March was more stunning every day. It was a sin that he could be this attractive and not be the person that she wanted.

"Seeing the House of Cruse on you again brings me much joy."

She flushed at the words. "I never thought that I'd see it again."

"Why did your father get rid of you in the first place?" he asked calmly. As if it wasn't a loaded question.

"I've only heard the story he's told the rest of the court."

"He buried you, Kerrigan. Yet you were safe in the mountain all along," he said, holding her tighter. "Why would he do that?"

"He just wanted to keep me safe." With the shift in her relationship with Kivrin, she couldn't help defending him. Even though she had wondered the same thing for years.

"Why didn't you come back? Why did you let us all think you were gone?" He drew her off the dance floor and into a private alcove. She glanced behind her, looking for the safety of the crowd. "Why did you let me think you were gone? You could have sent a letter… anything."

Kerrigan bit her ruby-red lip and didn't answer him. There was no reason for what she'd done. She could have reached out and let someone know. But she'd been so young and so afraid. She hadn't been wanted. It was enough to keep her in one place.

"Answer me," he snapped. Kerrigan balked at the tone. He hadn't used that tone with her in years.

"Don't speak to me like that." He grasped her arm and pulled her even farther away from the safety of the party. "March, stop!"

"I want answers, Kerrigan. I'm tired of tiptoeing around the situation. Give me what I desire."

"I don't *have* answers. I was abandoned as a child. I didn't know what was going on, and by the time I did, I'd been buried. What child thinks that they're wanted after that? I buried my life that day."

"You didn't bury your betrothal contract as easily," he growled at her.

She stepped back, but he still had her arm. "Release me."

"No."

"You're hurting me," she said, trying to wrench her arm back.

"You're a Society member. You've been through worse."

"What is wrong with you?"

"How long have you been *fucking* him?"

Kerrigan startled at the brutality of the question and the careless use of the vile word. It said so much and so little about what had actually happened last night. "I don't know what you mean."

"Everyone knows it. Don't try to play dumb."

"I don't know what you mean," she repeated.

March narrowed his eyes. He still hadn't released her arm. There would be bruises. She shouldn't have been afraid. She was much more powerful than he was. She had four other Society members here with her. She could stop this. And yet she felt ensnared. As she had all those years ago as a child when she caught him skinning the squirrel. The ruthlessness of the act and complete lack of remorse. She'd thought he might be different. That he might have changed in those years apart, but no, he'd just gotten better at hiding it. And she was frozen in place as time shifted around them... and fear took the place of her confidence.

"You went to the hot springs last night. You returned to his *rooms*," March snapped. "How long?"

"How do you know that?" she gasped. "Have you been spying on me?"

March searched her expression carefully, as if looking for guile. When he found none, he actually laughed. He laughed at her. "You know nothing about your own lands, do you?"

"What does that mean?"

March dropped her arm, and she stumbled back two steps. "Your father was in *disgrace* before you were born. He cut a deal with the House of Medallion and then disappeared for five years. We protected the lands and people with the understanding that we were allies. And allies *repay* their debts. That means, as soon as you were born and named heir to the House, you were tied to my house, to *me*. The House of Cruse owed the House of Medallion a marriage betrothal for everything that we'd done for you. To this day, your father has next to no standing army, and *we* have been securing your lands even after your supposed death."

Kerrigan blinked at those words. Realization dawned on her. That meant that the soldiers she'd seen in Lillington hadn't been for the House of Cruse at all. They weren't her father's men. They'd been March's lackeys all along. They were the ones to see her and Fordham head off into the woods. They reported what had happened to him. They had likely been doing it all week.

"Yes," he said, a cruel smile twisting his features. "You understand now."

She had never considered *why* she'd been betrothed to March. Her father had never mentioned any consequences to her breaking the agreement. Or what it might mean for the lands or the people if she withdrew.

"So, it's over," March demanded. "Whatever is happening with Prince Fordham is over and done with."

"You don't get to decide that for me."

"You're wrong about that. We're engaged. I could try you before a court for being a slut."

Kerrigan gasped at the word. "How dare you."

"Or I could just withdraw my troops, declare war, and slaughter all of your people. Maybe we only need three royal houses in Bryonica anymore."

Kerrigan's stomach dropped. She stared at him in shocked silence. He meant it. He meant every word of it. He'd really do it.

"Why?" she managed to get out. "Why do you even care? You don't even know me."

"I don't need to know you, but I know what you're *worth*. The lost princess, a Society member, first of her House. The king is on his last leg. My aunt will become a dowager, and there will be infighting if there isn't a clear winner." He arched an eyebrow. "Frankly, I don't give a fuck about you, but you'll make me king."

"You'll never get away with it. I'm part of the Society. I'll tell them..."

"What are they going to do? They don't interfere in intertribal wars. You'd be violating their law, and they aren't going to come to your rescue. From what I hear, you're on thin ice with them as it is."

Kerrigan stared Ashby March down. She was just one girl. She had power but not against this. Not against these machinations. He'd had years to figure out how to make this work if she ever came back. He'd never believed her father's lies, and he'd do anything to become king. Even use her to his advantage.

If she didn't want to watch the people and place she loved burn, she'd have to do what he said. She didn't see any other alternative. He had her entire world in the palm of his hand.

"Do you understand?"

She swallowed and nodded. "I understand."

She understood that she couldn't go through with this, and yet she had no idea how to get out of it. Her magic spun all around her as fear crept in stronger and stronger. It was the same sensation she'd felt after the capital attack when she was arrested. She'd assumed it had been a fluke, but here it was, swirling all around her.

March was speaking to her, but she couldn't hear him through the droning in her ears. She stumbled away from him, out of the alcove he'd sequestered them in. March reached for her, but then Fordham's face came into view. He looked concerned, but March swatted him away from her.

She tried to speak, but nothing came out. The bottomless of her magic rushed up at her, emptying like a sieve. Her vision went black, and she collapsed.

\*\*\*

"Kerrigan? Kerrigan, can you hear me?" Darby's voice said above her.

For a moment, Kerrigan could almost believe they were back in the House of Dragons. Darby was going to brew her one of her hangover-cure healing potions, like old times. Then, she opened her eyes and remembered what had happened.

*March.*

"Ugh," she groaned, blinking.

"You're okay. Take a breath. You collapsed at the party. Sonali and I had you brought back to your rooms."

"Oh."

She glanced around through bleary eyes but only found Darby.

"Sonali already left. She said you were stable. The only thing she could recognize was that your well of magic had depleted to an unsafe level."

"Oh," she repeated.

"What happened?"

Kerrigan shook her head and came up to one elbow. Darby offered her a glass of water, which she drained. "I don't know. One moment, March and I were arguing, and the next, my magic went on the fritz."

"Has this ever happened before?"

"No." Kerrigan sighed. "Yes. It happened when I was arrested. And it happened a lot during the tournament."

Though she didn't mention that it'd happened in the tournament because she was having visions. Here, she hadn't even *seen* anything. What was happening with her spirit magic if she was having the same circumstances of her visions but no vision?

"Okay. Well, this is *way* beyond me. I think you need to talk to Helly when you get back to the mountain and try to find a cause. In the meantime, you have a very concerned gentleman waiting for you."

She winced. "March?"

Darby shook her head. "Fordham."

"Right." Kerrigan sighed. "I do need to talk to him."

"Try to rest. I've been doing some reading about healing magical ailments, and anything that depletes your magic isn't good."

"Story of my life."

Darby smiled at her and then opened the door, letting Fordham inside. He closed the door behind him but didn't take the seat. He just stared at her with that guarded expression back on his face. She hadn't ever wanted to see it again, and now, she was only going to make it worse.

"Hey," she croaked.

"How are you feeling?"

She shrugged. "Like my magic depleted and I passed out."

"I see. Did you have a vision?"

"No," she whispered, staring down at the stone floor. "I didn't. This happened when I was arrested, too. I didn't have a vision then either."

"That's unusual."

"I'm supposed to see Helly about it when I get home."

"That's a good idea." He paused before taking a step forward. "What happened with March?"

She closed her eyes, wishing she didn't have to say what was about to come out of her mouth. "We're still engaged."

Fordham froze. "I see."

"It's complicated."

"I'm sure it is," he said on a sigh.

"He had guards in Lillington. They found us in the hot springs."

Fordham's gaze turned stony. "Of course he did."

"We were still engaged at the time," she breathed. "And he threatened…"

He held up his hand. "I know precisely what he did. You don't have to explain." He laughed brusquely and turned from her. "It's the curse."

"Fordham, it's not."

"It is. I should have known better, but I took the chance anyway."

"We can still…"

"We cannot," he said, his voice cold.

"You won't even let me finish? You won't even fight for me?"

"I'm letting you go before the curse kills you," he said, crossing his arms, guarding himself from her. "My feelings matter little if your life is in danger. We will still work together. I promise to help you with training and get you to pass the flying test when we return, but that's it."

She choked on a sob. "Fordham, I don't want this to happen."

His shoulders bunched. "It doesn't matter what we want," he said and then left the room.

Tears stung her eyes. She balled her hands into fists and tried not to cry. She didn't even hear as Darby came back into the room. Just felt her wrapping her up tight and holding her as it all came unraveled.

# CHAPTER 45
## *The Heart*

CLOVER

"Holy gods, did you hear what happened to Kerrigan?" Hadrian asked the minute he stepped into the house he shared with his mentor, Fallon.

Clover frowned. "No, she's not even back yet."

"She got back today," Hadrian said.

He patted the seat next to him, and she crossed the room to sit at his side. Fallon was gone for the afternoon, which meant they had the entire time all to themselves. She should have been dealing in the Wastes, but she'd ditched when she got the message from Hadrian.

It wasn't love. That was what she kept telling herself as she shirked her responsibilities to end up in his arms. It was just a fun thing to pass the time. It wasn't because he'd saved her life and they'd huddled together in that sewer for hours with only each other for company.

That wasn't the first time she'd endured something like that. Unlike Hadrian. When everything had come crumbling down around her when she was younger, she'd only had herself to rely on. Now, she had Hadrian. It filled a void that she hadn't known she was missing.

But it wasn't love.

A hundred percent *not* love.

His lips trailed down her jawline. "You stopped listening."

"Sorry. What were you saying?"

"She had some blackout at the court after an argument with March."

"Ew, March," Clover grumbled. "How did Fordham take it?"

"I didn't hear that much. Just the gossip."

"I'm worried for Red, especially after her arrest. Maybe I should go check on her."

He kissed her collarbone. "Or you could check on her after you leave."

She laughed and pushed him away. "You're insatiable."

His blue hair stuck up in a perfectly tousled way. Those big brown eyes staring straight through her. "I've never known anyone like you, Clove."

"That right, sweetheart?" she teased. "You should slum it more often."

Fighting with him still made her hot.

"Don't say that about yourself," he said, reaching for her again.

"Hey. I know my own worth. I'm worth ten of any Fae around," she joked. "I also know that I'm not a pretty, fancy noble like..."

The name that she didn't say lingered between them. Darby. She wasn't like Darby. Darby, who had turned her down. Who was currently sullying her perfectly beautiful self with some Fae male who would never appreciate her and who she had no affection for. All to make little Fae babies rather than making herself happy.

Clover's mood soured at the thought.

Hadrian stroked back the cut of her bob behind her perfectly normal human ears. "I like you just the way you are."

"Course you do," she said with a wink.

His finger moved to the chain she always kept at her throat, and he pulled it out from where the necklace nestled against her skin. She grabbed it back from him and tucked it away.

"Sorry," he said quickly. "You just never take it off. I was wondering why."

"It was my dad's," she said softly. The shape of the locket pressed firm against her skin. "It was the last thing he ever gave me. He told me to always keep it safe. That it... I would change the world." She laughed. "It's ridiculous. What's one girl going to do anyway?"

"Isn't that why you're part of Rights For All?"

"And look at what that got us," she snapped unfairly.

He held up his hands. "I just think you should give yourself some credit. You are changing the world. At least mine."

He pulled her close again, and this time, she didn't resist. She didn't want to resist him anyway. Men were so much more complicated than women. She never preferred one over the other. In fact, she'd always just been attracted to the person rather than their gender. None of that had ever mattered to her. But Hadrian was one of the few males she'd felt comfortable with for this long. And she wanted it to work... even as they hid it from everyone else.

"Hey," he whispered, tipping her chin up to look at him. He was a full head taller than her, which was a feat. She was tall for a human.

His lips grazed hers. She groaned and leaned against him, forgetting the world. They still had hours to themselves. She needed to stop arguing with him and use the time to their best interests. Neither of them heard the soft tread of satin slippers against the wood or the sitting room door click open. Only the pained gasp from the now-open doorway.

Clover's head jerked to the side to find Darby's stunned expression. Tears came immediately to her big black eyes.

"Darbs," Hadrian said, taking a step toward her.

But Clover could say nothing. Just stared at her as Darby witnessed what they had been trying so hard to hide from the world. They were together.

And Clover's heart still lay at least partially in Darby's hands. No matter how much she tried... she truly wanted them both.

Darby shook her head and then ran from the room. Hadrian made to follow her, but Clover stopped him and went after her instead. She reached her just as she flung the front door wide.

Clover yelled, "Wait!"

Darby stalled at the front steps. She even looked beautiful as she cried. "What?"

"Why did you come here?"

"I hadn't heard from you or Hadrian in weeks. I thought something was wrong. I didn't think *this*."

"Why not?" Clover asked, pushing her. She knew that she should back off, but she never could back down from Darby. "You said we couldn't do this. You said you were going to marry a male and pop out a brood of Fae littlings. You're in the Season, Darby. You have no right to be upset about this."

"Then, why didn't you tell me?"

"Would you have preferred I rub it in your face?"

"No," she said, swiping at her tears. "Of course not. But... I just thought..."

"What? You just wanted me to wait while you moved on?"

Darby looked pained and her lip quivered. "It doesn't stop how I feel about you."

Clover's anger cooled. She released a breath. "Me either."

Darby's eyes jumped to hers. "Then... why?"

"I've always wanted you, Darbs. You know that. But I want Hadrian too. I want you both."

"It doesn't work that way."

"It can," Clover said. "If you weren't so set on being someone you're not."

Darby pulled back as if she had been slapped. "If that's how you see it, then I guess I made the right choice. I hope you two are very happy."

Then, she slammed the door on her way out. Hadrian appeared at her side a moment later.

"How much did you hear?"

"All of it," he said, reaching for her hand.

"And you still want to touch me?"

"I already knew how you felt about her."

Clover met his gaze. "And how do you feel now?"

"I will take you however I can get you, Clove," he said in complete earnest. "If you want us both, you can have us both. I want whatever makes you happy."

"I don't think that will ever happen," she said as she glanced toward the door.

"Then, I'll keep you as all mine."

He covered her mouth with his. He had a way of making her forget everything. And she dived into it, mind, body, and soul. Anything at all to forget that look on Darby's face.

# CHAPTER 46
## *The Blackouts*

Fordham was true to his word.

Kerrigan scrubbed her face dry and met him for the next three days for training. And in that time, he scrapped everything they'd been working on. What was the point of bond training if she had no bond? He made her memorize the flying test as he remembered it so that she could fake the testing for Alura.

They didn't discuss what had happened between them or March. He never once changed from the military general she'd first met back to the caring man she'd fallen in love with. He was direct and unwavering. She hated every minute of it even though she knew it was necessary. Both giving up what they'd briefly had and focusing only on the training.

When they returned to Kinkadia, Alura ran her through her paces.

She shook her head when Kerrigan finished the test. There had only been one snag that was different than Fordham's impeccable memory, and she'd faltered but recovered.

"I must admit," Alura said when she reached Kerrigan and Tieran, "I didn't think ten days was long enough to make up for what we had done in a month, but you passed. You keep surprising me."

"Thank you, sir."

Alura circled her, pacing softly around the dirt-covered arena. "You practiced with Fordham?"

"Yes. We were in my home of Corsica for a week and used ancestral land to work on it."

Alura stopped just outside of Kerrigan's vision. "Corsica? Were you near Lillington by any chance?"

Kerrigan's heart hammered as she nodded. "Yes. We celebrated Geivhrea with the locals."

"Interesting."

"Your mother is from there, isn't she?"

Alura came into her view. "How do you know that?"

"My father told me."

"Your father is a swine," Alura snarled.

Kerrigan arched an eyebrow. "No argument there."

A smile cracked Alura's hard features. "My mother always said she would take me there one day, but it's never happened."

"You are more than welcome."

Alura narrowed her eyes. "My mother wouldn't be though."

"I think she would. It all happened a long time ago."

"Feuds sustain themselves," she said under her breath.

"Sir?" Kerrigan said.

"You're dismissed, Argon. Come back tomorrow with the others, and we'll get to work on formations."

"Yes, sir," she said and then patted Tieran's side before traipsing out of the arena.

She found Fordham, Audria, and Roake seated around the dining room table, chowing down on roasted chicken, vegetables, and bread. Kerrigan reached for a skin of water and took the seat farthest from Fordham. They might be back to how things had been, but it didn't make it any easier to see him. It only made it worse.

"You passed?" Audria asked.

Kerrigan nodded. "Formations tomorrow."

"Finally," Roake grumbled around a bite of chicken.

"Where's Noda?"

The three of them went silent.

Kerrigan glanced between them. "What? What am I missing?"

Audria sighed. "She's not coming back."

"What?" she gasped.

"She decided to return to Concha."

"But what about Avirix?" she asked about Noda's dragon.

Roake shook his head. "They sent her back to wherever she came from."

"Gods," she whispered.

Fordham finally looked up at her. "Her bond was weakening, and she didn't think that she could keep doing it. When she made the decision not to stay, it broke the bond. They wouldn't let either of them stay after that."

Kerrigan swallowed. Right. No one was allowed in the Society without a bonded dragon.

"That's terrible."

"They said one in three can't hack it," Roake said. He looked between us. "They guessed two would be gone."

They all gulped.

Audria shook her head. "Noda has been frazzled for months. Think about what she said—that she wasn't good enough. She could have made it if she had confidence. We all said we'd make it at the beginning, and we *are* all going to make it." Audria said it with such veracity, as if just by proclaiming it, it would make it true.

No one argued with her regardless. No one wanted to be next.

\*\*\*

It was late, and Kerrigan was at her desk, taking notes on her latest history assignment when there was a knock on the door.

"Come in."

To her surprise, Valia appeared.

"Valia!" Kerrigan gushed, rising to her feet. "I haven't seen you in ages. How was your holiday?"

"Hi, Kerrigan. My holiday was relatively boring. Everyone was out of the mountain on Geivhrea, and I had the run of the place."

Kerrigan frowned. "I'm sorry to hear that. It must have been lonely."

"I've grown accustomed to my own company. I did see several of the other stewards, and we exchanged gifts. Nothing big and extravagant like the Season party at Belcourt Palace," Valia said with a wink.

"Oh, it was... nothing really. I wasn't even there long."

"Don't downplay it. It sounded amazing."

Kerrigan laughed. "Thanks. What brings you my way?"

"Helly," Valia said as if it were obvious. "She said that she received a missive regarding you and to fetch you. Any idea what that's about?"

Kerrigan winced. She certainly did. It had been two weeks since she'd been back. She'd been back to flying every day, and she'd had no other blackouts. But she should have gone straight to Helly about what had happened at court. She'd just been so busy.

"Afraid I do."

"Well, let's go then. She doesn't like to be kept waiting."

Kerrigan looked longingly back at her history assignment. She'd be up all night to finish this, if she went to see Helly now. But if she didn't go to see her, it would only be worse.

She sighed and nodded. "All right."

They chatted about the holiday as they trekked through the mountain. Training had taken time away from all of her friends. She'd be glad when it was over in a matter of months and she could start seeing people again. It wouldn't be easier, but it would at least give her a less strict schedule. She could only hope.

Valia left her at the door to Helly's healing office. It was open, and Kerrigan knocked as she strode inside.

Helly glanced up. "Oh good, you're here."

"You sent for me?"

"Correct. And I wouldn't have had to do that if you had told me what happened at Geivhrea."

Kerrigan winced. "Yeah, sorry. It slipped my mind."

Helly arched an eyebrow. "Blacking out and having depleted magic slipped your mind?"

"If you haven't noticed, I'm on probation and trying to stay in the Society."

Helly waved a hand. "Yes. Yes. Sit. Let's look at you."

Kerrigan came over to the table and took a seat. Helly examined her eyes, ears, and nose before checking her heart rate. Then, she ran a few additional tests and shrugged. "You seem perfectly healthy to me."

"Sonali said that."

"So," Helly said, crossing her arms, "did you have a vision?"

"No, I didn't."

"Hmm... but these are the same symptoms, yes?"

"They are. And it happened once before too."

"When?" Helly asked, taking notes on a parchment.

"After I was arrested."

"And what were you doing right before you blacked out this time?"

Kerrigan swallowed. Helly was Lady Hellina, First of the House of Stoirm. She would know what it meant if she and March were arguing. She might even understand the political ramifications that Kerrigan had never been aware of.

"Well?" Helly asked.

"March and I were arguing about our betrothal."

Helly sat across from her and crossed her arms. "I see."

Kerrigan glanced down and offered a half-truth. "My dad offered me my dowry to give to him to break it off. He didn't mention that House of Medallion wouldn't see that as enough for a debt paid."

"Your father is woefully uninterested in politics. I suspect someone like Ashby March would have taken that very poorly."

"Yes," Kerrigan managed.

"So, you were in deep distress."

"Yes." Kerrigan glanced up at her. "Do you know what's happening to me?"

"For all intents and purposes, it looks like magic sickness."

"What?" Kerrigan gasped. "That makes *no* sense, Helly. Magic sickness only happens to the really old Fae who refuse their magic *all their lives*. I'm only seventeen!"

"I'm aware. However, what we know from Gelryn about your spirit magic makes me think that it's accelerating the condition. It could even be why spirit-casters inevitably go mad and die. Magic sickness does the same to those who are untrained in the arts of their own magic. They spend their lives ignoring what was given to them, and their magic poisons them."

"It's *that* accelerated?"

"You're a unique case," Helly said.

"I don't want to be a unique case," she said, flopping backward. "I want to just figure this out."

"I know. I'll try to get a message to Zina. I thought she'd already be back by now."

"Me too."

Helly touched Kerrigan's arm. "We still have time. I've made some improvements for those with magic sickness, and I can reach out to others who have had more contact with it in the south. Bastian might be able to help. Just try not to stress."

Kerrigan burst into laughter. "Try not to stress while I'm on probation and have Lorian breathing down my neck?"

"Let me deal with Lorian."

She sighed. "Right."

"It'll all be fine. You're doing well in your training. You and Tieran are a great pair. Work with him and focus on the bond." Kerrigan forced herself not to recoil at the words. "I'm sure it can only help in this situation."

Kerrigan nodded. Another problem that she couldn't voice. Another stressor she couldn't get rid of. No wonder her magic was trying to poison her.

# CHAPTER 47
## *The Symptoms*

Over the weeks, Helly's diagnosis of her illness became clearer.

She'd had three more blackouts since the ball, each one connected to a stressor. One after a particularly grueling water-magic exam. Luckily, she got back to her room before it completely took her over. The second time, she wasn't so lucky. She collapsed after a formations flying lesson, which she'd bombed—hard—and she fell over right on the dining table. Audria thought it was exhaustion. Kerrigan knew better. The last time, she received a letter from March, explaining that he would be in town for the spring Season event and he expected her to go with him. She took a handful of steps as her anger built, and everything dissolved. Fordham had found her on the ground, hanging out of her doorway.

"You can't keep doing this," he said. "You need to figure out how to fix it. The others think you're losing your mind."

"I am," she groaned.

"Don't say that," he snapped at her. "You give no one reason to doubt you. Not after all the work we've put in."

And it had been "we" since Fordham had been helping her pass much of the flying exercises by feeding her the answers.

"What am I supposed to do? Every time I get upset, I black out. I can't fix it. I don't have a spirit magic teacher, and no matter how much I scream into the spirit plane, I can't find Zina's signature. I can't reach her to tell her to come back. Helly hasn't heard anything."

"What about Dozan?"

Kerrigan balked. "Are *you* suggesting Dozan Rook?"

He paced away from her, running a hand through his hair. "I hate him, but he's useful. He has that healer, remember?"

"Amond," Kerrigan said. He'd healed her after she was stabbed by Isa, and he'd done it in a couple minutes rather than *hours*. Not to mention, he hadn't drained off an ounce of her magic. It had connected them somehow, but it had been safe and quick. "I hadn't thought of him."

"If he knows healing beyond the bounds of what Helly knows, then it's worth a try."

"Dozan won't do it for free."

"Then, give him whatever he wants," Fordham growled. "Your *life* is on the line."

Kerrigan crossed her arms at the words. They both knew what Dozan Rook wanted from her. It was something she could no more give him than she could give Fordham at this point. She wouldn't put it past March to know of her affiliation with Dozan as well. He might even have spies in the Wastes.

"Only one problem: I'm still on probation."

Fordham blew out a breath. "Well, you're not banned from leaving the premises."

"I'm sure that doesn't mean I'm supposed to go traipsing around the Wastes."

"Then, don't let anyone see you."

"Fine. I'll talk to him," Kerrigan said.

Fordham visibly relaxed at her words. As if he'd been imagining an argument about the whole thing. But she couldn't argue with him, not about this. He'd found her on the floor. Things were escalating, and she needed any solution to what was happening to her.

She shucked on her favorite black cloak and forced Fordham to be her lookout as she took the back way out of the mountain. She inhaled deeply as she walked the streets of Kinkadia. The mountain was home, but the city belonged to her in its own way. She hadn't really been out of the mountain since her arrest, except for the errand to Parris and flying into Rosemont. That certainly wasn't the same as being anonymous in the city.

She wove through the crowded roads, crossing over the divide from Central and into the Dregs. Taverns lit up the night, and music belched onto the streets. She wanted nothing more than to dive into them all and forget all the stressors on her. But first things first. Getting these blackouts under control was the main priority.

Crossing the threshold into the Wastes felt like coming home. Kerrigan had spent countless hours here. She hadn't realized she'd missed it.

Kerrigan kept her cloak hood up as she headed toward Dozan's private residence at the top of the Wastes. He lived and worked from on high. No one could be higher than the King of the Wastes.

"I'm here to see Dozan," she told a guard.

He grunted, "He's not taking visitors."

"Tell him Red is here, and he'll see me."

The guard's eyes bulged. "Red? The fighter?"

"Indeed."

"Man, I'm a huge fan."

Kerrigan laughed. She had *fans*. It was beyond surreal.

"Miss seeing you in the Dragon Ring."

Kerrigan missed it too. But that time was behind her. "So, can I see Dozan?"

"Yeah. Let me introduce you," he said, stalking up the stairs ahead of her. He knocked on the door, "Boss, Red is here."

An audible sigh on the other side of the door. "Let her in."

Kerrigan pushed past the guard and entered the dimly lit space. Dozan Rook sat behind his enormous mahogany desk and stared down at a set of throwing knives in front of him. Kerrigan had only made it two steps inside when one of those knives was poised at her throat as someone grasped her from behind.

"Red is a clever moniker," a woman rasped behind her. "I believe you owe me a debt."

Dozan didn't even look up. "Clare, release her."

"I told her the next time I saw her, I'd kill her," Clare Rahllins crooned.

This was easily one of the last people Kerrigan wanted to meet in Dozan's office. During the tournament, she and Fordham had infiltrated Clare Rahllins' weapons deal when they were trying to figure out who had killed Lyam. It ended up being Basem all along, and Clare was caught in the cross fire. After Clare's men finished torturing Kerrigan and Fordham, Kerrigan had managed to free them by using her spirit magic, and they'd walked away unscathed.

Kerrigan reached for calm. The last thing she needed was to black out right now in front of both of them. "Release me."

"You deserve this," she spat.

Dozan finally lifted his head. His eyes were narrowed, and his mouth twisted into a smirk. "If you damage her, Clare, then you will pay for it in pounds."

Clare gritted her teeth and then shoved Kerrigan away. "Fine. What is she doing here?"

Kerrigan clutched at the small trickle of blood that ran down her neck. "I could ask you the same thing."

"I'm glad that you're here, Kerrigan. It saves me the trip of sending Clover to retrieve you."

"For what?"

"Clare has generously agreed to help me find evidence about where Basem's magical artifacts were being delivered to," Dozan said, steepling his fingers.

"What does it matter?" she asked.

"Who can afford Tendrille steel with illegal magical artifacts embedded in them?" Dozan asked.

Kerrigan hadn't been thinking about Basem Nix at all. She had been so worried about so many other things. The question of who had the kind of money to throw around on that had never occurred to her. "Someone rich."

"Exactly. There aren't that many people in the city who could afford it, which narrows it down immensely. And with that kind of wealth, who would you guess was working with Basem before his death?"

"Lorian Van Horn," Clare grumbled.

Kerrigan's eyes rounded. "Seriously?"

"It appears Venatrix tribe is arming themselves with illegal objects. Think that should be enough to point the finger his way for Basem's death?" Dozan asked.

"I don't know," Kerrigan said. "Lorian holds immense influence."

"Which is where you come in." He waved his hand at Clare. "You're dismissed."

Clare looked like she wanted to launch herself at them both. She'd been brought low, and she clearly didn't like to be beholden to the King of the Wastes.

Dozan stood from his desk, stepping around it to lean back against the front. He crossed his arms and studied her. "I've been gathering the intel while you played faerie dragon rider. I have the means, and you inspire the crowds. It's time to take it public, Kerrigan. Not to the council, but to the people. They deserve to know what's happening and what the Society is willing to cover up."

She shook her head. "No way. It's too soon. It's not enough proof, and even if I did that, I'd be *out* of the Society. They'd kick me out."

"Then, your part is over," he said easily. "You don't have to continue on with the Society as one of their puppets. You can change the world from the outside."

"We'll have a better chance once I'm in."

"And then what obstacle will they put in front of you?" Dozan demanded, slamming his hand on the desk. "Then, what will they say to keep you quiet?"

Kerrigan squared her shoulders. "I can't do it. It isn't safe."

"And you think it's safe for humans and half-Fae to wait until you're ready?"

"It's not enough, Dozan," she snapped, getting heated. "It's just not enough. Knowing that Lorian hates us and had me arrested wasn't enough. Accusing him of orchestrating the massacre wasn't enough. A human admitting that he worked with Basem will mean nothing to them."

Dozan launched across to her, grasping her shoulders. "Which is why we don't go to them. We go to the court of public opinion. Turn the tide, princess."

She felt her magic building inside of her. The first signs of blackout hitting at the edges as the panic rose at the thought of what he was asking. She couldn't do it. She certainly wasn't ready. She'd never *asked* to be a symbol.

"I need to sit down," she whispered. "Or I'm going to black out."

She pulled out of his hands and sank into a seat. Her vision dipped around her. Placing her head in her hands, she rocked back and forth, counting backward from a hundred. She had to get this under control, or she wouldn't be able to do *anything*.

"What's wrong?" Dozan asked. He didn't precisely sound concerned, but it was as close as she'd heard him since she was twelve—when he'd carried her away from a brutal beating and taken care of her. Back before he was King of the Wastes. Back before everything.

"I'm having blackouts. That's why I'm here. I wanted to see if Amond could figure out what's happening."

"Your precious Helly can't figure it out?"

"She said it's magic sickness."

Dozan scoffed. "You're seventeen."

"That's what I said. But we don't know enough about my magic. It seems to be triggered by stress, but I can't exactly stay away from stress right now. So, I wanted a second opinion."

"Fine," Dozan said.

Her head whipped up. "What? Just like that?"

"Did you expect me to say no?"

"I expected to bargain."

He arched an eyebrow. "You're going to help me take down Lorian Van Horn, yes?"

She nodded. She wanted nothing more.

"Then, you're going to need to be well enough to do it. I'll fetch him."

Kerrigan gaped at him as he disappeared from his office. She'd never in a million years thought that Dozan would just allow her access to his personal healer. Not without a fight and enough sexual innuendo to cloud the room with lust.

A few moments later, Amond stepped into the room. He still wore the red vest and black shirt that marked him as one of Dozan's men. His light-brown skin was glossy and serene, and he had sharply pointed ears and full lips. She knew that he'd given up his tribe affiliation to work for Dozan, but she never found out why he'd done it. Or where he'd learned this sort of magic.

"Hello, Kerrigan," he said soothingly.

"Hi."

"I heard about your dilemma. Shall we get started?"

She nodded, and he gestured for her to lie down on the divan against the far wall. As soon as she was seated, he drew a blue ball of glowing light into his hands. Her eyes widened. She didn't think she'd ever get used to that. Healing magic didn't work this way. It was supposed to be a bridge between the magic of the healer and the magic of the injured. It would take time and energy to fix things, but with Amond's light, he could heal injuries that normally took hours in a matter of minutes. She had no idea how he did it.

First, he drew the glow down her body, scanning her for injuries. He frowned when he reached her center and then continued.

"What is it?" she asked.

"Well, nothing seems to be wrong," he said thoughtfully.

"Oh," she whispered.

"Except…"

He paused and then returned to where he'd hesitated. He pushed the glowy ball down into her gut. Just as the last time, it felt as if bugs were crawling around under her skin. It didn't hurt, but it was unpleasant.

"This doesn't make sense."

"Tell me about it," she said with a soft laugh.

"It appears you have magic sickness."

"Yeah," she said with a sigh. "That's what Helly said too."

"You're so young."

"I know."

Amond frowned. "I've treated magic sickness in older Fae before. It doesn't have a cure, but there are some things I can do that will ease it. You said that you had been experiencing blackouts. Tell me about that."

She described the feeling of her magic enveloping her and then draining away. How she would black out and that everything only happened when she was stressed out. And no, there was no option where she wasn't stressed. He listened curiously, moving the blue blob around all the time.

"I see," he said quietly. "What happens with magic sickness is, the unused magic slowly poisons the blood, causing mental instability and eventually death. However, here, it doesn't appear that your magic has moved into the blood at all. It looks like it's just *gone*. Which should be impossible."

"I love being one of a kind," she muttered.

He laughed softly. "Typically, I'd drain away the excess magic, and that would help for a time. Truthfully, I'm not certain what to do here."

Kerrigan groaned. "Great."

He removed the blue light. "If you have time, I would like to run some more tests. They might take a while. I could keep you here most of the night. Just because I don't have a solution, it doesn't mean that one doesn't exist."

"All right," Kerrigan agreed. "As long as Dozan doesn't care."

"Dozan doesn't care," he said, appearing in the doorway. "You may remain the night. I never minded before, did I?"

He grinned that licentious look at her. She almost laughed. At least he was predictable.

"Then, we will begin."

\*\*\*

Hours later, with the sun rising on the horizon, they were no closer to an answer than they had been at the beginning. Kerrigan promised to return for more testing when she could and stumbled blearily back to the mountain in the early morning light. She had, at most, an hour before she needed to report for dragon training. She had neither slept nor ate. Today was going to suck.

She stepped into the mountain through the hidden entrance. She wanted to catch at least an hour of sleep in her room. But as soon as she crossed over, she realized she wasn't alone. Her instincts were null from lack of sleep, so she could do nothing as the guards rushed her.

"Take her," Lorian said with a sick, twisted smile.

Kerrigan gasped. "No, wait, please…"

But it was all she got out before the butt of a sword hit her in the back of her head, and she collapsed forward, only half-conscious.

# CHAPTER 48
## *The Council*

T he last few hours were a blur. Kerrigan had succumbed to unconscious-
ness by the time she was dragged to an iron cell. She woke, shaking. The iron
couldn't touch her the way it did full Fae, but it still left her feeling unsettled and
disoriented. It certainly did nothing for the lack of sleep from the previous night.
The only comfort was that she wasn't back in magic-dampening manacles.

No one came to see her. Not even Lorian. Not even Helly.

She would have demanded information from a Society Guard if she'd
seen one. But iron did enough to keep the guards away as much as it kept the
prisoners within. When no one came for her, she lay back down to try to sleep.
Only just after she managed to finally relax enough, a contingent of guards
appeared before her.

"Stand up," one grunted at her.

She realized that she recognized this man. He was one of the guards who
had herded the protestors into the street. He was the one who had "disappeared"
when the Red Masks showed up.

He looked at her with such hatred. Seeing that look on his face told her she needed to play this very carefully. She slowly rose to meet him, calm and collected.

"Don't make any trouble," he said, roughly grabbing her out of the cell and hauling her toward the stairs.

It took so much effort to not back-talk him. Oh, how she wanted to.

But she had no idea what was going on or where she was being taken. She needed to try to figure it out and figure it out fast. Because she was starting to lose that calm, and the last thing she needed was to black out in the middle of this.

Kerrigan saw no one in the mountain. Whatever Lorian had orchestrated, he'd done it well. It left Kerrigan with only one option.

She dropped into the spirit plane, like dunking into water. Her feet still moved along at the even pace the guards were carrying her at, but she spent all of her focus on reaching out to Tieran.

He soared over. *Kerrigan? Are you hurt?*

"No. But I was detained. I don't know where they're taking me, but Lorian set this up."

*I was taken in the aerie. I'm being held in a guarded room. They won't tell me what's going on either.*

Kerrigan sighed heavily. Great. No easy escape. "Try to speak to Netta if you can. Tell her what's happening and to send Fordham. He can help get you out."

*Do you think this is the end? Am I going back to the Holy Mountain?*

"Not if I can help it," she told him.

He nodded once fiercely. *I'll reach out to Netta.*

Kerrigan bounced back into her body, a shiver of fear settling through her as the guards hauled her before the open council doors. All twenty members and the presiding officer sat in the chamber, wearing the black Society robes. She caught Helly's eyes across the room. She looked stricken, and for the first time, she didn't offer any comfort. Kerrigan looked to Bastian, who looked equally grim. Lorian looked smug as hell. But it was the forbidding faces of the other council members she was acquainted with that made her nervous. Masters Kress and Lockney didn't make eye contact. Master Boze looked perturbed that she was even in the council. Mistress Anahi kept twirling a box braid, her face perfectly blank. Even Mistress Alsia looked worried, and she had been firmly in Kerrigan's corner.

"Please step forward, Kerrigan," Presiding Officer Malwin Zoh said. He was a grisly, old Fae. Though he'd taken care to keep wrinkles from his face and gray from his hair. Rumor had it that he had personal healers on hand to keep him looking as young as ever. No chance he was going into the abyss anytime soon.

The guards released her with a little shove, and she stumbled forward into the cavernous council room. Not only was it large enough to fit the entirety of the Society if need arose, but the room also soared ever higher with places for dragons to be in attendance. Today, there were no dragons to speak for her.

She stopped at the podium before the twenty-one assembled elected officials. "Thank you, Master Malwin. Perhaps you could illuminate the reason for my detainment and being brought before the council."

"If I may, Presiding Officer," Lorian interjected.

"By all means," Master Malwin said.

Kerrigan bristled. That wasn't good. Having the head of the council defer to Lorian couldn't mean anything good.

Lorian stood. "As you are well aware, you were arrested for your part in a violent riot. You were put on probation for your crimes. You were also grounded from flying during that time." Kerrigan glared at him. Violent riots. What a joke. "Yesterday, you flagrantly ignored the terms of your probation by leaving the bounds of the mountain to meet with insurrectionists."

"I did what?" she gasped.

"You were seen walking into the area in the Dregs referred to as the Wastes," Lorian told her plainly.

"So? I've gone there before. It doesn't mean I'm working with insurrectionists."

"Did you or did you not meet with Dozan Rook?"

The council buzzed at the name. Clearly, they knew who Dozan was. Not good.

"Dozan Rook," hissed Alsia with a sneer.

"The so-called King of the Wastes," Lockney informed them.

"He killed his own family, you know," Boze said with a glare. He'd always been a toad-faced jerk. Kerrigan had never liked him. "Nothing but a menace."

"Miss Argon?" Zoh prompted.

Kerrigan gulped. "Yes, I was with Dozan Rook."

"And were you aware," Lorian continued, "that he had sympathies to the violent group, Rights For All?"

"I... yes, but..."

"And that he was funding their mission, which involved the events of the night of your arrest."

"I knew he was giving them money, but—"

He cut her off, "As you can see, ladies and gentlemen, she willingly went into the Wastes to meet with Dozan Rook. She is friends with another orchestrater, who goes by the name of Clover. She met with them despite her probation and broke the rules."

"I can speak for myself," she snapped back.

Helly stood and gestured to Kerrigan. "I believe that we should listen to what she has to say."

"Of course you do," Lorian sneered.

"No infighting," Malwin said with a wave of his hand. "Let's keep this civilized."

"I second Mistress Hellina," Lockney spoke up. He gestured to his notebook. "For the record."

Zoh nodded. "Tell us what happened last night, Kerrigan."

Kerrigan gulped. "I have been under an immense amount of stress due to Society training. Since I was grounded for a month, I had spent ten days in

Bryonica during the holiday training to improve. Mistress Alura passed me for all of my tests, but I was pushing myself to the point of blackout. I spoke with Mistress Helly about these instances," she said, leaning heavily on the truth, if not giving them everything that had happened. "She recommended a stress reliever, but it wasn't working. I wanted a second opinion." There was hurt in Helly's eyes. Kerrigan hated it, but she had to push through. "I wanted answers to help me complete my tests."

"Answers in the Wastes?" Lorian scoffed. "What are you, a *loch* addict now? There's nothing there but prostitutes, drug addicts, and gamblers. How dare you besmirch Mistress Helly's name in conjunction to some hack you claim exists in the Wastes."

Master Malwin banged a gavel on his desk. "Enough, Lorian. That's enough. I would like to hear more about this. Helly, is any of this true?"

Helly cringed. "Yes. I was treating Kerrigan for her blackouts. I was unaware she was getting a second opinion about the matter."

"And what was causing these blackouts?" Malwin asked.

Kerrigan's eyes pleaded with Helly not to tell them. Magic sickness was serious. She couldn't let the council know. Gods. But she also couldn't expect Helly to lie either.

"Early signs of magic sickness," she said calmly.

The council erupted in shouts. Many of the members were calling it impossible. The rest were looking at her in horror. Bastian tilted his head and kept his eyes level with hers. He'd remained silent through the whole thing, but he had to be on her side. She needed him to speak the sense he so often did. She begged with her eyes, but he made no move to help her. He leaned back in his seat and watched and waited as it all went down.

"Magic sickness," Master Kress said in shock. "Surely not."

"I'm quite certain," Helly said.

"How can that be?" Anahi asked with fear in her voice.

"She's unstable," Lorian bellowed. "Magic sickness in a seventeen-year-old is unheard of. It's impossible even. It must be a reaction to the circumstances of how she joined the Society. The bond pushing back against her. No one in the Society has ever had magic sickness."

"It's not been documented, but that doesn't mean…" Helly tried to say.

But it was too late. Lorian's mania had infected the rest of the council. People were jumping out of their seats to argue now.

"She's cursed!" Boze shouted in alarm.

"The bond is killing her," Lockney said. He began to scribble furiously.

"She's unstable, and she must be stopped," Kress said evenly. "Magic sickness is too severe!"

"We could never have someone like that in our ranks," another member shouted, who Kerrigan didn't even know.

It was all happening too fast. Everyone speaking up at once. Their own fears blinding them.

Master Malwin banged his gavel all he wanted, but no one was listening. Lorian had wrapped them all up in a frenzy. Even Helly couldn't get through to anyone.

"Please," Kerrigan managed. "I'm not trying to hurt anyone. The bond isn't *killing* me." But no one was listening. "Wait!" she shrieked. "Lorian is setting you up! He wants all half-Fae eliminated. He's responsible for Basem Nix's death. And he's been illegally smuggling magical artifacts. He wants you to kick me out. He doesn't want anyone else to oppose him. If you don't listen, then you'll be next."

Helly covered her face, as if Kerrigan had said the exact wrong thing.

"I have proof," Kerrigan tried. "Check his rooms and his Row house. It's there. I swear it is."

Malwin finally stood. "Enough! We will not hear any more of these accusations against one of our most esteemed. You are trying to save your skin with some veiled threat. That is not proof. It is hearsay." He held his hands up to quiet everyone. "To the matter of Kerrigan Argon, who here votes in favor of removing her from her position in the Society?"

Kerrigan gasped as hands went up all over the room. Helly kept her hand down. Bastian made no move to raise his. A handful of others didn't vote for her removal—Alsia and Anahi were two of them. Kress, Boze, and Lockney all voted for it. Lorian, of course. Kerrigan counted the hands furiously. A majority voted her out.

Malwin brought the gavel down. "Done. Kerrigan Argon, you are henceforth removed from your duties as a member of the Society. You will go to your room and clear out your belongings. A debriefing will take place in one hour. Dismissed."

Kerrigan was rooted to the podium. She couldn't believe the words that had come out of Malwin's mouth. It couldn't be true. It wasn't possible. She'd done everything right. She'd kept to her probation. No matter what they'd said about Dozan, that hadn't been why she was there to see him. And she was going to get her magic under control. That had been the point all along. Oh gods!

A guard appeared at her side and roughly grasped her elbow, yanking her away from the council. Kerrigan was numb. Completely in shock. She hadn't had enough sleep, and she wasn't supposed to be around stress. Her magic flickered at her fingertips. She tried to tamp it down, but it was a flood rushing through her. Ready to explode—or worse, disappear altogether. She couldn't black out. She just couldn't.

She reached the open doors, and Valia stood off to the side. Her eyes were wide with alarm.

"I am a steward of the Society. I can take it from here," Valia said confidently.

"I'm here to escort her to her rooms," a guard said gruffly.

"Come collect her in one hour for her meeting with the presiding officer," Valia said, dismissing them. "Come along, Kerrigan."

Kerrigan jerked out of the guard's grasp and hastened after Valia, trying to hold onto her magic. "What are you doing?"

Valia waited until they were far enough away before whispering, "Getting you out of here. Fordham found me and sent me to help you. Hurry."

Kerrigan didn't ask questions. She needed to be out of the mountain and find Tieran. If she was kicked out of the program, then that meant he'd end up back at the Holy Mountain. That was something she would never allow. But if Fordham had sent Valia, that meant that Tieran had gotten through to him. Hopefully, he was safe. She couldn't drop into the spirit plane to find out right now.

"Through here," Valia said. She pushed a hidden lever, and a hallway opened before them.

"You really do know all the ways in and out."

Valia shot her a grim look. "I hoped to never use them like this."

She rushed ahead until they reached a set of stairs that led down. They came out on the other side of the mountain near the greenhouses.

"Good luck," Valia said.

"Thank you. I owe you a great debt," Kerrigan said to the girl.

Tieran was waiting for her as Valia shut the door behind her. She rushed to him, throwing her hands around his neck. "Oh, Tieran, you're safe."

*For now. We need to go.*

Kerrigan ran a hand down her face. "I can't yet."

*What do you mean?*

"There's something else I need to do before I can depart. I want you to go somewhere and hide—somewhere they'd never think to find you—and I don't want you to tell me where you're going. Just get safe. I'll reach for you when I'm ready to go."

*I don't like this. We should go together.*

"I know. They think they can silence me, but I won't go easy. I can't. I have to do what I always should have done." She hugged him one more time. "Now, go. Find a place to hide."

He nudged her gently. *Don't be long. I'm just starting to like you.*

She laughed as tears welled in her eyes. Tieran took off, flying into the distance. What she hadn't said was that they'd be safer apart, where they couldn't be each other's liability or weakness.

Kerrigan still had her cloak and pulled it back up around her curls. She took the long way to the Wastes, knowing there might be eyes and ears watching for her. She even took a back way inside, disappearing into the afternoon rush and reaching Clover's table.

Her head popped up in alarm as she shuffled and reshuffled the deck in front of her. She motioned for the pit boss that she needed a break from cards and then dealt like a pro. There were only two people at her table, and both won. She was barely tipped and then rushed to her side.

"What's going on?" Clover asked. "Shouldn't you be in training?"

"No time to explain. I was kicked out of the Society."

"Scales!" Clover gasped.

"Tell Thea that it's time. I'm ready to be the symbol that everyone wants me to be," Kerrigan said confidently. "It's time the rest of the world knows the truth."

# CHAPTER 49
## *The Rally*

**D**ozan arched an eyebrow. "You're ready for this?"

"Don't I *look* ready?"

They waited inside his office for Thea to work her magic with her contacts. Getting a sizable enough crowd together on such short notice was a feat in and of itself. The fact that Kerrigan had demanded that it take place just outside of the Wastes was another matter altogether. Thea had tried to argue that it wouldn't reach the Fae and members of the Society that most needed to hear her speech, but Kerrigan was tired of speaking for those who wouldn't listen. If she was going to do this, she was going to do it for herself, for the humans and half-Fae, for the Dregs.

Dozan leaned back against his desk, seemingly unperturbed by the demand in her voice. "Last night, you were yelling at me that you'd never be ready. I'm trying to make sure you know what you're doing."

"Last night, they hadn't kicked me out of the program!"

"Fair. I can't say that I'm upset by the circumstances. You are better than they will ever be."

"Let's get this over with." She rubbed her hands together to bite back the chill. Spring was well on its way, but she'd forgotten how much colder it was outside of the mountain.

Dozan stood and came to her side. He brushed her hair behind her recognizably half-Fae ear. "That fire in your eyes makes me remember why I fell for you in the first place."

She scoffed. "You never fell for me, Dozan. You saw power. That's all you love."

"This look holds all the power in the world," he said, tracing her jawline. "I cannot wait to watch you conquer it."

She pulled away from him, her face flushing. His words kindled something deep within her and made her forget for a moment at least what she was about to do. Likely his desired effect anyway.

Kerrigan turned to the door. "Let's go find Thea."

"As you wish," he said, coming to her side with a smirk on his face that said he knew how much he affected her.

Kerrigan stepped out of Dozan's office and across the hallway to a large conference room, which she'd never used before today. Thea stood among the rest of the Rights For All leaders as well as Clover and Hadrian. To Kerrigan's surprise, they were holding hands.

She arched an eyebrow in her friends' direction. Clover shrugged, all nonchalant as she drew a loch cigarette to her lips. Hadrian looked chagrined, but he didn't pull back. Well, *that* was new. How little had she seen her friends if she didn't even know when or how this had happened. She'd have all the time she needed now, and she'd make up for it.

"Kerrigan," Thea said, drawing her into a hug. "How are you feeling?"

"Ready whenever you are."

Thea nodded. "We're almost ready. My runners have been all over Kinkadia for the last couple hours, and look." She drew back the curtain on Dozan's window.

Kerrigan could see the growing crowd beyond. Her jaw dropped. "So many."

"All for you, my dear," Thea said, beaming. "I'm so glad that you've agreed to speak out. I am sorry for the circumstances."

"It's time," Kerrigan said. "Long past time. Though I was afraid no one would come..."

"Yes, well, attendance has been much lower at our events since the riot. We've been keeping a lower profile. Plus, I can hardly blame them. This was what happened when Cyrene won the tournament. They always try to put us down. It's how they remain in control. But we're not going to stop this time around."

"No, we're not."

The volume outside was growing increasingly louder. A chant had been taken up by those nearest the front, and it moved backward through the crowd. She pushed the window open slightly to try to hear what they were saying.

*"Kerr-i-gan. Kerr-i-gan. Kerr-i-gan."*

She straightened her shoulders. She'd gotten the people here. They were chanting her name. It was time.

Thea must have seen the change in her demeanor. "Shall we? I'll introduce you."

"After you."

Clover appeared then, grasping her hand briefly. "Good luck out there."

"Thanks." Kerrigan tilted her head at Hadrian. "How long has this been going on?"

She shrugged. "Since the riot."

"Ah," Kerrigan said. "Does Darby know?"

Clover's head bobbed. "It didn't go over well."

"Do you love him?"

Clover glanced over at Hadrian and back. "I feel like I could love them both."

Kerrigan arched an eyebrow. "More power to you. If I tried that, someone would end up dead."

Clover snorted. "So true."

"It's time, Kerrigan," Thea said gently.

Clover released her with a nod, and then Kerrigan was walking through the Wastes. Dozan led the way, and Thea stood at her side. He opened the door to his private entrance, and Thea went to warm up the crowd.

She stood in the small space with Dozan. Tension was high as she waited for the moment of a lifetime.

"Kerrigan…"

"Don't," she whispered. She met his amber gaze. "Just… don't."

He smiled, an almost-genuine gesture. "You know you owe me big time for all of this, don't you?"

She snorted. "And there's the Dozan that I know."

"And love?" he countered.

She shouldered past him and out the door without a reply. She did owe Dozan for this. He was providing the space both inside and out of the Wastes without talk of payment. And he'd bolstered Thea's numbers by sending out his own birds to all of the taverns in the Dregs. He hadn't had to do that. And she still hadn't thought that anyone would come to hear what she had to say.

"May I introduce to you, Kerrigan," Thea said to the sound of uproar.

As she climbed the few steps that led to the wooden stage, she kept her face neutral instead of the utter shock that she felt. Not just at the half-Fae and humans who had attended previous Rights For All events and were here again. They were primarily the well-off bunch. The ones who had the means and spare time to spend fighting for their own rights. Those few were drowned out by the working class in attendance. Her people—the literal Dregs of Kinkadia—had come out to see her. The ones who had cheered her name in the Dragon Ring, who gambled with Clover, who had bought her drinks for her victory. They had shown up, and they had shown up in droves. The sea of people vanished in the distance to a ripple of bodies. And every one of them was here for her.

Thea had shown her the air magic to use to amplify her voice, and she spun the magic as she took center stage. She held her hand up, and eventually, the noise quieted.

"Today was a day like any other," she began, her voice carrying to the farthest reaches of the crowd with ease. "You woke up. You broke your fast. You went to work. You came home, expecting to wake up and do it all over again, weighted down by the judgment and prejudice against your existence. You feel it in the jeers about your ears and the pittance in your wages and the lack of respect afforded to you by the very people who are supposed to govern you. I have called you here because we cannot go on like this."

Kerrigan raised her hands as a cheer rose up. She waited until it crested before continuing, "Nearly a year ago, I was named a member of the Society. To all eyes, it appeared a step in the right direction. Today, they showed how truly threatened they were by that step forward. Any achievement by one of us is a threat to their power, and they will react in turn. So, they responded by kicking me out of the Society."

A gasp rang through the crowd. Apparently, word had not gotten out about what had happened. It had been a closed-door meeting. Kerrigan was supposed to have been "debriefed" by a council member and then shunted off somewhere to disappear. Oh, how wrong they were about her.

"Yes, it's true," she said with fire in her heart and eyes. "A half-Fae ascended to their government, and their response was to find the first available reason to get rid of her. The same excuses they use to keep you down, to keep you in your place."

She met the gazes of those near her. "I see the hurt and pain that has been done to you over the years. The oppression that has not only made you suffer in poor jobs for less pay, but has also broken your spirit. There is a life in Kinkadia for the rich. The rest can be swept away to the Dregs, where the Society doesn't have to pay attention."

People were nodding through the crowd. They knew this life. They'd lived it.

"Where the Society doesn't have to face the truth. And I think that time has ended."

More cheers and cries. She could hear her name rising up from the crowd once more.

"I am Kerrigan Argon. I was born a Fae noble. I was abandoned at the age of five for having the audacity to be half-Fae. I rose up in the ranks of the House of Dragons, their very system, and still, they cast me aside because I was perceived as less than. Still, I joined the Society. You all watched me come back with a dragon. *Finally*, a voice for us that we have always deserved. And now, they expect us to be silent? We can no longer be silent!" Kerrigan cried. "We have demands. We demand a seat at the table. We demand representation in the government. We demand equal treatment and pay in our work. We demand equal treatment by the Guard. We demand to be known and heard as *equals* in the great city of Kinkadia."

She increased the air magic, making her voice practically boom across the crowd. She wanted it to be loud enough that the mountain trembled.

"Only then—when all humans, half-Fae, and Fae live together as equals—will we rest. Only then will we be free!"

She threw her fist into the air to punctuate her closing statement. The crowd followed, pumping their arms and calling her name over and over again.

# CHAPTER 50
## *The Aftermath*

Thea came back onstage then and directed the massive crowd on where to begin the march. Kerrigan ducked back inside and pressed her back to the door. They'd argued about whether or not Kerrigan should lead the march down out of the Dregs to the base of the mountain. She'd wanted to do it, but considering that she'd just escaped, they didn't want to risk her being arrested again.

On the other side of the door, she heard the rallying cries of the beaten taking up for themselves for the first time in so long. And she was the one who had gotten them out there. She was glad to be part of the movement and terrified that she would walk a new group of people to their deaths.

She pushed off of the door. She couldn't let that weigh on her conscience any more than the last rally. It hadn't turned into a riot because of her. The deaths weren't hers either.

When she stepped out of the darkened hallway, Dozan Rook waited for her. "Bravo."

There wasn't an ounce of jest in his voice. And for a split second, they were back in time. He wasn't yet a king. She was just a girl, not a symbol. One word of praise from him would have meant the world. She let it fill her then and smiled back at him.

"Thank you for your help in this."

"Aye, princess," he said, slipping his hands into his pockets. "You'll have one more thing to thank me for."

"Oh?"

Fordham appeared out of the shadows.

"I didn't kill him when he set foot on my property," Dozan said.

He looked as formidable as ever. He was wrapped in black silk. Those storm-cloud eyes swirling like a tornado. Her heart skipped a beat at the sight. They'd been on such unsteady ground ever since Geivhrea. She wanted to fling herself into his arms but held herself back at the last moment. "What are you doing here?"

"I helped you escape, and you didn't think that I'd come find you?"

"What's happening at the mountain?"

Fordham shrugged. "Lorian is in an uproar. He swore that he would catch you and try you publicly for what you'd done. Helly managed to talk him down. She also kept from showing her pleasure at the fact that you'd gotten away. But she couldn't hide it from me. She asked me to check on you once things calmed down. I wouldn't be surprised if Lorian is knocking down these doors soon as well."

"Let him try," Dozan boasted.

Fordham shot him a venomous look. "You can't hold back an assault from the Society."

"You have no idea what I'm capable of," Dozan drawled.

"He has a dragon. He is on the council."

"He has no warrant to search the place."

"As if he needs it," Fordham said with a scoff. "This place is a heathen's den, and Kerrigan is a known quantity here. If he suspects that she's here, he'll walk right through the front door with or without permission."

Dozan eyed the prince up and down, as if he thought this was a fight he could win. "Is that a threat?"

"A promise," Fordham said. "Which is why we need to move Kerrigan today before he gets a whiff of that." He pointed to the sounds of the rally outside.

"She stays here. She's safe with me," Dozan said.

"You cannot protect her."

"Enough!" Kerrigan spat at both of them. "I will determine my own fate. All of your posturing is making me sick of you both."

But neither of them seemed to be listening. It was as if she had completely disappeared and the tension between Fordham and Dozan had finally boiled over. If she didn't do something, then it would come down to fists. And truly, she didn't want to see the outcome to that.

"I said, enough!" Kerrigan yelled.

She forced her way between them. Her already-erratic magic answered her call with zeal. She gasped as the energy from her spirit magic welled and shot out of her hands. Both of the boys were thrown across the room. Their backs hit the wall with a thud, and they skidded down the walls to the floor. Neither looked wounded beyond their pride. Both looked shocked by the outburst.

Kerrigan panted as the wave of energy took everything out of her. It had hardly felt like anything, and now, the magic sickness was taking over again. She could feel her vision dimming at the edges already.

"Oh gods," she whispered.

Her knees hit the ground. Despite what she'd just done, Fordham and Dozan rushed back to her side at once.

"Kerrigan?" Dozan asked.

"Is it happening again?" Fordham said.

She nodded. "Get... Amond."

Then, she toppled over as her world went black.

\*\*\*

*Mei pushed her back flat against the war tent. As if she could make herself invisible by force of will. All around her were men and women wearing the black robes of the Society. Commanders in the dragon riders army with pins denotating their rank. The best she could hope for was that no one would notice her.*

*But she was not that lucky.*

*Trulian's gaze shifted to hers so briefly that nearly no one would recognize that it had happened. Master Roan noticed though. He noticed everything.*

*"Girl." He snapped his fingers, and Mei jumped.*

*"Sir," she said, bowing slightly at the waist.*

*"Come forward."*

*Mei did as he'd said and stopped before the table. All eyes were on her now. She wasn't timid, but there were no right answers here. Only problems.*

*"You are the ambassador to the Dark Court?"*

*Mei cringed. "Tribe Charbonnet," she countered. "Or if you must... the House of Shadows."*

*The Dark Court was what the Society had decided to call her court for disagreeing with how humans and half-Fae were treated within. They weren't perfect, but it wasn't like the Society treated them any different. And a civil war wasn't exactly improving the conflict between Fae and the others.*

*Master Roan waved his hand dismissively. They were the enemy. He would call them whatever he chose.*

*"Point out the entrances to Ravinia Mountain."*

*Mei blinked and then narrowed her eyes. "Why?"*

*"That isn't your concern."*

*"I think it is."*

Trulian stepped forward, clearing his throat. "I think explaining the tactical advantage to her would be helpful, Commander."

Master Roan nodded at Trulian. A man, so thus someone he saw as an equal. Oh, how far the Society had to go.

"The war has dragged on long enough. If we can seal off the mountain, how long do you think it'll take for the bastards to starve?"

Mei didn't let shock show on her face. No, she was from Charbonnet after all. She would reveal nothing to these people. Only cold, hard fury.

"The stores are nearly boundless. A couple hundred years at least," she said with confidence. "If they don't dig themselves out before then."

Roan nodded. "Then, it's settled," he ground out. "Dismissed."

Settled. It was settled. What did that mean?

"What is settled, sir?"

He met her gaze. "If sealing them away won't work, then we'll bring the mountain down on them." He said it with not one ounce of remorse. This was war. He made decisions about who lived and who died. And today, he was condemning the lives of her people.

"There are civilians in the mountain, sir. Women and children," she said levelly. She knew he wouldn't respond to hysterics despite how she felt.

"All the better to end the war sooner by destroying their escape route." Roan raised his eyebrow, as if waiting for her to object.

Trulian intervened. "I'll escort the ambassador out."

"See that you do. And keep her quiet, Master Trulian."

Mei turned on her heel and stalked out of the tent. She knew what "keep her quiet" meant. Roan wanted her put down in a shallow grave. What would that mean for Zahina? She'd joined this ridiculous Society as well. Despite her best interest.

"Mei..." Trulian began.

"Don't say it, Tru," she barked. She continued forward, stomping through the mud. "I'm going to talk to Zina, and then we're leaving."

*"I cannot abandon my people."*

*Mei shook her head. "It's a short trip."*

*He sighed, but he could deny her nothing. It was how they had fallen in love in the first place. Trulian headed toward the dragons to find his beloved Androma.*

*Then, Mei went in search of her Zahina, tramping through the dirty war camp. She was in mud up to her ankles and wanted nothing more than to rid herself of this place. Nothing had gone as planned. No one would listen. Ten long years, they'd been at war with no end in sight until tonight. Tonight, the war could end.*

*It would end with the genocide of her people.*

*She brushed a hand back through her hair. She wouldn't even be here if it wasn't for her daughter. She had joined up like the rest of the youth who thought they could make a difference and had no idea of what war was actually like. So self-righteous and certain that they were going to change the world.*

*Fae should have been slow to go to war and quick to retreat. Their long lives afforded them space to see reason. But no one would see reason.*

*The tent flap shoved open before Mei could do so. Her daughter stepped out. They were nearly the same height with the same black hair and dark brown eyes. She had none of her father in her. Only twenty turns of the sun and dragon bound. How had she failed her so completely?*

*"What do you want, Mother?" her daughter sneered.*

*"You know why I'm here."*

*"I won't go with you. You're a coward."*

*Mei winced. The words hit hard despite the youth in them. She didn't know what Mei had sacrificed for her.*

*"You have no idea what you speak of."*

*"I know that I'm here to help us win this war against those barbarians. What are you doing, Mother?"*

*Mei clenched her hands into fists. She wouldn't rise to the insult. Zahina would never admit to having a mother from tribe Charbonnet. "Please, come with me."*

*"Where? Where are you running off to? How dare you run away from your obligation to the Society."*

*"I have no obligation to the Society," she snarled. "The Society only cares for itself."*

*Her daughter took a step backward. "You include me in that assessment."*

*"Yes," she bit out.*

*"Then, we're done. Trulian will never leave either. How does he not see you for what you are?"*

*"Your father has nothing to do with this."*

*Her daughter narrowed her eyes. "He is not my father."*

*"We don't have to go through this again."*

*"I have no parents."*

*"Please," Mei whispered, broken.*

*She knew what she had to do. She had to go to Cavour. She had to put up the wall that would end this war. She didn't know what would happen when she did it, if it was even possible. But she knew what would happen if she didn't try.*

*She had seen it.*

*Everyone would die.*

*"Please," she repeated.*

*"Good-bye, Mother." The girl turned away from her and flipped the tent flap back open.*

*"Zahina, please..."*

*But she was already gone.*

*And Mei had to save the world.*

*On the back of Androma, Trulian found her. She climbed aboard, and then they were flying. Mei clenched tight to the dragon. She feared little since the visions had taken her at such a young age. But dragon flying always made her dizzy. As if she were that much closer to the spirit all around her.*

*They landed outside of her hometown of Cavour. She had been no one when she was plucked from obscurity due to her affinity for spirit. For years, she'd trained with* the ambassador to take her place. Leaving her hometown for the city of Kinkadia, where she'd met and fallen in love with Trulian. But Cavour would always be home.

War had not been kind to the once-beautiful village. Dragon fire had destroyed near half the place in one go. Only the mountains had saved the people within, leaving the humans and half-Fae to fend for themselves against a war they didn't want.

"I am sorry," she said.

"Mei, are you sure?" a voice asked behind her. She had told him her plan on the way over. "These people... they don't deserve this."

"They don't." Mei whirled around. Her heart constricted.

Trulian had been the first to believe in her. His resistance meant that maybe even she was crossing the line.

"Can you even do it?"

She bit her lip and ran her hands back through her nearly black hair. "I don't know, but what other choice is there? You know what they're going to do if we don't stop them. You were in the meeting, Tru."

He glanced off to the mountains beyond her head. "This can't be the answer. They're monsters, but..."

"It's the only way. I've seen it."

"Seen it?" He frowned. "Again? You didn't tell me."

"Oh, Tru," she whispered, all the secrets that lay between them clogging her throat. All the visions she'd never dared to tell him about as her mind shattered day after day along the campaign.

"Please," he pleaded.

"Step back. I must work," she said. "To save our very souls."

And then before Trulian could talk her out of it, Mei lifted her brown arms toward the tri peaks of the House of Shadows. A bright, blinding light built between her palms, and she unleashed.

Power emanated from her hands and flowed around her home. Cocooning them. Protecting them. Isolating them. She poured all of her heart and soul into the spirit magic. Her *people would be safe. The Society wouldn't remember where the mountains were any longer. They couldn't destroy her home. They couldn't destroy everything.*

*"I'm sorry," Mei whispered to Trulian just before the magic took her life force with it, draining every ounce of herself into the wall.*

*Trulian shouted, having just realized that she was not coming back. But Mei was too far gone to stop. The wall would stay up. It would stay up until it was time for it to come down. And she would make sure of it, even in death.*

# CHAPTER 51
## *The Shift*

ARBOR

Wynter raised her hands over her head. "Do you feel it? Do you sense the shift? It is coming." Her voice rose. "It is coming!"

Arbor almost yawned as she stared out at the emptiness. The wall wasn't something she could see as much as Wynter claimed to be able to. But she'd dragged a dozen of her best acolytes out to the wall on horseback to watch her wave her hands around. The people were getting restless. It had been nearly a year since Kerrigan had been here and performed her miracle. Arbor had asked Fordham to return for Geivhrea, hoping it would reenergize the people. But he'd had plans.

She couldn't exactly explain her reasoning and why it was dire. The people wanted—no, *needed* something to believe in. Wynter was the face, but Arbor was making it all happen. The king was slipping from popularity. If she played her cards right, then she could depose him anytime now. Maybe they wouldn't even have to wait for Fordham and Kerrigan to return.

"It is coming!" the acolytes chanted.

Arbor glanced at Prescott on the other side of the clearing. He rolled his eyes at her. She tried to hide her smile. Pres didn't do the best job at hiding his disdain from Wynter. It hardly mattered. Sometimes, it actually made it better. Pres would come in all cold and aloof, and Arbor would bring the praise. It raised her in Wynter's esteem with little work.

As long as she could keep Pres safe. He was the only person she had anymore. She'd kill Wynter and end the rebellion before she'd let her hurt her brother.

She had just looked down at her battered nails, wondering how much longer she was going to have to endure this, when a gasp rose from Prescott's throat. She jerked his direction at the sound. It was so unfamiliar from his normal teasing voice.

Then, she gasped too.

"Are you seeing this?" she said, directed to no one in particular.

But Prescott was suddenly at her side, ditching the blonde who had been on his arm for the event. "I see it."

Wynter raised her hands high. "The time is now."

And the time *was* now.

Arbor watched in fascination as the wall came into perfect focus. It shone a bright blue light, and for the first time, she could see the map of veins that ran through the entirety of the endless wall. They weren't cracks, like Wynter had said. They were more like vessels to carry the energy through. And they were *beautiful*.

"What you see before you is the wall," Wynter said. Her voice was reaching a fever pitch. "As I have told you all this time, it is visible, and it is weakening. Even you can see it now with your own two eyes."

The acolytes fell to their knees before Wynter. They bowed and praised her for her magnanimous behavior. For letting them see the wall as she'd claimed.

But Arbor remained on her feet. Wynter hadn't done this. She was a prop for Arbor's rebellion but not worth anything more than that. How was this happening?

"Soon, we will be free!" Wynter cried. "Soon, we will stake our claim. Soon, we will show the *world* who we are."

Then, as Wynter turned to face the wall, the whole thing shimmered.

Arbor gasped again. It was as if she were looking up at a kaleidoscope of starlight. Then, the wall burst in the air and rained down all around them. She held her hand out, and a piece of the wall touched her and then disappeared entirely.

"Are you seeing this?" Pres asked her.

"I can't believe my eyes," she breathed.

Wynter stepped forward. "It is time, children," she bellowed. "It is time."

She crossed the divide where the wall had been for a thousand years. Pres slid his hand into hers, and together, they joined her outside of the wall.

*Outside of the wall.*

She'd never believed any of Wynter's ramblings. But here she stood, on the other side of the wall. Whether she had done it or not was irrelevant. She had a dozen witnesses who would say she had accomplished it.

Arbor smiled devilishly and looked to her brother. "It's time."

"Sister," he said, bowing at the waist and kissing her hand.

"Let's go show the world what we're made of."

# CHAPTER 52
## *The Sickness*

CLOVER

Clover found Amond where he always was—in the loch den. "Get up. Get up. It's an emergency."

Amond nodded his head and took another puff from the pipe. "Has Dozan sent for me?"

"Yes! And he'll have your head if you're too high to work your magic."

"My magic works because of the *loch*, little mourning dove," he said as he rose to his feet. "Surely, you, of all people, know that."

"Why would *I* know that?" Clover asked, hustling him toward the door. "I'm a human. I don't have magic."

"If you say so."

Clover shook her head and rolled her eyes. "My dad was a clockmaker. My mom was a littlings school teacher at the Laments church. No magic on either of their sides."

"Religion has a magic of its own."

She scoffed, "I have no religion either. It died in the fire."

Five years ago, when Kerrigan had been brutally assaulted, Clover had been inside the Laments church on the Square with the rest of the orphans. She was the only survivor, hiding among the dead in the catacombs. She made her way to Dozan after that. But magic hadn't saved her that night, just her own ability to hide.

Amond ignored her comment but thankfully followed her upstairs. He stepped inside, and Dozan ushered him forward. Amond revealed the blue orb of his magic and ran it over Kerrigan.

He shook his head. "The magic sickness is progressing rapidly. She won't last through the night if we don't find a way to stabilize her."

"Then stabilize her!" Dozan demanded.

"I am not trained in this. My expertise lies elsewhere. You would need a skilled Society healer for this sort of precise work. I am a bit more of a broad stroke," Amond told them with no ego.

Fordham crossed his arms. "I'm taking her to Helly."

"You can't!" Clover said. "She just escaped."

Dozan put a hand on Clover's shoulder. "I agree with Fordham."

Fordham blinked. "You do?"

"If we do nothing, she dies. I can't live in that world." Dozan stepped back. "Take her. Do whatever you can."

Fordham nodded, an understanding passing between them in that second.

"I can't carry us both through the shadows at that distance," he said. Clearly, that fact grated at him. "I'll have to call Netta."

"Well then, I'm coming with you," Clover said.

Fordham didn't object. He picked Kerrigan up in his arms and strode toward the door. Dozan followed behind them, his eyes never leaving Kerrigan. Clover had doubted his affection toward her friend for a long time. She'd wondered what exactly his game was. Had cajoled them both to just have at it again to try to get over this insufferable sexual tension.

But that look in Dozan's eye wasn't like anything she'd seen from him before. Under all of his bravado, he actually cared about Kerrigan.

They both did.

People still milled around the outside of the Wastes when Netta flew in. Gasps echoed all around them as the crowd made a dash to escape her landing zone. Fordham didn't break stride. He nodded at Netta and used his shadows to move Kerrigan onto the dragon's back.

"Are you coming or not?" Fordham asked.

Clover looked up at the imposing beast with a speck of fear. She'd seen dragons all of her life, but it was different than getting on one. She had to douse that dread for Kerrigan.

While Fordham arranged Kerrigan on Netta, Clover figured out how to make the climb and then settled herself behind Fordham. Without a word of warning, Netta pushed off of the ground and into the air.

Clover screamed as her stomach fell to her toes and then back up. "Holy gods!"

She couldn't believe her eyes at how *small* everything looked. It was both exhilarating and terrifying all at the same time. And over too soon.

Netta landed in an aerie empty of dragons. She wondered where everyone was. Fordham once again used his shadows to drop to the ground and marched forward without looking back.

Clover slid down the dragon's side and patted her. "Thank you."

*Of course. I look forward to seeing you again under better circumstances.*

Clover eeped at the voice pressing into her mind. She had known dragons did that, but whoa!

She rushed after Fordham. She was tall, but she had to jog to keep up with his long strides. Kerrigan lay unconscious in his grip. Her eyes were closed, but Clover could see her eyes moving under the lids, as if she were seeing something none of the rest of them could see.

They wound ever lower through the mountain. Clover knew the path to

Helly's apartments. She had been there before and ran ahead to knock.

There was no answer. Then after another insistent knock, Helly opened the door. Her face was pale, and her normal pristine appearance had faltered. Her hair was loose to her shoulders. There were bags under her red-rimmed eyes.

"Clover?" she asked. "What are you doing here?"

"It's Kerrigan."

Helly straightened her shoulders. "What about her? Have you seen her?"

Fordham stepped forward. "Can you help her?"

Helly's eyes rounded. The wreck she'd been a moment ago vanished. "Bring her inside." She let Fordham and Clover pass. "What happened?"

"She had another one of her blackouts. We had a healer nearby, but he didn't know how to stabilize magic sickness. He said that you were capable of that."

"Yes," Helly said, asking no other questions. "Put her on the couch. Clover, fill a basin with water. Fordham, I want you to hold her down."

"Hold her down?" he asked.

"Don't ask questions. Just do it," she snapped.

And no one asked any more questions. Not for the two hours that Helly worked on Kerrigan and tried to get her to stabilize. Not when she took magic from herself and fed it into her body. Not when she asked for Fordham's magic as well. Clover had nothing to offer in that regard, but she ran every errand Helly commanded.

Finally, she stepped back. "That's all I can do."

Fordham released Kerrigan, who had finally stilled. Even her eyes had ceased moving.

"Is it enough?" he asked.

Clover's nerves were raw at the question. There could only be one answer. Kerrigan had to survive. She had to.

"Only time will tell. We're going to need to keep feeding her magic every hour, on the hour. I have a few honeycombs that should help."

Clover's eyes widened. "Honeycombs?"

"The legal kind," she assured Clover. "They hold my own magic. I keep a stash for when I need to perform particularly difficult healings. I'll use them now to keep her stable."

"How long can she stay like this?" Fordham asked.

Helly shook her head. "I've never treated magic sickness in someone this young. I've never seen it in someone this young. It could be hours or days."

Fordham nodded. "Thank you for your help. I'll wait here with her."

"If you aren't in training, your absence will be noted."

He narrowed his eyes. "Then, make an excuse for me."

"You know what they'll think if you're gone. You can't afford it."

"I'll stay," Clover said, putting a hand on Fordham's arm. "You can trust me to look after her."

He deflated and nodded before departing. Helly and Clover exchanged a look once he was gone.

"How bad is it really?" Clover asked.

Helly sighed and shook her head. "We're lucky she's not already dead."

# CHAPTER 53

## The Spiritcaster

**K**errigan spun in a circle. She was in the spirit plane.

She wanted to scream and scream and scream. To fall to her knees and weep for what Mei had been forced to do to her own people. All this time, she had been told that the House of Shadows had been contained for their own good. A thousand years of isolation for their part in the Great War and the sin of wanting to continue with slavery. But it had all been a lie.

A pretty lie spun by the winners, as so often happened in history.

The truth was much worse.

The Society had been ready to bring down the mountains and kill everyone inside—men, women, and children. They decided it was easier than continuing the war with such high casualties. And they even asked the ambassador to the House of Shadows how best to do it.

After her years in Kinkadia, with a daughter and her lover in the Society, they believed she would choose them first. But she defied them all and put up the boundary around the House of Shadows to *protect* them.

She'd done it, knowing it might kill her. Knowing it would leave her daughter orphaned and her lover empty.

What she hadn't known was how the spell would morph. Yes, it was to keep their location secret from the invading army. To have the Society forget where exactly the boundary to the House of Shadows was. But it had an unintended consequence—trapping the House of Shadows inside.

And Mei hadn't meant for it to stay up forever.

Kerrigan couldn't even fathom it. Mei hadn't been a talented spiritcaster. She hadn't had proper training, but she had to be at least twenty years older than Kerrigan, and she hadn't lost her mind yet. Why then was Kerrigan suffering from this magic sickness so young? Why then was she stuck *here*?

She turned around again. She was still on the spirit plane. Still stuck in her head. She tried to drop back down into her body, but the drop never happened. Her body was unresponsive. Scales!

Never before had she been unable to find her way out of the spirit plane. It had become such an easy shift that she could almost pop in and out effortlessly. Why then could she not move?

She tried again and again with no success.

Eventually, she gave up. She wasn't getting anywhere with that. She might as well explore this world.

The spirit plane usually appeared to her as clouds, as if she were walking on high. When working with Zina, she'd been able to step out of her body and look down at it, but she preferred this visage when she did it herself. It was comforting to soar above the clouds. As if she were flying. No need for a dragon at all.

She pushed off from the cloud and found that she *could* soar instead of walk. She hovered over the clouds with her hands in the air and kicked out like she was swimming. She propelled forward, staring down at the clouds, rolling over to see the sky far above. The sun beat down on her face. It was a perfect day.

And yet, it wasn't.

"Hello?" she called out.

She thought she had seen a flash of black against the sky. Almost like a bird. But she'd never seen anything else on this plane. Just herself.

"Is something out there?"

She didn't see anything, but she couldn't shake the unease. She couldn't escape the plane. She didn't want to find out if something else was here.

Still, she was too curious to ignore it. She pushed off a cloud and soared toward the speck she had seen only a moment ago. But as she came around another cloud, she didn't find anything at all.

Kerrigan crossed her arms and landed on the cloud, puzzled. She turned in a full circle. She'd been certain there was something. Then, just as she finished her turn, a raven appeared. She gasped, putting her hand to her chest. It had come out of nowhere. Just popped into existence before her face. It tilted its head and cawed.

Kerrigan stepped back. She'd been helped by ravens on the spirit plane during the tournament, but that didn't mean anything. It hardly meant this one would be friendly.

"Can I help you?" she asked.

The raven cawed again. And then it rushed at her. She screamed, running backward, but in an instant, there were hundreds of ravens cawing and flying straight toward her. She screamed as their bodies connected with hers, and the cloud around her collapsed. Her scream turned shrill as she fell through the open sky. Seconds ago, she'd had complete control over the clouds and flying, and now, she could do nothing but fall.

She broke through the last cloud and realized she was plummeting toward a distant ground. Rolling hills and a far-off forest dotted the landscape she was hurtling toward. She'd never seen this before. She didn't know where in Kinkadia this was. But she didn't particularly want to find out what would happen if she landed. If she was injured in the spirit plane, would she die here?

She gasped and threw every ounce of air magic she had out to cushion her fall. It did nothing, of course. There was no magic in the spiritual plane. Nothing at all to save her.

Her fear clouded her mind, and the ground was getting closer and closer. She was going to die. Oh gods, save her!

No, she couldn't go out like this. The ravens were still at her side. No longer touching her, but soaring toward the ground, as if this were completely normal. She remembered Gelryn's words a year ago when she'd first entered the plane. If she was in the plane, it belonged to her. It listened to her command alone. This was her circus.

Kerrigan closed her eyes and drew in her magic, as she would in the physical world. Then, she pushed not with the air magic, but with the very essence of self. Something shifted, small but malleable. She drew on it until it became almost solid. Then, she grabbed it with both hands and pulled.

She jerked to a full stop. Her ears were ringing, and all of her hair whipped forward around her face. Her heart beat a staccato in her chest. Even though this wasn't real, it felt more real than reality.

Slowly, she peeled her eyes open and found she was a mere foot from the ground, held aloft on her stomach by the spirit magic she had conjured out of thin air. She gasped, and the magic dissolved. Then, she clumsily toppled forward onto the ground.

"Ugh," she groaned.

"Impressive," a voice drawled.

Kerrigan stumbled hastily to her feet and found a woman standing before her. She was easily six feet tall with white-blonde hair, braided like a crown around her head. She wore sturdy, scholarly attire but of high quality with a crimson sash across her chest with three slashes across the front.

"Who are you?" Kerrigan demanded.

"Who are you?"

"I'm Kerrigan."

The woman stared her down. "And are you the one making all the noise around here?"

Kerrigan blinked. "I… well…"

"Shouldn't you be in schooling?"

"Schooling? No, I'm seventeen."

The woman sighed. "So, you're from the country then? Don't know the first thing about how to get to the academy?"

"I have no idea what you're talking about."

"Oh Lords, help me," she said, crossing her arms. "What backward town are you from that you don't even know about the academy?"

"What? I'm from the city."

The woman walked a pace around her. "Don't seem like a city girl to me."

"Why are you on my spiritual plane?" Kerrigan demanded.

"My ravens brought you onto *mine*, girl," the woman grunted. "You've been irritating me for nearly a year in this place. I finally got sick of it when you used enough crux to level a mountain."

"Crux?" Kerrigan asked in confusion.

"You're a spiritcaster, right?"

"I… yes?"

"Well, who has been teaching you?"

"No one," Kerrigan said. "I've been kind of doing it on my own."

"Emperor on high," the woman said, looking skyward. "No wonder you've been so *loud*. We need to get you to Rhithymna as soon as we can. If you have no parental standing, it'll be hard to get you into Himera, but I'll do my best."

Kerrigan blinked. "Can we back up? What in the gods' names are you talking about? Who are you? What is Rhythm-uh-whatever?"

The woman stilled completely. It wasn't until that moment that Kerrigan noticed how much she had been fidgeting, shifting her hips, tapping her foot, adjusting her clothing and the like. "Where are you? What city?"

"Kinkadia."

She furrowed her brow. "Huh. Well, I guess that explains it."

"Explains what?"

"Why you weren't found earlier."

"Found?"

"I'll begin at the beginning. I'm Professor Cleora. I teach theoretical casting at Emperor's Academy in Himera College. I specialize in spiritcasting. Though there are so few of us anymore that much of my job is giving a more theoretical basis to the spiritual."

Kerrigan's eyes widened. "I don't know what any of that means."

"Obviously," Cleora said. Her brown eyes lit up, and she began to pace back and forth. "The answer is clear. If all possibilities exist on a plane, then it only makes sense that they could bisect without direction."

Kerrigan tilted her head. "What?"

She turned to Kerrigan, as if just remembering she was there. "It was all purely theoretical, but all good theories are rooted in fact. Yes. Yes. You and I are from different worlds." Cleora said it so simply, as if the fact wasn't life-shattering.

"Different... worlds," Kerrigan said slowly. "Like you're from Eleysia over the ocean?"

Cyrene had crossed from Eleysia to Alandria.

"No, child. There are no oceans to cross, but dimensions."

Kerrigan shook her head. "I don't understand. You mean, you're on a different planet? Like in the stars?"

"Close enough," Cleora said, tapping her hand against her side. "Yes. See, the spiritual plane isn't flat, like this." Cleora drew a line in the ground before them. "It's not flat like the physical world. It's more like this." She drew three circles around the line, as if each were teetering on an axis. "So, you could be here"—She pointed to one spot in one circle—"and I could be here"—and then a point in another circle—"and we could still meet."

"Okay," Kerrigan said disbelievingly.

Cleora wiped the image away. "It doesn't matter. I don't expect you to understand advanced theoretical casting. Most of my doctoral students don't understand it." She waved her hand. "What's important is that you can now get your crux under control so that you're not so noisy when I'm working."

"My crux?"

"Is that not what you call it in your world? Magic, spirit, root, essence, chi, frippery. Whichever word you want to use. Most have gone out of fashion, and crux is the most accurate anyway."

"So, wait, what you're saying is that you can teach me spiritcasting?"

"Teach you? Well, of course I can."

Kerrigan nearly did a twirl.

"If you come to Rhithymna, I'll enroll you, and we can get to work."

Kerrigan's heart fell. "But you said we existed in different worlds. Can't we meet here?"

Cleora was already shaking her head. "No, that's impossible. Teaching you here would only give you a sliver of your education. You can only reach the smallest amount of crux on the plane, such as manipulating centri—"

"I'm dying," Kerrigan cut her off. "I have what we call magic sickness. My magic is poisoning my blood because I have too much of it and can't use it."

"That presents a problem."

"If I don't figure out how to use my magic, then I'll die. I'd love to come learn crux from you, but I need to survive first to do it."

Cleora circled her once more before sighing. "Fine. We can meet here once a month at the lunar apex."

"A full moon? Are you sure it's the same time frame in my world as yours?"

"My lunar apex is in seven days, and yours?"

"Same," Kerrigan said with relief.

"Then, it's settled. You will cease to be so annoying and loud while I'm practicing, and we will meet every thirty turns to keep you that way. Now, go on."

"Wait," Kerrigan said before she could go. "Do you have dragons where you live?"

Cleora wrinkled her nose. "Of course we have the beasts. Hard thing to train they are."

Kerrigan didn't know what that meant. The hard part was training the riders, not the dragons. The dragons did all of that themselves.

"Do you have bonding and dragon riders?"

Cleora shrugged. "Of course."

"My bond failed with my dragon. I don't know what I did wrong. Do you think it has something to do with my spiritcasting? Or can you help me work on the bonding?"

"I'm confused," Cleora said. "You bond *yourself* to the dragon? How barbaric!"

Kerrigan winced. "That's... that's not how it's done by you?"

"Certainly not. The greatest among us use a coupling. They reach with their crux and hold a dragon with sheer force of will." She shook her head. "But only the emperor and their lot are that powerful. Most use a crux bond."

"What's that?"

"It's a way to control the beasts without the massive amount of crux necessary for a true coupling. My brother is a dragon trainer, and his crux bonds are superior to all others. He's even tied some off for officers to use. If you have sufficient magic, you can create a crux construct like so." Cleora used her spirit magic, and suddenly, a golden light appeared before her hands. She stretched it out until it made a long, thin line. "This is spiritcasting, but you can do it with other forms of crux. Just in the liminal space, you wouldn't physically be able to see what I'm doing. From here, you tether the crux bond to your dragon. It puts you in charge of the beast, and once you are through, you remove it quite like any other creature. Just make sure the beast is tied down before removing it. You don't want an accident."

Kerrigan wanted to try it and also feared it terribly. The way Cleora talked about dragons, she most certainly was from a different world. She talked about them as if they were just larger horses. Like they had no thoughts or feelings. Just animals to their core. Nothing at all like Tieran or any of the other wonderful dragons she knew.

But if what Cleora had said was true? Then, Kerrigan could crux-bond with any dragon she wanted at any time. There would be no need for an individual bond. Which was both exhilarating and incredibly invasive. She could never imagine taking Netta away from Fordham or Tavry from Helly. They were bonded for a reason.

"Go on, try. I know it's different where you're from, but here, even littlings can create a construct."

Kerrigan nodded and reached for the spirt magic—crux—within her. Found the space where she'd saved herself from the deadly fall and pulled a speck of gold light out.

"Good. That wasn't so hard, was it?"

Kerrigan shook her head. "No. It was almost easy."

"Easier off the plane too. Now, stretch it."

Kerrigan pulled her hands apart, and the light flickered and stretched slowly at first and then with gusto.

"Good. Good. Now, this is the important part. You must focus your intention on the bond. It is malleable and can bend to your will. So, you want to focus on it becoming a crux bond. You want to be in control of your dragon with all the proper properties. My brother's bonds are exceptional because his intention has been developed over the years. I could probably write an entire series of books on the importance of intention, but we only have right now. So, try that." Then, abruptly, Cleora turned away from her. "Lords, I must get back. Time is a slippery thing on the plane."

"Wait... what do I do now?"

"Tether it to your dragon. Once it's in place, they will follow your command until you remove it. If you're not in a place to attach the bond, I'd suggest running for cover. Dragons will always kill before allowing a bond. Good luck. I will see you in seven turns."

Then, Cleora popped out of existence as if she never were.

Kerrigan still held the crux bond in her grip. Could this actually work with Tieran? The bond was supposed to go both ways. Not leave her in complete control. Wherever Cleora was from, they must have different kinds of dragons because she could never use sheer force of will to hold any dragon, least of all Tieran.

She dropped her hands, the crux disappearing as easily as Cleora had. She'd found a spiritcaster teacher. Not the one she had been expecting. But nothing since the tournament had first started had been expected. At least if she had a teacher, she'd be able to use her spiritcasting and not have that magic poisoning her.

If she could just get out of here.

She took a deep breath and released it gently. Yes, she was ready. The world was waiting. No more lingering here.

She dropped. This time, the plane released her, and she fell into her body.

# CHAPTER 54
## *The Awakening*

**K**errigan woke to darkness. Her head pounded, and her throat was dry. Her stomach seized, as if she hadn't eaten anything in days. And though her magic felt tapped, the first press of it began to rise when called, reassuring her that she hadn't lost it entirely.

She had no idea where she was. She'd passed out at Dozan's and ended up in a fine bedroom that would never be found in the Wastes. She snapped her fingers—*old habits die hard*—and a weak flame appeared in her palm. Clover lay, curled up in a chair across the opulent room. She'd been here before. They must have brought her to Helly after she blacked out.

"Clover," she rasped, not quite trusting her feet under her yet.

Clover jumped straight out of the chair. "I wasn't sleeping."

"You were, but it's fine."

Her eyes widened, and she gasped, "Kerrigan! You're awake." Clover flung herself onto the bed and wrapped her arms around her. "Thank the gods, you survived."

Kerrigan patted her on the shoulder. "Uh, yeah, I'm alive. Fully intact.

Though a little worse for wear on my magic."

"Red," Clover said carefully, "you were out for three days."

"Oh," Kerrigan said. It had only felt like a matter of hours at most. Had she been in the spirit plane all that time? "Wow. I guess that's why I'm so hungry."

"Helly has been tending to you day and night. She stabilized you but has had to funnel you magic hourly since you collapsed. Speaking of, I should wake her. I don't want to since she's barely slept since you got here, but it's almost morning. I don't want her anger if I let her sleep longer." She looked back at Kerrigan. "You'll be okay?"

"I feel fine," she told her. Which was strange and miraculous all on its own.

Clover darted out of the room, and a minute later, a bedraggled Helly stepped into the room. She still walked with the air of someone confident in their place in the world, but she was running on empty.

"Kerrigan," she breathed. "It's good to see you awake."

"I hear that I have you to thank for that."

"It was nothing."

Kerrigan doubted that very much, but Helly was already turning to Clover. "Fetch Fordham. He'll want to know her condition."

"How did I end up here?" Kerrigan asked as Clover ducked out.

While Helly checked Kerrigan's vitals, she explained that Fordham had the sense to fly her to Helly immediately after her collapse. She made a noise of relief. "You're renewing your own magic again. That's a good step. I'd feared the magic sickness was too severe."

"I don't think that's going to be a problem anymore."

"I'd like to be that optimistic, but if this last episode was any indication…"

"I found a spiritcaster teacher."

Helly's eyes widened with barely suppressed disbelief. "How in the world did that happen?"

"It was an accident really. I was on the spiritual plane during all of… this," she said, gesturing around her, "and I was trying to figure out how to get back into my body. I guess it was noisy and irritating her."

Helly laughed softly. "She sounds like someone I'd like. Where does she live? We'll go there at once."

"Well, that's sort of the problem."

"Oh?"

"She's not from Alandria."

Helly sighed. "Should I prepare a way for you to use the portal to get you to Eleysia? I'm certain Cyrene would welcome you back."

Kerrigan shook her head. "As much as I'd like that, it wouldn't help. She doesn't live on this... world."

"This world," Helly repeated. "She's from a different world?"

"I'm really unclear, and she was spouting explanations for how we could have crossed dimensions on the plane." Kerrigan shrugged. "I didn't follow. Regardless, she agreed to teach me so that I don't die."

Helly looked skeptical. "That's awfully convenient. Are you sure that you can trust her?"

"Not particularly, but what other choice do I have? There hasn't been a spiritcaster here in a thousand years, Helly. Zina disappeared as soon as we got started, and she isn't her mother. I'm not progressing, and my magic is poisoning me. If this teacher can help, then it's worth a try."

Helly sighed. "Let's try for a controlled environment at least. Allow me to be there when you go under, so I can keep you stable."

Kerrigan glanced down and back up. "There's only one problem. I'm no longer welcome here."

Helly sank onto the bed next to her. "That trial was a sham. It was circus performers bellowing out fears and propaganda. Before you fled, I was planning to appeal the decision. Nothing is ever final unless the vote is unanimous, and it was far from that."

"Oh," Kerrigan said sheepishly. "I didn't know that."

"I gathered that by your quick escape. How did you even get out?" Helly asked.

Kerrigan buttoned her lips. "I'll never tell."

"Well, Lorian is furious. I filed the appeal, but the council left for spring holiday. Lorian was lucky that no one had left yet or else I could have called for a mistrial. They likely won't all be back until the spring Season event. The mountain is shockingly empty. Which is to our benefit. No one wondered where I was the last couple days, except Lorian when he found out about the appeal." She shook her head. "Regardless, we need to work together from now on. If you want to get back in the council's good graces and back into the Society, we need a plan. There's no guarantee, but..."

She was cut off by a sudden rush of feet at the door. Fordham and Clover dashed inside. Fordham took one look at Kerrigan, crossed the room, and fell to his knees before her. He took her hands carefully in his own and looked up at her as if she were a vision.

"You made it."

"Thanks to you."

He pressed a kiss to her hand. "I feared we were going to lose you."

Clover cleared her throat. "Not to interrupt, but there's someone else at the door."

Helly's brows furrowed, and she stepped out of the bedroom. "Zina!"

Kerrigan tossed the covers off of her.

"What are you doing?" Fordham demanded.

"I haven't seen Zina since the Night of the Dead. No news whatsoever. I need to speak with her." She straightened up and swung her legs over the edge of the bed.

"Do you think that's a good idea?" Fordham asked.

"Has that ever mattered?"

She rose to her feet, spinning slightly. She was weak after three days of being unconscious. But she had waited this long to hear from her. She wouldn't wait another moment. Fordham put his hand out to steady her, and she was grateful for his support. Clover darted to her other side. Though she looked worse for wear as well. Kerrigan wondered when she'd last had a smoke.

As if reading her mind, Clover said, "Helly lets me use her balcony. She doesn't approve, but I wanted her to focus on you, not me."

Kerrigan nodded, and then the trio was in the sitting room. Zina was gesticulating wildly, and Helly had her arms crossed. She looked alarmed.

"*You!*" Zina said when she caught sight of Kerrigan.

"Hello, Zina," Kerrigan said calmly. "Find what you were looking for?"

"Unfortunately, yes. I found it and more. Did you do it?"

"Do what?"

Zina floated toward her. Her magic so tight that she didn't even move her feet. She pointed her finger at Kerrigan. "Did you do it? Don't lie to me."

"I've been unconscious for three days. I've no idea what you're talking about."

"It's true," Helly said. "What is this about?"

"The wall came down," Zina said, clutching her hand to her throat. "The House of Shadows is free."

Fordham went preternaturally still at those words. "Excuse me?"

"Someone brought down the bloody wall, boy. Are you faint of hearing?"

"You must be mistaken. You can't even see the wall."

"Yeah, well, I have eyewitness reports of the wall turning a shimmering blue and dropping like falling stars. Then, poof, the three mountains appeared out of nowhere. People are talking about it for miles."

"How has this not reached us?" Helly asked.

"I have no idea. Maybe whatever magic kept the mountains hidden kept its destruction hidden as well. How the hell should I know?" Zina demanded. "All I know is that when I flew over to check it out for myself, the House of

Shadows military had already trekked out of the mountain and was on the way to Lethbridge."

Fordham paled. "Oh gods."

"What?" Kerrigan asked. "What's Lethbridge?"

"The closest known city to the original borders," Zina said.

"The humans who we trade with, the ones who managed to escape, they live in Lethbridge," Fordham said icily. His gaze was distant. "They're going to take the city."

"You're certain?" Helly asked, releasing the days of exhaustion and immediately stepping into the strong Society Council member.

"Yes. They'd do it for the insult of having to debase themselves. Even if expansion wasn't central," Fordham said. He met Helly's gaze evenly. "It would have been my first move."

She nodded, understanding instantly. "Then, we need to go."

Zina sighed heavily. "I was afraid you'd say that. You know that most of the aerie is empty?"

"Yes. We'll take who we have today to try to stop them at Lethbridge. We'll send who we can spare to the main tribes for support," Helly said confidently.

"I brought you a favor then. Actually, the bastard insisted after he saw what happened at the wall." Zina cupped her hands and yelled, "Come on in here and stop eavesdropping, old man."

The man who stepped through the door made Kerrigan gasp in shock. She'd know that face anywhere. Even old, completely gray with a scar puckering around one of his eyes, he was quite clearly Trulian.

"Master Trulian," Helly gasped, bowing deeply.

"Thank you for the warm welcome," he said as he returned the gesture. "It's a pleasure to be back at Draco Mountain. I thought I'd never see battle again. But from what I can see, you're going to need an old man for one more battle."

"We would be honored."

"Oh, honor," Zina said, waving her hand. "Let's get on with it. Sound the alarm, Hellina."

"Yes, of course. I'll rouse the Society."

"And you, girl. You're coming with us," Zina said.

Kerrigan frowned. "I'm not certain that the rest of the council will approve of that. I was recently kicked out."

Zina rolled her eyes. "I'll put this legend in front of them, and they'll all bow and scrape, won't they, Dad?"

Trulian scowled. "You're safe with us. If you're anything like my Mei, we'll need you."

"Then, I'm in."

Fordham interjected, "You just recovered from being unconscious for three days."

"It's battle, kid," Zina said. "We're running at an empty aerie. We're going to need everyone we can get. Training's over. Now, the fun begins."

***

Kerrigan and Fordham didn't argue. She hugged Clover, thanked her for all she'd done, and followed Fordham out the door. They all but ran back to their quarters.

Audria and Roake were seated in the main room, going over some assignment when they entered.

"Kerrigan!" Audria gasped. "What are you doing here? I heard what happened."

"No time to explain," she said, wheezing from the exertion.

"The House of Shadows has been released from isolation," Fordham said calmly. As if none of this affected him. As if he wasn't about to go to war with his own people. "They're heading to Lethbridge to take the city. We've been called to stop them."

"What?" Roake asked. "But we're still trainees."

"Not anymore," Kerrigan said. "There aren't enough members in the aerie. They need every last dragon in the sky."

"Gods," Audria whispered. "I know we've been training for it, but who thought we'd *ever* see battle?"

"Doesn't matter," Fordham said. He'd already seen battle. Civil war in his tribe was common. "What matters is that we answer the call. Get packed and get to the aerie."

Audria and Roake nodded. And for the first time in all of their training, Fordham moved into the natural leader position. Despite the fact that he'd always shown this aptitude, he usually fell back and let Audria take the lead. She was precocious and well-liked. She was the one that the Society wanted to be the leader. But what they wanted and what was reality were two different things. The head of their troop had given them orders. No one argued as they burst into activity to meet his demand.

Luckily, Kerrigan's room had been left untouched. Within minutes, she had everything she needed in her saddlebag. Then, she met Fordham in the armory. She strapped a sword to her belt and a staff to her back. Armor went in a second bag. She hoisted them both up, nearly toppling over at the weight of it. Her magic was refueling but slowly. She needed to eat and drink and sleep for another day. But she didn't have the luxury.

Fordham went to help her with the burden, but she stepped back. "I have it."

He nodded and went to help Audria.

With the few minutes alone, she dropped gracefully into the spirit world and called Tieran to her. "Come back to the mountain. The walls fell in the House of Shadows, and we're being called to battle."

*Are you certain? We were just removed from service,* he said when he appeared.

"I don't have time to explain, but I'll tell you on the way. Meet me in the western aerie."

*We're still not bonded.*

Kerrigan smiled. "I have good news. We don't have to be."

*What do you mean?*

"I figured out a way around it."

*This sounds like trouble.*

Kerrigan laughed. "Might be."

Tieran looked intrigued but just nodded and promised to meet her. She was back in her body when Audria and Roake were finished. Then, the four of them left the training quarters behind forever.

# CHAPTER 55
## *The Crux*

Tieran waited for Kerrigan in the aerie when they arrived.

She threw her arms around him. "It is so good to see you. We have so much to talk about."

*Indeed, we do. I came at your behest. I will fly into battle with you, Kerrigan, but I thought this was the end for us.*

Tieran anxiously looked around the aerie. Luckily, with the upcoming battle, no one paid a lick of attention to which dragons were and weren't present.

"It'll be okay. Helly said that she is going to appeal the decision on our behalf. Nothing is set in stone."

He huffed. *Then, why did they detain me?*

"Things changed quickly. I am sorry. You didn't deserve what happened. Can I explain the rest in the air?"

Tieran nodded, and she climbed onto his back. Helly appeared next to her, astride her dragon, Tavry.

"Ready?" she asked.

Nerves pricked at her. In the rush of getting ready, she hadn't considered what she was doing. This wasn't the first time she had flown into battle. She'd gone with Helly and Tavry across the world to protect Cyrene's homeland, but somehow, it felt different now that she was in charge of her own dragon.

"As I'll ever be," she finally said.

Helly smiled kindly. "You'll do just fine. Instincts will kick in."

Tavry touched her mind. *Just like we did in Eleysia, right?*

Kerrigan laughed. She loved Tavry so much. "Right. Let's do this."

One moment, they were all waiting, and the next, Trulian led them into the skies on the back of his beautiful dragon, Androma. Tieran took off in the middle of the pack. Fordham, Audria, and Roake formed around Kerrigan, settling into an easy formation with Fordham at the head. In practice, Audria had flown lead, but things had shifted, and Fordham had taken over.

It was a several hours' flight north to the House of Shadows and then east to Lethbridge. Trulian hoped to cut the House of Shadows off before they reached the fortified town. It had a large stone wall surrounding it, and if they took it, they would be in a much better position than if they were out in the open. They had no explicit ground forces. Lethbridge was Sayair tribe territory, but their standing guard would be much farther north, high in the Vert Mountains. Which meant that Bryonican forces would be called in and they were several days away by foot, maybe farther. Kerrigan hoped it wouldn't last that long.

Once in the air, the dragons spaced out. Kerrigan got her first glimpse of what an aerial army looked like, flying in formation. It was terrifying. Even with so few active dragon riders in the mountain, at least forty or fifty were flying out today with more on the way.

*I never thought that I'd see battle,* Tieran said in her mind.

"Our circumstances changed quickly—that's for sure."

*How did this come to be? Explain yourself.*

Kerrigan leaned forward on Tieran's back and began to recount her story of what had happened after she left his side. How she had inspired a march through the streets and then come back and blacked out, only to remain locked in her own mind on the plane for three full days, where she saw what had really caused the wall for the House of Shadows.

*And you believe that your blackout caused the wall to come down?* he asked carefully.

She shivered. Zina had suggested that she'd had some part in what happened. She'd connected to the wall when she was in the House of Shadows. She'd received the visions from Mei's memories. It was possible that she had also caused the wall to shatter when her magic was erratic.

"I didn't mean to do it, but… yes. I don't have another explanation."

There was no judgment in Tieran's voice, just curiosity. *That is very powerful indeed. And do you think you can put it back up?*

"No," she said immediately. "Mei sacrificed herself to do it. I'm not strong enough, nor do I have sufficient motivation, as she did. The wall is down, and it must remain so."

*You went into the House of Shadows. You are one of their people. What do you believe we will see when we reach Lethbridge?*

Kerrigan cringed at that assessment. She doubted it looked good that she and Fordham were part of the tribe they were warring with. Even if technically, she wasn't part of the House of Shadows, she'd made sure no one knew that.

"I don't know. They're prepared for this—Fordham is a good commander for a reason—and they hate the people of Lethbridge. They traded with them during all these years of isolation. I doubt they've forgiven that they needed help from humans."

*I see. You left something out of your story.*

Kerrigan smiled. "You noticed that?"

*I have been with you nearly a year. I know your pauses have weight. And you told me that you found a way to fix the bond. How did you discover this, and what must we do?*

Kerrigan liked that he knew her well enough to see it. She had been reluctant with Tieran from the start, but now, they were past that earlier antagonism. They were one and the same. "When I was trapped in my head after I had the vision of Mei, I met a woman, Cleora. She was also a spiritcaster but from a different world."

A *different* world?

"Yes, I found it difficult to believe as well. She agreed to train me in spiritcasting. We're to meet at midnight at the next full moon to begin training."

*That is in four days, and we fly into battle.*

"Well, I didn't know that when I met her."

Tieran's body rumbled. *Of course not.*

"I did ask her about dragon bonding though. There are dragons in her world."

He lit up at that. *Another world with more of my kind?*

"Yes." Not that she wanted to tell him that it sounded like they weren't the same kind of dragons at all. He likely wouldn't take kindly to knowing that they were just beasts. "And she told me how to use a bond through my spirit magic. She called it a crux bond. Should I try?"

*Might as well see if it works.*

Kerrigan gulped and sat back up, letting the chill from the clouds rush around her. She focused on reaching for her magic. It was still depleted, thanks to her blackout, but it rose to her. She sifted through it until she found that spot where her spirit resided. It wasn't readily available, but at least she could locate it. It was what allowed her to slip onto the spirit plane, which she would have thought would be enough energy to keep the magic sickness at bay but apparently not.

Then, she focused all of her energy on creating the small golden ball of light that Cleora had shown her. To her relief, it materialized as easily in the real world as on the plane. She took a deep breath and then stretched the ball into a long, thin line of light. It pulsed a little in her hand, and she shivered.

Cleora had made it seem like crux bonds were entirely one-sided. She would be in total control of the dragon she tethered this to, but she didn't want that. She wanted a two-way connection with Tieran. A makeshift bonding like the ones that the Society used. Even if Cleora had thought it was barbaric.

She focused her intention, shaping the bond. She had no idea if it was working, but she filled it with all the good feelings she had about being bonded. The sarcastic voice he used with her when she was being reckless. The wind in her hair as they flew as a perfect unit. The hours spent at Waisley fighting together. The relief at seeing him after their expulsion. She wrapped it all up in one perfect intention on the crux.

Now, she was supposed to tether it to her dragon. She had no practical idea of what that meant. She tried throwing one end of it down at him, but that did next to nothing. She tried wrapping it around the saddle, but that was futile. She frowned and considered why it wouldn't do whatever Cleora had said. Maybe because the intent was for them to both be connected, she needed to tether it to herself as well. She looped the end of the crux bond to her wrist three times and then stretched the end and wrapped it the same number of times around Tieran's neck.

*What are you doing?* he demanded.

"Tethering it to the both of us," she said as she finished the loop.

Then, she released both sides of the crux bond, and the gold light vanished. She gasped. "Oh my gods. Do you feel any different?"

*No.*

She tugged experimentally at her wrist and gasped again. Even though the tether was invisible, she could actually *feel* her connection to Tieran.

"Did you feel that?"

He pulled up slightly in surprise. *I did. It was like you were tugging on me.*

"You try!"

Tieran moved his head slightly, and she felt it all the way down to her wrist. Tears came to her eyes. It wasn't a real bond. Not like the ones that the Society had, but it was the most she had ever been connected to Tieran. And so long as it was in place, she would always feel him. She never had to remove it.

"I felt that," she said, leaning forward and wrapping her arms around him. "We're bonded, Tier. We're bonded."

\*\*\*

Hours later, they flew around the three great mountains that made up the House of Shadows. It was shocking to just be able to *see* the mountains. All those years, they had been hidden. When Kerrigan had flown here last time, she'd felt sick, just being *near* the mountains, and she couldn't even see them. Now, that was all gone.

The wall was truly down. No trace of Mei remained behind. It made her sad to think that she was gone entirely. But of course, she continued in her daughter.

The dragons veered east toward Lethbridge, and Kerrigan's heart sank to her stomach.

"Oh no," she whispered.

Smoke rose high in the distance. She couldn't quite smell it, but they all knew what that meant. Night was falling, and Lethbridge was under attack.

\*\*\*

The dragons landed in a clearing just west of Lethbridge. Scouts continued on to figure out what had happened. Alura was one of them. She'd landed long enough to deposit her bags and then burst into action again. They watched her fly away, knowing tomorrow, it would be them.

Kerrigan went about helping to set up the camp. She hoisted tents with

Audria, who seemed grateful for the last year. She'd never seen a tent before they went through battlefield conditions in one of Lorian's lessons. He'd ridiculed Kerrigan intensely even though she and Fordham were the only ones who knew what they were doing. And now, none of that mattered.

All that mattered was the battle to come. Not that she and Fordham were members of the House of Shadows. Not that there were people on the other side of that wall that she knew. Not that she might not be allowed to continue with the Society after this. Just tomorrow.

Trulian appeared himself after they ate dinner. "You," he barked at Fordham. "Come with me."

"Yes, sir," Fordham said. He didn't even ask questions. He'd defaulted to his military training.

Kerrigan wasn't so well trained. She jumped up too. "What's going on?"

"Maybe you should come with us too. If you have half as much strength as my Mei did, then you'll be an asset," he said. Then, he jerked his head and stomped back toward the largest tent at the center of the small camp.

Kerrigan fell into step next to Fordham. She hadn't had a chance to talk to him as they flew. He must be in turmoil at the thought of what was coming.

"Ford," she whispered.

He shook his head, and without a word, he tromped forward at a faster clip. He was a full head taller than her, and she had to all but jog to catch up. They didn't say another word. Trulian threw open the tent flap, and they followed him inside.

Kerrigan stalled, as if going back in time. The war camp in her vision had been larger, stabler, and full of men in black Society robes. But this was much the same. There were fewer people, and women dotted the space. A welcome change to a thousand years ago. Mei had been one of the only women in that tent. But this was still a commander's war tent.

Helly stood at a table. Who knew where they'd gotten it? Lorian was on her right. Zina floated in an almost trance in the back of the tent. Kerrigan recognized one of the other people in the room—Mistress Corinna, Head of the Guard. The rest of the faces were strangers. No other council members were in attendance.

"What is she doing here?" Lorian demanded. "Arrest her!"

Trulian waved the accusation away. "She's here at my command."

Lorian balked. "You are an esteemed warrior of the Great War, Master Trulian," he said, starstruck, "but I am a council member. She was ejected from our service and has no place here."

"I am also a council member," Helly said. "I invited her under Trulian's advice. Considering Trulian is the only other member here who has been on the council—and head of the council at that—I believe that we outnumber you."

Lorian glared at Helly. "This is uncalled for."

"We're in the middle of a war," Trulian snarled. "Arguing over one girl is pointless. We have exactly forty-two dragons and riders present and no foot soldiers. We are at least a two days, maybe more, away from any reinforcements, and you're arguing about one girl? She is trained in the art of warfare. We will use her as I see fit. Do you understand?"

Lorian looked very clearly like he wanted to argue with Trulian. But how could you argue with a legend?

"Understood," Lorian finally said.

"Good. Then, let's get on with it. One of the scouts is back. Alura, would you like to give your report?"

Alura stepped forward, her hands held stiffly behind her back. She didn't glance at her father once. "Yes, General. The city has fallen. The walls are barred. I counted roughly six thousand soldiers."

Kerrigan's stomach dropped. Six *thousand* soldiers? They'd moved them that fast? Holy gods!

"Any weaknesses?" Trulian asked.

432

Alura ground her teeth together and then shook her head. "None that I saw. They're carting large wooden crates and depositing them around the walls. I couldn't get near enough to see what was in them."

Trulian nodded and then looked to Fordham. "Well?"

Fordham inhaled sharply, as if realizing for the first time what Trulian wanted with him. He must have guessed from the start, but actually hearing it aloud was something else. "Sir?"

"They tell me you're the crowned prince of the Dark Court." Fordham clenched his jaw at the old insult. "Society before tribe. Tell us what we need to know."

"Sir, respectfully, we shouldn't be in this fight," Fordham said plainly.

"Explain."

"I believe that we should hold off on an attack and send in someone for negotiations."

"You believe they'll surrender?"

Fordham shifted on his feet, which was how Kerrigan knew that he was going to lie. It was his only tell. "Yes. I think they'd listen to me."

Trulian scoffed, "That doesn't sound like the court I remember."

"That was a thousand years ago, Trulian," Lorian interjected. "Perhaps the boy's information is more up to date."

"I'm well aware that I was fighting the Great War long before any of you were even a glimmer in your parents' eyes. What I want is the truth. What does negotiating bring us?"

"No more death," Fordham said.

"They started this fight. They understand casualties."

Fordham squared his shoulders. "I'm well aware. But it is their first taste of freedom. I would think that they would like to live to see it last more than a few days."

"I have to agree with him," Lorian said. "You fought them. You have your old prejudices. But are they really all that different than you and me? They're Fae. They want land. I can understand that. We can settle this without bloodshed."

Helly snorted at Lorian. "*He* has old prejudices? Last I checked, he was fighting for the end of the human and half-Fae slavery that you still support in your outdated ideals." It was the first time Helly had actively spoken out against him in public, but there were no other council members here. It was just her versus Lorian, and Trulian was backing her. She had the power.

"I don't support slavery," he said, offended by the accusation.

"Indenture is common in the Dregs among half-Fae and humans. Many are homeless. They don't feel like they have a voice. The Red Masks are running free. And now, you want to negotiate with the people who would put them in more danger? Are you out of your mind?" Helly turned to Fordham. "No offense to your people, but the last thing we need is more bigotry in Alandria."

Fordham stiffened but said nothing.

"Then, it's settled," Trulian said. "No negotiating with the enemy. Tell us if Alura's judgment is accurate."

Fordham balled his hands into fists. "It'll be closer to ten thousand soldiers. We've been fighting since we were old enough to carry a sword, and we know precisely what we're doing. These aren't young bucks. They'll stop at nothing. They'll slaughter us."

"They don't have dragons," Trulian countered.

"Oh, shut it, all of you," Zina said, jerking out of her trance. "Leave the boy alone. Six thousand or ten thousand. Dragons or no dragons. We're all about to walk into literal hell. Let them get a good night's sleep, and we'll figure it out in the morning."

"Zahina," Trulian barked.

"You know we have the advantage, General. If you're not going to give them the option of backing out, then what does it matter anyway?"

Trulian sighed at his daughter's words. "Fine. Fordham, you're dismissed.

Kerrigan, I want you to work with Zina on your casting."

"Of course, sir." Kerrigan bowed and then followed Zina out of the tent.

Fordham stomped off away from them.

"He'll be fine," Zina said. "He just learned a hard lesson about war."

"Yeah. Your dad is…"

"An asshole?"

Kerrigan laughed. "Um, I was going to say intimidating."

"He's just too stubborn to go into the abyss."

"I am sorry that you had to hear about your mother the way you did."

Zina shrugged. "He should have told me about her when it happened. Not a thousand years later. It was selfish. And look, it brought us right back to another battlefield." Zina hopped into another hover. "Anyway, I'm not training you. I used it as an excuse to get out of that tent. You know all that you need to know for tomorrow. Just follow that boy before he does something stupid."

Kerrigan's gaze landed on Fordham, still heading back to the tent. She was afraid that Zina was right.

# CHAPTER 56
## *The Negotiations*

"**D**o you want to talk about it?" Kerrigan asked when she found Fordham staring blankly into the fire.

Audria arched an eyebrow, but Kerrigan just shook her head. There was no point in getting her involved. Fordham's hurt couldn't be understood by someone who had never seen him with his people.

It was complicated. He hated the House of Shadows in a deep and personal way. He also loved his home and his people just as deeply. He was their crowned prince. He had always planned to serve as their king. Only everything had changed with his exile. He'd learned the hard way that things were both better and worse than he'd known.

"No," he growled.

"Okay. I can just sit here then."

"Aren't you supposed to be training?"

"Zina said I knew everything I needed to know."

He shrugged. "Probably true."

"And anyway, she didn't want you to do anything stupid."

He jerked his head toward her, and there was anger in his eyes. "Like betraying my people by giving information to defeat them to the Society?"

"Like betraying the Society and giving information to the House of Shadows."

"I would never do that," he snapped. "Society before tribe."

"In the abstract, yes. In reality, they're still your people."

He didn't say anything, just crossed his arms and stared into the endless flames. Finally, when she didn't speak again, he asked, "Did you take the wall down?"

"I don't know. Maybe? I was still connected to the wall through Mei." Kerrigan looked down and then met his mercurial gaze. "She was one of you, you know?"

"One of what?"

"She was from Charbonnet. She was the ambassador."

Fordham looked back at her, all defiance in his expression. "No, she wasn't. I would have known that. Our people wouldn't have done that to us."

"The Society was going to bring down the mountain and kill everyone inside," Kerrigan told him. "Men, women, and children."

He stilled. "They were going to destroy Ravinia Mountain?"

"Yes. Mei believed the only way to save you was to make the Society forget where the House of Shadows was. There were unintended consequences, and truly, I believe it lasted longer than she'd thought it would."

"It was done as protection... and not punishment," he said, as if tasting that for the first time.

"Yes. And when I learned that, I was connected to the wall, to her memories."

Fordham nodded solemnly. "It's good that it's down. People should have a choice."

"They should," she agreed. "I wish it hadn't come to this."

He nodded, and then without a word, he stepped into his tent and shut the flap. She closed her eyes with a sigh. She'd tried. He knew everything she did now. What he did with it was another thing.

***

Kerrigan wasn't sure what woke her up.

The camp was alive at all hours of the night. Everyone was on a rotating watch. Scouts were moving in and out. Not to mention, the rustling, groaning, and snoring that made up a war camp. It was dirty, smelly, and loud.

But something was different, and it wasn't the camp that had woken her in the middle of the night. Well before dawn—when they would convene for their opening attack. She grabbed her cloak and scrambled out of the tent. She stepped silently to the next tent. As gently as she could, she pushed the flap open to nothing but air.

Fordham wasn't here.

She *knew* it.

She and Fordham weren't bonded by anything more than trust and love and more. But she had felt connected to him long before they met in the hot springs. Whatever had brought them together, whatever part of her that had visions about him during the tournament, had pinged. And that usually meant one or the both of them were in trouble.

Kerrigan's gaze swept the camp. He wouldn't be in there. He'd be where the shadows were the darkest. And following that tug, she moved away from the heart of camp and toward the surrounding forest. She made it to the tree line when she heard the rustling of wings.

Her eyes caught on a falcon rushing down into the trees. She stalked across the forest as quiet as a mouse until she came upon Fordham with the bird on his arm.

His face shifted at the barest touch of her foot upon the ground, and then the shadows settled around his body.

"Wait, it's me," Kerrigan hissed, coming into plain sight.

The shadows vanished. "What are you doing out here?"

"I could ask you the same thing!" She crossed her arms. "I thought I said not to do anything stupid."

"I'm not."

"You're communicating with the House of Shadows. What if someone saw you?"

"They didn't."

She wanted to shake him. "Think for a moment what would happen if someone did."

"I've thought about it," he said icily. "Now, go back to the camp before someone notices."

She huffed. "I'm not going anywhere without you."

"You're not going anywhere *with* me."

"You cannot talk to them, Fordham. You're their natural leader. We need you."

"I can't," he said, whirling on her. "I have to do something. I cannot sit around and wait all night to slaughter my own people. Not without at least trying to save them. They will listen to me."

"And what if they don't?" she demanded.

"Then, fine. They will have sealed their fate. But not before I do everything in my power to end this."

Kerrigan sighed. She understood. Better than he knew. She was still betrothed to March to save her people. She hadn't found a way out of it that didn't involve him going to war with her people. She hadn't even been in Bryonica in twelve years, and still, she would do anything to protect them. She hardly expected it to be different for Fordham.

"Let me go with you."

"And have you get in trouble again?"

"Then, don't let us be seen," she said.

"I can't travel that far with both of us. And I'm not taking you."

"We have each other's backs. No matter what else has changed, Fordham, that remains the same." She crossed her arms and waited for him to refute that.

To her surprise, he didn't. He sighed. "We'll have to get closer to meet the rendezvous."

Kerrigan smothered her shock. He probably knew by now that she wasn't easy to get rid of when she set her mind to something.

They trekked through the woods, heading closer and closer to Lethbridge while avoiding scouts and patrols nearby. Once the city came into view and Kerrigan could see the incredible height of the stone fortress wall, Fordham called them to a stop.

"Okay, hold on to me," he said.

Kerrigan stepped forward into his arms. Her body fit against his like it was always meant to be there. She wanted to rest her head on his chest, but already, her body was reacting to his nearness. She needed to not think about the last time they'd been this close. Or how his body felt pressed against hers. Or anything else that involved a hot spring. Her cheeks colored, and she dipped her chin.

He cleared his throat, wrapping his arms tight around her. "Here we go," he said, his breath hot against her neck.

She shivered involuntarily, and then they were gone. The shadows enveloped them. Kerrigan gasped. Then as quickly as they'd moved, they stumbled to a stop on the other side of the fortress.

Two small figures appeared out of the darkness. "About time," Benton said with a smile.

"Oh my gods," Kerrigan said. She rushed out of Fordham's arms and toward the twins. She couldn't believe they were here. And also, the thought shuddered through her all at once. They were here. Which meant they could get hurt in the cross fire. "What are you doing here?"

"We were brought along to help with preparations," Benton said.

Bayton tugged her in tight. "The last time I saw you, you were saving my life."

"I cannot believe she threatened to kill you. I'm sorry that I couldn't take you with me."

"We're out now, my lady," Benton said. "And we suspect it's because of you."

Fordham ended the reunion. "We need to move. We're exposed."

The twins bobbed a hasty curtsy. "Yes, Your Highness," Bayton said. "Right this way."

Kerrigan and Fordham followed the twins through the darkened corridors of Lethbridge. Kerrigan knew little about the Sayair city, except that it was one of the largest outside of their capital. The fact that the House of Shadows had conquered it in a matter of days was terrifying.

Benton and Bayton stopped before a large wooden door and knocked twice. The door swung inward, and Prescott appeared before them. He caught Kerrigan's gaze, and his smile widened.

"You didn't tell us you were bringing the brains of the operation," Prescott said, hauling Kerrigan in for a hug.

She laughed, and Fordham scowled. "Let's get inside," he grumbled.

Prescott kept his arm wrapped around Kerrigan's shoulders as he drew them into the room. No one would know the city was at war here. Everything was resplendent with throw pillows and thick carpets. Candles lit the space with wax dripping down over large candelabras. Arbor lay out across a divan like a welcoming goddess and not a usurper.

"You didn't say you were bringing the girl," Arbor said, letting the lush red of her skirts fall to the floor.

"Change of plans," Kerrigan said. "I was instructed not to let him do anything stupid. So, here I am, doing stupid things with him."

Fordham's scowl deepened. "This isn't stupid. It's necessary."

"Yeah, Kerrigan," Prescott said with a wink. "Necessary."

"Pres, leave her alone," Arbor said.

He made a face at his sister and headed over to a table, where he poured red wine from a decanter. "A toast to our victory?" he asked, offering drinks all around.

Fordham and Kerrigan both declined. She liked Arbor and Prescott, but they were on opposite sides of this fight.

"Fine. Sister," he drawled, passing one to Arbor.

"Why must you instigate?"

"It's my best feature," he joked and then leaned back against the table.

"You said you were willing to listen," Fordham accused his cousins.

"And we are," Arbor said. "If you are as well."

"You have to stop this before it gets worse."

Arbor rose to her feet, and Kerrigan saw for the first time what she had missed all those nights in the House of Shadows. Arbor wasn't some forgotten puppy, falling after her cousin who had all the power. She aspired to power.

"Before what gets worse? Because as far as I can see, things can only get better. The wall is down, Fordham. It is what we always wanted. Now, we can leave the mountain and find a place of our own."

"By conquering nearby cities? By killing everyone inside?"

"We didn't kill *everyone*," she said with a feline smile. "And here I thought you were coming to join us. How easy it would be in this battle to take down your wretched father and claim your rightful place on the throne."

"I'm not interested in patricide," he said evenly.

"And it would never happen that way," Kerrigan interjected. "The Society is here. You can never hold out against us."

Arbor assessed Kerrigan and then dismissed her. "What are forty dragons against ten thousand trained fighters? This isn't our first war. We know what we're up against."

"I don't think that you do," Fordham said. "If you surrender now, then I can negotiate favorable terms."

"Surrender?" Prescott asked. "After we won Lethbridge in a fair fight? That's laughable."

"You will all be slaughtered," Fordham snapped. "I am trying to do the right thing. If you will not listen, then I will find someone who will."

"And who would that be?" Arbor asked. "Your father? He's wanted this fight longer than any of us have been alive. Do you think Wynter will hear you? Because I was there the day the wall fell. She had her acolytes around her as it came down. They think she's a prophet sent from the gods themselves to bring us salvation."

"Wynter didn't bring down the wall," Fordham said.

Arbor laughed and shook her head. "It hardly matters. What matters is that they believe her, and she believes her own rambling nonsense. She won't back down from this fight when she thinks it is divine."

"So, you would rather die?" Kerrigan asked.

Arbor narrowed her eyes. "There are ten thousand of us and forty of you. *Forty*," she repeated, as if speaking to a small child.

Kerrigan fumed at those words. They had no idea what the Society was capable of. What a unit of dragons would do, what they could all do. They had trained until they were nearly broken to get to this point. The House of Shadows might have military prowess, but they had no aerial assault. Nothing. It was going to be a bloodbath.

Before she could respond, Arbor turned to Fordham. "I love you, cousin. It should have always been you on the throne. Come take your rightful place and show them what we are capable of. That forty dragons are nothing compared to the might of our warriors."

Fordham stood his ground. "I thought that you two would be reasonable about this. That you would want to take the route least likely to cause harm. I guess I was wrong about that."

# K.A. LINDE

"I guess you were," Prescott said, coming to his sister's side.

"No matter how it happened, the wall is down. We deserve our chance at freedom. Has a year with them changed your allegiance so completely?" Arbor demanded.

Kerrigan was boiling over. She understood now why Trulian had dismissed the idea of negotiating with the enemy. It was futile. They would never make them understand. Fordham grasped Kerrigan's elbow, and she glanced up at him in surprise. Her fury was getting the better of her. He must have felt the shift. That she might do something stupid.

She backed down, letting it wash away from her. There was no point. Tomorrow, they would meet them on the battlefield, and Arbor would find out how wrong she was.

"Then, I believe we are at an impasse," Fordham said.

"I believe we are," Arbor said.

Fordham gave his cousin a quick bow. "Happy hunting."

"You too, cousin."

Without a word, Fordham wrapped them both in darkness. Kerrigan squeezed her eyes shut as they traveled, and then they were both back in the woods. Fordham put his hands to his knees, panting. He shouldn't have been using that power the night before battle.

"Are you okay?" she asked. "Will you be able to use this tomorrow?"

He coughed, wiped sweat from his brow, and then slowly straightened. "I've stretched the ability in the last year. I should have at least one jump tomorrow if I need it."

"Good," she whispered.

They trekked back through the woods, avoiding the patrols from both sides of the fight, and made it to the tree line. The camp was almost completely silent this late at night.

She glanced at Fordham. "Are you ready for tomorrow?"

444

He gritted his teeth. "I did everything I could, short of speaking to my father and sister, which would have only resulted in my capture. But I still had to go. I had to try."

"I know," she whispered.

"If they will not surrender, then I will be ready. For tomorrow, we go to war."

# CHAPTER 57

## *The River*

At dawn, the contingent of Society members formed up in front of Master Trulian. Many of them were still awestruck at the very sight of him. Kerrigan stood in her riding leathers, her sword strapped to her side. Fordham, Audria, and Roake surrounded her with Alura at the head. She was technically still their leader since she had been responsible for them during training. She didn't seem much pleased by that assessment as she would much rather be on the front lines, then babysitting the new recruits. Not that Kerrigan could blame her. She was a better warrior by far, considering she'd grown up in a war tribe.

Trulian ambled down the line of soldiers, nodding at people and speaking to the other commanders. Then, he stepped back and addressed the whole lot.

"Many of you have never seen real battle before. Many of you are thinking that this will be like the drills you ran. Many of you are walking in, sure that this will be an easy defeat," Trulian bellowed. "As someone who has fought this battle before, let me tell you, war is not fun or easy. It is hard, grueling work. They have superior numbers and a thousand years of rage."

The Society members shifted from side to side at his words. It certainly wasn't the speech Kerrigan had expected from him.

"I say all of this not to scare you or for you to lose your nerve. Quite the opposite. We are the Society. We are dragon bonded. We were chosen for our abilities. Then, we were honed into a razor's edge. We are the one thing standing between them and the next city they wish to conquer. It could be yours." He pointed to someone to the right and then the left. "Or yours. It could be any of our homes, our tribes. The people of Lethbridge did nothing to deserve this unprovoked attack, and the consequences of that are clear. We, the Society, will respond in kind.

"You have your assignments. Follow your commanders. Don't break ranks. Reinforcements will be here as early as tomorrow and troops within the week. Don't do anything reckless. You are our greatest assets." Trulian rose his arm into the air. "For the Society!"

Everyone raised their fist. Kerrigan joined them, feeling her blood pump as the adrenaline of the upcoming fight took over. And they shouted as one, "For the Society."

Alura whipped around as soon as the speech was over. "You lot are with me. We're to block off their escape routes. In the Great War, they would attack and then retreat back to the mountain when things got bad. We want to make sure that they can't get back or forward."

Fordham frowned. "They're not going to retreat. This isn't the Great War."

Alura stomped forward, getting right in his face. "What did you say, soldier? We have one job, and we are going to do it. If you have a problem, take that up with Master Trulian. Otherwise, you do whatever I tell you without any more back talk."

For a moment, Kerrigan thought he might not back down. He, of course, knew House of Shadows tactics better than anyone. But finally, he nodded and stepped into line.

"Good. Now, call your dragons, and let's fly," she snapped as Gemina appeared on the horizon.

Kerrigan gulped. This was the first time she and Tieran would use the bond since getting it into place. They'd tried it out some on the way here, but it was different. This was real battle. She gently tugged on the bond. To her relief, she felt it go all the way across the meadow to the space the dragons had carved for themselves. And Tieran answered in turn. She felt it straight to her tied-off crux bond on her wrist.

She wanted to cry. It was such an emotional moment that she could share with no one else. She hadn't even told Fordham that she'd figured out a way for it to work. There had been no time with everything going on. But he must have realized something was different because he tilted his head at Tieran heading their direction, even before Netta got the call.

"I fixed it," she whispered to him.

He looked like he wanted to ask so many questions, but now was hardly the time. Not unless she wanted Alura to know, and gods, did she *not* want Alura to know this little fact.

She was so grateful for Cleora. She never would have had time to drop into the spirit plane to call him when she was actually here. It had to be instantaneous, and it was.

Alura sprinted toward her dragon, letting Gemina grasp her in her claws and then send her sailing backward over Gemina's head. It was what they had practiced over and over again. There was no time for landing and mounting. The battle was ahead.

The rest of their team took off at a sprint. Kerrigan felt the bond strengthen as Tieran grabbed her and threw her backward. She landed into a crouch on his back, steady as an acrobat. A slow smile came to her face. She didn't care what her part in this was; she was just glad that the last year hadn't been a waste.

Then, they were soaring west, away from Lethbridge. The city itself was two tier—one level surrounded by the enormous stone wall that protected the House of Shadows and an exposed lower level. Most of the lower level had been decimated by the invading forces, but what still stood housed excess soldiers. On the northern side of the city was a small river that nearly drained during the cold months and filled to flooding as the snow melt ran off of the Vert Mountains. Right now, it ran at a trickle, as the snow wouldn't melt this far north for at least another month or two. But it was still wide enough to accommodate a few ships.

As they moved easily into formation with Alura at the lead, Fordham off her right wing, and Kerrigan off of his wing with Audria and Roake on the left, Kerrigan could see precisely what Alura had in mind.

Kerrigan was so caught up in where they were going that she didn't notice what was going on below until an arrow whizzed past her. She gasped and veered slightly out of formation.

"Shield up," Alura commanded.

Kerrigan fumbled for a second, disoriented. Then, she felt the gentle pull of Tieran's reassurance.

*Breathe. It's one arrow. We can take them out.*

She nodded, sending a tug back, and then dipped into her well of magic. It was still low compared to normal but enough to hold up a magic shield as they flew near their troops. Another arrow bounced harmlessly off of her shield, but she shuddered at the feel of it. The tips had been dipped in something that made her skin crawl. She could practically taste it.

Audria cursed violently, and Kerrigan glanced over to see her shield had dropped. "What the hell was that?"

"Oleander-tipped arrows," Fordham told them. "I forgot we still had those. They've been banned within our halls since I've been fighting. If the arrow doesn't kill you, the poison will burn out your magic."

Kerrigan's eyes widened. "Holy gods! What else do they have that you forgot about?"

He glanced back at her, his face hard. "Let's not find out."

A scream ruptured the clash of battle. Kerrigan whipped her head to the side and watched a dragon fall out of the sky. It was horrifying. She'd never seen anything like that. She tried to clear her eyes to make the picture make sense, but it simply didn't.

She was too far away to see where the rider was or if the dragon was okay. But the noise the creature made as it collapsed onto the battlements, crushing House of Shadows soldiers, was enough to make her stomach turn. The sound was deafening.

"Gods," she breathed. "We need to be in there. We need to be helping."

Alura didn't respond. She simply moved them farther from the archers and continued on their route. Someone else would be there to save that dragon. But Kerrigan's throat closed up as they moved farther away. Had there been more merit to Arbor's words than she had given credit?

\*\*\*

Alura stopped beside the river that wended through the mountains. She gestured for them to land. The shouts of battle were far behind them. Lethbridge wasn't a long distance from the mountains, which was how the House of Shadows had reached them so swiftly, but far enough for the battle to feel distant.

"Do you think they're dead?" Audria asked when they were once again on the ground.

"I don't know," she whispered back.

"Our mission is to dam the river," Alura said. "We'll use our magic and the dragons to hoist rocks in the way of the river. It won't do anything to stop it once the snow melts, but it's good enough for us right now."

It was grueling, backbreaking work. They quickly moved into an assembly line with the dragons hitting the stones to loosen them and the rest lifting them with their earth magic and depositing them in an array that slowly, throughout the hours, began to recede the river.

No one wanted to admit that they'd rather be in the thick of the fighting, prove to everyone they were worth it. It was hard not to feel like they'd been given this job to get them out of the way. The youngest of the lot of Society members, and they were farthest from the battle.

They spent days working on the dam. Each day, when they returned to camp and found more wounded, the feeling only grew that they could be doing more. But Alura stopped them from ever voicing that opinion. All work was valuable, and what they were doing would make a difference if the House of Shadows tried to retreat. It was a big if.

Because as far as Kerrigan was concerned, the House of Shadows was doing way better than they had predicted. Only one dragon and rider casualty, the one she'd watched fall, but they'd had barely any reinforcements come in. They were still waiting for the bulk of the dragons and the foot soldiers that they'd promised would be there. And still, they worked on the dam.

Kerrigan stretched her aching back. Her magic had already been low, and after days of work, it was down to sputtering. She felt useless as Roake and Fordham picked up the slack. She drank long and deep from her waterskin and ate a small lunch to try to bring back her bottomless well of magic. It was the wrong time for her to be pulling up short.

The food did help. She could feel herself managing to knit it back together, if slowly. But as she sat on a nearby rock with Audria at her side, she tilted her head.

"Do you hear that?" she asked.

"I don't hear anything, except us," Audria grumbled. She turned for the hundredth time back to Lethbridge, as if she could go to the thick of it by force of will.

"No, no, there's something."

She closed her eyes and listened harder. It was a whooshing sound. Like wind through the trees or an avalanche or...

Her eyes snapped open. "Get back!" she screamed. "Get away from the river."

She scrambled to her feet and tugged for Tieran to come to her. He broke free from his work instantly, rushing to her side.

"Get back to work!" Alura shouted. "I didn't say you could stop."

"I hear it now," Audria said. Then, she pointed north. "The river!"

Alura jerked around. Her eyes widened in horror. "Move, move, move!"

Kerrigan jumped on Tieran's back just as the first rush of water came flowing down out of the mountains. It was enough water to fill the river and then some. It was the flood that came with the first snow melt. It was easily a month early.

Tieran jerked straight upward, and Kerrigan clung to him with all her might as the river hit the top of the rocks and obliterated the dam in a matter of seconds. She screamed and closed her eyes as water cascaded all around them. Tieran leveled off when he was high enough to be out of the way and then circled back down.

Audria and Alura had gotten out, but Fordham and Roake weren't as lucky.

"Fordham!" she yelled over and over again.

A head bobbed up out of the water. Kerrigan recognized Roake and gestured for Audria to dive down for him. Roake's dragon, Luxor, had just pulled himself out of the torrent of water on the opposite bank and would be no help. But still, no Fordham.

She closed her eyes and concentrated. She'd thought so many times that she and Fordham were connected because of the visions she'd had. Even when she couldn't always tell what he was thinking, it felt like she could always sense where he was. She followed that, as she would the tether with Tieran, and directed Tieran back toward the mouth of the river they had been damming.

"There!" she shouted.

With one hand, Fordham clung to a rock on the surface. His face was half-in, half-out of the water.

Tieran dived toward him, going directly into the spray of the water and picking him up in his claws. He carried Fordham away from the river, depositing him safely on the riverbank. Netta appeared a minute later, coughing up water and checking on him.

"I'm okay," he said as they landed next to him. "Thank you."

Kerrigan nodded. Alura, Audria, and Roake were stranded on the other bank. She waved to them to give them the all-clear.

"How did that happen?" she asked when they were all together again in a clearing a short distance from the river.

"It's months too early for that much water," Audria spat.

"They must have melted it in the mountains," Alura speculated. "Is there a place they could do that?"

Fordham cleared his throat, spitting out more water. "We collect the snow melt every year. We have an underground well, but melted snow is safer for drinking."

Kerrigan shuddered at the thought of what they'd had to do all those years to survive. "Then, they must have released it. Does that mean they don't plan to escape?"

"We don't know what their plan is. All we can do is our next move. If we can't block the river," Alura said with a savage grin, "then we destroy the boats."

# CHAPTER 58
## *The Boats*

Kerrigan tapped her boot on Tieran's back as she watched the Battle of Lethbridge from the trees. She and Fordham had found a hidden space to the west of the docks. Audria and Roake were somewhere to the east. They waited for the signal from Alura.

"Do you think this is going to work?" she breathed.

Tieran tugged on the bond. He had been doing it reassuringly the last couple days. *It must.*

"I know. I know. But oleander-tipped arrows." She shuddered.

*We will work together, as we have always wanted to. Don't worry. You're not that bad.*

She chuckled. That was the Tieran she knew and loved. Always making fun of her. At least it kept her centered on the attack ahead.

Alura zipped out of the trees, heading straight toward the northern tower. Archers had been stationed at the top with enough arrows to keep anyone from getting too near the docks. Most of the fighting was taking place to the south, where the main gate was. The boats and the river had been mostly ignored.

As Alura drew within their range, the Fae were suddenly alert, and arrows volleyed down from the tower. Alura was a sight to behold. She maneuvered from Gemina's back with speed and agility. Kerrigan's jaw dropped as she watched her evade the first arrows with ease. One hadn't even scratched her shield.

"Wow," she whispered.

*Together, they are straight out of myth.*

Tieran wasn't wrong. The archers had enough time to pull another arrow and let loose. Gemina swerved to avoid the arrows. This time, just one grazed her shield but didn't break it. Not a direct hit then.

Then, they were there. Alura launched off of Gemina's back and dived headfirst into the tower. She pulled her sword from its sheath and cut two of the archers down before they even moved from their station. She flowed through the motions as if she were an element all on her own. Every movement timed perfectly to block and parry and slice. The archers were no match for a trained warrior, and Alura was one of the best. Within seconds—*seconds*—the tower was empty, and Alura jumped back down on Gemina, who slammed her body into the top of the tower, sending the roof tumbling inside. No more archers could come up and disturb them.

"That's our signal," Fordham said.

Kerrigan leaned into Tieran as he took off toward the city. They flew harmlessly over the burned husk of the outer ring. They came into range, and another volley of arrows shot toward them from the parapet. Kerrigan waved her hand, a blast of air knocking them off course. Fordham pushed forward, diving in while they were fitting another arrow to the bow, and Netta let loose a full blow of fire.

The majority of the archers were smart enough to duck behind the stone for cover, but a number were instantly set on fire and ran screaming toward the nearby water trough.

Kerrigan led Tieran into a steep dive as the archers were distracted with

Fordham. They came up on the first set of boats, and Tieran let loose his own breath of fire, whipping his tail into the first mast and sending it toppling into the second.

"Look out!" Fordham shouted.

She looked back, tugging Tieran far away from the battlement, and wrapped her shield harder around them. The first puncture of the arrow felt like a stab wound. She gasped as it knocked the shield out entirely. She jerked another one up in place, even as the poisonous oleander felt like it'd hit her personally.

Tieran circled as she caught her breath. Already, a team of water Fae attempted to douse the dragon fire. She wasn't strong enough in water to counteract them. And it didn't matter—no one was moving a ship with no mast.

Fordham regrouped near her as Alura made a second run, dropping onto Audria and Roake's side of the wall and cutting down archers like picking daisies.

"Second run?" he asked.

She nodded. Fordham flew Netta in for another run of the archers. They were smarter this time, and only one was still up when he came through. That one managed to get an arrow into Fordham's shield.

"Traitor!" The word echoed through the clash of battle.

Fordham used his air magic to nimbly grasp the arrow out of the sky. Then, he whipped around and threw it straight back at the Fae who had uttered that terrible word at him. The force of his throw, propelled by the weight of his magic, thrust the arrow straight through his throat.

Kerrigan gulped at the fury on Fordham's face. He was a soldier. This was what he was best at. She just hoped she could get him back after all of this was over.

While Fordham engaged the archers, sending the majority of them scattering when they saw their prince in all his fury, Kerrigan took Tieran down to blow fire on the rest of the western docks. Fae were trying to stop the spread of the fire, to douse the decks to keep them from going up in flames. But it did nothing to dragon fire.

Kerrigan was pulling out of the next turn when a stray arrow hit her shield. She gasped, feeling weak in the knees at the poison. Then, just as she was about to pull the shield back up, something grabbed ahold of her.

She tried to turn to see what the hell was happening, but she couldn't move. It was as if someone had grasped all of her limbs and frozen them in place. Then, with a yank like a rope around her middle, she was bodily pulled off of Tieran's back.

She screamed as she free-fell toward the docks. She couldn't even brace for impact because whatever had her was still locked on. Kerrigan prayed to the gods that she wouldn't die.

Then, Netta's body was underneath her, cushioning her fall and breaking whatever spell had hit her. Fordham grasped her round the middle, and the both of them rolled off of the dragon and onto the docks.

Kerrigan groaned. "What was that?"

Fordham shook his head as he came swiftly to his feet, pulling his magic close to himself.

Kerrigan was slower to get up. Whatever spell had been cast on her, it made her sluggish. She felt Tieran's tug of concern, and she touched the bond to let him know she was okay.

"Well, this looks great," Kerrigan muttered as she rose to her feet, the heat of the burning boats at her back.

Standing before them was a group of Fae in the black and silver of the House of Shadows. Each held a different color orb in their hands. Kerrigan's gaze shifted from one to the other in confusion and then realization. These were illegal magical artifacts. The same ones that Basem Nix had been selling last year to make him rich. The ones that Clare Rahllins had claimed they sold to Lorian Van Horn. And now, they were *here*.

She didn't know how that was possible, but illegal magic had never meant a good thing for her in the past. Basem had used orbs just like that to do all sorts of horrible things. Not to mention to make quick escapes in the way that Fordham did. The last thing they needed was for an easy escape for the House of Shadows.

Fordham straightened. "I am your crowned prince. Surrender, and I will be merciful."

The leader stepped forward. She was a beautiful female with raven-black hair and a cruel expression. "You were exiled for your involvement with those beasts, and here you stand, with one of them against us. You are no prince of mine."

Kerrigan didn't dare look to Fordham to see his reaction to that comment. She could feel the knife go through her own heart, and she had never truly belonged to the House of Shadows. But she knew abandonment, and this had the same shape and feeling.

"That's the thing about royalty," Fordham said, low and lethal. "You don't get to choose who your betters are."

Then, the shadows surrounded him. A second later, he was behind the lead Fae. He had her head in his hands. The snap of her neck pierced the air, and then she collapsed dead.

The fear in the rest of the group's eyes was beautiful. Kerrigan rushed in after him, drawing her sword at the same time as he did. She engaged the first soldier, feeling the hours and hours of practice snap into focus. Lorian had beaten her over and over again. He'd called her weak and pathetic. He'd spat on her confidence. But he'd also molded a fine soldier out of the dirt he ground her into.

She got inside the guard of the first, slicing through his ribs before he had a chance to use his magical artifact. The second one was ready for her, using the magic in her orb to cast terrifying monsters. Kerrigan stumbled as the first black creature came for her. She sliced through it with ease, and it dissolved into smoke. They were… illusions. Scary, potentially dangerous illusions but nothing more. She pulled deep from her well and blasted the illusions off of the docks and then ran the soldier through.

She reached Fordham by that point, and he'd taken out a half-dozen on his own. His sword was slick with blood, and his face was perfectly blank as he stared down the last pair.

"You are on the wrong side of this fight," Fordham growled.

"We fight with the king," he said, holding his amber orb aloft.

Kerrigan shuddered at the sight of it. Was it the same one that Basem had used against her in their final fight? She didn't want to find out.

"Don't let him…" she began.

But then he threw the amber orb at Fordham's feet and spoke the ancient Fae word to activate it, "*Carthai.*"

"No," Kerrigan shrieked as the world exploded around them.

She covered her ears as they both dropped to the ground. It was as if she were back in the Dragon Ring, back with Basem's knife at her throat, back at the riot with the Red Masks tearing down buildings. It always came back to this.

Her eyes watered as she reached for her magic. Her ears were bleeding, and still, she forced herself to pull the damn thing toward her. She got her hands on it, and it all evaporated in an instant. Then, she threw the damn orb into the river, so no one could ever use it again.

The pair of Fae stalked toward them, presumably to finish them off, but they missed Alura dropping in behind them. She swept the legs out from one and thrust her sword into the other, making a full three-sixty to plunge her sword into the gut of the second. She kicked the black orb, which Kerrigan guessed was their escape route, out of reach.

"Are you two insane?" Alura demanded. "We're not on the first wave of this battle. We're taking down the boats, not fighting! Call your dragons and get back in formation."

Kerrigan and Fordham stumbled to their feet. Her ears were ringing, but she was still there enough to see who stepped out of the fortifications to meet them.

"I believe this has been a long time coming, brother," Wynter said from the head of her acolytes.

# CHAPTER 59
## *The Shadows*

"**D**o not engage," Alura said as she drew her sword up and came between them and Wynter's dozen zealots. Aisling coming to stand just off of her lover's right side.

"You can't stop this one, Alura," Fordham said. "Take Kerrigan and go."

Alura snorted. "You must think me insane to leave you here to take on twelve soldiers and your crazy sister alone."

Two more bodies dropped onto the docks at their backs. Kerrigan whipped around, prepared to engage more fighters, but it was Audria and Roake. Audria sauntered forward, as if she were here for a party. "Can't let you have all the fun, now can I?"

"I guess we're all in this together," Kerrigan said.

Alura assessed the situation in a split second, and then to everyone's shock, she took a step backward, angling for Fordham to take lead. Alura was the best of them. She was their commander. She'd trained them for the last year, but she'd deferred to Fordham.

Fordham moved into position, as if the change in rank had no effect on him. He was the crowned prince. This was his battle, his sister, his people.

"It doesn't have to be this way," Fordham said in answer to his sister.

"Oh, I think it does. I felt your magic on the battlefield. I could feel your whore beside you. The wall is down, and you still want to imprison us," Wynter said. "We're not too happy about that."

"I want freedom for my people, not war and bloodshed."

"Then, you are not truly one of us any longer."

Wynter smiled dangerously and then raised her hands, pulling the shadows toward her. Fordham snarled and launched himself at her. The acolytes bellowed, and Kerrigan couldn't keep her focus on Fordham any longer. She raised her sword, letting the magic pull in close around her as she fought the first of Wynter's fanatics as Aisling went for Alura.

Kerrigan met sword to sword with the smallest female. Her eyes were rabid and hungry. Kerrigan couldn't believe her strength as she buffeted Kerrigan back.

"You are not worthy," she gritted out.

Kerrigan ignored her, pushing her back and then swinging the blade wide as flames raced up the length of it. She shot them toward the girl, who ducked and rolled out of the way. Water crashed into Kerrigan's side, and she tumbled sideways. Her sword went wide, falling into the river.

Kerrigan caught the edge of the dock before she could go into the racing water with it. Then, Roake was there, pulling rocks from the ground and hurling them at the acolytes, as if he were playing Dragon Eggs. They collided heavily with a pair of acolytes, bowling them over and crashing them into the wall. Kerrigan hoisted herself up and did a somersault to gain more traction as she threw a blast of air. One acolyte got caught in her storm and was whipped around in a cyclone before crashing into the water.

Audria had taken out a handful of their own while Alura clashed with Aisling. Wynter and Fordham kept appearing and disappearing with their dark shadow magic. Kerrigan hoped he had enough energy for that. He'd already pushed it further than he should. Wynter was probably well rested, waiting for this very moment.

Alura called out a command, and then they all engaged as they had been practicing for the last year. Together, they weren't the might of ten thousand soldiers, but it was the force they had to get through to be able to retreat to the safety of their dragons and get back into the fight.

Then with a shout, Aisling thrust under Alura's guard and slashed across her ribs. Alura cried out in pain. Kerrigan could barely look as she fought her own acolyte. They were well trained. Better than them maybe even. But she couldn't stop. Not even to help Alura.

Kerrigan had no concept of how the rest of the battle was going. Just this moment as she hit, blocked, parried. Her magic didn't wane. It responded instinctively. Air, water, fire, earth. A marvel of combinations that pushed the acolytes farther and farther back, away from the burning docks and to the door into Lethbridge.

Alura was wounded. She struggled forward but retained her military prowess. Then with a performance Kerrigan had never witnessed, Alura whirled and drove her sword through Aisling's heart. The great warrior fell backward, felled like a tree.

Wynter appeared then in the middle of the fight. Her scream of torment ached everywhere. Aisling was her lover, if not acknowledged. Her eyes were glowing orbs of death and destruction as she leveled her sword at Alura.

"You."

Alura rose stiffly to her feet and beckoned Wynter forward. But Wynter had no intention of fighting fair. She threw a blast of straight black power into the center of Alura's chest.

"No!" Fordham roared as he materialized before Wynter. He struck his sister across the face and center her stumbling backward, but it was too late.

Alura had taken the brunt of Wynter's attack and was thrown backward.

She tumbled a few feet before collapsing entirely. We all yelled as one, and Audria finished her fight long enough to dash to Alura's side.

"She's alive," Audria said. "But I don't know for how long."

"Get her out of here," Kerrigan cried.

Audria tried to get away with Alura, but suddenly the acolytes engaged them again. There was nothing to do but leave her there and hope for the best.

"She deserved it for what she did to my Aisling," Wynter snarled.

"Then let us finish it," Fordham said.

He was flagging. Wynter panted but looked as maniacal as ever. Perhaps more than normal.

She threw the shadows at Fordham, as if they could cut through him. He pushed them away, as if they meant nothing, and thrust his sword out toward her. Wynter made a sword of solid air and parried every thrust. She was a marvel. They were an even match in every way. Raised in the same way. Honed to be deadly.

Wynter knew every one of his tricks. Except one.

Kerrigan ignored the remaining acolytes. Fordham needed her help or Wynter would end him too. She rushed to his side. She had no sword. Only her powers to sustain her. But Fordham was not best on his own, as he had always been trained to be. He was best with his team. He was best with her.

"Get out of here," he barked at her.

"I'm not leaving you." She met Wynter's gleeful strikes with her own magic. "I'll never leave you."

"I can't protect us both."

"Then, let me help," she snapped.

He shot her a look of recognition. They had learned new ways to move, new ways to exist together in the last year. Wynter was one lonely girl who thought herself special. Wynter's mania was pure ego. She thought she was blessed. She believed wholeheartedly that she had been chosen for this and that she was their savior, carrying them out of the isolated mountains, and that she would always reign triumphant.

Well, Kerrigan actually *was* special. She'd taken the wall down. She had visions of the future and ones that told her of the past. She was the one Wynter couldn't understand, had only tried to use.

"Together," Fordham said, and they launched forward.

But Wynter hadn't prepared for what Fordham and Kerrigan could do together. And for a fraction of a second, that mania slipped into fear.

Wynter had control over the black shadows that Fordham used for short jumps. Kerrigan had seen him use them once to take down an assailant. Wynter seemed to have no gumption against using them, and she threw the shadows like knives.

Kerrigan smiled as she met Wynter's black shadows with the four elements. Air to blast the dark power away from them. Water to douse them where they crawled. Earth to pull Wynter from her feet. And fire to distract her long enough for Fordham to close in.

"You were never good enough," Wynter snarled at Fordham, coiling her shadows in like a whip and striking at him. "It should have been me!"

He dodged and then drew the edge of his Tendrille blade across her magic, disrupting the shadows. "Perhaps it would have been you, Wynter. Maybe it even *should* have been. You had more control," Fordham spat. She wrapped the dark around his ankles and tried to pull him off his feet. Kerrigan stepped in, using her Dragon Ring fighting skills to slice the air down and sever the connection. "But you were always crazy."

"I am the chosen one!" Wynter roared.

Kerrigan snorted. "Chosen for *what*?"

Fordham actually chuckled. It sounded good on him, and it threw Wynter off-balance. "Your cult followers can't make you the next queen."

"No," she agreed, her eyes narrowing. "All I have to do is kill you."

Wynter put her hands to her chest, tipped her head back, and threw her arms wide. Black ink released from her chest like a torrent. Kerrigan dropped to the ground as it enveloped the whole of the docks in a burst. Fordham didn't move. He stood stoic in the darkness of Wynter's magic. The magic that had kept his family in power for thousands of years.

Kerrigan could barely breathe in the flood of night. She had no idea how Fordham could stand it. Let alone stand against it. But he put one foot in front of the other until he was directly before his sister.

"You have long lived in the shadows. You have let them consume you when you should have been looking to the light," Fordham whispered through the roar of her power.

He took that final step and thrust the sword toward her. Wynter's eyes widened, and at the last second, she jerked away but not fast enough as the sword sliced through her shoulder. She screamed. Her black shadows intensified, sending Kerrigan facedown onto the docks. Then, the shadows disappeared in a rush.

Fordham yanked his sword from Wynter's shoulder. He hesitated for the span of a second. Even though Wynter deserved death, he still hesitated. And in that second, Wynter pulled a knife.

Kerrigan gasped. Without thinking, Kerrigan sank as deep as she could go and pulled on that place where she entered the spirit world. It snapped to attention, and she shouted, "Fordham, down!"

Fordham didn't hesitate at her command. He dropped to the stones, and Kerrigan unleashed. A boom shook the docks as her spirit energy collided with Wynter. She was thrown backward, her body crashing into the stone battlement. To Kerrigan's shock, the rocks moved with the force and began to crumble. Shouts sounded overhead as the entrance to Lethbridge collapsed. Soldiers fell from their posts, and Wynter was buried under the rubble.

"No," Fordham shouted and began to dig through the stones to get to his sister. "We deserve justice."

But Kerrigan wasn't looking at the wreckage. Her eyes were fixed beyond—to the hundreds of soldiers who had waited on Wynter's command and were now forcing their way through to attack.

"Ford, we have to go," she shouted.

"What in the gods' names was that?" Roake asked.

Kerrigan whipped around to find Audria already on Evien's back with Alura cradled against her. Roake rose slowly to his feet. He'd never seen her spirit magic, and every instinct in her body told her that she couldn't tell him. They couldn't know. Kerrigan opened her mouth, having no idea how to explain to them what she'd done.

"Some help over here," Fordham interrupted.

Kerrigan grabbed his arm. "We have to go. Look."

His manic gaze shifted to the Lethbridge gates. His face paled. "Gods."

"Call Netta. Let's go."

Kerrigan tugged on the bond with Tieran, dragging Fordham away from the advancing soldiers.

"Was it one of those magical artifacts?" Roaked asked in confusion.

"Yes," Kerrigan said, glad to have been given an out.

Fordham frowned. "Kerrigan and I have seen them back home."

"Good thinking," Roake said.

Roake narrowed his eyes. "I didn't see you holding anything."

Kerrigan shrugged. "I picked one off of the first group before you landed. I knew what it was better than they did."

Fordham shoved his sword back into its sheath. "We'll come back for my sister when this is over," he promised. "She'll pay for what she's done." And then he ran as Netta approached.

"Head back to camp. We'll regroup from there," Kerrigan yelled as Roake got on his dragon.

Kerrigan felt shaky, like she might pass out. There was no way that she could do a running mount. She let her current feeling flow through Tieran, and he responded in turn, diving down toward her and picking her up. They soared over the river before he released her on the bank. She climbed onto his back and collapsed forward.

They made it into the skies when the sound of wings carried across the wind. Hundreds of dragons flew in formation in the distance, heading toward them. Kerrigan's heart soared. Reinforcements were finally here. The stomp of feet drew her attention away from the Society. Then, a line of navy-blue soldiers crested the hill toward Lethbridge. Her heart caught as she recognized the Bryonican uniforms. Her people had heard the call and come to help.

The fight had only begun, but the odds were turning.

\*\*\*

Reinforcements swelled their camp from a meager forty to thousands. Kerrigan barely registered the difference because as soon as her feet hit the ground in the clearing, she passed out. Hours later, she gasped awake, rushing out of her tent to find dozens of campfires still lit.

"Hey, you're okay," Roake called. He was seated before the fire but scrambled up to assist her. She waved him off.

"I'm okay. How's Alura?"

Roake grimaced. "She's with Helly. The healers are keeping her stable, but she hasn't woken yet."

"Gods," she breathed. "Will she wake?"

"We don't know yet."

"Scales," she said gruffly.

Roake sat back down. "I'm on watch."

"It's the same day?" she asked with a wince as she flopped in front of the fire.

"Same day," he confirmed.

"What happened?"

"Nothing much. We retreated when the reinforcements came since it was almost dark. We're going to break through the line and into Lethbridge tomorrow at dawn." He pushed a plate toward her. "We saved you dinner. Thought you might want it when you woke up."

"Thanks," she said, digging into the food with abandon.

"Helly checked you over after she stabilized Alura. She said it wasn't the magic sickness. They wanted to bench you tomorrow. She said it looked like exhaustion and you just needed to sleep."

She bit her lip. "You think she was telling the truth?"

Roake shrugged. "Who knows? You're in it tomorrow with us at least."

Kerrigan sighed and glanced up at the moon. She gasped when she saw it was full in her sky. Was it time for her to meet with Cleora? Had she gotten her days right?

"You should get some more sleep," Roake said. "I'll wake Audria in a few hours."

"Thanks."

She finished her food and then crawled back into her tent. With a breath, she dropped into the spirit plane. She left the clouds immediately and landed on the stretch of land where she had met with the spiritcaster. She turned in a circle and called out, "Cleora?"

But there was no answer. Cleora had been certain that their moon cycles matched, but perhaps they had been wrong. Maybe wherever Cleora's world was, day was night, and night was day. Maybe they were drastically off from each other. Kerrigan had no idea. She'd never met anyone from a different *world*. Cyrene had been strange enough, and she'd come from a different continent.

"Anyone here?"

Kerrigan sighed in exasperation and then sat down to wait. It could be that she was just early... or late. She'd give it an hour. Unfortunately, she couldn't sit around and wait forever. She would need to get some actual sleep to fight tomorrow. Already, her body hurt in places she'd never imagined. And that was after a full year of training.

Then, after a few minutes, a piece of paper appeared before her. Kerrigan jumped like the thing was set to explode. When it gently swayed to the ground and landed harmlessly, Kerrigan picked it up between her fingers and read what was on it.

*Emergency back home. Meet next full moon.*
*—Cleo*

Kerrigan huffed. Of course, right when she could really *use* spiritcasting to help win this battle, Cleora was absent. Well, at least Kerrigan hadn't missed her.

Kerrigan folded the note and put it in her pocket before dropping back down into her body. She reached into the folds of her nightclothes and was surprised to find the paper had come with her. What kind of trick was *that*?

Next time, she'd find out.

She shoved the paper into her bag and promptly passed back out. Spiritcasting would wait for her. The battle tomorrow would not.

# CHAPTER 60
## *The Battle*

Trulian called Kerrigan and Fordham into the commander's tent before dawn. They dressed in haste, only stopping briefly to see that there was no change in Alura, before crossing the clearing to the tent. Fordham said not a word. His eyes were dark and a little lost. He knew the cost of what was to come. Kerrigan stifled a yawn as she followed him into the tent. Her eyes scanned the room that had been nearly empty. Now, all twenty-one of the council members were in attendance.

Helly frowned at her entrance. Bastian hung back with Kress, who stroked his ginger beard as he listened to whatever Bastian was saying. Anahi read the notes over Lockney's shoulder. Alsia checked and double-checked her weapons, pulling knives out of various places on her body. Lorian stared off into nothing. He must have taken the news of his daughter hard.

Then, another figure stepped out of the crowd. Kerrigan stopped dead in her tracks when her fiancé appeared before her.

"March," she said flatly.

He shot her the most dazzling smile he could muster. "There you are." He swept forward, taking her hand in his and pressing a firm kiss upon it.

"When I heard that my fiancée was among those set for battle, I came as fast as I could."

"You're... with the military?" she asked, pulling her hand back from his.

"Lord March brought the foot soldiers," Helly said with an arched eyebrow.

"The House of Medallion is at your service," March said.

"Oh," Kerrigan whispered. Her stomach roiled. She was glad to have the reinforcements, but she had never considered that March would lead the charge.

"You can leave the reunion for later," Trulian said gruffly. "You lot have proven your merit against the opposition. I'm putting your contingent in my regiment on the front lines."

"They're new recruits!" Helly objected.

"I agreed with you when we got here. Now, they're veterans as far as I'm concerned, and we'll use them where they can be best utilized," Trulian said, rejecting Helly's worries. "They took down the princess. Let's cut off the king's head."

Fordham didn't even blink at the talk of killing his father. He hated the man for all he had put him through, but still... it was his father.

"To your stations. We fly with the sun."

Trulian dismissed them, and Kerrigan hastened out of the tent before March could say anything else.

She grasped Fordham's arm to slow him down. "How are you feeling?"

He glanced at her. "Fine. I'll do what must be done."

"Fordham, yesterday..."

He jerked her into a faster clip. "I have to appear completely unaffected, Kerrigan," he said low into her ear. "They see me as the traitor in their midst. Trulian is only moving us to the front lines to keep an eye on me. So, no, I cannot discuss my *feelings*. My feelings don't matter. All that matters is that they do not remember that I am the crowned prince of the enemy. That they do not turn on me."

Then, he released her and stomped away. Her heart broke for him, but this was war. There would be time to fix this once they won.

\*\*\*

Clouds rolled in, dark and ominous, as the army prepared for battle. It felt wrong to leave Alura behind, but they had no choice. So, Kerrigan called Tieran and climbed onto his back.

*Are you ready for this?*

"Ready as I'll ever be." She sent a pulse of adrenaline down the bond. It mingled with her feelings of unease and excitement. She was on the front lines. She was in the thick of it. She had to succeed.

Tieran sent back his own mixed feelings. The exhilaration of war and terror that she might get hurt and fear for the future. It was all the same feeling, and she felt comforted to know that he was in the same mindspace as her. That they could share this.

Kerrigan pulled into formation with her group. Fordham leading as the four of them drew into Trulian's regiment. She couldn't even believe that she was part of this.

She recognized Society members who were brilliant soldiers. Master Cannon, who she had fought during her training, looked eager to get started. Master Kress was in full armor, throwing a ball of flame aimlessly around, as if none of this concerned him at all. Others she only recognized by reputation. She was not even a full member, and she flew here with them. Whether or not it was because Fordham was seen as the enemy, they were making a name for themselves today.

And as the ground troops marched, angling for Lethbridge's gate, the Society dragons fanned out to take the city. Kerrigan could just make out March at the head of his soldiers in a plumed helmet. She couldn't hear the words of encouragement as his horse galloped before the lot of them, but she knew he could be inspirational. So long as he valued a person as more than an object of his ascension.

House of Shadows soldiers swelled before the doors that led into the city. Powerful Fae waiting with swords raised to take on their enemy. No sign of the king. He would be behind the gates. Their real prize.

Trulian held his own sword high and then bellowed, pointing the sword toward the city beyond. The dragons flew as one while the soldiers below moved into battle. The clash of swords against shields was deafening. The roar that came from the magical artifacts was almost worse. But it was the dragons that did the most damage.

Kerrigan dived into her magic as she faced the onslaught and then threw everything she had at the soldiers. Dragons picked Fae off the ground and dropped them from on high. Some barreled straight through the lot of them. Fire bloomed over and over on the field. Within the hour, it was a bloodbath. Disorienting and terrifying and thrilling.

She remembered the feel of riding on Tavry with Helly into battle. But nothing compared to this. She understood the year of training better than ever. The shielding and fighting and flying and formations were second nature once she was in the thick of it. If it hadn't been, she would have been lost. The world was chaos, and all she had to follow were the commands ingrained in her head. Fordham was her lead; she was his wing.

A powerful boom tore through the normal buzz of war. They circled around and found March's soldiers had a battering ram thunking against the doors of Lethbridge. It hit again and again against the seemingly impenetrable doors. Then, the wood cracked, the doors caved inward, and the war shifted.

They were in.

Soldiers pushed through the giant doors, trampling over the enemy and flooding the upper tier of the city. They'd taken out most of the archers, which left the dragons free rein to fly inside. Trulian veered inward, his eyes forward, and they followed in his wake.

Kerrigan could feel the tide of the battle turn. Before the reinforcements had shown up, they hadn't been able to get past the battlement. It was too early to say, but it already felt like it was only a matter of time. And with the boats burned yesterday, there was no escape for those inside.

Trulian vaulted from his dragon, landing heavily in the central square with his blade extended. "Samael!" he taunted. "Come fight me, you coward!"

The rest of the riders dropped into the square with him and immediately engaged the soldiers. Trulian hacked aside soldiers as if they were made of paper instead of flesh and blood. His magic flowed like a living, breathing thing. Kerrigan had never seen anything like it. Over a thousand years of carefully honed magic. A man so powerful that he'd fought against the abyss all these long years after his beloved's death.

"Samael!" he roared again. "Your soldiers die for you." He hacked down another Fae. "They die, and you *hide*! Your father would be ashamed of you. At least Braidien fought his own battles."

And then, from the far opening to the market, King Samael Ollivier stepped from the shadows and materialized out of thin air. The same trick both of his children had inherited but that he alone had truly mastered.

"You dare decry my father's name," the king jeered. He removed a blade as black as night from a sheath at his waist.

Trulian knocked aside the Fae before him and stepped into the center of the madness that had cleared for them. "Oh, I dare!"

"Who are you but some lowly Society bastard?"

"I might be lowly," Trulian said, leveling his sword at Samael, "but I am your doom."

Samael jumped from his spot at the entrance to stand before Trulian in the space of a heartbeat, using those clever shadows to his advantage. But Trulian hardly blinked. He raised his sword and met the king against his blade. Their magic sang a symphony as they came apart and collided back together. Both were utter masters. Circling, rebounding, throwing strikes Kerrigan couldn't even see in the blur. It was as if the edges of reality had shifted. And all the while, the conflict raged around them, soldiers unaware that their fate was being determined in this one fight. A battle that should have ended a thousand years ago, coming to fruition at the heart of a dying city.

Kerrigan took down another Fae, who seemed surprised that someone so small could pack that much of a punch. She was constantly underestimated for her size. But as she turned to face her next opponent, no one was there. The space was open wide as Trulian and Samael fought.

She didn't know who moved first or which opening happened. All she saw was Trulian's blade pierce Samael's defenses as he stabbed him through the stomach. The king stumbled, shock registering on his face. Fordham jerked toward the fight, as if for a split second, he thought he could stop it. But there was no stopping it. He knew that as much as anyone. Maybe more.

"Your time is over," Trulian told him, twisting the blade.

Samael fell onto the stone. A gurgle escaped his mouth. Blood ran freely from the wound. "You... will... pay for this," he managed to get out as blood came out of his mouth.

"No. This is what I have waited all this time for. I should have never let my love keep you safe," he growled.

Samael glared at him, and then with his dying breath, he shot a bolt of shadows straight at Trulian. It was just as Wynter had done to Alura, but infinitely worse. A thousand years of carefully controlled magic from the king. Trulian had no chance of dodging the magic. There was no escape. The bolt slammed straight through his chest. Trulian went stock-still before toppling over at the feet of his greatest enemy.

"No!" Kerrigan screamed.

She dashed through the open space and skidded to her knees before Trulian. She turned him over onto his back. But then Zina was there, appearing at her side out of the crowd. Her eyes were haunted as she reached for her father's pulse.

"He's dead," she muttered.

Tears clouded Kerrigan's eyes. "No, no, no, I'm so sorry."

"This is how he would have wanted to go. He was ready to see Mother."

Something hard came into Zina's face as she saw her father lying dead on the stones. And then with a fury Kerrigan had never seen from her, she screamed at the top of her lungs, and every single person on the square froze to stone. She held them in her grasp. Not differentiating between friend or foe. They were all just there. The people who had led her father back into a battle that would take his life.

Kerrigan couldn't even blink. She watched as Zina's great power rippled from her in such a force. Then, Kerrigan felt around the shape of the magic to her spirit beyond it, and she dropped out of the physical.

Zina was hunched over, sobbing onto her father's figure. The feelings she couldn't process in reality couldn't be contained here. She'd frozen the outside world, only to try to come to grips with what was in front of her.

Kerrigan came to her feet and put her hand on Zina's back. She gasped and jumped away from Kerrigan.

"You don't understand," Zina cried.

"No, I can't. I lost a parent before I could feel the sting of their absence. But I know what it is to be abandoned by someone you love. I know how it can fester and burrow deep until you feel like you can never touch that place within you. And I know it's harder to move on, harder to see them as people who made choices, than it is to just be angry."

Zina wiped her tears. "He lied to me about my mother. He lied, and now, he's gone. I'll never get those years back."

"You're right. What he did was wrong. There's no excuse, but there's a

477

reason. He wanted to protect you. He might not have been the best father. In the end, he made the choice he thought would hurt you the least. He did that because he loved you."

"I know," Zina finally said, looking so small in that moment. "He wanted this fight. He *wanted* it."

"Mei took this final battle from him. Maybe you should honor him by ending it."

Zina nodded, tears forming rivulets down her cheeks, and then held her hand out. "Let's end it then."

They came back into reality together. Zina released her magic in a rush, and everyone collapsed to the ground, gasping for breath. She held her head high above the lot of them and magically projected her voice.

"Your king is dead. Lay down your weapons and surrender, or you will find no mercy," Zina said, her voice reaching far beyond the walls of the square to the soldiers out into the field.

The Fae before them shook with terror at her ferocious power and laid down their arms. They fell to their knees in surrender. Dishonorable for their people, but better than every single person dying.

She heard the clatter of weapons all through the city. And at the top of the tower, a white flag was hoisted over Lethbridge.

# CHAPTER 61
## *The Defeat*

ARBOR

"They're rounding us up," Prescott said frantically. "We need to get out of here."

Arbor pressed her fingers into her temples. "How are we supposed to do that?"

She wanted to shriek at him. They were finished. Everything she had worked for was gone. Fordham and Kerrigan had killed Wynter. She was buried under the rubble, and what was Arbor supposed to do with that? Queen Viviana had surrendered in a hurry after Samael had been killed, and there was no one else to take his place. He'd finally kicked the bucket, and she didn't even have a person to put in his position. All her work for nothing. It wasn't as if anyone would accept *her* as queen. Not with her bloodline. Not without Fordham or Wynter for her to puppet. Gods, she was really and truly screwed.

"I don't know. You're the genius," he barked. Uncharacteristically Pres.

It set her teeth on edge. "We need to figure it out, or they're going to kill us."

"They don't seem to be killing people."

"I don't care," she snapped, grabbing a bag and stuffing enough valuables in it for them to get by. They'd barred the door long ago, but surely, this old city had a secret passageway. "Start looking for a way out."

She pushed against the walls, and Pres went to the closet. They touched everything they could find. But if there was a way out, she didn't know it. And she certainly didn't find it before the door burst open and a man walked inside. He looked as self-important as all the rest.

"Come on out," he said, sword aloft. "Every one of you needs to be accounted for."

She opened her bag and showed him a diamond the size of his palm. "I'll give you this if you leave this room and act like you never saw us."

The man ignored the diamond and grabbed her arm. "Don't care for your bribes. Just move along."

"Pres," she gasped.

"Unhand my sister."

"You come along too," he said, throwing Arbor bodily into the empty hallway.

Her shoulder collided with the opposite wall, and something crunched. She gasped in pain, her eyes watering.

She had never been a part of the military, much to her cousin's chagrin. She knew battle magic but hadn't used it in so long that it didn't even come to her naturally. Prescott had more than her, and he tussled with the man before also being casually thrown out of the room.

Pres pulled his magic to him, ready to throw something at their attacker.

The man thrust his sword against Prescott's throat. "Try me."

"Roake!" a voice boomed down the corridor.

"Down here," Roake called back.

And then their cousin stepped into the hallway. Fordham eyed them as if he had no idea who they were. Not a single clue. Gods, he had always been a good actor.

"Audria needs help with some nobles on the hallway over. She asked for you. I can take this lot."

Roake scoffed, "Good luck. This one"—he pointed his sword at Arbor—"tried to bribe me. The other is a sore excuse for a magic user."

"Then, I'll have no trouble."

"You know them?" Roake asked, eyeing Fordham.

Fordham's jaw tightened. "I know everyone," he ground out. "And they're all prisoners of war until the council can come to some treaty agreement with the queen."

Roake shrugged, sheathing his sword. "Fine. I'll go see what Audria needs."

Fordham clapped him on the back as he departed. He waited until Roake was out of earshot and then sighed.

"You should have listened to me," he told them.

Prescott sneered, "We had superior numbers!"

"It didn't matter," Fordham cut him off.

Arbor held her head high. "Are you going to take us to the dungeons?"

"Of course not," Fordham said. He shook his head. "Look, I have one more jump in me. I can get you outside of the city. But then you need to disappear. I cannot be responsible for you after this. Go underground."

"You're really going to help us?" Arbor asked.

"Unless you want to become a prisoner of war for who knows how long. I can get you out. Others got out on their own."

Arbor and Pres cut each other a glance before nodding. "Do it."

Fordham pulled his shadows tight to himself, and then they surrounded them both. Arbor tightened her grip on her cousin, clinging to him and her brother as they disappeared. She hadn't thought that Fordham's magic worked this well. He'd never been able to jump this far before, let alone with two people.

But then they were on the other side of the river in the safety of the trees. Arbor looked at Lethbridge from the outside for the first time and gasped. The city was nothing like it had been when they first came to conquer it. The walls were caved in. The place was a disaster. The docks burned. It would hardly be livable from here.

"Go. Be safe by disappearing," Fordham said, and then he jumped back across the river.

"Well, sister," Prescott said, leaning against a tree, "this wasn't in the plans."

"It was not."

"What are we going to do now? Go underground?"

She snorted. "Hardly. Someone in the Society sold us those magical artifacts. Someone in their ranks is sympathetic to our cause. We just need to show them how valuable we are alive."

Prescott grinned. "I love the way you think." He held his hand out, and she put hers in his. "Shall we?"

She nodded, and they slunk out of the view of the city.

Today was a defeat but not the end of their schemes.

# CHAPTER 62
## *The Treaty*

"I never found her," Fordham said in frustration. He and Kerrigan stood before the commander's tent and waited for the reading of the treaty that had been signed with Queen Viviana.

"Wynter?"

He tersely nodded. "I pulled apart the entire rubble. Dug everything out myself, and she wasn't there."

"How is that possible?"

He ground his teeth and shook his head. "I don't know. I should have found a body if she was dead."

"Do you think that she used her magic to escape? Jumped somewhere?"

"I thought she was sufficiently incapacitated." He sighed. "But she must have."

"Gods..."

"It's not the last we've seen of her."

Kerrigan gulped. That was not a good sign. Not at all. Wynter was powerful. And the last thing they needed was a loose cannon with that amount of power as an enemy.

The crowd grew silent as Presiding Officer Malwin Zoh stepped forward to read the treaty. It had taken a full day of negotiations and the approval of the council for Queen Viviana to sign her seal on the document. And it was a litany of demands.

*1. The House of Shadows will become the thirteenth tribe of Alandria, sovereign to the Society and hereto known as tribe Charbonnet.*

*2. All full-Fae will remain within the arranged boundaries of Charbonnet for a duration of five years with no standing army.*

*3. A Society occupation will exist within the bounds of the tribe until the Society dictates that they are able to rejoin the greater world.*

*4. No member of tribe Charbonnet will be permitted to enter the dragon tournament or join the Society for a period of one hundred years.*

*5. All held slaves will be immediately released and slavery abolished in all forms.*

*6. Any and all illegal magical artifacts will be handed over to the Society for destruction.*

*7. A fine of a million marks a year will be paid to the Society for the rebuilding of the city of Lethbridge and reparations for lives lost.*

Kerrigan winced with each new infraction added. The Society had all the bargaining chips on their side. They could and, apparently, had asked for everything. And the queen, in an effort to keep her people safe, had given it all away.

Fordham said nothing. He hardly even blinked as his people were stripped of everything that had made them what they were. She wanted to reach out to him, to offer comfort as the army cheered their victory and his demise. But he had been so adamant that he didn't want them to turn on him that she had no way of doing that without putting a spotlight on him.

He should have been in those negotiations. He should have figured out a way to help those he cared about. But he hadn't stepped forward as king even though he was the rightful heir.

And when the treaty was finished being read, he didn't cheer with the others. He just stood there and watched as everyone celebrated. Then, he turned and walked away. Kerrigan didn't know how to help him. So much of it was excessive. The House of Shadows had already lost so many lives. To confine them to the mountain they'd been isolated in felt cruel. To not permit them a place in the government they were now forced to be a part of was even worse. And what did that mean for Fordham? He was already part of the Society. Would he not ascend to an official position because of this treaty? It seemed ridiculous since he had fought for the winning side.

Kerrigan stepped forward, hoping to speak to Helly about it, but she was dismissed from the commander's tent before she could even get inside.

She huffed and whirled around, determined to do something. Kerrigan's eyes landed on another council member, Master Kress. He was in charge of the list of prisoners and working out who was and wasn't a slave to be released. Something would have to be done with all the humans and half-Fae within the House of Shadows, as they could obviously no longer remain where they had been enslaved. Which gave Kerrigan an idea. She just wished it weren't Master Kress.

"Sir," she said as she approached him.

His eyes swept to her, and he sneered. "What is it, Miss Argon? Can you not see that I am busy?"

"Yes, sir. Of course. I was inquiring about two half-Fae slaves—Benton and Bayton."

"Why?" he demanded.

"I'd like to request that they be released to me."

"To you?" he asked. "You're going to have two half-Fae slaves?"

She balked. "Of course not, sir. I was hoping to help them find work and a place to live in Kinkadia. They're going to need a lot of help. There should be sponsors from within the Society for this, sir."

He looked at her for a moment and then softened. "Too true. If only we could get more Society members to offer such." He shrugged. "I'll find them on my roster and have someone collect them. They should be ready to fly when we leave here."

"Thank you, sir."

"Maybe spread it around that we're looking for more sponsors."

"Of course, sir," she said with a brilliant smile. Kress had voted for kicking her out of the Society. She might have just turned one council member in her favor. One down, a dozen to go.

\*\*\*

There was so much more work to do before they could all fly out. She helped round up prisoners and clear rubble from the city. She cleaned out burned buildings in the lower quarter, salvaged what she could of the boats she'd destroyed, and ran missions to nearby cities for supplies, mainly food. She was weary and ready to go home and not think about war for a hundred years or more.

But she knew that even when she returned, she wouldn't really rest. She had started a movement for humans and half-Fae in the city. Bringing in all the displaced refugees from the House of Shadows would only swell their numbers. The Society might see them as a problem, but Kerrigan saw it as an opportunity. These people might be refugees, but they deserved fair treatment and a voice in the government as much as anyone else. And if no one else would take up the mantle, she would have to do it.

She was so lost in her thoughts that she didn't even realize she had crossed from the Society holdings over to the gap of land that led to the Bryonican soldiers until one of them hollered, "It's Lord March's fiancée!"

She froze at the word. *Fiancée.* It still left a bitter taste in her mouth.

March stepped out of his tent at those words. A smile lit his face as he found her gaze. She didn't return the gesture. In fact, all she wanted to do was run as March purposely strode across the camp in her direction.

"Have you come to see us off?" March asked as he got closer.

"Are you leaving then?"

"We've done our part. The Society is giving the House of Medallion a reward for our work here." He beamed. "And I'll be awarded a medal of honor."

March, the war hero. Just great.

"Congratulations," she said. "We'll remain for a few days to clean up."

"Hear, hear," he said with a laugh.

It was maybe the most normal conversation that they'd ever had. He was jubilant. Not an ounce of the venom that he'd had that night at the winter Season party in Rosemont. If she didn't know he was a snake, she might have even enjoyed his company.

"Well, I'll just…" She gestured away.

"No need to run off," he said, catching her hand. "We got off on the wrong foot. You've lived your life, and I've lived mine. I want to apologize for how I acted this winter. I was… jealous." He ducked his head, as if he were a fool in love. Gods, he was a triumphant actor.

"It's fine," she said, pulling herself free. "I was under an immense amount of stress from the Society. I wasn't myself."

"I realize that. You're brilliant," he said with a smile. She looked at the edges, waiting to see it for false, but it wasn't there. "I watched you flying and in battle. I have never met a woman such as yourself. If you'd permit, I would like to get to know you more, my lady."

"I thought that you didn't care about me," she said, anger returning to her voice. How dare he treat her like trash and threaten her people, only to try to court her favor.

"Can't we do this in a way that's more agreeable?" he asked, stepping forward. "You are as fierce and deadly and beautiful as a nightshade. Truly, I am besotted, Lady Argon. We are to be joined. It does not have to be unpleasant."

She swallowed and watched herself swimming in his blue irises. How easy it would be to love this man if he were anyone else. He had spoken the words to entrap her, not understanding that he had already lost every single ounce of her goodwill at a party on Geivhrea.

But she had taken strategy classes in her government courses the last year. They had taught her all the history and philosophy of modern warfare. Perhaps what was happening with March was no different. A new sort of war. And if she wanted to win, to keep herself from being weak ever again, then she had one job. Convince him that she wanted this too.

Slowly, she released her anger and looked to the ground and then up at him through dark lashes. All the coquettish lessons she'd suffered through with Darby coming in handy.

"Maybe it could work out," she said softly. "I would like that."

His smile only brightened. And then to her shock, he grasped her around the waist and planted a firm kiss on her lips. She gasped, and he took advantage of the opportunity to slide his tongue in and meet hers. Every instinct in her body told her to escape, to scramble away. Instead, she went loose as jelly in his embrace and told her mind she could endure one kiss to get away from him forever.

Cheers and catcalls and whistles rose up from the army all around them. The Bryonican soldiers seeing exactly what they wanted. Their general planting one on his intended, their future lady. Maybe their future queen.

He released her slowly, a lustful smile on his pretty lips. She staggered backward with a forced laugh.

"I shall see you at the spring Season," he called out to her as she fled. "Then, we will discuss wedding dates."

The crowd cheered louder. She had to keep the embarrassed smile on her face for ages. It wasn't until she was safely ensconced in her own tent that she let it slip, and anger covered everything else. She would beat March at his own game. She would bury him before this was over.

***

As promised, Benton and Bayton appeared at her tent the morning the Society intended to return to Kinkadia. Her eyes filled with tears when she saw them. She rushed forward and threw her arms around her friends. "They let you out."

"All thanks to you, my lady," Benton said.

"We'd still be displaced without your help," Bayton added.

"Kerrigan. It's just Kerrigan from now on. You're no one's attendant anymore."

Benton and Bayton exchanged glances. Benton spoke up, "Actually, miss, if you'd please, we would like to work for you as our thanks."

Kerrigan gaped. "What? I... I don't think that I can cover your expenses. Plus, I live in the mountain, but I don't have my own quarters yet. I was going to help you find work."

Bayton waved that all aside. "We understand the circumstances, but we still feel that we owe you our support. And truly, you need some looking after."

Benton clucked her tongue at the camp. "Allow us to take this down for you, miss."

"Call me Kerrigan, please. I can't have attendants that I can't pay. That's not how it works."

"I'm sure you will figure it out, miss," Bayton said.

"You always do," Benton said and then went to work, taking down the tent and packing all of her belongings.

Kerrigan shook her head.

Fordham appeared then out of his own tent and stared at the twins in shock. "What have you done?"

"I'm sponsoring their release," Kerrigan said. "I've been offering the opportunity to other Society members to reduce the potential refugee situation."

Fordham gaped. "You didn't mention it to me."

"And when would I have? This is the first I've seen of you."

"I've been working."

Benton bowed deeply to Fordham. "Your Highness, may we help with your campsite as well?"

Fordham flinched at the royal title and looked around to see if anyone else had noticed. "No, I can do it."

"Absolutely, Your Highness," Bayton said and then began to deconstruct his tent as well.

Kerrigan shrugged. "They don't listen to me either."

"Because you both need looking after," Benton insisted.

Fordham pursed his lips. "We'll have to pay you."

"Of course, Your Highness," Bayton said dismissively.

He ground his teeth and looked to Kerrigan as if this were her fault.

"You'd have known about this if you were doing anything but penance," she hissed at him. "You should have been in that tent, negotiating for your people. You should be at the head of discussions for the refugees. These are your people, Fordham."

"Don't," he snarled. "I am dealing with it. You deal with your fiancé."

She glared. "I *am* dealing with my fiancé. I am dealing with how to get rid of him. That is my main objective."

"I saw you kissing him in front of the entire camp. Forgive me if I don't believe you."

"Believe what you want. You always have made assumptions about me, haven't you?"

"This is not at all the same thing."

"Then, what are you doing about everything right now, Fordham? Why are you on the sidelines?"

"It's the curse!" he barked. "This whole bloody thing is because of me."

She startled. "When are you going to stop blaming yourself for everything that happens and start trying to fix it?"

"I tried that with you, and look where that led us," he said, placing another foot of space between them. "The minute that I feel anything at all, it is stolen or killed in front of me. My mother is dead. Dacia is dead. My father is dead. Half of my kingdom is dead! I will not interfere and have the rest die with it. And if you marry March, then good riddance."

Tears came to her eyes at the harsh words as his cold gray eyes fixed on her with all the built-up anger and frustration. Then, he disappeared in a cloud of shadows, leaving her to pick up the pieces of her heart.

After they had finished with Fordham's tent, Benton and Bayton carefully bundled her in a blanket, sitting her before the dying fire. Bayton brushed free the snarls in her curly hair and then plaited it back out of her face. Neither of them said a word, but the caution and worry in their faces said everything.

When the camp was packed, Kerrigan shrugged off Fordham's anger and called Tieran. Audria had agreed to carry one of the twins to redistribute the weight. Over the next couple of weeks, the remainder of the refugees would be brought into Kinkadia by foot or in caravans.

Benton held on tight, only screaming a little as Tieran rose into the skies and headed south toward the city. Bayton looked to be in a blissful state just getting to be near the dragons, let alone to ride on one.

It was a few hours back to the city. Fordham even flew with them. Alura was being carried by a healer back to Kinkadia. Now, it was just the three of them, and Audria wearily took point. A few hours later, they landed in an aerie, and with Benton and Bayton's help, it only took one trip to get her belongings back to her room. She'd have to figure out where they could stay, but there was plenty of space within the mountain.

Kerrigan returned to the aerie to see if they needed help with any of the remainder of the supplies. She followed Mistress Corinna into the room. She veered straight for Helly, whispering furtively, and handed her a document. Kerrigan kept chancing glances at them, wondering what was going on.

Then, Helly sighed heavily and nodded. Kerrigan read the words on her lips. "Do it."

Corinna moved into action, and the Society Guard who had been carefully placed around the aerie formed up behind her. She stepped up to Lorian, who had just landed and stood by his dragon, Oria.

"Lorian Van Horn, you are under arrest by order of the Society council for possession of illegal artifacts and treason. Anything you say and do can be used against you."

Lorian jumped backward toward his dragon, as if he were going to flee, but a rush of guards dropped him to the ground. A set of magic-dampening manacles were fixed around his wrists, rendering him inert.

Lorian gasped. "What is the meaning of this? I didn't commit treason."

He was still shouting as Corinna dragged him away, reading him his rights as a Society member to appear before the council to plead his case. Kerrigan crossed to Helly, who was silently crying.

Helly glanced up. "You were right. I had a team check his home and study, and there were artifacts as well as letters with the House of Shadows all this time. He was the mole, and he cost us good men and women in this war."

Kerrigan pulled Helly into a hug. No matter that Lorian had caused her so much grief, he had been friends with Helly for years, and his treachery would have lasting repercussions.

# CHAPTER 63
## The Trial

**K**errigan hastened into the council chamber. Her eyes flitted around the room until she found Audria and Roake seated off to the side. "Sorry I'm late. I was looking for Fordham. Have you seen him?"

Audria shook her head. "He wasn't in his room when I left. Roake?"

"He said he'd be right behind me. Must be late."

But Fordham was never late.

"Huh," she muttered. She bit her lip and sat back. He'd show up. He had to. Kerrigan and Fordham had both received notices about a formal meeting with the council after Lorian's fate was decided.

She had never seen the council chamber full before. Every Society member in the mountain was in attendance for Lorian's trial. He stood at the podium, straight-backed and unblinking. Someone had the decency to clean him up, but she could see the strain the last few days had on him.

"Have either of you spoken to Alura?"

Alura awoke yesterday. Helly had informed Kerrigan that Alura didn't wish to have any visitors. She wouldn't tell her how she was doing medically either.

Audria and Roake shared a look, and Audria said, "Helly wouldn't let us see her. But can you imagine how she's feeling right now?"

"Terrible," Kerrigan whispered.

But Alura wasn't in attendance. Surely if she was awake, she would do everything she could to be at her father's trial.

Then the council door opened one more time and two figures stepped through. Kerrigan gasped, and she wasn't the only one. Alura had one hand on a cane and the other wrapped around her mother. Anya's eyes were puffy and red, but she helped her daughter maneuver through the council room, looking at no one save her husband.

But Alura... Alura was *not* okay. She had woken up, but she hadn't recovered. She leaned heavily on the cane, limping every step and taking an interminable amount of time to cross the room. Despite it all, she was as blank-faced and straight-backed as her father. No pain crossed her visage. Only clear determination. How could someone whose entire identity had been their strength and skill in battle have been decimated so thoroughly? Who would Alura be without it?

Alura and her mother took their seats to a series of whispers cascading around the room. But no sign of fear gave them away. Not even a single tremor.

Then, Presiding Officer Zoh called the council into session.

"Silence, please." He raised his voice, amplifying it around the room.

The rustle of wings above revealed just how many dragons had come to hear Lorian's case. The council looked as ill at ease as the dragons high above. Helly was grim-faced. Bastian had his arms folded. Kress couldn't seem to make eye contact with anyone. He just stared off into the distance. The secretary, Lockney, was furiously writing on a piece of parchment. Anahi's careful box braids had been removed for a new style, and she kept reaching up to twirl a braid and finding it gone. Her gaze was disoriented and uncertain. Alsia just looked haunted. It was only Boze, who sat forward, smug, as if he had already made up his mind. The slimy toad.

"We're here for the case of Lorian Van Horn, a Society member and council member. He has been accused of the following: treason, conspiracy, murder, possession and trafficking of illegal magical artifacts, falsifying documents, lying to the council, and resisting arrest. How do you plead?"

"Not guilty, Master Zoh," Lorian said. He stood, square-shouldered, before the podium.

Kerrigan had stood there. She knew the weight of judgment in that position.

"Mistress Hellina has filed the charge," Zoh said. "She will provide the evidence."

Helly stood from her seat on the council and came forward to address the entire court. "After the death of Basem Nix, an investigation began into who could have possibly infiltrated the Society's defenses. It became clear to those involved that his death had to have been an inside job. Only someone with access to the dungeons could have done this without anyone noticing. The investigation quickly went nowhere, but against the wishes of the investigators, I continued my own search.

"I had many members followed and discovered that Master Lorian had been meeting with some suspicious people. I had no evidence that he had done anything untoward, so I did not bring my concerns before the council. Then, an accusation came forward that Lorian had been selling illegal magical artifacts. The same ones that were connected to Basem Nix. We took this accusation seriously and had his home and study searched under a warrant from the presiding officer. We found illegal artifacts hidden in his study and home along with correspondence with the House of Shadows, detailing the sale of crates of them over the last year. Artifacts that many of us saw firsthand on the battlefield in Lethbridge.

Helly took a deep breath. "Thus, the evidence asserts that Master Lorian murdered Basem Nix in Society custody to hide his involvement in his illegal possession and trafficking of weapons to conspire with our enemy. An act such as this is treason, and I call for the council to determine the appropriate punishment for his actions."

She nodded her head at the presiding officer and returned to her seat.

"You have heard the accusation. You may speak for yourself, Lorian, unless you have hired counsel to speak in your place," Zoh said, already dropping the title Lorian had earned all those years ago.

Lorian had no counsel. He looked steely-eyed at his peers, tilting his chin up and not backing down an ounce. "This is a wonderful tale," he said, clapping his hands slowly. "The clues all line up, leading you to believe that I must have done precisely what the honorable Mistress Hellina has said. Except that the facts are a fiction and this trial is a farce. I have never owned or sold an illegal artifact. In fact, if you remember correctly, I was the one who introduced the legislation for which artifacts needed to be taken off of the streets. I have no idea what you found in my study or in my home, but they did not belong to me. Nor have I ever communicated with the House of Shadows. I wouldn't even know how to reach them or until the wall fell, where their home was."

"You did argue on behalf of negotiations with the House of Shadows though," Helly added. "You were the only one who wanted to speak with them."

"Is it wrong to want to keep the killing to a minimum? Yes, I come from Venatrix, a war tribe, but I do not enjoy death and destruction, especially not at the scale of which we saw at the Battle of Lethbridge. I would keep that from happening if I could. I would always argue for an open dialogue before war." He swept his arm aside, as if he could clear his name as easily.

"You have similar sympathies as the House of Shadows," Helly countered. "You have cut down all legislation related to humans and half-Fae. You had one of our now-veteran soldiers kicked out of the training program due to your dislike of her heritage. You blamed the riot on the protestors because of who they were. These are all sympathies that were outlined in the letters we read from the House of Shadows, a Fae tribe known for their barbaric treatment of humans and half-Fae."

"I am not the only person in this room who wants to see Fae continue to be elevated above all else. I certainly am not the only one who sees these protests as outlandish ways to incite violence in our city. And I would only ever kick someone out for their failures, which were well-documented. My sympathies aside, I would never commit treason or help a group I went to war with. That is absurd."

Round and round it went. Several of the other council members got involved in the cross-examination, but it all seemed to point in one direction. At one point, Alura swayed uneasily as she jumped to her feet to defend her father. She was cut down and threatened with dismissal.

And while it all happened, Kerrigan watched Lorian. She had observed the man for the last year. She knew his wrath. All the ways that he hated her. All the ways that he twisted his words. But here, he seemed... sincere.

It made no sense. Because all of the accusations that had been put forth laid Lorian bare. He had obviously done it. Had he deluded himself so much into believing that his actions were justified? Had he twisted it all up so much that he thought himself in the right?

Kerrigan had always believed herself a good judge of character. She had hated Lorian as long as he had detested her. She saw him for who and what he was. But here, he was not pleading for his life. He was not begging. He didn't look twitchy or even worried. He was *certain* that the council would believe him.

So, when the verdict came down, Lorian's shock was the truest thing to happen in the court.

"The council finds you guilty of all charges. We have agreed to death by hanging the day after tomorrow," Master Zoh confirmed. He banged his gavel, and the Society was in an uproar.

But Lorian... he just looked stunned. As if he never thought it would happen.

As if he hadn't done anything wrong.

Anya doubled over, sobbing big, heavy tears as the majority of the Society filtered out of the room. Alura sat ramrod straight. Her eyes glassy. Her arm around her mother.

Lorian reached for his wife and was jerked away by a contingent of guards. Zoh waved his hand, and they released Lorian long enough to allow him to wrap his arms around her one last time. He kissed her frantically, reaching for Alura. The words of comfort were lost in the drone, but Alura finally cracked, tears streaking her face.

"We should go," Audria whispered.

"I have my meeting after," Kerrigan said.

"Oh, right. Do you want us to stay?"

Kerrigan bit her lip and shook her head. "Still no Fordham?"

"No. He has a meeting too, right?"

"Yes," Kerrigan said.

Audria frowned. "I'm sure he'll turn up."

Kerrigan nodded and watched everyone trickle out. Eventually, even Lorian was pulled from the room. Alura and Anya passed Kerrigan on their way out. Alura leaned heavily on her cane as she tried to keep her mother upright. Anya looked devastated, but Alura was furious.

She snatched up Kerrigan's arm. "Speak to them for him."

"What?" Kerrigan gasped. "What would I say?"

"I don't know, but for some stupid reason, they listen to you. They listen to you, and that is why he was sentenced. Speak for him."

"He had me kicked out of the Society, Alura."

"And now, you're back in, and he's dead. That is not a fair trade," she snarled.

Anya tugged her daughter back. She wiped her face, and then she pulled Kerrigan in for a hug. "Alura, leave her alone. She is not responsible for this."

"She sure as hell is part of it," Alura snapped and then hobbled off.

Kerrigan winced as she watched the once great woman have to use a cane.

Anya sighed as she watched her daughter. "She is grieving. For her body and her father. Forgive her." Kerrigan nodded, and Anya patted her arm. "And tell your father that I said hello, will you?"

"Um… sure."

"Alura mentioned that I might be welcome back in Lillington."

"If you'd like."

"I think I might need a rest after this," Anya whispered. "I can't imagine going back to Venatrix without him." She choked on the words. "Perhaps I will reach out."

"I am so sorry."

Anya smiled sadly and then without a word followed after her daughter. The door closed behind her, leaving Kerrigan alone with the council and still… no Fordham. Where the hell was he?

"Kerrigan Argon," Presiding Officer Zoh called out.

She stepped up to the podium. "Yes, Presiding Officer."

"Where is Fordham? We also called him to this meeting."

"I don't know, sir. The message was delivered to him."

Lockney tutted. "We won't wait for him."

Bastian sighed and steepled his fingers. "We can give him a few minutes. The boy has surely had a trial after seeing his people die."

"Killing them himself," Helly added softly.

Boze sneered, "He's the crowned prince of the enemy."

"We have a peace treaty with them," Alsia reminded him. "They are not the enemy."

"Bah!" he called. "We just went to war with them, and we've been to war with them before."

"Fordham is a Society member," Helly cut in. "Watch your tongue."

"Helly is correct. Fordham fought bravely," Bastian said. "He should not suffer the same consequences as the rest of his people."

"Then, where is he?" Boze demanded.

Zoh cleared his throat. "That's enough. We're not here to argue. Fordham is a Society member regardless of his affiliation, regardless of being the crowned prince. He fought for us. He is one of us."

Kerrigan fought back tears at the words. She wished that Fordham had heard them. He'd been so worried all this time that everyone would turn on him, but they saw him for the man that he was and not just the throne.

"Alas, if Master Ollivier is not present, we will begin with you," Zoh said confidently. "Your case is more pressing, is it not?"

"Sir?" she asked.

"Before this court, we removed you from your training in the Society. This happened based on the word of Lorian Van Horn. He testified that you had magic sickness and were unstable. Thus, unable to fulfill your duties to the Society. Additionally, that you had ties to insurrectionists within Kinkadia. Yet you answered the call to battle, and you fought bravely alongside us at the Battle of Lethbridge." He motioned to Helly.

"Furthermore, all signs of magic sickness have been eliminated from her body. Whatever the cause, it was clearly a temporary case due to the stresses of training along with... harassment from one of our own." She met Kerrigan's gaze with a nod. "Harassment that we now know was due to his undue sympathies against the Rights For All organization and humans and half-Fae more broadly."

"More than that," Bastian continued, "your accusations against the convicted were true."

Kress leaned forward. He stroked his beard. "Without your information, we would not have investigated further into the magical artifacts. However did you know about this?"

Kerrigan gulped. "Master Kress, I had information from the people you believed to be insurrectionists but are actually just people. People who want desperately to be heard by this council and the Society as a whole."

Boze sniffed. "We went off of the advice of some insurrectionists."

"And it turned out to be true," Anahi said. "Which adds merit to her words."

For a moment, the conversation went down a rabbit hole about whether her information was valid and whether they should have been able to know before then. Kerrigan stood still and waited for all twenty members of the council to give her permission to speak again.

Zoh finally called it all to order. "This is not a debate, council. Silence." Everything settled back down, and Zoh nodded at her. "This is a meeting to decide your fate. Before we brought you in here, we called for a vote on whether to introduce you back into the Society due to your heroic actions and help in discovering the mole in our midst."

Kerrigan nodded, holding her breath as fear crept in.

"And we have agreed to give you full robes and make you a Society member," Zoh said.

Her face broke into a smile. "Oh, thank you!"

"With conditions," he clarified.

Her smile dropped. "Conditions, sir?"

"The terms of the treaty with the House of Shadows states that no new Society member may be admitted from tribe Charbonnet for the next hundred years," Lockney said, reading directly from his notes on the treaty. "As you would be admitted as a new member, we simply cannot break the bounds of the peace treaty for you."

Kerrigan gulped. *Scales.* "But... what about Fordham?"

"He was already a member of the Society at the time of signing," Lockney said as if it were obvious. "The training group was granted full member status by the council before embarking to Lethbridge for battle. You, however, were not."

"Oh," she muttered.

"We have come up with a proposition," Bastian said, nodding at Zoh. "If you renounce the House of Shadows as your tribe and give up your affiliation, the council will grant you leave to return to the tribe of your origin."

Kerrigan blinked. They'd found a loophole to let her back in. And that meant... that meant she would have to leave the House of Shadows. Leave the very tribe that Fordham had given her when she had nowhere else to go. But also the tribe that had never wanted a half-Fae in the first place. She had never officially been a member of the House of Shadows. The king had never, would never recognize her. Though Fordham, as king, obviously could... if he ever took up the mantle.

But if she renounced it, she would have to return to Bryonica, to the House of Cruse, to her birthright as the lost princess. The thought of returning to the House of Cruse didn't bring the same sense of terror that it once had. She had come to a truce with her father. She'd returned to Waisley and seen the people of Lillington. She had found hope in her lands and people. She had already decided to do anything she could to save them from a terrible fate. In fact, she had worn the House of Cruse livery to the winter ball. What difference would it make if she made it all official again?

March, of course, was the reason behind all of her problems. This would all make it easier for March to marry her. She sucked her teeth as if she'd tasted a lemon. This would make her plans for him much more difficult. But what other choice was there?

"I accept. I'll return to Bryonica." She held her head high and added, "Though I have some conditions of my own."

Boze scoffed, "The audacity."

"And what are these conditions?" Zoh asked, waving Boze's objection aside.

"Two things. One, I would like start a sponsorship program for displaced refugees from the House of Shadows. Those people will be arriving within the week, and they are going to need help assimilating."

"Ah, yes, Kress told me about you adopting two previously enslaved half-Fae."

"Yes. Well, I didn't adopt them, but I am helping them find living arrangements and work where they will be paid for their skills. And I would like to see more Society members step up to help these people in need."

"I think it's an excellent idea," Kress said. "I suggested it on the battlefield, but so much was going on."

Zoh sighed. "Fine. That should be no trouble. We will set you up with people already doing social work. You said a second objection?"

"Yes, sir. I would like the council to consider the implications of what you have done in your peace treaty with the House of Shadows."

The council shifted uncomfortably at the weight of her words. Lockney glanced up at her and quickly back down. Bastian arched an eyebrow at the gall.

Zoh was red in the face. "That treaty is the only reason we did not slaughter their people. They should be happy by what we allowed them."

"Certainly. They had no bargaining chips at all. So, why not take them for everything you could?" she said, forcing the words out despite the stares of disbelief.

"That is how negotiations work," Boze snapped.

"Yes. Of course. But then why did we admit them as a tribe at all? Why give them special dispensation to continue to exist? It makes no sense if we are then going to punish them for their existence. We made them join a government that they cannot be a part of for the next hundred years. That's a long time for resentment to grow while we occupy them." She took a breath, meeting each of their gazes in turn. "We can't change it now. The treaty is in place. I will renounce my place with them. But there is a reason there is unrest in this city. Do you really want there to be more with another tribe? Perhaps there is a long-term way to ease the anger. A way to find a solution to this growing pain with anyone who is not a member of the Society."

Alsia cleared her throat. She was stern but fair with her judgments. She leveled her eyes on Kerrigan, and then a smirk formed on her face. "If I didn't know better, I'd think you were campaigning for a seat at the table."

"Hear, hear," Bastian said with a smile.

Kerrigan blinked at what Alsia had said. "I..."

"The election is this summer," Alsia continued over whatever objection Kerrigan was going to voice. "And we're down one member. I, for one, would be interested in what might happen if you threw your hat in."

Helly grinned ear to ear. "As would I."

"She's a first year," Boze groaned.

"Oh hush," Anahi snapped at him. "Ambition is ambition. Talent is talent. And this girl, no matter her age, has them both."

The rest of the council shifted uneasily at the suggestion. Zoh looked disturbed that it had been voiced in his chamber. He'd been making demands, and now, she was. Something he was certainly not used to.

Zoh banged his gavel. "The election is another matter. I will consider the second request. Hellina has been given your official robes. Congratulations. Council dismissed."

Kerrigan sagged in relief as Helly rushed over to her with black robes in her arms. She pulled her into a hug. "I knew you would do it."

"I'm Bryonican once more."

"More than that. You're a member," Helly said, helping her into the robes. "And who knows... maybe by the end of the summer, you'll be on the council as well."

It was inconceivable. And yet, as terrifying as it was, she wanted that council position. She was going to do everything she could to get it.

\*\*\*

Kerrigan headed out of the council room in a daze, the weight of her new black Society robes around her shoulders.

"Mistress," Bayton said, dipping a curtsy.

Kerrigan startled. "Just Kerrigan, Bay, please."

"Yes, I will never get used to that."

She fell into step at Kerrigan's side, which was a vast improvement from her walking two steps before or behind her. "Why are you here?"

Bayton bobbed her head. "Miss, while you were away, we were requested to pack up your belongings, and you have been relocated."

"What for?"

"Was this not acceptable? It was a missive from the Society, and the rooms are far superior."

Kerrigan shook her head in confusion and followed Bayton away from the council room and up, up, up, deeper into the mountain. Kerrigan's hands shook as she realized where they were going—to the member suites. Hers were far from Helly's elaborate quarters, but still, they'd known she would accept.

"Here we are, miss." Bayton opened the door, and Kerrigan stepped inside her own private Society chambers.

She clasped her hands over her mouth in shock as she took in the plush living room. It was already furnished with more elaborate furniture and belongings than she had lived in since leaving Waisley as a child.

"Oh, Mistress, you made it," Benton said, fluffing a pillow. "We have already unpacked your belongings and hope that you find the room adequate. It still needs some cleaning, but so far, we approve."

"It's wonderful."

Benton gestured to the back hall. "This is the formal bedroom that connects to a bathing chamber. There is a formal study as well as two additional bedchambers. If you permit, we will share the smaller of the two rooms. So, your guests will still have space to enjoy your company. Unless you would prefer to find us a place elsewhere. In which case, we entirely understand.:

"Shh," Kerrigan said, giddy with laughter. "Take both rooms."

Benton blinked at her in confusion. "But, Mistress…"

"Kerrigan," she repeated. "Just Kerrigan. You have lived long enough in shadow. I want you to each have a room. If I have guests, they can sleep on the couch or the floor for all I care."

"That is most generous," Bayton said. "Too generous."

"It's the least of what you deserve." Kerrigan very well could have been them if she had been born a thousand years earlier. Things weren't that much better now, but it wasn't slavery. It wasn't what the twins had endured at the hands of tyrants. She wouldn't subject them to that ever again. "They're yours. Do with them as you will."

"Yes, Miss… Kerrigan," Benton said, stumbling over her name. "Also, this was delivered for you."

She held out a plain envelope, but Kerrigan recognized the calligraphic writing as Fordham's. She took it out of Benton's hand and stepped into her new living quarters, tearing the envelope and retrieving the letter from within.

*Kerrigan,*

*I've started this letter a thousand times. I have never been one of many words and always felt that I could express myself better on paper. Thus, I write to you today to express my deepest regrets about what I must do. I will speak plainly: I am leaving the Society.*

*Netta and I are still bound, and I will not let her suffer a terrible fate by leaving her behind. By the time you read this, we will have already left the aerie with Kinkadia far behind us. Do not look for us. We do not wish to be found. Not when the potential for harm is so great with our continued existence in the mountain.*

*My biggest regret is that you will read this letter and be hurt by the contents. I wish with all my heart that I could stay behind. That we could live a faerie tale, as we had that week at Waisley. Though it was not reality, and I can no longer pretend that being near you does not endanger your life.*

*Loving you is the best and the worst thing that ever happened to me. You challenged me to be a better version of the male that I am. Together, we were so much more than we ever could be apart. Which is why I must leave.*

*The curse hangs heavy over my heart. It is only a matter of time before you fall prey to it. So, I go in search of a way to break this abomination once and for all. Know that I do this for you, for us. If I survive, then I hope I am not too late to fight for you.*

*Yours always,*
*Prince Fordham Ollivier*

Kerrigan stepped carefully back into the living space. Benton and Bayton stared at her curiously but dared not ask. More conditioning.

"How long ago was this delivered?" she asked.

"Before we moved your quarters, miss," Bayton whispered.

"Hours ago," she gasped. She choked on the thought.

"What is it?" Benton finally asked, helping Kerrigan to a seat.

"Fordham. He's... he's gone."

# CHAPTER 64
## The Execution

"What are you doing here?"

Kerrigan swallowed and stepped deeper into the prison beneath the mountain. Lorian's face looked as determinedly irritated as ever. They'd stripped him of his Society robes. He was in a filthy beige shirt and black pants that clung to him from sweat and grime. Kerrigan had never seen him in anything but his robes. He was fastidious about his hygiene as well. It was shocking to see him like this.

"I wanted to see you."

"You've come to gloat. Your plan worked. I am the one behind bars now." He came slowly to his feet and stepped up to the ironwork. "Is that it?"

"No," she said carefully. "I didn't do this. That was all you."

He huffed and rolled his eyes. "If that helps you sleep at night."

She took a deep breath and released it. "I don't know why I'm here. Something didn't feel right. Alura was so adamant of your innocence, and I've never known her to be a liar."

"Maybe because I didn't do it."

"The evidence said you did it. The council voted."

He sighed and slumped back against the cot. "My daughter is not a liar. I am not a liar. If you believe me to be so, then you can leave. I don't wish that my last hours be disturbed by you."

Kerrigan bit her lip and turned to leave. But still, something nagged at her. It had nagged at her for two whole days as she waited for the execution to take place. She just didn't know what it was. Lorian wasn't telling the truth. Surely, he knew what he was doing. Twisting his words so that she had sympathy for him.

"Who were you working with in the House of Shadows?" she asked, her back to him.

"I assure you that I was not working with anyone. Why would I go to war against a group that I helped?"

A good question. But there was an easy answer.

"You did it to save face. If you tell us who it was, then maybe we can still plead your case. Get you sent t…"

"Prison for life?" he asked. "No, thanks."

"Think of Oria," she snapped.

He dipped his head. Surely, thinking about how his dragon would also suffer the same cruel fate today.

"I have thought of her. Speak with my dragon. She will tell you my heart."

"The council already did."

"Then, leave me. I have no information for you that I did not have for the council." His head tipped up, and he looked at her with those same eyes that had always haunted her steps in the mountain. "I am innocent."

Kerrigan didn't know why she had bothered. He wasn't going to give her anything. She trusted her gut. And her gut had said that she needed to talk to him to find out if what he had said was true. But he was determined to see this through.

"The gods be with your soul," she whispered and then stepped out of the prison.

Guards passed her on her way back up to retrieve him for the execution. It was going to be a private affair due to his high role in the government. Only council members and family would be allowed to be present. It was a luxury, considering the treason charge.

Kerrigan didn't want to be in the mountain when it happened. She'd told Ben and Bay she'd be back any moment, but she couldn't go to those rooms and be okay when nothing was okay. Yes, she had her position and a good in to get a nomination to run for council. But Fordham was gone. The refugees were a mess waiting to happen. Humans and half-Fae still had limited rights. And something told her that Lorian was not the end of the violence he had started. That this was only the beginning.

She meandered away from the center of the mountain toward the eastern grounds. She could have gotten lost in the city, but today was not the day for a half-Fae to be wandering. Already, there were counter protests for Lorian's death. He had been beloved in the city. Instead, she headed toward the greenhouses.

She touched the door and then retreated, moving away from the interior, where she had shared a heated kiss with Fordham. She walked the grounds, and a tug came from Tieran, checking on her. They'd gone flying the last two days to help her escape her thoughts, but it hadn't been enough.

She sent a pulse back to let him know that she was wandering today. He seemed increasingly concerned, but she couldn't deal with it right now. She shut down her side of the bond and felt the sinking failure seep over her. Tieran thought they had won. She didn't want to continue to bring him down when she couldn't process her own emotions.

With a heavy sigh, she stopped in the shade of an overgrown tree along the hillside. A figure approached her along the same walk. That was unusual, considering that no one came this way. Only the naturalists ever really ventured outside of the city limits like this. She pulled her magic in taut, fear clouding her judgment.

War had changed that. She reacted now without provocation. Screamed herself awake in the night as she was caught in another nightmare of slaughtering Fae before her eyes. It had been necessary. That did not mean it didn't haunt her.

But as the figure came into view, she released her unease in measures. "Valia," she said in surprise. "What are you doing out here?"

"Looking for you," she said, tucking a strand of her honey hair behind her ear and looking back the way she had come. "I thought you'd be in your rooms. Your attendants sent me to the dungeons."

Kerrigan flushed. "Yes. Did you need something?"

Valia looked around again, as if she expected someone to jump out at them.

Kerrigan pulled her magic in once more. "What is it? Were you followed?"

She gulped. "I don't think so. But I need to speak with you."

"About what?"

Then, to Kerrigan's shock, Valia burst into tears. Kerrigan gaped at the stoic girl who had been nothing but fierce the entire time she'd known her.

"Valia, what is it?"

Valia shook her head. "I can't tell you. They'll... they'll kill me." She hiccupped.

"Who?"

"The Red Masks," she whispered.

Kerrigan swore she hadn't heard her. "*Who?*"

"Please don't make me repeat it."

Kerrigan stepped away from the girl in horror. "Who are you?"

"I'm so sorry, Kerrigan. I was placed here. I was supposed to... I was supposed to gain your trust. Then, I was going to kill you." She said it so matter-of-fact and somehow, without malice.

Then, it came back to her. That night in her room during the tournament. A vision had warned about a person with honey-wheat hair in her room. Kerrigan had thought nothing of it, because it had only been Valia. She'd been worried for no reason. But the warning had been real, and Valia *was* a threat. "That night during the tournament."

"Yes," she croaked. "I lost my nerve. I couldn't do it."

"You've been spying on me all this time," Kerrigan said with a dawning realization.

"Please, I didn't want to. They'll kill me before letting me go."

With the force of her magic, Kerrigan yanked the girl off of her feet and threw her backward into the tree. Vali cried out, fresh tears coming to her eyes. Kerrigan pushed her hand against Valia's throat and held fire in the other hand. "Tell me why I should not do the same?"

"You should," Valia whispered. "I deserve death."

"Who are they? Who sent you? What do they want?"

"I'm sorry. I was raised in the organization. I was just a child. A daughter of the Father. They want... they want to wipe out humans and half-Fae."

"I know what the Red Masks are," she hissed. "But if you are truly one of theirs, then let's go to the council right now and tell them all you know."

"No! No, we can't do that. They'll kill everyone I know. They're so deep, so insidious, that it won't hurt them. But you won't have me any longer."

"That sounds good as far as I'm concerned."

"But you need me."

"I don't think that I do."

"I can help you," she gasped. "And... I understand why you'd hate me."

"Do you?"

Valia nodded and started crying again.

"How can you help me?" Kerrigan demanded. Then she thought for a second. "Do you know Isa?"

Valia gulped. "Yes. She's another daughter of the Father. She failed at killing you. So, I was supposed to do it. We were both punished for our failure."

"And who *is* the Father?"

"I don't know." Kerrigan pushed the fire hotter, and Valia screamed. "I swear I don't know. He wears a Red Mask at all times. It molds to his face so that even in death, we'll never know who he is. Isa may know who he is, but I do not. I'm not sure anyone else does."

"It's not Lorian?"

But Kerrigan already knew the answer. She knew it before Valia started shaking her head. Lorian wasn't the leader of the Red Masks. He was just a bigot. One who would suffer for the sins of others.

"Did Lorian do the things that he was accused of?"

A tear streaked down her cheek. "No," she choked out. "It was a plant."

Kerrigan released her in a rush. "We have to stay the execution."

Valia grabbed her arm before she could go dashing back toward the mountain. "It's too late. He's already gone."

"You let an innocent man die!"

"Lorian Van Horn was not innocent," Valia said. "He was not a Red Mask, but he was hardly innocent. You can't save everyone, Kerrigan."

"I can damn well try," she said, shaking her hand off and heading back toward the mountain.

"I'm offering you a chance!" Valia rushed after her.

Kerrigan turned back to face the real traitor in their midst. "A chance at what? Leading me astray again? You said yourself that they'll kill you for this."

"Yes, if they find out. Like if you barge in there right now and explain how Lorian is innocent. But"—Valia raised her chin and met her head-on—"if we work together, maybe we can stop Father before it's too late."

"How do I know that this isn't another trick? How do I know that the *Father* didn't send you to do this?"

"You don't," she said, swiping at her tears. "You have no way of knowing, but I swear to you on the grave of my mother that I am telling you the truth."

"I could never trust you."

"No," Valia agreed with a sigh. She dropped her chin to chest, a wash of shame coming to her cheeks. "But you could still work with me." She lifted her head again and met Kerrigan's stare with one of matching fury. "I'm done watching the world burn and doing nothing about it."

Kerrigan looked at the girl and saw her for the very first time. She had blood on her hands and weight on her shoulders. She'd been raised to be a spy and an assassin for a broken man. Kerrigan might never have this chance again. It would mean she would be trading Lorian's life for information to bring down the whole bloody organization.

"If you betray me, I will unleash on you a thousand fold."

"I know," Valia said with a smile. "I know you, Kerrigan."

Kerrigan might regret this later, but it was necessary. She held her hand out. "We take them down."

Valia hesitated only a second before sliding it into hers. "Together."

# CHAPTER 65

ISA

Isa leaned over the side of the wall where the dragon's typically observed council meetings to watch Lorian's head be released from his shoulders.

No dragons had come to see the show. So, she had the entire upper quadrant to herself. Her hands dug into the cliffside while her feet had light purchase against the stone. She shouldn't have been able to see into the chamber from here. There were no official doors, but she knew how to not be seen. She'd climbed up hours ago in the pitch-black and waited like a spider spinning a web.

Only council members and family were present for the execution. Father watched impassively from his seat among them. He'd done so well with this one. Exactly as he'd always planned. And soon, it would all come to fruition.

The chamber emptied. The body disposed of. The blood sponged from the floor. And then Isa released from her hiding spot and went in search of Father.

He sat at his study in the heart of the mountain. A king ready to ascend to his throne.

"Father," she breathed, dipping her head.

"Isa, how did you like the show?"

"Well done," she said. "It was brilliant. Strategy like I've never seen before. The way the pieces just fell into place. Exquisite."

She had wanted a way out. Her father was manic. He was always one breath away from killing her as easily as he'd played Lorian Van Horn. But his genius was unparalleled. She would rather be in the shadow of genius than dead.

"Good," he said, reaching into his desk for the Red Mask that hid him from the rest of the world. "It is almost time."

"Yes, Father."

"We must prepare for what is coming."

"How can I help? Shall I kill the girl?"

He glared at her. "Do not lay a hand on Kerrigan Argon," he snarled. "We have discussed this. She is mine. She belongs to me. If you do anything to jeopardize this, then I will end you in a similar fashion."

She gulped and stayed stock-still. "As you wish."

"The girl is at the heart of what is to come. She will lead us to everything we deserve." He rose to his feet, towering over her small frame and sliding the mask into place. It melded to his face, and his smile turned deadly.

"Yes, Father," she said, sinking to her feet before him.

Her stomach twisted at his evil genius. She could have gotten out. She could have escaped. He would turn his gaze to her, and then it would all be over. The menace rippling from him only made her cower more. And gods, how she hated cowering.

"Stand, Isa," he commanded.

She rose to her feet, and he put a hand on her shoulder.

"My time in the shadow is almost over. I want you at my side when we take our rightful place in the world." He faced the window that overlooked the city of Kinkadia. "It is almost time to cast off this mask."

Her eyes stared up at the Father in worship. "Yes... Father."

He flung aside the Red Mask. "Soon, I will no longer have to be *Master Bastian*. By the end of the summer, this will all be *mine*."

**The End**

## ACKNOWLEDGMENTS

*House of Dragons* was a tough act to follow. So, when I started on *House of Shadows*, I had all these fears about getting it right, but also excitement that I was back in this glorious world again. I had so many ideas for this story, and so many twists and turns planned. At some point, it almost felt like too much to hold in all at once, too many strings, too many storylines. But thanks to a lot of people holding my hand and telling me I could do it, I created this second even more in depth fantastical book.

Important people who made this book what it is today: Staci Hart, Rebecca Kimmerling, Diana Peterfreund, Bethany Hagen, Nana Malone, Rebecca Gibson, Devin McCain, Anjee Sapp, Mari Mancusi, Jovana Shirley, Sarah Hansen, Kimberly Brower, and my wonderful husband!

And last but never least, YOU! Thank you reader for picking up this book. There are millions of books and you chose this one. I can't wait to take you back to Alandria in the third book, *House of Curses* with more dragons and Fae and a crazy terrorist group. I wouldn't be able to do this without you. You're my #1!

USA Today Bestselling author K.A. Linde grew up as a military brat and has a Master's degree in political science from the University of Georgia. She creates fantastical stories based off of her love for Disney movies, fairy tales, and *Star Wars*. In her spare time, she loves traveling, binge-watching *Supernatural*, playing piano, and dancing. She currently lives in Lubbock, TX with her husband and two super adorable puppies.

Kyla is the author of more than thirty adult novels, but does not encourage anyone younger than eighteen to pick those up.

Visit her online:

www.kalinde.com

Or Facebook, Instagram, Twitter, & Tiktok:

@authorkalinde

For exclusive content, free books,
and giveaways every month.
www.kalinde.com/subscribe

Printed in the USA
CPSIA information can be obtained
at www.ICGtesting.com
LVHW090934061123
762866LV00004B/81